He Was There

Efharisto !

Christina Dooley

He Was There

A Novel of Danger and Destiny

Christina Dooley

Printed in the United States of America
First printed edition 2019
Published by Christina Dooley
www.hewasthere.org

To those who have gone before… and to the
One who has brought us this far and will never leave us

ACKNOWLEDGMENTS

I wish to express heartfelt thanks to my aunts, Anna Baker, Areti "Toula" Pearson, Marika Harris, Sophia Stover, Uncle John Pearson and parents Bill and Eva Dooley. I cannot tell you how much I appreciate you and all you have done to help with this project. I couldn't have done it without you.

Thank you to my siblings Chris Dooley and Angie Durham and to ALL my family for all your help and support.

Special thanks to Bill and Eva Dooley for your extensive assistance in editing and guidance in this journey.

DISCLAIMERS

Although most would consider this work rated for general audiences, for some conservative readers (especially young children), content such as wartime violence, somewhat graphic accidents, emotional grief and adult situations may not be appropriate. There is no foul language, and adult situations are mostly implied.

Please do NOT try any "home remedies" mentioned— most have no proven benefit and many could cause harm. This book is not intended as a substitute for the medical advice of physicians. The reader should regularly consult a physician in matters relating to his/her health and particularly with respect to any symptoms that may require diagnosis or medical attention.

The drama portrayed is of extraordinary situations in a unique time and place and the author does not wish to condone conflict or violence, excessive or underage alcohol consumption, excessive child labor, exploitation of animals or any use of tobacco. Do not attempt any risky, prohibited or dangerous activities mentioned in this book.

Chapter 1

Nikolas Stavrolaki dismounted from his horse and took a deep breath of the brisk sea air. The ocean waves on the north shore of Crete were calm and rhythmical, lulling to sleep the builders taking their afternoon rest under the nearby tree. He gave his horse some water after the long journey from his hometown of Lithos and then walked towards the nearly-completed structure.

They had made great progress. In his mind, he could already smell his grandmother's famous *moussaka* [casserole of seasoned potato, tomato, eggplant and sometimes meat], lemon chicken, and *baklava* for dessert. Combine those with fish grilled straight from the sea, a beautiful view of the ocean and close proximity to the ancient Minoan ruins, and he was sure to have a successful *taverna* [casual restaurant].

Karidia at the beginning of 1935 was a sparsely-populated paradise, with only about three villas spread out within the region. They were mostly used as summer homes for residents of the big city of Heraklion, about two hours west by wagon. Both the area and the endeavor were a departure from the agricultural community of Nikolas' family about an hour inland, to the south. The mountainous terrain did not make travel between the towns and villages easy, but his excitement grew as he dreamed of all the possibilities in this new venture.

As he walked down to the sandy beach, he wondered if his little brother would have been proud of him or thought he was a little lofty in the head. He probably would have thought that Nikolas already had enough to manage with his hauling business, as well as his growing produce for the market. How he missed his brother who was also his best friend. Many years ago he had passed away of pneumonia as a twelve-year old boy. His grandmother and father were unquestionably supportive. His mother— well, she was complicated.

"Should be ready on Saturday," said the contractor, walking up behind him, "but it will need a few days after that for the plaster on the inside walls and maybe even some of the cement holding the stones together on the outside to set completely." Nikolas was elated, "Thank you! I will bring the final payment in a couple of days when it is done." They shook hands, and Nikolas rode away to check on the crops in one of his fields nearby.

***

Arianna Kazandaki continued to crochet. She wished there was enough light in the cellar to read. She had only attended school for about a year, but thanks to her grandfather's teaching, her reading had gotten much better. She really should be outside with her older brother Konstantine, planting the vegetables for the market and for her parents and ten siblings.

It was silly really. Why would her presence jeopardize negotiations between her older sister and her suitor? Arianna had been told that she is beautiful, but this seemed a little ridiculous. And why was it so important that the older daughter be married first, although Arianna had no desire to get married yet. Her mother had been married at fourteen years old. She was lucky to be several years older than that and still free.

It was hard for her to sit still when there was daylight remaining and work to be done. After a while, she started to feel a little uncomfortable. She thought to herself, "How much longer? There is no bathroom down here."

She tried to concentrate on the crochet pattern that she was experimenting with. She was fascinated with creating new designs. Mother had always told her she was like Konstantine in her ability to put things together in new ways. Konstantine was architecturally creative as a craftsman and stonemason.

2

They were also alike in their work ethic. With their two oldest brothers in Heraklion running a building materials business, their father working as town mayor, butcher and shoemaker and their mother operating the café and taking care of the large household, the care of their many fields primarily fell to Konstantine, herself and her younger brother Antonios. "I'm surprised Kosta hasn't come to my rescue," she muttered under her breath.

Finally the cellar door opened, "You can come up now— your sister is engaged!" squealed her mother. "*Endaxi* [Okay]!" Arianna ran up the cellar stairs and straight to the outhouse in their courtyard.

***

On Saturday Nikolas, his father and grandmother journeyed with excitement to the new *taverna*. "When do you think you will open?" his father asked. Nikolas replied, "I think next weekend. I have to go to Heraklion to pick up the several dozen place settings that I ordered. We can bring the furniture and cookware sometime next week, and then we should be set." He thought a minute and continued, "I am not sure how much business we will have at the end of February, but I am too excited to show off Grandmother Georgia's legendary food to put off the opening until spring." Nikolas smiled at his grandmother, who patted his hand fondly.

While Nikolas completed the transaction with the builders, his father and grandmother walked around and started cleaning. Later, Nikolas joined them and said, "After we open, I can gradually bring my stuff into the living quarters below the *taverna* and move out from your place in Lithos, Grandmother. The builders did a really fine job finishing everything like I wanted it." As he said that, he thought it was almost too good to be true. "I'm proud of you, Niko," encouraged his grandmother. "I couldn't do it without you," he told her gratefully.

Monday around three o'clock in the morning there was a sudden sound like a rumble of thunder and a violent shaking. Nikolas jumped out of bed and ran to check on his grandmother, who was already on her feet. "*Panayia mou* [my Virgin Mary]!" she said as they ran outside. Nikolas' mother, father and younger sister emerged from the adjacent house.

After a while, the earthquake stopped, although they themselves were all still shaking. Nearly the whole village was outside asking if everyone was okay. A few had found lanterns and were checking for major damage. Nikolas looked towards Karidia. If he could go check... but no, he wouldn't risk it for the safety of his horse. The village would have some repair work to do, but nothing that couldn't wait until morning. Nikolas wondered if he could sleep.

The next morning confirmed his fear— not his worst, since there were no deaths or major injuries in the area— but his new *taverna* by the sea had been leveled to the ground. He wandered around the rubble. They hadn't furnished and stocked the *taverna* or the living area yet, but he would have to start building all over again. He examined several of the stones. Some may be salvaged.

Nikolas briefly wondered if the earthquake was a sign of his dreams becoming bigger than reality. But then he pictured families and friends having a great time with good food, music and swimming at the beach. No, he knew this was a sound business enterprise and something he would really enjoy.

He thought about the building's position near the edge of the six-meter cliff leading down to the ocean. He may need to consult with more experts to make sure every precaution is taken structurally for rebuilding. But first he would have to strategize about his income.

***

Arianna's oldest brothers, Petros and Markos Kazandaki, left their business in Heraklion for a few days and traveled to Prasinos Kampos to check on the family after the earthquake. They were relieved to find everyone okay and only minor repairs needed at their home.

So the brothers joined their father in checking on all the residents in the area. They chuckled that even in a time of crisis, their father the mayor, meticulous with tradition and proprieties, was dressed in the traditional Greek pantaloons, ornate vest, bright sash and cap. They made their rounds, helping their neighbors, starting with the widows and the elderly. Although their father sometimes protested the position that he never sought (as every year he was elected by acclamation), he did the job well since he genuinely cared for people.

After a long day, the mayor returned with some neighbors that they had found to be in need. "My lady, I trust you have plenty of bread, as usual," he addressed his wife. "Yes, my lord," she replied respectfully. It was not uncommon for her to bake sixty to seventy loaves of bread to be able to share meals with neighbors, family or those passing through. They gathered around the large table, gave the Lord thanks and caught up on all the news.

After they reported to the others that they had found some earthquake damage but for the most part had been lucky, the brothers from out of town congratulated their oldest sister on her upcoming wedding. Markos admired the ornately woven basket their mother brought in with fresh homemade bread. "One of Arianna's new creations," their mother said. To which Petros replied, "You know it's these little touches that we are missing in the city. Our business has grown, and we are getting more involved in the community. We need to entertain more, but Markos and I find ourselves pretty helpless in domestic areas. Father, what would you think of allowing one of our sisters to live with us in Heraklion?"

Konstantine spoke up, "You can't have Arianna; she is my right-hand girl." He winked at her and she smiled. His father looked at his daughters thoughtfully. He was about to lose one to marriage and couldn't quite accept the idea of letting another go just yet. "We will think about it. There is still a lot of work to be done. Konstantine may be needed more with stonework damaged by the earthquake, leaving more to be done in the fields. We will see." Arianna thought to herself, "I wonder if I would like big city life."

***

Since the scattered stones were unsightly and he didn't know if the government would permit him to delay very long, Nikolas felt the pressure to rebuild the *taverna*. But he considered how he would pay for the materials and labor all over again. His mother had a lot of money, but a loan from her was not an option in his mind.

Nikolas pondered, "Grandmother, what would you think of starting a smaller restaurant temporarily? There is a place for rent across the road from my vegetable field to the east, not too far from here but on the other side of the Minoan ruins. It's not right along the beach, but we can fix it up quickly and maybe have a small room in which to stay in case we serve late. We can use the fresh vegetables from the garden across the road, and maybe I can buy a boat and find fishermen willing to split the catch." Georgia mulled it over and said, "I think that is a good idea. We can start slowly and see how it goes."

Nikolas began to set his plan in motion. It was not difficult to find a boat and fishermen to partner with. The restaurant took more time to get in order, but he worked hard and was able to open it for the peak summer season. Although it was small, with the location near the Minoan ruins and his grandmother's sumptuous recipes, the venue started to prosper.

When things ran smoothly at the temporary restaurant, he began to turn his attention to rebuilding the *taverna*. One fall day Nikolas decided to take a trip to Prasinos Kampos, about a kilometer east of his hometown of Lithos. There was always a little friendly rivalry between this village and his, but there was a stoneworker of high repute there. Getting his dream on firm footing was worth any funny looks he may get by being there.

Nikolas was directed to the café in the square to find Konstantine Kazandaki. The stonemason was resting at a table outside, with his tools set aside and a *komboloi* in his hand. A young girl from the village ran up and asked him, "Why do you play with that? It almost looks like a necklace." Konstantine smiled, "These are my worry beads. As I move them with my fingers, my worries go *plop*! All gone." She laughed and ran to play with some other children.

"Are you Konstantine Kazandaki?" Nikolas asked. "That's me," Konstantine answered. Nikolas introduced himself and explained his project and predicament. "You may need more support beams. I can come out and help and you can pay me when you can," said Konstantine. Nikolas was relieved, "I am a man of my word and will

6

pay you in installments as quickly as I am able. We can put a schedule in writing."

"Kosta!" Nikolas heard from behind. He turned and looked over his shoulder and saw the most beautiful girl he had ever seen, standing with a large basket at a distance. "My sister, Arianna," Konstantine explained. "Time to exchange these stone working tools for harvesting shears." The men arranged a time to meet in Karidia and said their goodbyes.

Nikolas stood there a few minutes, a little stunned. Up until then he had been so focused on his businesses that he usually didn't notice women, but he couldn't get Arianna out of his mind. He suddenly became more determined to make a success of things.

Chapter 2

A year later, Nikolas' businesses were thriving. He wished he had thought of the fishing boat idea earlier— it brought in profits as well as fresh fish for the restaurant. The horses and wagons for hauling produce, wine or olive oil to market were contracted to laborers who could hardly keep up with the demands. The temporary restaurant had taken off, and his grandmother's cooking became famous in the area. Some had even visited from Heraklion, so word was starting to spread there too.

Best of all, the restaurant by the sea was completed. This time as he made the final payment, he said a quick prayer acknowledging his dependence on God and asking for His protection and blessing. As he reflected over his life— his brother dying of pneumonia, his grandfather and aunt dying of the flu, how his mother had changed after that and her own issues as a young girl, how he broke his back in his youth after a wheel fell off his wagon, the earthquake… so much was out of his control. Yet he was alive, had the ability to work hard, and God willing, would persevere, trying to keep a positive outlook even through the tough times.

***

The next summer, Antonios and Arianna picked figs in one of their distant groves. They had been harvesting since morning, and Arianna was grateful for the shade from the fig trees and the mountainous cliff behind them. She was not looking forward to picking grapes in the hot August sun in the coming weeks.

Konstantine rode up to them and dismounted, "Looks like a good time for a break. You've done more than I expected!" They didn't argue. As Arianna passed some bread and figs to her brothers, Konstantine teased, "Hmm, I could use some of your good *spanakopita* [spinach and feta cheese baked in fillo dough] to go with this." Arianna countered, "And when would I have time to

8

make that, since I am slaving out here all day?" Konstantine replied, "I have seen you handle many more things at once than that. Should be no problem for you, Miss Energy."

Antonios begged, "Please don't talk about foods we can't eat during the fast." The Greek Orthodox Church observed the death of Virgin Mary in the middle of August and fasted from dairy, sweets and meat during the first two weeks of the month. "Did you get the extra workers lined up to help us pick the grapes?" Antonios asked Konstantine. "Yes," Konstantine assured him, "but since you two don't seem to need my help, I'd better go get a team together for making the raisins. Thanks for the snack!"

As Konstantine put one foot in the stirrup, a stray dog suddenly barked loudly from behind him on the rocky hill. The mule jumped in fear and tore off running with Konstantine's foot caught in the stirrup, dragging him behind. "Whoa!" Konstantine yelled and tried to reach up and grab the reins. He tried to loosen his foot from the stirrup. "KOSTA!" Arianna screamed, terror filling her whole being.

Antonios ran to try to catch the mule, but it was already far ahead of him. Antonios shouted back to Arianna, "Go get help!" Arianna ran as fast as she could back to the village. Konstantine kept trying to calm the mule but he could barely speak from being dragged a horrifying distance over rough terrain.

After what seemed like an eternity, the mule slowed a little. Konstantine was able to release his foot from the stirrup, but he twisted free within the mule's path, and the mule's hind legs stomped heavily onto Konstantine's stomach. Antonios' heart went from panic to dread.

He reached his brother, who was curled up in pain and barely conscious but moaning softly. "It's going to be okay— help is coming," Antonios tried to soothe him in spite of his own fear.

A few minutes later they heard a horse and wagon racing towards them. Their father, mother, uncle and Arianna jumped out of the wagon and ran to Konstantine on the ground. "Oh, my baby!" his mother cried out. "It's bad," Antonios said. "We need to take him to the hospital right now."

They lifted him carefully into the wagon and traveled as fast as they could the fifteen kilometers to Heraklion. Arianna and her mother used pieces of cloth to stop the bleeding from cuts all over his body. As they would hit bumps in the road, Konstantine would scream out in pain. "It's his stomach," Antonios explained.

They finally reached the hospital. The doctor examined him and did not have good news. "He has massive internal bleeding. I don't think there is a lot we can do." Arianna and her mother started sobbing, their hopes deflating. "Can you do something, surgery?" his father asked. "We can try, but it's risky," the doctor warned. "Antonios, go get Petros and Markos," his father directed. "Let me go," said the uncle, already walking towards the door.

After some discussion, the family opted for surgery, and each said a comforting word to Konstantine. Arianna pleaded, "You cannot leave us, fight hard." The family members could hardly sit still as they waited and prayed during the operation.

After the long surgery, the doctor informed the family that they had taken out Konstantine's appendix, but he also had a perforated small intestine. They repaired it as well as they could, but the damage was extensive and there was also risk of infection. They sat with him a while and then came up with a schedule to take turns staying with him, but Arianna wouldn't leave his side.

Days after the surgery, he started to develop abdominal swelling and a high fever. He called Arianna over to him, "I'm sorry to leave you with so much work to be done. You will be the oldest in the home now, and I know you can handle the responsibility. You have been my right hand and my best friend. Such beauty and so capable... Don't cry for me, I am going to a better place. Carry on and make me proud." Arianna cried softly and said, "You have been everything to me. I don't want to see you go, but I don't want you to worry. I will do my best for the family to make you proud of me."

They called for a priest to give Konstantine his last communion. The next day, with all his family gathered around, Arianna heard him whispering, "Praise the Lord. Praise God in His sanctuary, praise Him in His mighty heavens. Let everything that has breath praise the Lord." Then Konstantine breathed his last breath. Arianna let out a small scream and sobbed. His mother started wailing. His father held his hand and quietly whispered, "Take care of him, *Christe*," as he choked back tears.

***

Nikolas had made a name for himself, although not really by choice. He enjoyed making his big dreams a reality, even if it took working from sunup to sundown. He had acquired more fields in addition to his other businesses. He was friendly, well respected and well liked. He was teased sometimes during times of celebration when he decorated his horse and wagon with things like beads and flowers. Maybe that was a little much when not everyone had a horse, but as he looked out at the ocean from the *taverna*, he knew that he admired beauty and wanted to enjoy life.

He became aware of the time and got a little nervous. A friend had told him that he and an acquaintance of his from another village were going to come by the *taverna* with his daughter that he wanted Nikolas to meet. They were all to come in the middle of the afternoon when business slowed so they could talk at leisure. Nikolas hastened to make sure everything was in order.

At last they came, and he welcomed them warmly. His grandmother served a few *mezethes* [appetizers] and wine while they sat out on the balcony overlooking the ocean. "It's really beautiful here," Barbara began. "Thank you," Nikolas said, "The ocean is calm today; sometimes it can get a little rough." Barbara was certainly pretty, but he wondered how she would weather life's turbulent waters. Maybe he was judging too prematurely by her delicate, unspoiled hands and complexion.

They visited until the early evening crowd started coming in. The guests from the other village said their thanks and goodbyes, while Nikolas' friend stayed behind a few moments. "Well, what do you think?" he asked Nikolas in private. He replied, "She seems like a very nice girl, but I don't think there was a real connection. I can't really explain it. But thank you, I enjoyed meeting them and had a good time." "You are a good catch, but don't be too picky or wait too long," his friend advised as he departed.

Nikolas couldn't explain it to his friend, but earlier as they were all talking, Arianna's face came to his mind. He hadn't seen or thought about her in a long time. He had heard of Konstantine's sudden and tragic death and grieved for her. He knew the pain of losing a brother who was also a close friend. He had wanted to go to Konstantine's funeral, but he didn't know him that well and didn't want to intrude on the family.

He then heard that Arianna had gone to Heraklion to keep house for her older brothers. Why should he think of her now when he would probably never see her again? He shook her from his mind and went to help his grandmother serve the customers.

***

Arianna was fascinated with the city. There was so much more to see and do, and the daily tasks were a lot less physically taxing than work in the fields. She quickly learned that her brothers were well respected in the community. And for a month now, she had been a help to them— ironing their shirts, cooking and cleaning. It was good for her to have a change after Konstantine died. Her brothers tried to coax her lively spirit back as much as they could, but she didn't think she would ever have the same zest for life after losing her beloved Kosta.

One evening, Antonios came from the village into the city. He joined his older brothers at a restaurant in Heraklion for a dinner with some businessmen. After introductions were made, they sat down for the meal. They spoke of family, business and politics. "Have you heard of this guy named Hitler in Germany?" one of the businessmen asked. "Yes," another answered, "not sure what he is up to. It seems like he's one that should be watched."

After the three brothers returned to Petros' home, they sat with Arianna in the living room. Antonios disclosed the reason for his visit. "You know Dorothea as the next oldest has helped me in the

12

fields some. But she has been getting a skin rash from the sun. They have tried different things to treat and prevent it, but she is really uncomfortable. I think you have enjoyed it here, Arianna, and I hate to ask this, but is there any way you can change places with her and come back to help me with the harvests and planting?" Arianna's heart sank in disappointment, but she thought of her promise to Konstantine. "I'll go if that is really what is needed of me," she said.

Arianna was home before the end of the grape harvest in early fall. She joined in the reaping with as much enthusiasm as she could muster. There was a young man named Vasilis, a friend of her cousin, who especially seemed intent on making her laugh. She found that she enjoyed working with him. They took breaks with the others under the shade tree.

After the grapes were picked, Arianna did not see Vasilis in October during the pomegranate and fall vegetable gathering. But in November during the olive picking, he and her cousin were both back to help. He worked up in the trees with the men. With sticks they knocked the olives down to the blanket below for the women to gather them. At times, the ladies grabbed the edges of the blanket and carefully flung it up in the air so the leaves would blow away, leaving the olives on the blanket.

During breaks, Vasilis again tried to charm Arianna. She was used to men trying to capture her attention and flatter her. Most of them seemed insincere and more interested in themselves. But Vasilis seemed genuinely nice, and she was in good spirits because of the cooler autumn winds.

Over the next few months, Vasilis thought of Arianna. Conscious of customs prohibiting direct interaction, he enlisted her cousin to send several messages and coordinate a few escorted "accidental" encounters with Arianna.

In the early spring, Arianna's cousin approached her privately. "How would you feel if Vasilis' family went to your parents about arranging a marriage with you?" She thought for a moment, pondering her desire for independence. But she wasn't entirely unfettered at home, and Vasilis was handsome and the nicest young

13

man she had met. At last she said, "I think I would like that." It didn't take Arianna long to begin to dream happily of her new life with Vasilis.

***

Nikolas knew that Arianna was back in Prasinos Kampos. He also knew that she was the prettiest girl in the area and that other men would be trying to arrange a match with her. If he was going to approach the family, he had better do it now. He wasn't sure of his chances. They would probably prefer someone they knew better from their own village, but then again, he had done pretty well for himself, so maybe... He couldn't get Arianna out of his mind, so he had to at least try to pursue a relationship with her.

Having made his resolve, Nikolas almost wished he could immediately appeal to Arianna's father. But on the other hand, the culture's tradition of using the subtle intimations of go-betweens could protect his feelings, should he be rejected as an outsider from a disregarded town.

As he considered what he thought was his biggest impediment, he remembered that Arianna's Aunt Alexandra also lived in his hometown. While he did not know her too well, her intervention could help to bridge the rift between the two villages. As for his side of the negotiations, although he was close to his father, maybe he was a little too close. This bond, along with a little Greek fervor, could make the situation too volatile. His Uncle Elias would be a more suitable advocate.

Uncle Elias was a shepherd of his own large flock of sheep. Even though he could have been resented by jealous neighbors for having gone to America in his younger years, Elias was so gentle and kind that he was well regarded. He cared for his sheep and even more for people. He loved to roam the countryside with his flock, gaze at the earth in its stillness and daydream. His temperament would be perfect to represent Nikolas.

Nikolas lost no time in searching out his Uncle Elias. After finding him and exchanging a few pleasantries, Nikolas revealed his heart's desire. His uncle looked at Nikolas searchingly. "Are you sure that is

14

what you want, my boy? She is beautiful, to be sure, but do you know her character well enough to unite your life with hers and even lay down your own if necessary?"

Nikolas respected the wisdom in his uncle's question and thoughtfully answered, "I don't know her as well as I would like, but I have seen her loving loyalty to her family. She seemed to handle tragic grief without bitterness, sacrificed her own dreams for the needs of her loved ones, worked harder in the fields than I have seen some men do and had a twinkle in her eye in teasing her brother, showing a sense of humor that can be valuable in a life partner. I would love the opportunity to gain her respect as her husband." Uncle Elias smiled, "Quite a speech…" After they both chuckled, Uncle Elias slapped him on the back and promised, "I will do what I can to help you."

It was agony waiting over the next weeks for Uncle Elias to inform him of how he fared with Arianna's Aunt Alexandra. Nikolas tried to distract himself with work, but after a little while even his laborers began to look at him funny. He decided to take a swim to clear his head. Spring had barely begun so the ocean waves were cold and invigorating. He felt so insignificant in its vastness, yet a calm sense of purpose settled over him. He left his destiny in the hands of a very big and capable God.

Unbeknownst to Nikolas, Uncle Elias had already had an effective meeting with Aunt Alexandra. He was presently working on the next stage of conversations. Uncle Elias and Aunt Alexandra intended to approach Antonios as Arianna's eldest brother in the home.

When the time with Antonios had been successfully arranged, the two matchmakers praised Nikolas' hard work and successes as well as his unselfish devotion to Arianna. Antonios asked several questions and then requested time to consider it and speak to his parents. They agreed on a future appointment for continued discussion.

One afternoon, Uncle Elias came with his flock of sheep to visit with Nikolas at the *taverna*. Nikolas brought him a glass of water and joined him outside under the shade tree. Seeing the anxiety on

Nikolas' face, Uncle Elias sought to put him at ease, "We have a meeting with Arianna's father on Sunday afternoon." Nikolas was surprised and relieved, "How…?"

Elias explained that he had met with her Aunt Alexandra and that they both had met with Arianna's brother Antonios a couple of times. Nikolas peppered him with questions, and after answering them, Elias said, "You have found favor, my boy. Now her father wants to meet you before it is finally decided."

A little apprehensively, Nikolas, accompanied by his Uncle Elias, called upon Arianna's father the next Sunday afternoon. The mayor had heard quite a bit about Nikolas but now with Nikolas' petition sought to understand his character. They sat for an hour discussing life, goals, family and business.

When the older man perceived Nikolas to be humble, respectful and God-fearing, he asked what Nikolas would require as a dowry. Nikolas replied, "I really don't want anything. I would be more than blessed to have your daughter as my wife." Arianna's father insisted, "I must provide a wedding gift. Is there a piece of land that you have had your eye on?"

Nikolas said, "There is a villa across the road pretty near the *taverna* that is for sale. I would like to have a place for my family that is separate from the business. If you like, I could pay for half and if you wanted to contribute half, we can put the deed in Arianna's name as a present for her." The mayor, appreciating his unselfishness, agreed to the gift and to the match. Nikolas felt his heart take flight as they shook hands and said goodbye.

***

"I can't believe you have done this to me," Arianna shouted at her father and mother. "You didn't consult me at all— I don't even know who he is!" Her mother tried to soothe her, "Your father has spent some time with him. He is of good character, has many respectable businesses and seems to really care about you."

"You don't understand," Arianna countered, "Vasilis is who I want to marry." "Vasilis? Do you know him so well as to defy your

16

father's wishes?" her mother asked. "I spent some time with him during harvests and, anyway, I know him better than this stranger," Arianna answered, completely frustrated. Her father spoke up, "Vasilis is a nice young man who may do well for himself, but Nikolas is already established. Regardless, I have given my word."

Arianna, sobbing, stormed out of the room. She thought about appealing to her older brothers in the city, but she knew their sense of loyalty to their father and the family name. If only Konstantine... She grieved afresh at the loss of her older brother and best friend.

Her mother sought her out several minutes later, "I'm sorry, Arianna. But it is a woman's duty to follow her family's wishes. Your father has given his word and you know how his honor rests on this. A God-fearing man who will provide for his family— what more do you need? You will learn to love him, as I did with your father." Arianna objected, "It is so unfair. I will never force my daughter to marry any man she doesn't want to."

***

Nikolas' mother had one purpose in her visit to the Kazandaki family— to secure for her son more riches than he had asked for. She had never really understood Nikolas and his selflessness. The history of Crete with its various conquerors was such that you took what you could before someone else took it from you, at least from her perspective. She and her son may not have been close, but her own family pride was at stake, and she could be a force to be reckoned with.

Immediately after she introduced herself at their home, she demanded, "What are you going to do for my son?" Arianna's father was taken aback, "We have agreed to an arrangement about a villa that we will both give my daughter." She retorted, "That is not enough. Nikolas is the most respected and prosperous entrepreneur in this whole area. He could have any girl he wanted, with a much bigger dowry. He offers her much more than you give. You insult our family with your greed for all that he has acquired."

The mayor was stunned at her arrogance and materialistic mindset. He thought to himself, "What kind of family is this? Maybe I

17

misjudged Nikolas' character." At his silence, she continued, "Don't you think that as the mayor of Prasinos Kampos you owe more than that?" Arianna's father had had enough, "The deal is off and you may tell your son so."

After she left and his emotions calmed, Arianna's father hoped he wasn't unjustly judging Nikolas, but he thought it was better to be safe than sorry when it came to his daughter. Plus, it opened up funds that were needed for his daughter Dorothea's upcoming marriage to Demetrios in Heraklion. Demetrios had found a property that had a place for his business downstairs and residence upstairs. He would transfer the money to him immediately so they could secure the building before it became unavailable. At the same time, he thought it best not to tell Arianna anything just yet.

***

On Palm Sunday afternoon, Nikolas excitedly went to the Kazandakis' home laden with gifts and foods for Arianna and her family. It was the custom for the groom or his family to give valuable jewelry for the bride, as well as the wedding dress. The bride's family would take care of the groom's suit and wedding reception.

Nikolas was greeted with a puzzled look from Mr. Kazandaki, "Your mother didn't tell you?" Nikolas hesitantly replied, "No, I haven't seen my mother." The older man explained, "She came here and demanded a bigger dowry. I told her the arrangement was off." Nikolas felt like he had been kicked in the stomach. He looked so stricken that Arianna's father invited him in to sit down. Nikolas said, "I am sorry. I am very close to my father, sister and grandmother, who raised me, but my mother…"

In his distress, his mother's whole troubling past came tumbling out, "Maybe it isn't all her fault. As a child she fell from her hanging crib and her hand became crippled. I sometimes wonder if that accident in some way also crippled her perception of all that she later went through. As a young girl, she faced the loss of her father from the flu and resultant move to her mother's hometown, which she took very hard. A few months later she was devastated when her beloved sister—her only confidant in the new village— also suddenly died

18

from the flu. Not long after that, a man returned from war and wanted to marry her widowed mother, whom he had known before. But her mother adamantly protested saying that she was born once, baptized once, married once and would die once."

Nikolas took a deep breath and continued, "So instead the family arranged for him to marry her daughter, my mother, who was around twelve years old and still playing with dolls at the time. My mother fought the agreement bitterly. She was so young when she had me that I was raised by my grandmother. As the first child of that marriage, I try to steer clear of her in order to not provoke her."

"All of that to say I am very sorry if she did not represent our family well, but she does not speak for me and has little to do with me. I will be crushed if she has ruined my chance of happiness. I really care for your daughter, sir, and don't want a single thing from you other than her partnership in marriage." He choked up at the end of his speech, realizing how feeble his sincerity must look in the face of his mother's insults. He humbly said a silent prayer, "Please God, let them have mercy on me and not hold my mother's offense against me."

Arianna had been listening in the background, and her heart towards Nikolas softened. Having recently felt betrayal by her own family, she could sympathize with his feelings, and he seemed to have it far worse. She could also empathize with his mother's losses and unwanted marriage arrangement at such a young age.

At any rate, Arianna had already made her apologies to Vasilis and had reconciled herself to her family duty. Previously, the only thing she had known about Nikolas was that he was a rich man with a famous house in another town. Now through his vulnerability, she couldn't help but be impressed by his character. In spite of his being wronged by his mother, both in his upbringing and in her sabotaging his engagement, he apologized, understanding her difficulties. In surroundings known for family feuds, Arianna knew that many other men would have been proud, angry or bitter in a similar situation. Suddenly Nikolas no longer seemed like a stranger but a likeable gentleman worthy of respect, and she began to feel a stirring in her heart to want to help him.

Arianna's father hesitated, "The money I had promised you for the villa I have given away as a dowry for my younger daughter. Even if I were to agree, I can't offer the same arrangement." Nikolas saw a glimmer of hope, "I honestly don't want anything but your daughter's hand. I will work hard to provide for her and love her."

Arianna's father looked over and saw his daughter hidden in the hallway. She gave him an almost imperceptible nod. He turned and smiled at Nikolas, "Welcome to the family." Overcome with relief, Nikolas forgot proprieties and impulsively jumped up and hugged his future father-in-law. Wiping a stray tear from his eye, Nikolas turned the attention to the gifts that he had brought, including the biggest fish anyone had ever seen. "Let's celebrate," the mayor said. "Come meet the whole family."

When Nikolas was able to steal a private moment with Arianna, he gave her a gold necklace and matching bracelet. With love written on his face, he assured her, "I promise to do everything I can to make you happy." Arianna accepted the gifts with a smile and a sincere, "Thank you." She still felt some turbulent emotions, but deep inside felt at peace about her future alongside this man who loved her.

Chapter 3

The day of Nikolas and Arianna's wedding dawned beautiful and clear. They had chosen to have the ceremony at a small church in Prasinos Kampos since the large church that Arianna's father and grandfather had helped build in the main square was not completed yet. Arianna wore a long light pink dress, the first time she had worn anything other than black since her brother died. Her silky skin, delicate features and sparkling eyes, highlighted by long dark eyelashes and well-defined eyebrows, were framed by her beautiful long dark hair braided into a crown.

Arianna's father and mother escorted her to the front door of the church and left her to walk down the aisle to the waiting groom. Her parents held their breath, knowing several brides who turned around and walked out the church door. Arianna reflected during her brief moments of freedom, standing between her father and her husband-to-be. A feeling of tranquility and security outshone her sense of duty. As she got closer and looked into Nikolas' eyes, rather than seeing the pride of a conquest won, she discerned a genuine sacrificial love, and this gave her comfort. Nikolas beamed at his stunning and spirited bride, scarcely believing the wonderful gift God had given him.

At the altar, the priest began the wedding ceremony with prayers to the eternal God for the bride and the groom. The priest then asked for the rings from Uncle Elias, who served as Nikolas' *koumbaro* [best man and sponsor]. The priest blessed the rings and holding them in his right hand, made the sign of the cross over their heads and betrothed the servants of God, the bride to the groom. The *koumbaro* exchanged the rings three times, representing that their lives were forever entwined in the Father, Son and Holy Spirit.

The priest held the *stefana* [two wedding crowns, or thin white decorated bands linked by a long ribbon] and prayed, "O Lord our

God, crown them with glory and honor." He placed one crown on the groom's head saying, "The servant of God, Nikolas Stavrolaki, takes as his crown..." and then placing the other on the bride's head continued, "the servant of God, Arianna Kazandaki, in the name of the Father, Son and Holy Spirit." The *koumbaro* exchanged the crowns three times, surrounding and sealing the union in the Holy Trinity.

Following a Scripture reading on the wedding in Cana and teaching about the responsibilities of marriage, the priest gave them walnuts for strength mixed with honey for sweetness, as well as a shared cup of wine. "May their joys be doubled and their sorrows halved because they will be shared."

Still wearing the *stefana* and holding hands, Nikolas and Arianna took their first steps together as husband and wife while hymns were sung. The priest, holding Nikolas' hand and the Bible, led them (symbolizing the couple following the Word of God as they start a new life together) around the altar table in a circle (signifying the eternity of marriage). The procession continued around the table three times, representing the Holy Trinity. The *koumbaro* followed behind them, holding the *stefana* in place.

When the circular procession ended, the priest blessed them and removed the *stefana*. He used the Bible to separate the joined hands of the bride and groom, demonstrating that the only thing that should be able to divide them was in God's hands. In conclusion, the priest offered a benediction prayer for a long, happy and fruitful life.

At the door of the church, Nikolas and Arianna greeted the guests as they exited and gave them a *boubouniera* [white candy-coated almond wrapped in tulle tied with ribbon]. As they proceeded towards the town square, the sound of the *bouzouki* [metallic-sounding guitar/mandolin] signaled the beginning of the celebration. The aroma of marinated lamb and chicken that had been roasting slowly over a fire pit wafted enticingly.

All kinds of vegetables, breads and wines were attractively arranged alongside homemade *spanakopita* and *dolmathes* [lemon-drizzled steamed grape leaves stuffed with seasoned rice and sometimes meat]. For appetizers, they enjoyed varieties of cheeses, fruits, nuts and olives.

As was the custom, Arianna proudly displayed on a table her handiwork demonstrating her homemaking skills— lace tablecloths, embroidered pillowcases, crocheted doilies and brightly colored woven linens. The ladies enviously exclaimed over her original creative designs and asked for instructions on how to copy them.

Nikolas came to the showcase table and found Arianna for their first dance. "You are the most beautiful bride," Nikolas whispered to her fondly. Nikolas held a white handkerchief that could be twirled in the air or clasped to join two dancers. Nikolas led Arianna in a traditional dance, at first slowly, just the two of them; then others joined in a circle, with arms linked and hands on each other's shoulders, as the music intensified. Arianna's older brothers brought out some plates for those who wanted to throw them on the ground in carefree celebration. Nikolas, leading the semicircle, showed off by first squatting low then springing high with a kick and a slap to his heel. "*Opa!*" people yelled as the music became faster and livelier. Nikolas twirled his bride around, thinking it was the happiest day of his life.

The music and dancing continued for several hours. Arianna's mother began serving the wedding cake, a thin honey-flavored sponge cake. A selection of other desserts, such as *baklava* [layers of thin fillo dough and nuts topped with a cinnamon-honey syrup] and *kourabiethes* [flaky butter cookies topped with powdered sugar], and Greek coffee accompanied the cake.

Arianna's father found Nikolas and handed him a handwritten deed to some land in Prasinos Kampos, saying, "I am sorry it couldn't be more, but I wish you and Arianna long life and happiness." Nikolas replied, "Thank you for this gift and for your blessing, as well as this celebration. I will do everything I can to provide for your daughter and make her happy."

They might have lingered longer into the night, but they had more than an hour's journey over the mountain toward the sea to their new home together in Karidia. Nikolas brought his horse adorned with flowers and a beautiful specially-woven blanket and helped Arianna up to ride sidesaddle. Family and friends sent the couple off in traditional merriment as Nikolas led the horse. Many from the village followed part of the way in procession, cheering and singing joyful wedding melodies. Having walked most of her life, Arianna felt especially proud to be honored by this elaborate bridal celebration.

The next day, Nikolas found Arianna sitting outside their home on the beach. "It's perfectly beautiful here… so peaceful," Arianna said. "I am so glad you like it," Nikolas replied, "I would like for you to make our living area downstairs exactly how you want it. If there is anything you would like or need, just ask." Arianna responded gratefully, "Thank you. I will unpack and organize some things and then you can show me how to help at the restaurant." He suggested, "We can take it easy for a week or so." Arianna admitted, "I am really not good at sitting still without doing anything. I would like to learn what my new life will be like and also help with your responsibilities."

Nikolas showed Arianna around the *taverna*. It was modestly sized, made of stone, but the inside walls were covered with plaster. Nikolas had hired an artist to meticulously paint the walls with various detailed picturesque scenes, with the uniform top border tying the themes together and matching his specially-ordered dishes. It was essentially one room, but there were partial walls coming in from both sides, dividing it into four sections. Tables and chairs were set up in each area and out on the balcony. The back left section had a fireplace with shelves built all around it for storage of pans, cooking oil and spices. The back right section had a door leading out to the balcony. To the right of the *taverna* were two large trees. Behind them near the edge of the cliff were steps leading to the ocean or to the lower level of the house, which was partially outdoors.

In the lower yard against the cliff, on the left near the steps were two bathroom stalls. There was an underground septic tank further away that needed to be emptied every now and then. Towards the center of the lower level, in the open air was a wood-burning oven, with an adjacent table for laying bread or other food on top of it. Furthest to

24

the right was an enclosed room that Nikolas was using for living quarters.

After looking around the home-business, they decided to take the horse and wagon around to see Nikolas' various properties, starting with the closest one to the house. He called it *Sterna*, and it was about a fifteen-minute walk east of the house past the Minoan ruins and further inland. It was a large field where he grew all kinds of produce like tomatoes, cucumbers, beans, squash and peppers, and on the north side was a section of grapevines.

Near the center of that field was a well with a windmill that pumped water through pipes to a large cistern on the south side of the property. The cistern was made of stone and cement and had a spout at the bottom that could be closed or opened to irrigate the plants. Depending on the crop and season, Nikolas would dig channels directing the water systematically.

Nikolas explained that this was the closest well for clean water for drinking, washing and cooking. He had also built a smaller cistern at the house that collected rain water for other uses. Arianna thought these constructs were very modern and clever. In such a remote area, without Nikolas' advancements, they would have had to walk a lot further to a communal well of one of the distant villages for household water, and watering the plants would have been a lot more difficult.

They then took the wagon a little over an hour south on the winding dirt road over the mountain to Lithos, his hometown. Nikolas told Arianna, "There is a footpath straight over the mountain, so walking might be a little shorter than riding in the wagon around the mountain." In Lithos, he had two large areas of land. At the top of the hill in a windy area was a threshing floor for grains. Wheat, barley and oats were planted among olive trees. Then also among the olive trees were several rows of grapevines and an area to make raisins. That big plot of land he called *Milos*.

Across the road near a creek were walnut, almond, orange, lemon, plum, pear and fig trees that produced in various seasons. Among them he planted crops such as potatoes, onions, artichokes and melons. That area was called *Lemoni*. Nikolas showed Arianna which side of the lemon tree had sweet lemons and which had sour, since it had been grafted to have both. Arianna smiled appreciatively. He also showed her around the village and where that town well was.

Nikolas looked toward the east and told Arianna, "I don't need to show you the area of land with grapevines and a few olive trees that your father gave us in Prasinos Kampos, a kilometer that way." He pointed then asked, "Did you have a name for it?" She answered, "We called it *Petra* since it was near my grandfather's house that was built into a rock."

Then they rode further south an hour to Topos, the village where Nikolas' mother had grown up before they moved to Lithos. The piece of land really belonged to Nikolas' father and had a threshing floor, grains, and some vegetables. Nikolas explained that he may be needed to help here during the summer harvest and she may be needed to help bring food for the workers. Arianna realized that was probably about a three-hour walk from the house.

On the way back, Nikolas explained to Arianna his hauling and fishing ventures, which pretty much ran themselves. He told her, "At various times, I contract both of my horses and wagons and a fishing boat to day laborers who for the use of my vessels bring me a share of the profits. Also, if they are around during mealtimes, I usually try to give them something to eat."

When he got close to the house, he turned east past the Minoan ruins and traveled two kilometers to the small town of Asprada, where the nearest school and the main church were. Nikolas told Arianna, "Karidia is too new of an area to have a regularly assigned priest, but every now and then one comes to hold a service in the usually vacant, small church there. So the church here in Asprada might be our usual church." Arianna thought to herself that a forty-five minute walk would not be easy but could be done since church and school were so important. But the walk might take more like an hour for children, especially since there was a sizable hill along the way.

After her tour, Arianna was impressed with all that Nikolas was handling. Her new husband was certainly not lazy, and in many ways he was innovative. Arianna was used to hard work, but she wished that more of his properties and their families' villages were closer to their house. It would be no small feat to climb up and down that mountain each way, especially when they were carrying supplies or produce.

In time, Arianna became more accustomed to her kitchen duties. Growing up, the household tasks had usually fallen to her older sister, and Arianna helped in the fields during the day and did her handiwork at night. Here Nikolas had laborers to help with the field work, but she needed to bring them food and also cook for the restaurant. Nikolas' grandmother was an invaluable teacher for her in her new role.

Arianna was grateful for those first few months of dedicated learning before she became pregnant. Nikolas soon realized with his grandmother getting older and Arianna with child, he needed to find another cook for the restaurant. He found a woman from the area who was skillful and also flexible for whatever work was needed.

Arianna also came to love the ocean and its different moods. It would thrill her to see turtles or seals come to the shore on rare occasions. She began to anticipate the weather by observing the kind and color of the clouds at sunrise and sunset. Nikolas would catch different kinds of fish that at first she didn't quite know what to do with. Once an octopus crawled out of the bucket and started to sneak away before she could decide how to prepare him. As she screamed and started to call it names like "rapscallion" and "slimy fellow," Nikolas laughed and caught it for her.

One morning, months later, as Arianna looked out onto the beach, she saw a tent near one side of the house. She woke Nikolas and they went down to see who was there. A rubber inflatable boat was aground nearby. As they got close, a couple emerged from the tent and waved to them. The couple seemed to know very little Greek, but Nikolas and Arianna understood them to be tourists wanting to walk around the area. The lady introduced herself as Brigitte and pointed that her husband was Dieter. As they left them, Nikolas gestured toward the house and indicated that they were welcome anytime.

The next several mornings, Arianna brought the tourists some bread and fruit before they left their tent. Each day she looked forward to visiting her new friends and tried to ask where they were going that day. Brigitte vaguely indicated, "Oh, here and there to look around." Arianna noticed that they were gone for most of the daylight and thought that they must be seeing a lot.

One morning Arianna came a few minutes earlier than usual and saw some papers with sketches of the area. Trees, ditches, wells and large rocky areas were all drawn with precision. Arianna thought they were very clever and almost said something, but Brigitte hurried to cover up the documents and divert Arianna. A few days later, Arianna woke up and looked out on the beach and the tourists were gone. She felt disappointed because she thought that they had become friends, and they didn't say goodbye.

When Arianna complained to Nikolas about Brigitte's sudden departure, he empathized with her and then tried to distract her with preparations for the coming baby. "You know with Grandmother not able to work much in the *taverna* anymore and with the baby coming, what would you think if we moved upstairs into the back half of the restaurant and make that into our home? We can start to slow down the business in order to have more family time," he said. She thought for a moment and replied, "If you think we'll be okay with less business, I would like that." He apologized, "I really wish I could have purchased the villa across the road when it was available, so we could have kept the business and family completely separate. But if you are willing, this might work. We can use the downstairs area more for a barn and for storage."

Nikolas and Arianna took their time getting re-settled upstairs. By December, Arianna had things the way she wanted them and prepared for their first Christmas together. They spent some time with each of their extended families. The time they shared alone was special and simple, mostly looking forward to the gift of their first child.

In the middle of March, Arianna began to have some pains. "Should I get the midwife?" Nikolas asked anxiously. "No," Arianna replied, "but can you go get my mother?" Nikolas urged her to rest, then sped off with the horse and wagon to Prasinos Kampos for his mother-in-law. The next day, Arianna's mother told Nikolas to bring the midwife.

After many hours of prayer while pacing and fetching water or doing whatever other tasks he was instructed to do, Nikolas heard a baby's cry. With a sigh of relief, he ran to check on his wife. Arianna was smiling as she told him, "It's a girl!" "How are you?" he asked anxiously. "Happy," answered Arianna. He looked at his baby girl with overwhelming love in his heart and asked, "What shall we call her?" Arianna suggested, "How about Georgia after your grandmother?" Nikolas choked up as he said, "That would be perfect!"

Arianna's mother and the midwife continued to take care of Arianna and the baby. As soon as Nikolas was allowed to, he held Georgia proudly. He looked at Arianna and teased, "I have a present for you, but you can't have it for a few months." Arianna was curious but thought no gift was greater than the one he was holding right then.

Soon afterwards, Nikolas rode out to Lithos to tell his family about the new baby. He was saddened to find his grandmother very weak and tired. When she heard the good news, her face became radiant, "I could not be more proud of you, Niko, my grandson— really more like my son. And I am honored that your daughter bears my name." Nikolas was glad she was touched, "I owe so much to you. You have been a mother, benefactor and friend." A few days later, Grandmother Georgia passed away quietly in her sleep. The community mourned her death, as she was well respected and admired.

Arianna took it easy right after the baby was born. Gradually she returned to helping the cook prepare food for the workers in the field. Later when she felt stronger, she began taking food to them. She noticed there seemed to be fewer laborers than usual and asked Nikolas about it. "With the talk of war, some of the men have returned to their homes," he told her. She had heard some rumors but didn't think that it would affect Greece, and certainly not Crete. Surely they just wanted to be closer to their families.

Arianna saw all of the work to be done and started to help with the late spring and summer harvests. Initially, Nikolas and the baby wouldn't let her do too much at a time. While she worked, she put baby Georgia on a saddle turned upside down on the ground under a shade tree. While she didn't particularly enjoy the manual labor, it gave her a rewarding sense of accomplishment, and she enjoyed being outdoors. They had much to do all the way through the fall. In September, they heard that Germany had invaded Poland, but that seemed too far away to affect them much.

When Arianna became pregnant again, Nikolas brought her the present he had told her about at Georgia's birth. He hoped it would divert her a little from the field work. He led her outside where a beautiful black foal was tied. Arianna loved her immediately. Nikolas told her that the horse was born on the day Georgia was born and he had bought it from Arianna's uncle. She was pure-bred Arabian. He handed Arianna a small sugar cube to make friends. "She will need special attention since she has recently been weaned," he told Arianna. The foal nuzzled underneath Arianna's arm looking for more sugar cubes, so Arianna talked and played with her a little before settling her in the barn area.

As time passed, Arianna settled into a new routine with her baby and the growing foal. During Georgia's naptime in the afternoon, she often found herself under a shade tree in the front yard, reading whatever she could find. She had a prayer book, and others had written down many of her favorite Old Testament Bible stories that she had heard from her grandfather. She wished that books were more plentiful. She had heard that many books, especially Christian books, were hidden in the ground during the past Turkish occupation in the early 1900s. She also knew that every now and then someone would find one, and she wondered how many were still buried in forgotten places.

Occasionally some ladies from the area walked by and saw her and stopped for a visit. When they asked what she was reading, she either read to them, or from memory told some of the Bible stories

30

with great enthusiasm. Many of the ladies were not able to read, and not all of the narratives were told in the usual Greek Orthodox liturgy. They were all fascinated to hear the stories and message come to life. Some of the ladies told other friends about their visits, and soon it became a regular Sunday afternoon event, with some also coming other days of the week. On Sundays Nikolas surreptitiously tried to sit close enough to overhear.

Nikolas loved when Arianna told her favorite story. The emotion in her voice conveyed her tender heart as well as her strong convictions. "With every step up the mountain, Abraham fought his human emotions with his faith in the promises of God. He pondered the command of God to sacrifice his promised son with whom God had miraculously blessed him in his old age. His son, Isaac, was truly beloved. After reaching the top of the mountain and building an altar, Abraham looked into his son's meekly questioning eyes. Knowing that God is God and must be obeyed completely, Abraham raised his knife above his trembling but trusting son. Abraham began to lower his knife but God stopped him and provided a substitute, a ram caught in a nearby bush. Abraham and Isaac rejoiced at their salvation provided by another."

While some of the ladies wiped their eyes, Arianna further expounded, "Another beloved but purely *perfect* Son, Jesus, gave Himself as a sacrifice, becoming a substitute for us, for the death penalty of sin that we, who are *imperfect*, deserved. God loved us so much that He went through with this enormous sacrifice." Although most kinds of self-sacrifice were foreign to the historically oppressed people of Crete, they could understand the strong bond between a father and son. They were impacted by both the foreshadowing and the fulfillment that conveyed the essence of the Holy Bible— Love.

Chapter 4

The summer of 1940 brought to Crete more insinuation of war as times were becoming tougher. Arianna could hold back her fears no longer, "Will your slightly stooped shoulders from your back injury exempt you from a draft if it comes?" Nikolas always thought honesty was best, even if it hurt, "No, I don't think so. I can do everything that I was trained to do in the military. How about your family?" Arianna replied, "Father is too old, but my brothers..." She couldn't finish the sentence.

As the time of the delivery of their second child drew nearer, Arianna's mother came to stay with them a little earlier than she had with the birth of Georgia. Georgia was a little over a year old and was becoming a handful. Their friends and extended family were sure that this next baby would be a boy. A son to carry the family name and help shoulder the physical burdens was vital to cultural status.

Many were surprised when Arianna had another girl. She was beautiful and healthy and Nikolas was happier than if he had a thousand boys.

The designation of a godparent was something that Greek families took very seriously. In addition to lifelong spiritual guidance, godparents were expected to pay a sum of money to the church and shower the child with gifts, such as gold jewelry. Nikolas and Arianna had a difficult time finding a godparent for the new baby since the baptism expenses were prohibitive for many experiencing difficulties stemming from the surrounding unrest.

They found a gentleman who was willing, provided they name her after his mother. Nikolas and Arianna agreed, but the name was so unfamiliar to Arianna that she had to write it on a piece of paper and fasten it to the baby. When a kindly neighbor would look in on the baby and ask her name, Arianna would peek at her nametag. They decided to informally call her by an alternate form of that name, Ioanna, which was much more familiar.

The fall season brought the inevitable faster than anticipated. Seemingly, Prime Minister Benito Mussolini of Italy was not to be outdone by the conquests of Chancellor Adolf Hitler of Germany. Word began to spread of the Greek government's firm "No!" to Mussolini's ultimatum to let Italian forces occupy some regions of Greece. The proud Greek citizens began to celebrate October 28th as "*Ohi* [No] Day." War was declared and immediately Greece dispatched troops towards the northern area of the mainland, near the Albanian border.

Suddenly the town crier in Karidia announced the draft of both Greek men and supplies. The local constable made his rounds door to door with specific orders. Arianna felt like her life was falling apart. She was still adjusting to her husband's different world and to having two small children. She couldn't bear the thought of being separated from her husband or losing any more brothers. What were several countries doing getting into a war anyway— hadn't everyone learned how horrible the first world war was?

When Arianna heard from her neighbor friends that the military was taking horses, she reached her last straw. She exclaimed "No way!" and decided to hide her favorite pet indoors. The small horse already thought she was a member of the family. She followed Arianna around since she would occasionally give her sugar cubes. In Arianna's estimation, the only thing she couldn't do was talk, she was so smart.

When the constable and some soldiers came to their home, they immediately took the two larger horses and one of the wagons used for their hauling business. They also told Nikolas to report to the Heraklion military facility in two days. Nikolas tried to joke with Arianna, "Guess you should have tried to hide me instead of the horse." Arianna hit him playfully then slipped away and cried.

Days later Nikolas departed with his regiment for the Greek-Albanian border. He was concerned about leaving Arianna and two

33

very young girls, but he felt better knowing the fighting was not in the islands. When Petros' wife offered to stay often with Arianna and the girls, he was relieved and grateful, even if it would just distract Arianna from worrying. He couldn't forget the look in Arianna's eyes as he and her brothers rode off.

Nikolas scanned his fellow comrades. Most were a lot younger than his thirty-three years. It had been over a decade since his initial mandatory months of military training, and the time reviewing the latest machinery and getting outfitted in Heraklion was extremely brief. He wondered if he was up to this physically and also mentally since he had never seen real combat.

By the time they sailed to the mainland and traversed its length to the north to reach the front, fighting had already begun, with some progress by the Greeks in moving the Italians northward. His unit mobilized immediately. Nikolas was assigned as a machine gun loader. The initial adrenaline of dutiful adventure disintegrated into a transient illusion. War became very real very fast. It seemed to Nikolas that they were outmanned and out-supplied. But he also witnessed the unequaled fierce determination of Greek men defending their native land, and they were slowly gaining ground.

It was becoming a bitterly cold winter, and Nikolas was not used to the snow and ice of the north. He and his infantry fought long, hard days and into the nights. Nikolas was used to hard work, but this with the extreme weather and toll of seeing his comrades fall right before his eyes was a shock he had never before encountered. Thinking of his wife, daughters and beautiful homeland was the only thing that kept him going. God's presence seemed far off in this wasteland, but Nikolas knew that whether he lived or died was in His hands, so he fervently said a quick prayer when conflict was especially intense.

One evening after a particularly exhausting day, Nikolas started to doze off during the artillery fire. He felt his mother shake him and heard her say, "Wake up!" He awoke and shifted position, and as he did, a bullet whizzed past him to the exact place he had been. His heart pounded as he realized what had just happened. He took a moment to look towards heaven and say, "Thank you. I am not sure

34

why You have chosen to spare me, but I will look for Your purposes in whatever the remainder of my life may hold."

***

Arianna, as much as she was able, tried to maintain what produce she could without hired help. She worked as hard as she could to provide food for her family, sell what she could and even in the tough times give to others in need. She was preoccupied with thoughts of the war, but other than rare brief letters from Nikolas, she knew little of the developments. Arianna did know how to drop to her knees, though. In her mind, sometimes there was no time to wait for a priest to come around. She appealed in humility and faith directly to Jesus for Nikolas' protection. She felt comforted by His presence.

The *taverna* was all but closed, with business down and the cook that they had hired back with her family. Petros' wife was a great help and support. She helped with the housework and care of the girls when Arianna was in the fields. During one of those times, she peered into the small crib and admired Ioanna sleeping contentedly. Suddenly she felt sick. She turned aside and vomited. It was at that moment that she realized she was pregnant. She felt elated at the thought of having her first child but also anxious at the timing with the war. When she was let in on the secret, Arianna was delighted and certain that God would take care of them.

***

It was a terrible winter. Nikolas was horrified to see most of his battalion killed, either by gunfire or from freezing to death. Many were on the ground, covered in snow, making it tragically difficult to distinguish the dead from the living. Nikolas continued warfare late into the night. He had never been so cold and so thirsty. His fingers could barely manipulate the bullets. He thought that he would die from thirst.

When the fighting slowed and he could stand it no longer, he staggered throughout the vicinity, searching among the fallen for a canteen that wasn't frozen. He kept shaking canteens, but nothing was shaking. He finally found one canteen that made a sound, so he thankfully thought, "There is water here." So he took it, and as he drank thirstily, he realized it was pure alcohol. He thought to himself, "My goodness, if the shells don't kill me, maybe this will." He saw a few other medical supplies around and thought this might have been for disinfecting wounds. He faltered to the ground, overcome at last by exhaustion, frost and alcohol.

So he was for the rest of the night until morning, when some comrades found him, most of his body frozen in the snow. In the light of day, a unit had come to reconnoiter and found him alive. It was a miracle that he was not wholly frozen to death since the alcohol lowered his core body temperature, but his legs and feet were dark purple and blue, frozen from the hips down.

The men loaded him onto a stretcher and took him to a medical camp to the south of the battlefront. When a medical team was finally able to look at him, they determined that both of his legs had to be amputated. Those assisting hastened to prepare for the operation.

**

Arianna was planting winter onions mid-morning at the *Sterna* property, not too far from the house. All of a sudden, she had a strong feeling that Nikolas was in danger. It was so pressing that she dropped her tools, crouched on the ground with her face in her hands on the earth and pleaded to the God of heaven to save him. "Protect Nikolas, O God. Watch over him and provide a way safely home. Keep him whole, body, soul and spirit, by Your mighty power. Thank You, Jesus, our Savior." She began to sing quietly as she resumed her planting, trusting Nikolas in the hand of the Father.

**

The physician picked up the instrument to begin Nikolas' amputation. As he moved closer to begin the procedure, a flurry of activity stopped him short. A wave of critically wounded soldiers was brought to the camp. The doctor quickly threw the tool aside, "This will have to wait." He ran to assist the gravely injured troops.

When Nikolas awoke from the chloroform and saw his legs and then felt their numbing pain, he was both relieved and anxious. Maybe he had a chance to recover fully, or maybe this chance was going to

36

take his life. Time wore on with so many more men in serious condition. At long last, they decided to send him closer to home to wait his turn for surgery— if he was still alive.

Nikolas was sent by train to Athens. When he eventually reached the hospital, the wounded were overflowing beyond the facility walls. His case was of little concern to the medical doctors, since there were so many other men who were bleeding profusely. The doctors ran to control the hemorrhaging or surgically remove bullets from those about to die. So they put Nikolas to the side and gave him a blanket and a small ration of food. He overheard a doctor walking away utter "If he lives, he lives; but if gangrene sets in, well…"

There were so many people ahead of him that they finally decided it would be better if they sent him home to his family. "Better that than die here now from frostbite or later on when we finish with all this other massacre and try to remove his legs." So they put him on a boat and shipped him to Crete.

***

Late one afternoon, Arianna heard a wagon coming towards the house. She went outside and saw two men she did not recognize slowing a mule to a halt. The driver went around to help the passenger climb down and handed him a walking stick. The passenger had long, unkempt hair and beard and appeared frail and filthy in a long, light green coat. She thought to herself, "Who is this unsightly stranger?" Then when his eyes met hers, she uttered a quick scream and ran to embrace him, "Nikolas!" The driver explained, "He has a bad case of frostbite in his legs. A military officer found out that I was headed this way and asked if I could bring him."

They helped Nikolas inside and to the bed. Arianna told the driver, "Sit down and I will fix something for you." He replied, "I'm sorry, I can't stay." So she gave him some bread and olives to take with him and wholeheartedly thanked him for bringing her husband home.

After expressing sincere sentiments of love and relief to each other, Nikolas tried to forewarn Arianna, "The doctors at each base thought both legs needed to be amputated, but they just didn't have time to do it. They were afraid for my life and advised I find someone in this area…" Arianna gasped sharply as she felt her chest tighten. She felt his head for fever and then carried a bucket of hot coals from the fireplace closer to make him warmer.

Needing more light to examine Nikolas' legs, Arianna lit an oil lamp and brought it near him. She had never seen anything so bad. Both legs were mostly bluish purple with purple blood blisters here and there. But she didn't see much black, there was no unusual odor and he had some feeling. He had no fever or sign of infection that she could see. She fed him some soup and bread, which he ate gratefully.

When she felt he was stable enough, she ran over to *Sterna* to draw some water from the well. After warming the water over the fire, she gently washed his legs, carefully preventing dirty water from flowing onto the wounds. When he was clean enough to let him soak, Arianna brought a large metal tub and kept bringing more warm water to make sure the lukewarm temperature was kept constant. Afterwards, he rested in bed. This bathing routine was repeated with Arianna's watchful care over the next several weeks.

Christmas was a simple event that year. Petros' wife, who mostly remained in Prasinos Kampos after Nikolas came home, went to church with Arianna's parents, but Arianna stayed home with Nikolas and the girls. Although there were no gifts or fancy foods, they were happy spending the holiday together. They said their own prayer of thanks for protection and the gift of God's Son.

Georgia was almost two years and Ioanna was six months old. Nikolas was so happy to spend time with them. He laughed as Georgia ran around the house, chasing their small cat. For their sakes, he did his best to push his thoughts of the war aside, but he couldn't suppress the nightmares. Arianna hardly slept, worrying about his physical and emotional condition.

Around the first part of the new year, Nikolas could walk short distances on his own and normal color was returning to his legs. He began some mild stretching exercises, and Arianna gave him light massages. His night terrors were lessening, with Arianna gently soothing him back to sleep and silently praying for him.

As spring began, Nikolas was doing so well that they began to worry that he might be called back to the war. He was able to work short periods of time, with Arianna overseeing so that he would not overdo it. They felt fortunate to still have their young horse for transportation or carrying small loads.

In April, they found out through Arianna's father that the Germans were joining the Italians in the fighting in Greece. A few weeks later they learned that Greece had surrendered. As Nikolas and Arianna shared their feelings, they had a mixture of relief that Nikolas would not have to return to war and her brothers would come home, but also the disappointment of defeat mingled with defiant pride and apprehension about the future.

Overall, they were thankful that the war had not touched them more. They had heard horrifying reports of what was happening to the Jewish people. Arianna knew that Greek history had seen its share of brutality, but this was a new kind of enemy. The Greek currency continued to lose value, but they had food and shelter.

In May, the men who had been deployed from Crete returned home from mainland Greece. Nikolas and Arianna gladly helped welcome her brothers home. Arianna's father gave praise to God for keeping the men safe and for Nikolas' recovery. They discussed hearing that there may be some British soldiers on the island, mainly near three larger cities, including Heraklion, but for the most part that was reassuring. None of them felt safe enough to travel unaccompanied, but other than seeing Greek soldiers pass through every now and then, they were left alone.

On the afternoon of May 20th, Nikolas and Arianna relaxed on their balcony with Petros and his wife. Arianna brought out a plate of freshly harvested cucumbers. "First batch of the year," she told them. They looked out at the ocean and spoke of the weather, the crops, babies— anything but the war. They started to hear a distant roar from over the ocean. Nikolas flashed back to a memory of the battle near Albania but then shrugged it off.

39

He picked up Georgia, who had just awakened from her nap, bounced her on his knee and quoted a children's rhyme that mentioned cucumbers, *"Pezome tiri ke agouri, pame pera sto Papouri. Posa avga efaes* [Let's play cheese and cucumber. Let's go to Papouri. How many eggs did you eat]?" The others smiled as she giggled and reached for the cucumbers. "I can't believe she's already two and Ioanna is almost one," Petros' wife said. Arianna agreed wistfully, "Time goes by so fast. In a little while, you will be due."

The roar was becoming louder. "Maybe you ladies should take Georgia into the house and see if Ioanna is awake," Nikolas suggested, starting to get a little concerned. Petros and Nikolas exchanged worried glances. The ladies had no sooner gotten up when suddenly they heard an aircraft approaching and then a deafening *BOOM*! "Get inside, quick!" Nikolas shouted, "Take cover!" The sky was full of aircraft, flying from the direction of Heraklion in the west. It was like nothing Arianna had seen before, and she was frozen in terror.

Nikolas pushed the women and Georgia inside the door as another bomb exploded on the beach near their shore. "Jesus, save us!" Arianna screamed as she ran to Ioanna, who was awakened by the commotion. They crouched under a large table in the front section of the house, beyond the stone wall separating it from the back half of the home. The women were crying and shaking from fright while the men were contemplating what to do.

After a time Nikolas asked, "Do you think we should try to get down into the enclosed area below near the animals?" Petros countered, "Should we try to make a run for my family's place in Prasinos Kampos?" Nikolas thought aloud, "It is further inland and more sheltered by the mountains..." Nikolas continued, "We will have to get the horse. Do you think we can make it with the wagon?" Petros replied resolutely, "I think we have to try."

The roar from the aircraft was constant and jarring, but the bomb blasts were lessening. Nikolas and Petros ran to hook up the horse to the wagon and bring them around to the front of the house. They quickly loaded the women and children. As they hastily rode off,

40

another wave of planes came through and began shelling along the shoreline. Enemy bullets punctured the rooftop and sides of the house. Nikolas pressed the horse faster until they reached an area near the mountain where they felt more protected. They slowly ascended the winding road up and around the mountain.

A while later when they neared an overlook, they looked back towards the house and saw the most amazing sight. The sky had opened up with a panorama of multicolored parachutes. At first they gasped at the enormous magnitude of the mystifying contraptions, as well as the vivid beauty of the scene with the magnificent seascape in the background. Then suddenly they were struck with the realization and fear, "The Germans are here."

Chapter 5

The Kazandaki relatives were speaking loudly and all at once. Arianna exclaimed "How do we stand a chance against so many? You should have seen the number of invaders coming from the sky!" One of her brothers expounded in amazement, "We heard that some even had motorcycles. But we also found out that many were unarmed since they sent their weapons down in separate parachutes, and our forces and Allies rallied quickly to shoot many of them down."

Another brother added, "And there are people from New Zealand and Australia here to help in addition to the British. But then again, we don't have many weapons." Arianna's father spoke up with pride, "We Greeks know how to fight, even if it is with pitchforks or whatever we have. But for now, we must hide and take care of our families."

It was decided that the Stravrolaki family, Petros, Markos and their wives would stay at the house that used to belong to their grandfather. It had been built into a cliff at the edge of the village of Prasinos Kampos. It was not large but had two stories. Like many houses in the area, the outside walls and door looked like a traditional home, but the entrance led into an open-air courtyard with enclosed sections on both sides. It was mostly used for storage, so they had some cleaning and organizing to do.

Arianna was grateful that their *Petra* piece of land was nearby and had some produce that they could harvest and continue to cultivate. "I wish we could have brought our chickens. And I really need cloths for diapers," Arianna told Nikolas. "I don't think we will be here long enough to need the chickens, but maybe in a couple of days we can go check things out. If it's safe, we can get a few supplies," he offered.

Nikolas first ventured out to his hometown of Lithos, over a kilometer westward. He found that everyone was okay, and no one had seen any signs of war in their area. He gave his relatives an account of all that he had seen and heard, and they were glad that his family was alive and safe. He then worked a little in his two fields in that area, bringing back a large basket of fruits and vegetables that he collected.

The next day he and Arianna left the girls with their aunts and carefully traveled by foot back to Karidia. When they neared the house, Nikolas told Arianna to wait at a distance until he went closer and determined it was safe. He was relieved to find little damage and no enemy soldiers in the area. He summoned Arianna. He checked the roof and outside perimeter and fed the cat and chickens while she gathered a few supplies on the outside doorstep.

Throwing out the molded cucumbers, Arianna shivered, remembering the moment they had left them. She was determined to clean her house spotless, regardless of who may find it next. She washed the dishes, straightened the bed and mopped the floor, walking backwards to make sure she wiped after her own steps. Nikolas chuckled softly as he saw her. Arianna snapped defensively, "With all the bombing, the door might open and I don't want anyone to peek in to see a dirty house!" She stopped at the door and looked in every direction. Everything was perfect.

"We have to go. It's getting late," Nikolas urged. They left with a few supplies that they could carry on foot— a couple of dining sets, food and diapers, all gathered in a quilt, and a potty chair. "The house has a little damage from the shelling, but it isn't very bad," Nikolas told Arianna on their almost five-kilometer walk to their temporary home.

A few days later, the family started to realize that the conflict on their island might last longer than they had thought. They heard very little of battle, but it appeared that local and support forces were resisting Axis occupation in many different areas of Crete. They thought that they should prepare to stay in Prasinos Kampos for a while.

Arianna was perplexed, "Greece officially surrendered weeks ago. Why are they bothering us, and with such a big commotion?" Nikolas guessed, "As the largest Greek island and one of the biggest islands in the Mediterranean, Crete is probably strategic for military operations." Petros added, "They were probably interested in our ports for their ships and large land areas for their planes. Maybe they knew there were Allied troops here and wanted a show of strength in achieving their objective."

Nikolas and Petros started discussing another trip back to the house. They decided to bring the horse so they could load up the saddle with as many belongings as they could. Arianna insisted on coming along. They left the girls with Arianna's mother and cautiously made their way toward the sea. All appeared quiet, so they made haste to gather clothes, pans and whatever else of use or value, and secured everything to the saddle on the horse. Nikolas tied the chickens' legs together and hung them upside down to have them ready to take with them, while Arianna chased after the cat.

Suddenly, planes swooped in overhead and began shelling rapidly. The horse whinnied and jumped in fright. The saddle flipped around to her belly, spilling most of their belongings onto the ground. Arianna was terrified and confused and ran towards the horse to try to pick things up. Nikolas shouted, "Get down! Get out of the open yard!" Arianna started running around in circles, confused and calling for the cat. Petros yelled, "Come this way, get in the house!" The low-flying planes kept shooting near her.

When she saw Nikolas taking steps towards danger to try to save her, Arianna finally came to her senses enough to run towards the house. They pulled her inside and ducked down within the shelter. Nikolas and Petros wanted to yell at her, they were so mad and frightened, but they were too relieved she wasn't hit and were still alarmed about their current predicament. They looked at her face and saw that she was shaken.

After a while, they realized that it was getting later and the shelling was not lessening. Nikolas told Petros, "You take the horse and run, and we will take the way winding through the wheat fields to hide

44

along the way." Petros didn't like that plan for any of their sakes, but as sitting ducks, any moment they could be captured or killed.

The men made sure to secure any paper currency or few gold coins that they had. Nikolas took the Greek flag he had from the *taverna* and their sieve, and Arianna grabbed a glass framed picture of Jesus. They left everything else behind. "The chickens! The cat!" Arianna lamented as they weaved through the wheat field. The shelling came close to them and Arianna fell, breaking the glass frame of the icon and cutting herself. "Get into the ditch!" Nikolas shouted.

As she lay in the ditch, Arianna's thoughts flashed back to the drawings of the countryside that had been sketched by her foreign friends camping on the beach shortly after she married. "That must have been what they were up to… German spies! Planning this attack!" The realization was startling. She and Nikolas had provided kindness to those who could have hurt them at the time and were oppressing them now.

Arianna's extended family was relieved when all of the foragers finally returned. When Petros told them about the traumatic experience, they were alarmed and glad that God had protected them. The fright was enough to make them forget about returning for a while. They settled in to village life in their close quarters. Shortly after that, they learned that Crete had fallen and was now occupied by the Germans. A new apprehension of how their lives would be changed pervaded their thoughts.

After a time, a healthy baby girl joined Petros and his wife. Arianna remarked that it would be helpful to have some pieces of furniture for storing clothes and supplies and a table and chairs to sit. Nikolas and Arianna's brothers discussed whether it might be safe enough to try to bring the wagon to Karidia to load some furniture. They did some scouting in between times of working the various fields. Finally, they felt it was calm enough to attempt.

When the men arrived at the house in Karidia, there were signs that the Germans had been there. Wine barrels were rolling down the road. The many dishes for the *taverna* and Arianna's valuable china had mostly been taken but some were left broken. There was no sign of the chickens or cat. Arianna's finely embroidered pillowcases had been cut and apparently used as swimming suits.

A local man passing by stopped in when he saw them and said that the Germans had been in and out of the area and had helped themselves to their wine. "The drunken soldiers took your wedding *stefana* and put the two crowns on donkeys, paraded them around in the road and made a mockery of our culture and traditions," he told them. Nikolas shook his head at the lack of common decency.

Nikolas also couldn't help but think about how immaculate Arianna had left the house after their first trip back. It was hard for him to see the things that they meticulously worked and cared for destroyed. But he was glad that the house was still intact and most of the furniture remained. They loaded everything they could, taking the bed but leaving the mattress that the Germans had slept on.

Arianna was thankful when they returned safely with several pieces of furniture. She didn't know whether to cry or scream when she heard about the condition of her house and her things. Sometimes it was very hard to be a lady and a Christian.

Arianna's sister Dorothea, who had taken her place in Heraklion years before, moved back to Prasinos Kampos with her husband Demetrios when the war in Crete began. Demetrios, Petros and Markos made occasional trips back to the city to try to maintain a little business, but their families stayed in Prasinos Kampos. Not long after the men retrieved the furniture from the Karidia house, Petros' wife asked that Petros return one more time for a few belongings that she had left when she was staying there. Demetrios volunteered to go with him.

When they came to the house, they ran into a German officer. It was too late to hide. Demetrios thought quickly. His German wasn't perfect, but it was probably their best shot. He immediately engaged the man with a friendly and respectful smile, "Hello, sir, nice day!" The officer was taken aback and pleased to hear his native German being spoken in a foreign land, and by a regular citizen. They spoke a little while and the officer came to see that Demetrios was well educated, and he liked his genial personality.

46

Demetrios told the German officer, "This is the home of my brother-in-law." The man looked at it a minute and saw that it was sturdily constructed. He noted the flat roof and proximity to the ocean and thought that it could be a strategic vantage point for firing upon any enemies. He then said, "Don't worry, I will see to it that the house will stand. I will paint our symbol on the roof, and we will use it as one of our headquarters." Demetrios thanked him and they left, not wanting to push their luck for more belongings.

When Demetrios told the others what had happened, Arianna was upset at the thought of the Germans in her home and the German symbol tainting her roof, but Nikolas marveled at the favor they had with the enemy. They could have been killed, yet because of the encounter with that officer, their house would be saved. Who knows if they would be able to live in it again, but there was hope. Another hope that came their way was a new baby to come the early part of the new year. In spite of the worries, Nikolas was ecstatic at the news.

The months passed relatively calmly in the quiet, remote village. The extended family worked the fields when they could, although not enough to maintain a marketable business as before. They cultivated what they could to have food to survive. The girls had fun playing with other children, mostly within the concealed courtyard. Arianna did what she could with very limited supplies to prepare for the baby when not cooking, cleaning, watching the children or working in the fields. Because he was the only one in the village who had a horse, Nikolas kept very busy. He worked his and other people's fields and helped neighbors with emergencies.

Nikolas and the horse also took an evening job at the olive press. From high up, the olives were funneled onto a circular slab that had an edge. Large circular stone wheels were attached to thick wooden spokes, which were attached to a central rotating pillar. Attached to the pillar was a long plank that the horse could pull around in a circle to roll the stones over the olives.

Then the crushed olives would be folded into a blanket made of goat's skin and placed on a press. When the men forced the press downward to squeeze the olives, the oil poured out through a spout. The leftover dense olive cake was used or sold to make soap or fuel for heat. Nikolas was paid with olive oil and olive cake. By the time Japan and America entered into war and the conflict was escalating, the Greek currency was practically worthless. Some even used the old bills as toilet paper or kindling to try to cook or keep warm.

That winter was a very cold one. It was one of the rare times the area had snow. The young girls were fascinated with it, even though it wasn't enough to really play in. Several times Nikolas was called upon to take sick or injured people to find the one doctor they had in the territory, or in more serious cases to Heraklion for medical care. Arianna worried both for his safety and his own health.

On the return from one of these trips, Georgia ran outside and yelled, "Look, *Mama*, the horse is white!" The horse's nose, mane and tail were dusted in snow. Nikolas greeted his daughters playfully then cared for the horse, giving her food and water and covering her with his thick army coat because she was both sweating and shivering. At night that coat covered the girls since they only had the one quilt they had brought from Karidia.

In the midst of this cold, Arianna went into labor. Nikolas immediately hurried to get the midwife. As Arianna was waiting she prayed, "Please don't let him get killed or allow the horse to get confiscated..." "*Agghhh...*where is he?!" When she had time to think of something other than the pain and worry, she felt so uncomfortably out of place and yearned for her home.

Arianna felt restless— it was confining in their close quarters, and they had so few supplies. She had cut Nikolas' old, torn shirt to make a single long shirtdress for the newborn. Any other material remnants she had were needed for diapers. Finally Nikolas and the midwife got there. "You'd think that after two children, the third would come easily," Arianna complained to prevent them from seeing how worried she had been about their arriving unscathed.

In the wee hours of the night, a little baby arrived, and it was the long-awaited boy. Arianna wanted to wake up the whole village to

48

share their triumphant news. All other trials seemed to disappear as Nikolas and Arianna cradled their newborn son.

In the morning, they showed Georgia and Ioanna and all of the clan their treasured new family member. Even Nikolas' mother came, beaming with pride and demonstrating surprisingly pleasant behavior. The relatives came and went, passing him around, sometimes checking to make sure he was a boy. "Leave my son alone," Nikolas said, "it's too cold for that."

A couple of days later, the midwife came back to do the circumcision. She warmed herself at the fire and wondered if her hands would stay warm enough, it was so chilly. Soon after that, Nikolas noticed that the infant seemed to feel warm. Arianna brushed it off saying that they had to keep him warm. Then he started to have difficulty breathing.

The baby's symptoms progressed rapidly, so the doctor was quickly summoned. "I am sorry, it looks like a severe case of pneumonia. There is no medicine— I don't think there is anything we can do," the doctor told them regretfully. "No!" Arianna groaned, a heavy weight of despondency settling over her. She prayed fervently, "Please don't take my baby."

They hastened to make baptism arrangements, but they had a hard time finding a godparent since times were so hard. Arianna pleaded with relatives, "Please, we don't need any gifts— nothing— I just want a meaningful sign that my baby belongs to Jesus and I will see him in heaven." Finally Arianna's aunt offered, "I will arrange something with the priest, but I have no clothes or jewelry to give him. And I know the custom is to give him his grandfather's name, but I would like you to call him Angelos." Arianna grabbed both of her hands and kissed them. "Thank you, whatever you want; a baptism is all we ask. Thank you!" Arianna said with relief.

Georgia perceived that her little brother was sick and that both of her parents were sad, and her mother had been crying. She sensed that something was very wrong. Nikolas took turns picking up both of the girls, trying to distract them from the sadness. At the same time, he wanted to spend every precious moment with his son.

Because they didn't want to draw attention to themselves during wartime and also since it was forbidden for a mother to enter a church within forty days of giving birth, the priest and family observed most of the traditions of the baptismal ceremony in the home of Arianna's grandparents. Georgia felt protective of her little brother and had begged to go along, but she and her sister were compelled to stay with their aunt.

At the beginning of the ceremony, the priest asked the godmother, who was holding the baby, "Do you renounce Satan, all of his angels and all of his works?" She answered, "I do." He asked, "Do you unite yourself unto Christ?" She replied, "I do." The priest made the sign of the cross over the infant. The godmother recited the Nicene Creed then pledged herself to do whatever was necessary to educate him in the Christian faith and set a good example. The priest asked, "What shall his name be called?" The godmother answered, "Angelos."

Normally they used a baptismal font, a metallic basin with a pedestal, but in the home they used a ceramic bowl. The priest immersed the naked child in water three times saying, "The servant of God, Angelos, is baptized in the name of the Father, and of the Son and of the Holy Spirit." He placed the child in the godmother's arms in what was supposed to be a clean white sheet representing purity, but they did the best they could with what they had. The priest then placed oil on the child's hands, feet, ears and mouth to consecrate them to the service of Christ. Then the godmother rubbed oil over his whole body that he may be able to escape the grip of sin.

While Angelos was being dressed into his shirtdress that had been made out of Nikolas' shirt, a candle was lit. The priest and the godmother, holding Angelos, walked around the makeshift baptismal font three times, reflecting that the angels in heaven were dancing at his salvation. The priest sang, "As many of you as have been baptized into Christ have put on Christ."

Since Angelos was too young to take communion, the priest concluded with a Scripture reading, "Or don't you know that all of us who were baptized into Christ Jesus were baptized into His

50

death? We were therefore buried with Him through baptism into death in order that, just as Christ was raised from the dead through the glory of the Father, we too may live a new life." Arianna sobbed, not wanting to think of the likely imminent resurrection of Angelos into heaven. Nikolas put his arm around her, his own eyes tearing at the thought.

Following the baptism, the family gathered at Arianna's parents' home. After spending a little time together, they left Nikolas and Arianna to have some privacy. The baby was wheezing uncomfortably. Arianna could hardly sit still. She was beside herself, trembling and pacing. "God, please, save my little boy!" Nikolas could hold it in no longer and started sobbing himself. When he could speak, he took Angelos in his arms and told him tenderly, "You are the most perfect, most precious little child and we love you very much." Arianna screamed after Angelos took his last gasping breath. They sat together and wept.

In due course, the other family members came in. When they realized that little Angelos had gone to be with Jesus, they began wailing and sobbing. After a time, the family tried to console themselves that he was no longer suffering, and that maybe Konstantine was able to welcome him to his new home and introduce him to his loving Savior, Jesus. Arianna's mother tried to comfort her, "You can't imagine anyone loving Angelos more than you, Arianna, but Jesus does, and He will take care of him now."

Nikolas carried lifeless Angelos on a pillow as they brought him home. Georgia had awakened from her nap, and she ran to the door. She would never forget the tragic sight of her motionless brother in the arms of her disconsolate father. Another wave of grief assailed them as they realized he would never take another breath here, play here or know his sisters. They struggled to keep their composure as they did their best to explain what they could to Georgia and Ioanna.

Still feeling numb and confused, they knew they must start to prepare for the baby's funeral. Arianna was heartbroken that she did not have something fitting for him to wear for his burial. She thought back to all of the intricate designs she had created just a few years ago, but nothing was left, and there were no materials to make anything new. She had nothing special to give the most precious thing in her life. She resented the war more at that moment than she ever had before. Arianna asked the Lord, "Why? Why give him to me to take him away?" Then she stopped herself, "No, Lord, thank you for giving him to us, even if it was just for eight days."

The girls were sad and insecure and didn't want to be apart from their parents, but they were protected from going to the emotional funeral. Arianna had never thought she could be in more anguish than she was with Konstantine's death, but it was many times worse to lose her child. Arianna was dreading that the time was getting closer to lay Angelos' body in the ground. When the time came, Nikolas and Arianna made their way to the church, which was next to the cemetery on the outskirts of town.

After a brief service, they laid his tiny body to rest, commending his soul to Jesus. The priest sprinkled dirt in the shape of the cross over the box as the family members wailed and sobbed. Then he pronounced the benediction and said to the family, "May God give you strength to bear your loss." "Only by God's strength," Arianna whispered to herself, almost passing out in emotional and physical exhaustion, "only by God's strength."

Chapter 6

In the days following the funeral, Nikolas and Arianna felt unsettled at their borrowed accommodations in Prasinos Kampos. Nikolas thought a change would be good for all of them and began to look for a place closer to his hometown and larger properties in Lithos. He first approached his mother, thinking that with the death of her grandson, she may be sympathetic and want to spend time with her granddaughters, but no way. She was not interested in sharing her home. Nikolas felt a little betrayed— she did have a large house after all, and a war was going on, with strangers finding refuge with strangers. But he did not press the issue. If she wouldn't be happy with the arrangement, he didn't want any bitterness to poison his family life.

The homes of his other relatives were already filled with added displaced kin. He continued to ask around, but places were limited, since many had fled Heraklion to the safer villages where they could grow their own food. Likewise, supplies were not obtainable to try to build something modest.

Provisions, other than what they could cultivate themselves, were scarce. However, predominantly, they felt secure. The people of their community struggled to remain inconspicuous with the occupying forces. They avoided the main roads, traveled in very small numbers with minimal tools to not appear threatening and did not keep lanterns lit in their homes for long in the evenings.

They heard a few accounts of acts of heroic resistance in other towns that resulted in retaliatory torture or firing lines, even of priests, women and children. Though they were proud of the courageous spirit of their countrymen, the townsfolk of Prasinos Kampos were anxious for their families and wanted no part of the cruelty.

The dark cold of winter metamorphosed into the dawning of spring, in more ways than one. Arianna's unremitting black mourning clothes reflected a deep feeling of emptiness, but she started to take more of an interest in daily life. Their beloved horse delivered an adorable foal. Arianna liked to watch it wobble and then frolic in the springtime air.

Arianna also came to realize that she was with child again. The family was concerned for Arianna's health, with it being so soon after her last pregnancy. Her recent grief, in conjunction with wartime stress and undernourishment, increased their anxiety. While they expressed their joy, they resolved to help her in any way that they could.

Three-year old Georgia, after being confined indoors most of the winter, ran outside to play the first moment she could. There was so much to explore. After running around for some time, she slowed down enough to become curious. She unearthed some interesting-looking wild mushrooms. She smelled them and thought they might be a pretty good snack. She ate two good-sized ones before Nikolas found her, "How many of those did you eat?" She held up two fingers. Nikolas didn't recognize them to be too dangerous, but they were not particularly safe either, especially for a young child. "Let's go inside and find *Mama*," he suggested. They gave her some bread and milk to add some fiber and coat the stomach and hoped she would be all right.

Georgia woke up from her nap complaining of a headache and stomach ache. Nikolas and Arianna looked at each other. They weren't sure what to do. The doctor was never easy to find, and more than likely he couldn't do much but let it pass. Poor Georgia couldn't keep anything down for weeks. During that time Nikolas found a place in Lithos for them to relocate, but Georgia was too sick to move. She had no energy, had chills while sweating and seemed slightly delirious.

The doctor came around and stressed the importance of giving her liquids. "If she has any seizures, send for me immediately," he added. Arianna started to really worry. She had just lost one child, now surely not another! They gave her fluids, tried to keep her comfortable and prayed relentlessly. Arianna's family supported them, affirming that Georgia would be okay and helping with the household duties so that Arianna would not be overburdened. Gradually, Georgia started to retain food and regain some energy. Arianna exhaled a sincere prayer of thanks.

"This has been too much," Arianna confessed to Nikolas, "I think I am ready for a new beginning once Georgia is back to her normal self. Is that place in Lithos still available?" Nikolas answered, "I can inquire, but you know it's not much of a home. It may have been a house a while back since it has a fireplace and a window, but a wealthy woman has been using it as her barn and for storage. It's basically one room, but of sufficient size, and it has a few steps leading to a small open loft." With Arianna's encouragement, he pursued an arrangement. For his labor several times a year tilling the landlady's fields with his horse and his plow, he was granted her structure for lodging.

They decided to leave most of the heavier and more valuable pieces of furniture in Prasinos Kampos. The last thing they moved was the horse so that her foal could be weaned. Arianna's father had his eye on the foal, so he offered them a baby goat in exchange, apologizing that it wasn't a fair trade. "Your family has provided us lodging and support for a year; you shouldn't be giving me anything," Nikolas protested. "I am happy to give you something that will eventually provide milk to my grandchildren," his father-in-law returned.

Arianna organized her new one-room home and cleaned the best she could, considering she had a dirt floor. She cleaned out the fireplace and stored food in baskets hung by rope from the exposed beams of the roof. They swept the leftover hay from the loft and made beds for the girls using rugs and Nikolas' military coat. They would keep the goat indoors while it was a baby and during the winters but hid the horse in a neighbor's barn.

Not long after they got settled in Lithos, the German forces became more visible in the villages. At first, troops filed through to make their presence known and to survey the area. Later small contingents were stationed throughout the various districts. The German command was enflamed by the tenacious and fierce Greek resistance

55

which was being aided by local citizens. Even children would zigzag along their well-known rocky paths and shortcuts through the mountains to deliver supplies or messages of troop movements.

The patrols started to enforce rules upon the Greek citizens. Anyone bearing a weapon would be shot on sight. Citizens were required to salute and say "Heil, Hitler" to the German soldiers. Permits were needed for travel during the day, and strict curfews were enforced in the evenings.

Nikolas, still one of the few men in the area with a horse, often needed a permit in order to help sick or injured neighbors in need of a doctor. With his lanky frame and jovial, laid-back personality, he did not appear much of a threat to the Germans. On rare occasions when he would come across one or two by themselves, he even offered them a snack of any goods that he had on him. He took care not to travel frequented roads with noticeable quantities of produce to avoid tempting them to seize an entire load.

Nikolas also helped the people of the village with their plowing, transportation or various tasks. He never required payment, but they would pay him with whatever they had— a handful of potatoes, some eggs, even a chicken. Nikolas and Arianna recognized that their cherished horse was a blessing from God to provide for their family and the community during the war. This horse was especially prized since their other two horses and the wagon that had been confiscated were never returned.

In addition, Demetrios somehow got his hands on a large bag of sugar, which was a rare commodity, and shared some with the Stavrolakis. Their landlord gave them honey from her honeycombs in return for odd jobs. So the Lithos residents sometimes offered Nikolas trades for sugar or honey, especially for mixing into medicinal preparations.

When the family sat down for meals, they sincerely thanked God for their blessings and provision of food and asked Him to meet the needs of others. They had heard troubling stories of starvation in the cities. Arianna worried when Nikolas was out on errands for others or for themselves, especially if he ran a little late, but was so thankful that God used many of these missions to provide for them.

As time progressed, Arianna had some difficulty keeping her food down. This pregnancy was her most difficult thus far. Nikolas was concerned over her small frame. She should be larger by now. He knew that seeing the Germans every day added to her anxiety and tried to shield her from contact with them or thoughts of war when possible.

This became harder to do when a young man from Albania deserted to Lithos and took refuge in Nikolas' mother's barn. He had shown up on her doorstep frightened, hungry and thirsty, and she took pity on him. He knew a little Greek but wasn't fluent. For her kindness to him, he innocently called Nikolas' mom "Matero" instead of the Greek word *Mitera* [Mother].

He tried to blend in, gratefully working hard for Nikolas and his father in return for food and shelter. One day in the fields, he caught a bit of unspoken conversation between Nikolas and his father. Instead of saying, "*Ohi* [No]," Nikolas slightly nodded his head upward and made a soft clicking noise (almost a kissing sound) with his mouth. At the Albanian man's perplexed look, Nikolas chuckled, "We Greeks have the reputation of being pretty fired up, but sometimes we can be rather laid back. That gesture is another way to say 'no.'"

Nikolas' father stepped in, "There is a popular joke about two shepherd friends who were on two different mountaintops separated by a large chasm. One shepherd slowly and emphatically shouted at the top of his lungs to his friend, 'Hey, have you seen my missing goat?' The friend glanced over in the other man's direction, tilted his head up slightly and uttered an almost inaudible, '*tsk*.'" The Albanian laughed at the tale with the unique mannerism.

The man from Albania was a humble, likeable fellow, but they knew that his presence put them all in danger. Nikolas carefully helped the man smuggle a letter back home to his family who didn't know if he was alive or dead. All the time that the foreigner worked, he kept his ear to the ground for a way of escape back home, but it was too dangerous without legitimate paperwork in fully-occupied Crete.

Once when the Germans randomly inspected men's papers, he snuck away to his temporary quarters, thankful for the piles of recently harvested sheaths of wheat to hide in. When for a period of weeks the Germans permeated the village, it became necessary to continue to use this extraordinary measure to temporarily hide the refugee. Nikolas and his father carved out the middle of the wheat stack, leaving a small hole for him to breathe.

Nikolas' mother left her chickens and eggs near that area so that it didn't look unusual for her to visit several times a day to smuggle food and water. The man felt claustrophobic in this protective prison in the stifling heat of summer. At night he was relieved to be able to get out and hide in the open air of the dark barn for several hours. He was even more thankful when the German ranks thinned out in the area so he could go back to concealing himself reasonably.

That fall, like the previous year, the Stavrolakis thought it too risky to try to make wine, but they were able to pick some grapes. They had some for the table and to share with their families and those in need. They were also able to make a small batch of raisins to store for the winter. Afterwards came the olive harvesting. This time, Nikolas with the horse helped crush olives into oil at a mill in Lithos.

Christmas came and went yet again with simplicity but gratefulness. Nikolas took some time to play *kokoli* with the girls. He would sit on a chair, cross his leg, put a child on his dangling foot, take her hands in his and swing his leg back and forth saying, "*Kokoli, kokoli.*" The girls laughed and kept begging for more turns until Nikolas was worn out and tried to distract them with something else.

When the first few weeks of the new year rolled around, Arianna was not always in good temper. She was due any time, and the confinement with two girls underfoot in their one-room dwelling in the middle of an occupation was trying her nerves. When Arianna tried to pick an argument with Nikolas one day, he laughed it off saying, "I know better than to mess with Greek women— they are

58

known to go after their enemies with pitchforks and win!" Arianna knew what he was referring to, having heard stories of some women from another area of Crete aggressively defending themselves against soldiers during the war.

"Did you hear about the seamstress and the German?" Nikolas asked. When she said that she hadn't, he told her that a woman was approached by a German soldier who wanted her to fix the emblem on his shirt collar. Nikolas grinned, "First, he asked if her husband was there. When she said that he wasn't, the German started to tell her that he had a big collar... But she misunderstood him to say 'a big *kolo* [rear end].' She took off after him, waving a stick and shrieking a string of infuriated indelicacies in Greek. She chased him all the way down the road!" Nikolas told the story with such animation that Arianna had to laugh. Then she sighed, "How much longer until this war is over? I want to go home." Nikolas didn't know what to say, so he just held her in sympathy, wishing the same thing.

Arianna's family had been worried about her and the baby's health since she first told them shortly after Angelos died that she was expecting. Realizing that it was becoming increasingly common to lose both the babies and mothers during wartime deliveries, they redoubled their prayers as the time drew closer. Not knowing if the baby would come past curfew, they weren't sure if Arianna's mother would be able to come for the birth. Since Demetrios spoke German, he was chosen to go with her, and together they managed to get a permit for a few days.

In the middle of the night when the time came, Arianna had a very difficult delivery. It was all the midwife could do to control the bleeding, and Arianna became very weak and incoherent. Nikolas pleaded, "Please, Lord, don't take her from me." Arianna gave birth to a tiny baby girl. Her head and torso could fit in Nikolas' hand. Arianna's mother cleaned her quickly and wrapped her snugly to protect her from the chilly room. Nikolas hung a bassinet by rope from the rafters near the fireplace. Eventually Arianna's bleeding decreased and she began to recover. Nikolas breathed a sigh of relief and gave thanks to God.

It took a while for Arianna to get back on her feet. The baby was so small that they weren't sure if she was going to make it. Arianna kept her covered, both to protect her and because she was almost embarrassed to show her tiny form to anyone. Georgia and Ioanna were so happy to have a baby sister and were enthralled with her tiny fingers and toes. Arianna cut a pair of old pants given by Nikolas' father to make diapers and clothes for the baby.

They thought it prudent to baptize the baby as soon as possible. They weren't able to find a godparent among the relatives since many of Arianna's siblings also delivered babies during the wartime downturn. Nikolas asked their landlady, who agreed, provided that they name her Stella. Since there was some concern about the occupation, and it was also very cold outside for a tiny baby, they brought the priest to their place and baptized baby Stella under the loft.

The weeks wore on. Arianna was feeling much better, and Stella was slowly gaining weight. But Nikolas started to feel ill. At first he thought it was an irritation or chafing on his backside and legs. But before long, they realized he was breaking out into enormous boils. They developed into fiery red, pus-filled blisters that were unbearably painful. Ghastlier still, they started turning black in areas. Arianna wondered if some of the poison from his severe frostbite from years before was working itself out. He developed a fever and became bedridden.

Suddenly they heard pounding at the door. Frightened, Arianna opened the door to German soldiers with guns. Through gestures and a fraction of Greek mixed with German, they demanded that the man of the house be seized. Terror engulfed Arianna. With a faltering voice, she tried to explain, "He is too sick." The Germans did not understand and became more belligerent. They stomped over to Nikolas, and Arianna lifted the sheet. The men jumped back when they saw the grotesque sores. Visibly stunned and standing back, an officer asked to see Nikolas' identification. After covering Nikolas back up again, Arianna stood frozen in silent, pleading prayer.

Nikolas told Georgia, who was closest, to get his wallet. Georgia looked at him confused. Nikolas shifted in the bed in order to point

60

to his wallet and winced in pain. Knowing they could all be shot right there, he repeated himself with urgency, "Hurry up! The wallet, bring me my wallet." She still didn't understand and looked up at the Germans with innocent and frightened eyes. The officer showed a fleeting glimmer of sympathy. Nikolas tried again, "The small holder of my papers, bring it to me!"

Finally, Georgia got the idea and brought the wallet to Nikolas, who struggled to hand it to the officer. The officer looked at the papers, gruffly gave some orders to the soldiers (probably to leave him there to die) and gestured for them to go. They looked relieved to get out of there, not knowing if his infirmity was contagious.

Nikolas and Arianna were trembling with relief when they left. After the near miss, Arianna couldn't help but break down and sob. They had heard that the Germans were known to randomly take citizens to the edge of town for a firing squad. They gave thanks to God for the ironic means of emancipation— the boils saved his life.

When she could pull herself together, Arianna turned to making a home remedy to try to speed the healing of Nikolas' boils. She took half an onion, carved out the center to make a bowl and added into it a mixture of ingredients like crushed wheat, olive oil, beeswax, honey, bamboo scrapings and olive oil soap shavings. After making several of these, one for each of the larger-sized boils, she put them over some warm embers until they boiled and the onions became soft. When they cooled enough to put on the skin, she placed them on the boils, wrapped them in a bandage and left them overnight.

In the morning, the pus was near the surface, ready to be carefully lanced. Since his boils were severe and he still had some fever, after lancing them, she dabbed them with strong medicinal alcohol and covered them with a clean bandage rather than leaving them in open air to heal. Nikolas winced with the pain from the lancing and the alcohol, but soon he began to improve.

Arianna was grateful for the hints of spring that allowed her to occasionally open their window to air out their lodging. She changed Nikolas' bandages periodically and carefully sterilized the materials and sheets in boiling water. Before long, Nikolas was able to ambulate to some degree.

When he was able to walk greater distances, Nikolas cautiously walked into the village to hear any news of the war. He knew that there were a few on the island who had wireless radios, and that there were teenage boys that ran as couriers between the villages. When he visited with some of the other men, he found out that most of the German soldiers had evacuated, and there were rumors that they may be bombed.

Applying his past military training, Nikolas pondered what might be a good emergency plan to keep his family safe. With the help of his father and the Albanian man, he surveyed an area of the towering hill across the road from their place and dug into it a cave-like area for his family to be able to retreat into. Other neighbors did the same. They were barely deep and just wide enough for a few people to squat into so that the hideouts weren't obvious from the road. Tall grasses and other natural outcroppings also helped camouflage the caves.

A few days later, they heard the town crier hollering at the top of his lungs, over and over again as he walked throughout the village, "Tonight we will be bombed; make sure there are no lights!" Nikolas and Arianna debated whether to go to the cave that night or not. They thought that with no lights, their structure may not be seen to be targeted. But it was a full moon, and their lodging was on a hill next door to the schoolhouse and across the road from the church, both of which could be spotted.

So they decided to take the girls to the cave and play it safe. From there they heard the planes coming and tried to cover the girls' ears as the bombs fell and exploded, one after the other. After several moments, the bombing stopped. They waited a little longer in case there was to be a second wave, but no other airplanes loomed. They anxiously returned to their accommodations but, providentially, all appeared to be intact.

All was quiet for the next couple of days. Nikolas and Arianna took a moment to sit outside with a few neighbors and family. There wasn't much coffee or snacks, but it was nice to sit and visit. They caught up on each other's families, and then the conversation turned to the struggle. "Our village was lucky that there wasn't any major damage from the recent bombing," someone remarked. They all agreed, and some made the sign of the cross over themselves as they thanked God.

Nikolas' father informed them, "The town crier just acquired a hand-cranked siren to warn us of an impending air raid or any other trouble." Arianna was a little shocked— such a forceful and modern departure from their peaceful countryside. She could understand the value of warning everyone sooner, but she dreaded the additional traumatizing intonations of war.

A neighbor told them a story that happened days before during the bombing. "At dusk, just before the planes came, a woman on the outskirts of town was taking down some laundry from a clothesline. Her baby was in a blanket on top of a large brick placed on the ground. When they saw others start to run for the caves, the woman ran to get the other children, and the husband took the baby, bundled in a blanket. When they got to shelter, they opened the blanket to check on the baby, only there was no baby, just a brick inside the blanket."

The others exclaimed, "What happened?" The neighbor continued, "Of course they were astonished and alarmed and ran back home. Mercifully, they found the baby unharmed and sleeping. They figured that another blanket must have fallen from the clothes that were being collected onto another brick. Somehow in his haste, the man scooped up the other brick and blanket by mistake." Nikolas and Arianna felt the relief on behalf of the parents. It was too close a call and too close to home for them to be amused, although they felt that someday it may be a vaguely humorous tale.

The men started talking to Nikolas about trying to construct a community shelter. They discussed some possibilities and decided that a large barn that had been built into a foothill could be cleared out on the inside and camouflaged from the outside. It was not quite in the center of the village, but that was probably advantageous in order to not be a target. They thought that it wouldn't be too far away for most people to run to. The men recruited more help and got the refuge ready in the next few days. The town crier spread the word to everyone about the new shelter and warning siren.

Stella was still too small to be outside for very long, but Nikolas and Arianna were looking forward to being in the fresh air and cultivating the spring and summer produce. Nikolas said to Arianna, "I'm thinking of planting potatoes next to the onions and broad beans we planted last winter among the fruit trees on the *Lemoni* property. What do you think?" Arianna replied, "That sounds good. We haven't had potatoes there in a while, they are hearty for us and can be mashed for the children." So Nikolas planted a fairly large area of the field with potatoes.

One evening in the late spring, out of nowhere came a blaring siren. Nikolas shouted to Arianna, "Get the baby! I will get the other two." He flung Georgia on his back and picked up Ioanna as they ran towards the community shelter.

"What's happening, *Baba*?" Georgia asked as she looked back and spotted up in the sky some big, loud things making a "V" shape. "Everything will be okay," Nikolas tried to reassure them. Ioanna was looking over Nikolas' shoulder as he carried her. Her eyes were wide as saucers as she saw small scary things zipping down from the sky at everybody and everything. She was so worried that the flying things would hit her mommy and daddy.

The shelling continued as they ducked into the obscured shelter. Ioanna started crying as they all packed into the dark, unfamiliar hideout. Nikolas soothed both girls saying, "Everything is all right now. This is a safe place." More people kept scurrying inside. Arianna tried to find some friends of the girls to help put them at ease and keep them quiet.

After it seemed like most people were there, they tried to count everyone and see who all had made it. As they were being noted, the silent companions looked at one another. No one wanted to think about what may have happened to anyone who was missing.

Chapter 7

The people of Lithos, clinging to the feeling of security, remained in the shelter longer than they needed to. But they realized that they had to get out since the children were getting sleepy and there might be people needing help. They discovered that most of those who didn't go to the shelter either had elderly family members or lived further out. They had felt it was safer to take cover in their homes or their closer caves than try to evade the shelling along the roads to try to get to the shelter.

Among the citizens, there was a twisted ankle, some lacerations and one man's shoulder had been grazed by a bullet. The midwife bandaged his wound and put his arm in a sling. Then she provided aid to the other injured, and they all counted themselves fortunate. That evening Georgia and Ioanna were so happy to be back in their rug beds and slept contentedly.

The next day, however, an unfortunate repercussion from the previous day's events caught everyone by surprise. A young boy, a distant relative of Nikolas, was outdoors and noticed a shell on the ground. He was not old enough to have had any military training, and he was intrigued with the adventures and mysteries of war and weapons. He wanted to pick it up to examine it, but first he kicked at it. The unexploded shell suddenly exploded. The boy yelled in pain and then went into shock seeing his mutilated leg. Help was near so they were able to stop the bleeding and preserve his life, but he lost his leg.

This accident and the recollections of bullets so close to all of them tormented Arianna. She asked Nikolas, "Is there anywhere safer we can go?" They contemplated other options, but with the Germans occupying their house by the sea and knowing the Germans were targeting both cities and villages, they could not think of a better plan that was any more certain than their current situation. So they counted their blessings— they had food, their health, the horse for work and the goat for milk— and went back to work in the fields. Nikolas carved out a hidden cave nearer to the area between the *Lemoni* and *Milos* properties, since they would spend a great deal of time there during the summer and fall harvests.

Before long it would be time to gather the wheat on *Milos* and fruits and potatoes on *Lemoni*. One afternoon Nikolas made some trips back and forth from the village well to water the potatoes. Arianna examined the potatoes and urged Nikolas, "Let's go ahead and pick the potatoes. They are a little small but ready, and we could use them." Nikolas answered, "No, it's getting a little late. What's one more day? I would rather collect them all together." Arianna snuck a few in her apron for the children.

The next day, they went to *Lemoni* to pick the potatoes. They stopped and stared. Not one potato was in the soil. For several minutes, they couldn't comprehend what was going on. "Somebody stole all the potatoes," Nikolas sighed. Arianna was confused, "We haven't seen enemy soldiers in a while." Nikolas replied, "It must have been people from the area or transients." Arianna couldn't believe it. She had always been taught to not harvest an entire crop but leave a portion for the poor. She felt that was fair and right, but this… This was stealing their food, livelihood, time and toil.

Arianna started gathering whatever plums, cherries or lemons that were close to being ready. Nikolas turned his attention to the wheat and decided to harvest as soon as he could. Some wheat had been sown both in *Milos* and also *Sterna*, closer to their home in Karidia. He also had an idea, "What if I make a little hut out of bamboo for us here, and we camp out closer to the crops?" Arianna liked the idea of being out in the open air instead of being cooped up in their quarters.

So Nikolas constructed a small teepee-like dwelling out of bamboo. They brought some of their things, as well as the horse, goat and chickens. The girls thought it was a great adventure moving to the outdoors.

66

After they got settled, Nikolas started cutting the wheat in *Milos*. When it was time to harvest the wheat in Karidia, four-year old Georgia begged to go along. She knew that their real house was in that area and was impatiently eager to see it. Nikolas would have to bring the horse and wagon anyway to bring the wheat back to the threshing floor, so he agreed to let her go.

They started out too early for Georgia to see anything in the morning. Once they got to the *Sterna* field, Georgia was captivated with the windmill, but something didn't look quite right. "Why is the windmill tied up, *Baba*?" Nikolas answered, "We aren't here very much to take care of it. The wind can be so strong that it could break it if we don't tie it." Georgia helped gather the wheat after he cut it. They put in a full day, but Georgia persevered, knowing that she would get to see her dream home soon.

On the way back, she sat on top of the horse and got so excited when they reached the top of the mountain and saw the sea. Nikolas pointed to their house far off in the distance. Such a thrill she had to catch a glimpse of the genuine home of her daydreams. Even more fascinating was the ocean and how it was level with the ground below. "How come the water doesn't come all the way to the mountain?" Nikolas was not quite sure how to answer that so he said, "God made it that way."

"I want to go closer," Georgia pressed. "I am afraid we can't right now. Maybe someday," Nikolas hoped. The ocean beckoned to him every time he was in the area. But the cannon he saw poised on top of their roof was a stark reminder of the war. Would there be a day when this nightmare would be over and... He couldn't bring himself to imagine what life might be like in the future. For the time being, he was very thankful for a successful wheat crop.

Although they had a small threshing floor at the *Milos* property in Lithos, they decided to take the wheat-filled wagon south an hour to Nikolas' father's property in Topos. Nikolas' father was getting older and needed help harvesting his wheat. Additionally, his threshing floor was bigger and he had two large oxen that made the threshing easier. Nikolas and Arianna cut some St. John's wort,

67

which was tall and soft, and let it dry in order to make a large mattress.

While Nikolas helped his father harvest his wheat, Arianna and the girls spread their harvested wheat in bundles around the edges of the nine-meter circular dirt floor. This allowed the wheat to dry while having it accessible for the threshing. The oxen were yoked together and hooked up to a wooden platform that had sharp stones implanted on the bottom of the wood. There was a chair on top of the wood for someone to sit and drive the oxen. The oxen would go around the circle, pulling the wood with the sharp stones that in the intense dry heat would cut the top of the wheat from the stalk below. It would also cut the top into its many kernels.

While one person was driving the oxen, others would periodically sweep the wheat that had been cut into the center of the circle and add more uncut wheat to the outer circle. One of the girls stood close by with a bucket, watching vigilantly for the ox to give the warning signal. When the animal would stop short and spread its legs, the girl would run quickly to hold the bucket strategically in order to catch any unwanted "fertilizer." At one point, it was Ioanna's turn to ride on the back of the wood to stabilize it. After going around and around for hours in the hot sun, she fell asleep on top of the plank.

Once the wheat was cut, they winnowed it. They took pitchforks and tossed the wheat and stalks up into the air. The wind blew the lighter stalks away from the area, leaving the heavier kernels of wheat, which were later collected. At night they spread the quilt on top of the pliable weed mattress. The girls slept in the middle with the parents on each side. Sometimes the adults would eat garlic to try to keep the mosquitos or other small intruders away from their open-air campsite.

After a few days, they returned to their Lithos bamboo tent with their kernels of wheat. The girls would later clean it by fingering through it to sort out any rocks or dirt and then store the kernels in a large barrel. Little by little as they needed it, they would take some to the mill to crush it into flour. Lastly, Arianna passed the flour through their sieve, leaving any husk remnants on top and the good flour below.

68

After they were finished with the wheat, Nikolas and Arianna concentrated on harvesting the vegetables. They gathered from *Lemoni* a large crop of onions and some lentils and beans that they had left on the plants longer in order to dry for the winter. Arianna showed Georgia and Ioanna how to braid the stalks so that one or two dozen onions could be bunched together and hung for storage. They spent the evening braiding the onions and laid them out to dry on the ground overnight.

Very early in the morning, from their bamboo hut, they heard marching and cadence calling. Arianna whispered to the girls, "Stay hidden." Nikolas and Arianna poked their heads out to see a large troop of soldiers hungrily eating their onions. Arianna started to rise, "Our onions!" Nikolas held her back, "It's okay, as long as we stay safe." Nikolas could hear a few of them talking and said to Arianna, "*Italee* [Italians]." Arianna shivered, realizing their danger. However, after they ate the onions, the army marched away.

When it was safe, the family emerged from the hut to survey the loss. They had left most of the dried lentils and beans behind, but all of the onions were gone. Georgia asked, "What happened to the onions?" Nikolas answered, "Some men were very hungry and needed them more than we did." Arianna was relieved that their family was safe but shook her head, "I don't know how anyone can eat so many raw onions so early in the morning."

A little later they heard the bleating of sheep. "Uncle Elias!" Georgia and Ioanna shouted excitedly. He ran to hug them both, "My how you've grown!" He then greeted the adults and little Stella. Nikolas told his uncle how the Italian army had just marched through and commandeered their onions and observed, "You must be doing a good job of keeping those sheep hidden. If the enemy devoured all those onions, imagine what they would do to your sheep!" Elias replied, "Yes, I probably shouldn't stay long in case they are still in the area."

The girls had been darting in and out of the dozens of sheep. Ioanna pointed out the largest sheep in admiration. "That big guy is the boss when I need a break," Elias explained. Georgia said, "I don't think you ever take a break. They follow you everywhere." Elias laughed, "You're right. They know that they can trust me to take care of them. They know my voice and follow, just like it says in the Bible about the Good Shepherd. But we have to go now, so say goodbye to them." The girls said goodbye, trying to hug one or two sheep as they frolicked around. Heading in the opposite direction as the Italians, Elias left with the sheep following after him.

In the fall, the Stavrolakis moved back into the made-over barn in Lithos. The summer air and exercise had been good for the health of the older girls. Stella was doing well but still was small for her age. Arianna decided to start her on soft foods, but the only thing she liked was boiled and mashed broad beans.

It was Georgia's job to shell the large, coarse pod and peel each bean within. Many times she used her teeth for the job. By the end of fall, almost five-year-old Georgia was so frustrated with the task that she blurted to a lady visiting Arianna one day, "I am so sick of fixing beans every day!" The kind lady smiled and praised her, "You are such a good big sister and a help to your mother." Georgia grinned and ran off proudly.

After a little more casual conversation, Arianna's friend asked her, "Did you hear about the plane crash in Prasinos Kampos?" Arianna was shocked. The lady told her that an airplane had crashed on the mountain near Prasinos Kampos. The people of the village hurried there with pitchforks, shovels and whatever else they could find, not knowing how many planes or enemies they would encounter. But there was only one man who had parachuted safely. When he saw the local citizens, he raised his hands and said, "English, English!" So instead of harming him, they took him in and provided food and aid.

Arianna's mind couldn't help but imagine what could have happened to her family or friends if that had been an enemy soldier, or if there had been more of them swooping in on her hometown. For the past two and a half years she felt as if they lived in a constant fear of "what next?" Moreover, the German soldiers had returned to the villages. Maybe that meant the possibility of fewer air strikes, but the threat of firing lines might be worse. Arianna's heart stopped every time she heard an officer shout, "Halt!"

That winter, they were extremely short on supplies. After much deliberation, Nikolas decided to risk his safety in order to take a load of wheat into Heraklion to trade it for what they needed. Although he had acted confident in front of Arianna, Nikolas almost had a change of heart as he approached the soldiers for a day pass into the city. He had already escaped the firing squad once, and now he was presenting himself in much better condition, along with his desirable assets of a horse and wagon.

He thought of his family's needs and said a quick prayer. The soldier eyed Nikolas' gaunt, slightly stooped form and meek, pleading eyes as he ascertained Nikolas' intended quest with the mention of Heraklion. With a dismissive grunt, the soldier gave him the permit and waved him along. Nikolas felt like running, but he thought he'd better not raise suspicion.

Having escaped the potential danger and with the satisfaction of being able to meet his family's needs, Nikolas felt free to enjoy the scenic ride. The way was winding and narrow, with the ocean precariously below on one side and jagged mountains on the other. That stretch of road was called "*Kako Oros* [Bad Mountain]" because it was so dangerous. But Nikolas knew the road well, and there were surprisingly few checkpoints.

He found that merchants in the city were eager for food, so he was able to negotiate fair trades for the things that the family needed. Passing a bakery, he felt drawn to stop and get a special treat for the girls. Sweets were not sold in the villages, and he was surprised that the city even had some during wartime. Excitedly, he selected for each of them a *koulouraki* [ring-shaped cookie/pastry]. After watering his faithful horse, he embarked towards Lithos. The wind had gotten much colder. Although he still had time to make the two-hour trip home before curfew, he hurried the horse along as safely as he could.

Nikolas was startled when about halfway along his journey, he rounded a corner and suddenly heard a German officer yell, "Halt!"

Panic seized him. This was not a regular checkpoint. He stopped obediently. The officer motioned Nikolas down from the wagon and began ordering and gesturing to a few soldiers. Nikolas gathered that they had run into some sort of difficulty and needed his wagon to transport some heavy equipment. He again wondered what was to stop them from shooting him right there so they could permanently take his horse and wagon. Nikolas tried to slowly back out of their way, but the officer motioned for him to help them load the wagon.

Afterwards, the officer pointed back towards the previous checkpoint, indicating that Nikolas should haul the equipment back towards Heraklion. One of the soldiers rode in the wagon with him. All the while, Nikolas dreaded to think what would happen to him once they decided he was expendable. And if he survived the experience, he worried that he would have to make the perilous cliffside journey back in the dark. He only had a daytime permit. If he were accosted without special permission after curfew… He began to pray in earnest.

***

Arianna had been uneasy all day. When curfew came that night, Nikolas still hadn't returned. Arianna fed and washed the girls and put them to bed upstairs in the loft. Trying not to sound too frightened she told them, "You girls pray, let's all pray that God will bring your *baba* safely back." The little girls knelt by their rug bed and with pure and sincere hearts asked the Lord to bring their daddy safely home. Then, having the faith of children completely trusting their heavenly Father, Georgia and Ioanna crawled into bed. In perfect peace, Georgia went to sleep.

From her bed aloft, Ioanna could see her *mama* below light the *kandili* [thick glass filled with water and a layer of oil with a wick secured on top] and put a bucket with holes over it to shield the light from the Germans. Growing up, Arianna had never had a Bible. But when Nikolas returned from the Albanian front, he had a Greek Gideon Bible comprised of the New Testament with Psalms and Proverbs. She took the Bible and started reading. As was her practice, she read the Bible out loud, "I am the Light of the world. Whoever follows Me will never walk in darkness but will have the

Light of life." Upstairs in the loft, Ioanna was falling asleep, gazing at that flickering flame and hearing the Word of the Lord.

All of a sudden, she saw come out of that light the full figure of the Lord Jesus, whiter than white, purer than the light. He came and stood by the girls' bed. He spoke to Ioanna's spirit and assured her that her *baba* was okay. He was going to bring her daddy home— he was coming back okay. Then she felt like He took a blanket and covered the girls, but the cover was more than a physical blanket. It was His love, His grace, His complete protection. It was like a flood of love, and she was a happy girl to be in that kind of love.

To assure her, He brought her a *koulouraki*, and one also for Georgia. He told her, "I will leave them downstairs for you to find when you get up in the morning." She saw Him go down to the kitchen and hang them on nails on a wall rack.

In the morning, Ioanna woke up the happiest girl, jumping all over the place. Jesus was her friend and He loved her! She dashed downstairs, not at all surprised to see her daddy, and went directly to her gift. The *koulourakia* were right where Jesus told her they would be. She pointed to the top one, which was hers, and asked, "*Mama*, who put that there?"

Arianna was so grateful that Nikolas had returned safely and knew that every good gift (including delicacies as well as a merciful curfew exemption) comes from God. Instead of answering Ioanna that her daddy brought the treat, Arianna said, "Jesus!" Thinking that everyone had seen what she had seen, Ioanna took Arianna's answer to confirm in her heart the miracle that she saw and felt. Nikolas and Arianna, though unaware of Ioanna's special encounter and foretold meaningful gift, were once again immensely grateful for God's provision and answered prayer of protection for Nikolas and his horse and wagon.

Chapter 8

The new year brought renewed hopes that the war would soon end. It was unnerving not knowing what was going on in the rest of the world or what would happen to them. The Stavrolakis had no way of guessing which power or powers would win the war. They did hear that many of the Italians had moved out of Crete, and they thought that was a good sign. Nikolas joked with Arianna that eating so many of their raw onions so early in the morning must have made the Italians march right off of their island. Whenever they could, they chose to color their isolation with optimism and tried to get on with everyday life.

One day, Nikolas' younger sister Zoe came over and offered to take Georgia and their goat out for a walk. Arianna thought this was a little unusual— Zoe typically didn't have much interaction with them, but Arianna consented. Since it was still somewhat cold outside, she told Georgia, "Put on your coat." Georgia obediently put on her coat that had been made out of burlap, and she tied it with a string.

Georgia had her usual places where she would take the goat to find some scrub to eat, but Zoe suggested that they go further down away from town. Georgia was happy to go for a longer walk. After a few minutes Zoe told Georgia, "Wait here, I will be right back." Zoe was gone for quite a while and then came back with a pastry. Georgia's eyes widened. She didn't know which tree or bush produced pastries, but Aunt Zoe must know where to find them. Zoe was in a giddy mood as they sat on a log and split the pastry, which delighted Georgia.

This ruse was repeated with walking the goat, filling the clay water jug at the well, picking a few artichokes or any other seemingly innocently-concocted plan. Arianna was not able to surmise much from naïve Georgia. But with the sparkle in Zoe's eyes when she returned, along with whispers from the village, Arianna began to suspect that Zoe had a secret romance. She watched her in her few interactions with the others in Lithos. She moaned when she deduced that Zoe had set her eyes on Spiros. Arianna knew that neither of their mothers would approve of the match, each thinking the other's child was not good enough for her own. She didn't know the details, but supposedly there had been a previous conflict between the families.

Arianna thought that she would stay out of it until Spiros approached her with a favor of giving Zoe a letter. Arianna was too surprised to think of a pretext not to take it, so she accepted it. When she gave it to Zoe she said, "I am not sure what is going on and I don't want to get involved, but I know that while it is best to marry for love, it also is much easier if you have your family's blessing." Zoe was so glad to be able to confide in someone that she gushed all of Spiro's great qualities and all of their plans to Arianna. Realizing things had progressed even further than she had thought, Arianna didn't offer too much comment. She could see that Zoe was in love and determined. "This is not going to be easy," Arianna thought to herself when Zoe left.

The next time Zoe came back with Georgia, instead of a pastry, Zoe had a ring. She advertised broadly in the village, "See what I found in the woods? Did anyone lose a ring? Whoever it belongs to can come and claim it." By this time, Zoe's mother suspected something, but she had no way to prove it. So Zoe wore the ring. Over time, the talk in the town escalated to where the relationship was impossible to hide. "If you are even thinking of having any kind of relationship with that Spiros, you can forget our blessing," her mother warned her.

Knowing how Zoe's family felt, the couple thought that it would be no use for Spiros to ask for her hand. "We have to elope," Zoe told Spiros impulsively, and he agreed. Zoe asked Nikolas for his help, but at the same time his mother adamantly opposed his involvement and threatened to disinherit both of them. Although Nikolas was not very close to his mother and she didn't always treat him well, he was mindful of the commandment to honor his father and mother and wanted to stay out of it. But he saw the deep commitment of the couple and thought it was better to have them live with God's blessing— even if the wedding had to be performed by magistrate instead of a priest— than to live in sin.

When Spiros and Zoe eloped, Zoe's mother kicked her out of the house without letting her take anything. Nikolas pleaded for his mother to be sensible— her clothes had little value, but his mother said, "Better I burn them than give them to her." Nikolas and Arianna did what they could to help, but they had so little themselves to give them. Afterwards, Nikolas and Arianna marveled to each other that even the life and death of war wasn't enough to overcome a hot-blooded family feud. But they consoled themselves that Spiros and Zoe really loved each other.

Arianna soon had other distractions. She found out that she was again expecting. "Surely this one will be a boy," she thought. Her youngest, Stella, was a year old and was able to state emphatically, "*Thelo koukia* [I want broad beans]!" Arianna thought, "Thank goodness for broad beans or Stella might not have survived." But she was finally healthy enough not to worry.

The older girls were growing too, and Arianna fretted about how to clothe them. There was no fabric to be found. Arianna did not have an extra dress and what she had was wearing thin. Arianna approached Nikolas sadly and asked about the Greek flag he had taken from the *taverna*. Nikolas reacted, "No way, that is unthinkable! The flag is our pride. Is it not enough that we are occupied by the Germans and cannot display our flag but must hide it, after our countrymen have bled and died for it? What now… are we actually forced to *cut* it?" Arianna understood and said nothing.

Two days later, Nikolas came to Arianna holding the flag. He almost choked up but said, "The girls are more important. Just don't make me watch as you cut it." Arianna did her best to try to disguise that Georgia's and Ioanna's dresses had been made out of the Greek flag. When the dresses were finished, their friends suspected but were sympathetic. The girls were proud of their outfits. Georgia even had a matching bow for her hair, although it was always slipping out of her soft hair. Ioanna's hair was curly, attracting the attention of the older village girls who loved to play with it.

76

One day while he was out in a field, Nikolas found an old piece of a German tent. He concealed it and brought it to Arianna. He told her that if she did something with it, it would have to be kept hidden or they could be killed. The Germans periodically inspected the homes in Lithos, and if anyone was found to have any item belonging to the soldiers, there was no excuse— they would all be shot. Arianna decided to make it into underwear for Georgia and Ioanna. She had just enough for one pair each, but she cut the heavy material generously to make sure they had growing room to wear them for a while.

Before she could get them sewn, she heard someone outside say, "The Germans are coming! They are on the other side of the village headed this way!" She grabbed the material and ran next door where there was a little yard. She quickly dug a hole and buried it. She wiped her hands and strolled back to their place. When they had gone, she breathed a sigh of relief and dug up the material.

When Arianna finished sewing the underwear, the girls tried to be thankful. The material was rough and was made so wide in between the legs that it rubbed their legs painfully when they walked. Worse yet, everyone could hear them coming from the *crryvpfb*, *crryvpfb*, *crryvpfb* sound the underwear made when they were on the way. For the rest of her life Georgia never liked tents.

One day in early August, Georgia and Ioanna took the goat to a field belonging to Nikolas' mother. They left the goat to forage and saw that her fig tree up on the hill had ripe and beautiful figs. They both loved figs, so they had a great time enjoying themselves— the figs were so yummy. They also had a few grapes from her vines.

At four and five years old, they didn't know that figs and grapes can have a laxative effect. They soon felt a strong discomfort, and, strangely, their gas seemed wet. Ioanna looked at Georgia as if to say, "Where is this coming from?" Georgia shrugged back at her like "Don't look at me." It was soon an overflowing situation. Ioanna thought to herself, "As big as this underwear is, it doesn't seem to be holding anything." "I think we ate too many," Georgia said. They stood there a while and then Georgia bemoaned, "*Mama* is going to be so mad. Now we are going to get it for good!"

Ioanna thought a minute and said, "Let's use the fig leaves to clean ourselves off." Georgia thought that Ioanna was so smart. In cleaning themselves off, they realized that fig leaves were even more scratchy than their underwear made from a tent. But that was better than facing *Mama*'s wrath. They had quite a job trying to clean themselves, their new underwear and even the messy business that had rolled down their legs and down the hill. They did their best but somehow felt it wasn't quite satisfactory.

Georgia and Ioanna retrieved the goat and shamefacedly waddled home. The poor girls were not only squeaking and reeking but dreading what their mother was going to do. They were so forlorn and repentant that Arianna had sympathy and helped them clean up. She did not yell at them but took the opportunity to share a life lesson that they learned well, "Remember not to eat too many figs or grapes at one time." They both answered solemnly, "Never again, *Mama*!"

That year it was Ioanna's turn to go with Nikolas near Karidia to the *Sterna* field. This time Nikolas was picking grapes. Ioanna helped gather some grapes with him but then took a rest among the vines while Nikolas worked in another area. Ioanna knew well not to eat too much fruit, so she busied herself playing.

She was interested in cooking, so she collected some tender grape leaves and pretended to make *dolmathes* by filling the leaves with dirt. She had carefully rolled several when all of a sudden, she heard sirens. Ioanna knew what the sirens were, but she didn't think she was in danger hidden in the grapevines, so she kept playing.

Planes flew overhead, and then unexpectedly, she noticed the strangest sight. A bunch of shirtless men with sunburned backs were crawling like snakes among their grapevines. They were as surprised to see four-year old Ioanna there by herself as she was to see all of them on their bellies amongst her "*dolmathes*."

78

Suddenly the planes swooped low and started shelling the field that the pilots had seen the soldiers escape into. *Ptchoo, ptchoo, ptchoo, ptchoo, ptchoo, ptchoo, ptchoo*! Bullets were hitting everywhere on the ground around them. One of the soldiers grabbed Ioanna and dove on top of her to shield her. The shelling continued several minutes, and then they heard Nikolas running and shouting frantically, "Ioanna! Ioanna! Where are you? Ioanna!" The soldier let her go and she ran, crying, to her father. He held her tightly in relief.

Nikolas tried to express his gratitude to the soldiers as best he could without knowing their language. He pointed to a bucket of grapes but they smiled, shook their heads, waved and went on their way back toward the sea. Nikolas couldn't believe what a close call they had. He was glad that they were okay but also that none of the soldiers had been killed right in front of Ioanna. He was so shaken that they left without finishing the harvesting, taking whatever they had collected thus far.

Although he downplayed the situation to Arianna since she was five months pregnant, he took opportunity to tell Georgia and Ioanna how to distinguish the airplanes. "The ones with a circle are friendly planes, but the ones with a cross are dangerous. If you see those, try to run and hide in a cave if you can," he told them as he drew their different symbols on the dirt with a stick. As he thought about it further, Nikolas supposed that some friendly planes could also try to target enemy areas. He added, "But if you see *any* planes or if you hear the sirens, it's best to hide or stay close to Mama or me."

Looking back, he reflected that he didn't know who was doing the shooting recently. Since he was too busy ducking for cover to look at the planes and didn't see the soldiers in their full uniforms, the men who were willing to save Ioanna's life in the grapevines could have been allies *or* enemy soldiers. He knew that there were good men on both sides of the conflict. He wrestled with the perplexities of war for some time afterwards.

In the fall, there were rumors that some of the Germans may be leaving Crete. While they didn't want to count on that, Nikolas and Arianna discussed the possibility of school for Georgia. At that time, the culture valued agricultural or house work over schooling, especially for girls. Boys were thought to need some education for their later military training. During a war, there were even more excuses for the children to go without education. But Arianna treasured her ability to read and wanted that for her girls.

Since the schoolhouse was right next door to their temporary home in Lithos, they thought that it should be safe enough for her. They could always run next door to take her out if they needed her for something or for her protection. So they enrolled Georgia for her first year of school.

There were very few school supplies to be salvaged. Georgia had a small chalkboard and one small piece of chalk. There were no books or materials, so learning anything was extremely difficult. After a while, her small piece of chalk broke beyond use and she was blamed for not taking care of it. She was given a pad of paper but no pencil, so the other kids tore off pages to use since she couldn't use them herself. Despite the obstacles, she persevered the best she could.

Often Ioanna told Georgia that she missed her when she was at school. They each told one another what the other had missed during the day. Ioanna told her once, "I took the goat to the field next to the big fallen tree. But there was a lady there this time, and she must have planted something there because she came after the goat and me with a stick and was yelling at us." Georgia was baffled, "I guess we shouldn't go there again." Ioanna asked Georgia, "Are you so smart now from school?" Georgia replied, "Not really, but I think now I know my letters."

On a cold night in early December, Nikolas went to get the midwife. Arianna put the girls to bed, "You girls go to sleep now. Maybe in the morning you will have a new brother or sister, but stay in bed and go to sleep." Nikolas returned with the midwife and his cousin. A while later Arianna screamed in pain and all of a sudden the baby was born, immediately crying.

Georgia pretended to be asleep, but she had to find out what kind of baby was here. Nikolas' cousin said sarcastically, "It's another girl."

80

Georgia's elation was dimmed by the way the birth of her sister was announced. First of all, how did she know— *Mama* was the one who was supposed to have the baby, not her. And anyways, she didn't sound too excited about it. Georgia was comforted when her father replied to her, "So what? I love my girls!" She drifted off to sleep happily.

The next morning the three older sisters were overjoyed to meet the new baby. Arianna's mother also came to help and to visit her new granddaughter. They all decided to call her Sofia. She was beautiful and healthy. "Four girls!" Nikolas got teased a lot, but he didn't care. He was proud of them and very grateful that they were all healthy.

Nikolas brought all four girls to see his ailing father, who had recently suffered a stroke. His father kissed all of them and said, "Ah, the smell of my children is like sweet, hot bread!" He then blessed each of the girls individually. He later asked Nikolas, "Will you feel a pain in your heart when I go?" Nikolas' voice faltered when he answered, "Yes, I will." His father pronounced, "With the same measure that you feel about me, your children are going to feel toward you. You are a good father, Niko. And I am extremely proud of you, son."

That was the last time the girls saw their grandfather alive. The Stavrolaki family mourned a man who was very patient with his troubled wife and very supportive of his children and grandchildren. Nikolas felt like he had lost the best friend that he had had since his brother died. Arrangements were swiftly made for his funeral and burial. It appeared as though the tide of the war had turned enough to lessen the conflict in their area, so they thought it was safe to coordinate the use of the church for the service.

Before the funeral, Nikolas and Arianna brought the girls to the house where his body was laid out. There was a step up into the room, and Georgia tripped and cracked open her toe. Blood was everywhere and Georgia was crying from the pain that radiated up her leg, so Arianna took her home with Stella and the baby.

Nikolas and Ioanna stayed with the family and later proceeded to the church and graveside services. They did not have a casket, so he was laid on a door, covered with a sheet and lowered into the grave using ropes. Ioanna did not really understand death, but she took it all in—the people crying and her father and his male cousins lowering the body. She did comprehend that her grandfather had died and thought back to what she overheard her grandfather say, that her father was going to die too. Ioanna cried, but not so much for her grandfather, but for her father. She thought, "Who is going to bring my *baba* down? There had to be a son, and there wasn't one. There are no girls doing this. Who is going to lower my daddy down to the grave? He is too heavy for us."

Back at their quarters, Arianna had no idea of the tender burden Ioanna was carrying, but she did wonder if she may have been too young to go to a funeral. Arianna was glad that the church could be used again. A little distractedly, she bandaged Georgia's foot. It was a pretty deep gash so she instructed Georgia to rest and try to keep it clean. She contemplated about her need to be home during the funeral, but she could not have attended the church part of it anyway since she was within forty days of having the baby.

For that reason, Nikolas and Arianna delayed baptizing Sofia, so they could have the baptism in the church. They again had a difficult time finding a godparent for the baby. Nikolas finally arranged something with a lady he was doing some farming for, but she wanted the baby to be named Barbara. "But we have been calling her Sofia," Nikolas protested. She was resolute, so they changed her name to Barbara.

Arianna was disappointed in the name change but knew they had no choice. She started to reflect to Nikolas, "Didn't you have a girlfriend named Barbara?" Nikolas chuckled, "Hardly a girlfriend. It was a setup that didn't work." Arianna teased him, "So that's why you want to name our daughter Barbara, to remember her. Maybe you would have had a better life with Barbara." Nikolas grabbed Arianna around the waist and assured her, "You are the only one I want to spend my life with. You have been my right hand through some of the most difficult times I could have ever imagined. I couldn't have done it without you."

82

After Barbara was baptized, Arianna shifted her focus to potty training Stella. She still had the potty chair from one of the trips back to the house, which seemed like ages ago. They had no bathroom inside, so she tried to get Stella to use the potty chair. For some reason, Stella only wanted to go in one area outside by the school.

One day, Georgia opened the door and Stella looked out to see white everywhere. That was the first time Stella discovered snow. She was fascinated and wanted to go check it out, but Georgia held her back. "No, let's wait for *Mama*. It might be slippery and we don't want you to fall or get messy."

A little while later, Arianna knew that Stella needed to go. They took off her clothes, but she ran away from them and wouldn't cooperate with using the potty chair. She ran around, crying with frustration. She lost her balance and fell onto the metal bucket with hot coals that they used to heat the area away from the fireplace. Stella screamed in pain. Arianna ran over to her and Nikolas said, "I'll get the midwife," and ran out.

Soon the midwife arrived, looked at the burn briefly and then started to make a cream out of ingredients like beeswax, milk, wheat and egg whites. Before they could put it on, they had to carefully peel off the pieces of coal that had stuck to her skin. Stella shrieked in anguish and tried to pull away from them. Her skin was already starting to blister.

It was an agonizing night for all of them, but finally they got her cleaned, the cream applied and area bandaged. Not long after that Stella calmed down and soon fell asleep from exhaustion. After that, Arianna had a challenging time trying to potty train her without irritating the wounds.

Gradually, winter turned to spring. One splendid day in May of 1945, the unbelievable happened. The church bells from all of the villages nearby joined in triumphant cacophony. The town crier announced, "Hitler is dead! Germany surrenders! Europe is free!"

Chapter 9

When they heard that the war was over, Nikolas and Arianna looked at each other in shock. They found it almost too hard to believe. After four long years in Crete without much hope, could the nightmare actually be over? Involuntarily, a movie reel of the births, deaths, near misses, illnesses and extreme sacrifices played in their heads. The enemy that had appeared so formidable in their lives had actually been vanquished? People were dancing, laughing and celebrating in the streets.

Once they dared to accept the news as true, Nikolas and Arianna gave thanks to God for saving and delivering them during the most tumultuous time of their lives. And yet they knew that they could not immediately step back into their old life. It would take time to rebuild and heal. They also didn't know when all of the foreigners would vacate the island. They decided to remain camped out near their orchard and garden for the time being.

When the fall season approached and it started to get cooler, Nikolas and Arianna decided it was time to return home to Karidia. They did not want to be obligated to their landlady any longer and did not want their house by the sea to be open to squatters. Reports circulated that Japan had also surrendered and the war was really over. The next chapter beckoned them to take a courageous step towards eventual normalcy. They were not sure what they would find when they unfolded the curtain, revealing the vestiges of an even more intense battle stage. Structurally and militarily, would it be safe to return?

The family put in almost a full day to gather as much of the remaining harvests that they could. Then they packed the wagon with their crops and few possessions that they had in Lithos. Nikolas planned to take the loaded wagon the long road around the mountain while Arianna would take the girls the shorter and steeper foot path over the mountain.

Arianna was not sure that she was really prepared for the long journey. The path was dangerously rocky and steep and usually only wide enough for one person. She wasn't sure if she could manage four young girls, all six years old and under, over about four kilometers of rough terrain. And if possible, she wanted to try to make it most of the way before dark. She said a quick prayer for safety and strength.

Emboldened, Arianna tied the goat to her waist and called to the girls. She put Stella on her back and carried Barbara in her arms. Georgia carried the sieve, which Arianna didn't want to get broken in the jarring wagon. Ioanna carried a metal bucket of food, water and cloth diapers.

Arianna tried to get the girls excited about the adventure to inspire them along the journey, "Today we get to go home! We have a long way to go, but just wait until you see the ocean! It is so beautiful! Take care, now. Here we go! Be careful so you don't fall and hurt yourself or break what you are carrying."

The beginning of the trek was the most strenuous. Because it was uphill, they were forced to take many breaks. Arianna was thankful that she had packed some refreshments. The snacks helped to revive the children and to give them shorter destinations to look forward to.

They were almost to the summit when the baby started crying, and the girls murmured that they were hungry, thirsty and tired. Arianna encouraged them, "We are almost at the top. From there we can see the house and the ocean!"

When they almost thought that they could walk no more, they reached the top of the mountain. The girls looked down and saw the house, their promised land. Feelings of joy, hope and belonging surged in their hearts. The girls took it all in and then jumped up and down in anticipation. Arianna was relieved too. But although it was downhill from there, they still had almost half the journey in front of them and it was starting to get dark. Arianna paused for a brief moment to sit down and feed the baby. The girls again asked for something to eat or drink, but she was out of provisions. So she took a cup and milked the goat to give to the girls.

Refreshed, they continued onward. The girls tried to keep the house in their sights, fearing that it might fade from reality if it faded from their gaze. There was a time that they couldn't see it from the path that they had to take. Then suddenly they rounded a corner and they could see it, still at a distance, but closer than before. Georgia and Ioanna jumped up and screamed with excitement. They really were going home! They were going to make it. It was a picturesque fantasyland in the glowing sunset, and they were so proud that this marvel was their home.

As they trudged along wearily, the house began to disappear into the darkness, but Arianna assured them that it was still there. Yet Arianna worried that she had seen no sign of Nikolas at the house. She became alarmed, thinking of Nikolas and the horse with the loaded wagon and steep trails in the dark. "What if he takes a wrong turn? What if the horse gets injured or a wagon wheel falls off? What if the overloaded wagon goes too fast on a downslope?" Arianna's mind kept portraying the perils.

As Arianna got closer to the house, she wondered if they would come across dead bodies on the ground. How would she explain that to innocent children imagining a perfect paradise to come home to? With her thoughts on the dead, she was startled out of her skin when she heard a living voice demand, "Who are you? What are you doing here?" She was too frightened to answer at first. They had thought that all of the occupying forces had left the island, but what if they were wrong and they would all be killed?

But realizing that she had every right to be there and must defend her daughters, Arianna summoned up her courage and retorted, "Who are you?!" The voice softened and asked, "Arianna?" Arianna was so relieved to recognize the son of a local landowner that she would have hugged him if her arms weren't full. "Oh, I am so relieved to see you!" she told him as he began to take some things to carry from the girls. Then she continued, "Is your family okay? Is this area safe?" He answered her, "They are all fine, but you must be very careful of landmines in this area. They are everywhere, especially near the beach."

A new fear confronted her. How would they be able to walk anywhere knowing at any time they could trigger an explosion and… she couldn't think of it. How was she going to manage keeping young children still? Could Nikolas and the horse avoid them? The war was supposed to be over, yet she was coming home to an insidious enemy in her own yard. "Oh, Jesus, keep us safe!" she whispered.

The young man walked them home and she thanked him wholeheartedly as he left. The girls were so happy to be there that they started kissing the walls and jumping up and down, laughing. Arianna saw that the door and most of the windows were gone. She peeked into the house and from the darkened view saw that it was trashed with plaster rubble from the walls, and there was garbage everywhere.

"Let's just sit and wait right out here for your *baba*," Arianna told the children. They all sat down on the ground with their backs to the front wall of the house, the goat still tied to Arianna's waist. Stella and baby Barbara soon fell asleep. Arianna continued to worry and pray for Nikolas. The wind began to whip up from over the mountain, and Arianna shivered. She had nothing with her to warm the girls.

She heard a sound like a horse trotting and at first thought it could be Nikolas. But she saw that it was two strangers on mules passing through. The travelers seemed startled to see a family and a goat there outside the house, just as Arianna was surprised to see strangers traveling their way at night. Arianna called out to them, "Hello! Have you seen a man with a horse and wagon along the way?" They came over to her and said, "No, we haven't seen anyone."

Arianna and the travelers chatted a minute and then Arianna asked if they had a match. They did and offered it to her, so she started to walk carefully towards the way they had come to gather some wood. Arianna told the girls, "You stay right there and don't any of you move anywhere." The girls sat as still as statues. Arianna explained to the strangers that there may be mines in their area. She found some kindling and started a fire. The strangers warmed their hands and then wished her well and headed on their way as she thanked them.

Georgia and Ioanna dozed off now and then amid the silence that was only suspended by the calming rhythm of the ocean. Arianna tended the fire to make sure that it did not go out. Out of the stillness at last they heard the sound of a wagon. Arianna and the older girls jumped up, overjoyed. Arianna shouted to Nikolas, "I am so glad to see you are okay. Be careful where you walk— I was told there are landmines everywhere."

Nikolas jumped down and carefully led the horse ahead to an area that he could tie her with a short leash. He unhitched the wagon, then took out of it a bucket of oats and fed the horse. He hugged Arianna and the girls and said, "It is good to be home!"

Arianna explained that the house was too cluttered to sleep inside. As he looked around, he thought it would be better if they weren't all camped in plain sight. They thought that the balcony should be safe from mines, so they moved the girls there, as well as the goat. Nikolas found the quilt and a bucket of coals that he lit from Arianna's fire and brought those to the balcony. There was no lower barrier on the balcony to prevent them from rolling off onto the ground below. So Arianna again warned the girls not to move, and Nikolas and Arianna slept towards the edges of the balcony.

When Georgia awoke the next morning, she sat up, at first confused about where she was. Then she saw the most beautiful sight. The sun was rising out of the ocean with brilliant colors. She gasped in amazement and then shook Ioanna, "Get up, get up! Look, here the sun is inside of the ocean!" Ioanna began screaming along with Georgia, "Wow, so beautiful!" Nikolas and Arianna had seen it many times, although not for years, and it was so good to be there with the children. Nikolas told the girls intuitively, "This is something you will remember for the rest of your lives." After taking in the spectacular sunrise and immense ocean, Ioanna looked down below the balcony and saw a wood-burning oven. In awe, she thought to herself, "We've come home to a palace!"

Everyone was most curious about the condition of the house. Arianna reminded the girls, "Remember to stay close. You can walk on the balcony but don't step into the yard or beach unless you are holding our hands." They all walked closer to the house and Ioanna hugged the walls and Georgia followed suit.

Nikolas told them, "Let me check inside first." When he came back he told Arianna, "It is not suitable for them. There is inappropriate graffiti on the walls. I will need to get some coals or something to color over it. There is also excrement in the rest of the mess. I need to walk to *Sterna* to get some water. I want to make sure there aren't any bodies or anything, so stay here and see what you can find in the wagon to feed the girls, and I will be back with some water."

As Nikolas walked, he took in the surroundings. Having such an appreciation for the beauty of God's creation, he was dejected to see ugly reminders of the war. Along the road towards Heraklion were crates of unused shells, hand grenades and other explosive materials stacked waist high. The villa across the road that he had once wanted to purchase was flattened to the ground.

Nikolas turned and walked the other direction towards his property to the east. Here and there he saw burned tanks and other vehicles. Across many of the fields were wooden crosses marking makeshift graves. All of this plus the vandalism inside their house and the landmines around their house was overwhelming. He thought back to how he had built and rebuilt his *taverna* and home. It was as if the war had littered all over his dreams. Nikolas struggled to focus on what he had to be thankful for— at least they had survived, were in good health and the would-be conquerors were defeated. As he walked along, he saw a few other leveled buildings and marveled again that their house had been spared.

On his way to the well, he scoured the countryside for any cardboard or suitable boards to cover the open windows and door. Once at *Sterna*, he found no dead bodies, dangers lurking or contamination to the well or to the cistern. He breathed a sigh of relief. With healthy water, they could endure to get everything else into shape… eventually. However, he noticed a massive unexploded bomb embedded in his field with a large crater around it. Pieces of metal were strewn throughout the area, perhaps portions of exploded bombs. Disappointment overcame him. Intruding upon a large portion of his valuable property was another silent snare to his family— one he was powerless to extricate by himself.

Nikolas returned with water and scraps of cardboard. He informed Arianna of all that he had investigated. Arianna listened with interest, but her main concerns were that her family would not stumble across any dead bodies or step on any landmines. She also couldn't stand the thought of her home in shambles. Nikolas and Arianna decided to focus on getting their house in order. Initially, they left the girls with strict orders not to move from the balcony so that they could clear the most dangerous and inappropriate parts first.

When Arianna first stepped into the house, she looked around and couldn't help but start crying. Even though Nikolas had prepared her, it hit her hard to see the house that she had taken such pride in ruined. The beautiful, meticulously-painted designs that Nikolas had taken such satisfaction in— now half of the plaster was on the floor, revealing the stones underneath, and the other half had been desecrated with vulgar drawings. The sight of this along with the stench and offensiveness of feces everywhere was sickening.

They rolled up their sleeves and went to work, but Arianna's tears continued to flow. Nikolas tried to remain stoic, but it was tearing him up inside— not only for his own dreams, but to see his family exposed to this type of situation in a place that was supposed to be their refuge. They removed any sharp or dangerous objects from the floor and then began to clean up the excrement that they could reach within the rubble. Then they took some coals and colored over the drawings.

Once all of this was done, they found a safe place to walk and dump the pieces of plaster and trash at the front side of the house. They called for Georgia and Ioanna and showed them exactly how to walk to this area as they helped empty the buckets that Nikolas and Arianna kept filling. This process continued for several days.

During their breaks, Nikolas tried to survey at least a few paths where they could safely walk. He didn't find any mines in the front of the house or along the road. It seemed that most of the mines were on the sides and at the back of the house along the beach. He realized that their positioning probably made sense as the Germans' attempt to protect themselves from any enemies trying to approach by sea. As he walked to the west of the house, Nikolas found their wooden door and window shutters as well as one of his garden tools. They were a little dilapidated and dirty but usable, and he was thankful.

When Nikolas assured Arianna that it was safe to cross the road to the area where the villa had been, she decided to take a break to get some fresh air. She took Georgia and the horse for a short walk. When she faced the villa in rubble, Arianna recognized how blessed they were that their house was still standing, even in its deplorable condition. Remnants of what had been a beautifully decorated villa with its columns, pottery and painted designs were strewn among the high grasses. Nothing was left standing. There was a hanging rope that had been tied to a nearby tree. Georgia thought that she could use that as a swing, but Arianna first wanted to check out the area better.

Arianna tied the horse to graze on the weeds and carefully walked around and peeked under one large raised piece that had been the roof, in order to make sure there wasn't a dead body underneath. What she found instead was a beautiful array of fragrant lilies. The beauty amid the destruction overwhelmed her and she began to cry. "Look at the pretty flowers, Georgia!" The young girl, in awe, reached out to pick some, but Arianna stopped her. "Leave them so I can get the bulbs and plant them. They can remind us to persevere in the hard times."

Georgia saw a wooden cross nearby, "What is that?" she asked, pointing to it. Arianna didn't want her to think of a dead person buried there so she told her, "The people are looking everywhere to find a good place for a church. Everywhere they find what might be a good place to build one, they put a cross." Georgia was happy that there may be another church nearby. Later when she walked more of the vicinity, she came to think that they found lots of good places for a church.

Arianna's walk was a good respite for her soul. She faced her formidable obstacles with renewed vigor, starting with trying to organize her kitchen area. She was sad that her good china, along with Nikolas' many dish sets were mostly taken and the rest broken. She saved a couple of the bigger pieces and threw the rest away. Most of their possessions had been taken, including two large portraits of historical royal figures.

Nikolas propped up a makeshift table. There were only two chairs so Georgia and Ioanna stood for meals while the younger girls sat in their parents' laps. Nikolas carved some bamboo into two-pronged forks and they used some layers of onions as spoons. Arianna was glad to find her rock water tub intact outside of the home. A large stony rock formation had been chiseled into a hollowed-out basin. Water could be poured into it in order to store it or wash clothes or use as a trough.

After Arianna fashioned a broom out of some branches of brush, she swept the best that she could. When most of the dust had been aired out, Nikolas boarded the windows with cardboard and shutters and reinstalled the scuffed door. He noted several areas where bullets had punctured the stone on the outside of the house, but it was nothing that jeopardized its stability.

Nikolas climbed onto the flat roof and was pleased that although it had been chipped in many places and bullet fragments were everywhere, it also was structurally sound. He was also very glad that the cannon had been removed. But after all that they had been through, it was difficult to see a huge red swastika tarnishing his roof. He tried to turn his sinking feeling and his desire to not be marked by the war into thanksgiving that his house was preserved, even if by this symbol. Most of the others in the area had to rebuild from the ground up. Since he didn't have the means to cover the symbol at that time, Nikolas reluctantly turned his attention to removing most of the loose bullet fragments and shells. He then

92

cleaned out and repositioned the cistern for catching rain water from the roof.

One night when they were all inside, it started raining. As it began to rain harder, all of a sudden came loud explosions, one after the other, *Boom! Boom! Boom! Boom! Boom!* The whole family jumped at the sounds, mostly coming from the beach area. Arianna screamed and paced in circles, wringing her hands and muttering, "*Panayia mou!* They have come back for us... Can we ever escape... What more can we face?" The baby started crying. Georgia and Ioanna were frozen in fright, and Stella ran to hold onto Arianna's leg.

Nikolas was dazed, wondering how the war had started up again, or was it their allies bombing his house because it had a swastika on the roof? Nikolas gathered his wits enough to cautiously look out into the back yard. He finally realized that the rain was triggering the landmines to explode. He told Arianna and the girls, "It is okay! We are safe inside— it's the mines going off in the rain." He reasoned to them that maybe it was a good thing that they went off that way so that they were safe from those later. Their hearts were racing too fast for them to comprehend much, but they felt a little reassured by Nikolas' calming tone.

When the rain stopped and things calmed down, they realized that the rain had washed away some of the sand, exposing more *unexploded* mines along the beach. There were different kinds of mines, but most were round, about a third of a meter in diameter. Nikolas started to place rocks all around the mines to warn everyone of their position.

But Arianna decided that she couldn't wait for the government to come to their rescue. She did not want those things all over her back yard. She made sure the kids stayed back, and she grabbed a hook, attaching it to a long rope. Nikolas protested, "No, Arianna, it's too dangerous! Just leave them, I will mark the area." She was not to be deterred but told him to stand back and reassure the girls. Those pesky deathtraps were not going to trespass on her domain.

First, Arianna dug trenches around each mine and filled the tunneled areas with water in order to soften the sand and lessen any resistance. She then carefully slipped the hook onto the handle of the first mine. From a safe distance, Arianna slowly pulled the rope. Since she was able to pull it from the hook and didn't drop it, the triggering mechanism on the top was not disturbed. She carefully pulled them out of the sand or dirt, one by one, and placed them in an out of the way area on the far side of the house.

After Arianna sequestered several mines, she and Nikolas barricaded them with a sturdy rock wall along all sides. Arianna felt a little better, but they both knew that they would have to continue to be careful, since there were probably more hidden mines. Still not finding any mines in the front yard or near the road, Nikolas explained to Arianna his theory about their placement along the beach and in the ground along the sides of the house. "At this position, the Germans were probably more worried about defending from surprise attack from the sea than from the land they had already conquered and needed to navigate themselves."

It took weeks of cleaning and repairing the best they could with limited supplies for the house to start to feel a little more like home. Nikolas and Arianna sat outside on the balcony after sunset one night after a hard day's work. Nikolas asked Arianna, "How do you feel being back here?" Arianna admitted, "I thought that it would be easier to put the past behind us. The contrast of being here now without having anything— our beautiful things or our practical daily tools— is a constant reminder of the war. But it is even harder to continually be haunted by the terrifying memories of all the close calls that we had. I understand a little better what you went through with your nightmares after you came back from the fighting in Albania, now that I have them too."

Nikolas confessed, "I keep flashing back to the planes shelling near you and the loaded horse in the front yard and also near Ioanna in the grapevines." Arianna nodded and added, "All of us running through gunfire to the shelter in Lithos, and the boils… I was so afraid that the Germans were going to take you and shoot you anyway." A tear slipped down Arianna's cheek and Nikolas gave her a hug. It was a little better to talk about it, but Arianna wondered if they would ever really be the same.

Chapter 10

Arianna tried to focus on going forward. But her nightmares continued, even of the anxiety of trying to find her cat when trying to evacuate their house. Another recurring dream centered around forgetting to lock the door of her Karidia house against the Germans, as if locking the door might have prevented the war from happening. More serious were the ones of Nikolas or the girls being shot at, only with different outcomes. She often woke up in a cold sweat. Throughout the day, she found herself distracted and jumpy.

Even Nikolas was overwrought with the memories and wondering if there could have been a better way to keep his family safe through the war. He also felt the pressure to bring stability to his family now. It was harder for him in the fields than it had been. He was further away from most of them now, and the one he was closest to had a bomb in it.

There was a need to not only feed his family but also sell greater quantities to pay for all of the things they had lost. There were fewer day laborers, tools and seed available. And there were so many things they needed— practically everything. At least he had been able to trade some food for material right after the war ended so the girls didn't have to wear the Greek flag and a piece of German tent. But he had to get so many more materials and supplies. After the scare with the mines going off and realizing the possibility of friendly fire, new whitewash for the roof also became a higher priority.

Nikolas needed to be everywhere at once. He prioritized the fieldwork to try to generate income, but the other burdens of retrieving their furniture from Prasinos Kampos, painting over the swastika on the roof and removing the bomb from the crater in *Sterna* weighed on his mind. He knew that he wouldn't have time to get everything accomplished before winter.

Nikolas put one foot in front of the other, but his thoughts were a swirling daze. Arianna was in her own fog, distracted by memories, lack of sleep and wondering if the war was really over or would something else happen. She also felt the pressure of winter approaching and mostly worked in the fields.

Georgia and Ioanna were happy to be at their new and permanent home. They also perceived that their parents were having a difficult time coping. With the outlook of those who have achieved a dream come true, together with a great love for their parents, the girls stepped in to do whatever they needed to do to help.

Georgia and Ioanna had been told how to spot mines and where not to go in order to get around on their own. They each took turns babysitting their two younger sisters while the other would perform other duties. They walked up the mountain to find wood for the fires, carried it home on their backs and prepared meals for their whole family. Both of them stepped in as field hands, walking back and forth for kilometers and putting in such long hours in the fields that their tender hands blistered and sometimes bled.

One day when she was out in the grapevines, Ioanna looked around and pondered the situation. Even at five years old, she knew something didn't seem quite right. She was picking as fast as she could, but she was hardly getting anything done. There should be a lot more people helping in a field this big. She had heard her father and mother talk of workers who used to help them and wondered where they all were. How hard this burden must be on her daddy, who seemed to struggle from sunrise to sundown. And for all of their hard work, they never seemed to have much. She knew that he did everything for her and her sisters.

Ioanna stopped a moment and prayed "Lord, would You please take care of my sisters? I do not want to see them poor. Please take care of my family and I will give You my life." She resumed her tedious task, resolving to do her part of the bargain, with both her promise and her labors, to make that desire come true.

Another day, Georgia and Ioanna needed to prepare dinner. They couldn't find anything to cook except potatoes. There was a big frying pan handy, so they decided to make French fries. They peeled and cut the potatoes and put them in a bowl of water until they were ready to fry them. Ioanna found the olive oil. Georgia brought a chair for them to stand on to reach the elevated fixed-wall fireplace. She gathered the wood and placed it between two bricks inside the fireplace. Ioanna put the frying pan on top of the bricks and poured in the oil. Georgia lit the fire. She didn't know how hot it needed to be, so she kept adding more wood.

When it seemed hot enough, Ioanna brought the wet potatoes over. Georgia stood up onto the chair, reached over and dumped them into the pan. Flames and oil spewed upward in a sudden explosion. Georgia was so terrified that she jumped off the chair and ran out of the house and down the road. At first Ioanna was immobilized by the astonishing explosion. She watched Georgia take off running. Then Ioanna sprang into action, trying to find a pan to smother the fire.

When Arianna found out about the incident, she was relieved that neither of them was hurt. She examined Georgia carefully, but miraculously there were no signs of burns. She instructed them about drying the potatoes and not having the oil too hot. She wanted to tell Georgia that problems weren't solved by running down the road, but half the time she felt like running herself. They were so young; it wasn't their fault. She wished that she didn't have to depend on them so much.

Nikolas was also alarmed when he heard about the accident. But he comforted them, "I am so glad you are okay. What a tremendous help you are to the family!" With understanding and approval, the girls felt like they could face the kitchen and other work again. They were appreciated and weren't messing things up too much.

One day, Nikolas came home with a surprise for Arianna and the girls. He proudly installed new glass windows, replacing the cardboard that was covering most of them. Arianna asked him, "How did you manage it?" Nikolas smiled, "I worked something out." Arianna appreciated how Nikolas was so resourceful and worked so hard. She knew that he had some friends who owned a factory in the city, and he must have arranged some sort of trade. She loved the light that the windows brought in, and the girls were excited to be able to look outside.

As winter began, Nikolas took the horse and wagon to Prasinos Kampos to try to retrieve their furniture from the small house where they had stayed for the first year of the war. Arianna and Georgia decided to go along. Arianna was excited to have something that she was proud of back in her home again. With the war over and Arianna's older brothers and their families back in Heraklion, the Prasinos Kampos house had reverted back to a storage area and barn.

Arianna went straight to her wooden buffet with glass shelves. Looking past the dirt and a broken piece of glass, she proudly asked Georgia, "What do you think of this beautiful piece?" Georgia had very few memories of that house, and with the stark poverty that she had experienced during the war, she wasn't aware of the intended elegance of a buffet. She noticed that chickens had taken up residence in it so she replied, "That is a nice place for chickens to live and lay their eggs!"

Arianna, who prized that particular wedding gift, felt personally wounded by the insult of her treasured symbol of life before the turmoil. Her innocent daughter wasn't even aware that the impudent invasion had thwarted a more civilized upbringing. Perhaps a little crisply she replied, "No, chickens aren't supposed to live in there. That is my most cherished piece of furniture that is supposed to display pretty things." Georgia looked at it sideways and decided to take her word for it.

With the help of his brothers-in-law, Nikolas was able to load their bedframe, a table and the upper section of the buffet in the back of his wagon. A couple of Arianna's brothers took this load back to the home in Karidia. Nikolas tied the lower section of the buffet to his blanketed horse. He walked it slowly through the Prasinos Kampos town square. With every few steps of the horse, the buffet leaned to one side and then to the other. The townspeople laughed, toasted him with *raki* [concentrated alcohol] and teasingly sang a song they normally sang for a bride and groom during farewell celebrations from the square.

98

Nikolas wasn't sure if they were mocking, thinking that he was marrying his horse or buffet or if he just looked like a groom transporting furniture. Either way, as much as he enjoyed a good joke, he was a little embarrassed but smiled and waved. It took him most of the evening to get home. He gave the horse plenty of food and water and a rubdown as soon as he was able to remove the buffet from her back. He praised the horse, "You always come through for me, ol' girl. I couldn't manage without you."

With the furniture restored to its rightful place, fresh weeds gathered and dried for mattresses and months of cleaning, repairing and organizing, the house started to feel like a home again. Arianna kept a warm fire burning and tried to make it as cozy as possible during the cold months. Reminders of war persisted in the sting of poverty and the fear of the mines.

Nikolas and Arianna's hearts filled with dread every time they heard an explosion off in the distance. Sometimes animals would trigger the mines, but other times people did as well. It was gruesome to happen upon pieces of flesh everywhere. Grasping that some person was ambushed by a cruel death was horrific, and the trauma was intensified by the agony of identifying who it was. They constantly worried for friends and family members.

One day, Arianna's brother Antonios came to their door. When Arianna saw him, she knew that something was wrong. "What happened?" she asked him apprehensively. He told her that a young cousin of theirs had been killed by a landmine. "She was out visiting a friend who had just had a baby and lived not far from the beach. Her scarf blew away in the wind and she ran to catch it and accidentally triggered the mine." Arianna gasped at the tragedy, tears running down her cheeks. Antonios hugged her and said, "It was instant. She did not suffer."

They had heard of numerous other injuries and deaths from those abominable snares lying in wait, but none had hit so close to home. The war had been over in their area for over half a year and yet it was still killing her loved ones. "One minute she was full of life and the next…" she lamented to Antonios and Nikolas, who arrived and heard the news. Nikolas was vigilant with each rain or windstorm to try to spot any newly uncovered mines and, by using the hook and rope, remove them. In addition to guarding his family, he kept the animals pent up and safe.

Nikolas, Arianna and all of the sisters celebrated Barbara's first birthday and Christmas with more gratitude than lavishness. They focused on how God was faithful to bring them that far and not on what they did not have to embellish the occasions. They had a home, vegetables to eat and most importantly each other. Near the beginning of the next year, they were happy to learn that a new baby would join their family.

When spring approached, Nikolas was asked if he could loan his horse and wagon for a wedding in Prasinos Kampos. Although the war had ended, the young girl was still referred to as a war bride and had very little with which to celebrate. Arianna and the girls were happy to collect spring flowers to adorn the horse's mane and the wagon. The small town pulled together to make the day special for the young couple.

When they were getting ready to leave Prasinos Kampos, Georgia and Ioanna begged their parents to let them stay the night at their grandparents' house. Arianna asked them, "Are you sure? It's not close to home if you change your mind." When they assured her that they wanted to and wouldn't change their minds, Arianna asked her parents, who were delighted.

Georgia and Ioanna liked to be around all of the activity at their grandparents' home. They had many aunts, uncles, cousins and neighbors coming in and out. Provisions were not enough to re-open the café, but neighbors and those in need knew that the Kazandaki table was always open with such as they had. Georgia wandered around to the area where her grandfather cobbled shoes. She was fascinated with all the different foot-shaped sizes of the solid wood shoe molds, but she thought to herself, "I wonder how all the people get their feet in there?"

In the kitchen area, Ioanna watched her grandmother and grandfather run their busy but orderly household. She marveled that without

100

saying anything to one another, they seemed to be in perfect unity. Ioanna asked, "*Yiayia* [Grandmother], why do you call *Pappou* [Grandfather] 'My lord'?" She answered, "Your grandfather was sixteen years older than I was when I married him at fourteen years of age. At first it was a sign of deference because I was grateful that he protected me from dangers going on at the time. But then I came to really respect and honor him for who he is."

Ioanna had seen glimpses of many dangers in her young life but was protected from the stories of her grandmother's day, when Turkish men would kidnap young, beautiful Greek women for their harems. There would be fighting and bloodshed if they were overtaken, but more often their children would grow up and be trained to fight for the Turks against the Greeks. On the other hand, if the women were married, the Turks respected the marriage and the women were safe.

Ioanna observed the many qualities of her grandfather. In spite of having so many children and grandchildren, he treated each one specially and had time for everyone. She knew him to be loving but was also captivated by his commanding presence and dress. As she watched him at the basin washing his hands saying, "Wash me that I might be clean; wash away all my iniquity and cleanse me from my sin," she admired his humility that almost contradicted his flamboyant appearance.

Her grandfather's vest with shiny buttons and bright red sash and cap were proudly worn, despite wear and mending from the insults of the recent war. His boots were made out of soft leather and were tied above his knees. Ioanna saw no buttons or zippers, so she wondered how he got them on and off. Most interesting of all were his pantaloons. Although they were thick, they were soft, with piles of material hanging below his seat. They were tighter at the knees, allowing them to be tucked into his boots. Ioanna tried to imagine her father wearing something like that as he worked out in the fields and then laughed. What seemed so fitting for her grandfather didn't seem to suit her father at all.

Georgia was summoned from the other room by her grandmother, "Come get a quick bite to eat. Before long it will be time to get ready for bed." Since they had just come from a wedding, the family and friends who had gathered did more talking and laughing at the table than eating.

After a leisurely time, the women got up to clear the table. Confident that Georgia could find her way on her own, they sent her upstairs to get ready for bed. When she got to the storage room on the way to the stairs, it was so dark and cold. Something kept brushing her on the head as she walked forward. She looked up and saw obscured shapes of creatures everywhere and started screaming, "Help, help! The *baboulithes* [boogeymen] are here!" She was so scared that she couldn't look up and couldn't move but kept screaming.

Finally her grandmother came in, along with Ioanna. "Those are just wineskins hanging from the ceiling. They can't hurt you," she said and held her hand the rest of the way up the stairs with Ioanna. Georgia was familiar with wineskins since her father had several, but seeing so many of them in shadowy form in a dark, unfamiliar room, all hanging over her and pummeling her blindly was another proposition entirely.

Each vessel had been made out of a whole goat, carefully skinned as a single piece, starting from the throat. The large goatskin was then cured with salt. They used them primarily to transfer oil or wine or to take to sell rather than to store for long periods of time. Seeing such a sight, Georgia wasn't convinced that they weren't boogeymen and didn't know how she was supposed to go to sleep knowing they were right below. But she knew that she had promised her mother that she wouldn't ask to be taken home.

Georgia eventually felt comforted when her grandfather came upstairs and began his nighttime prayers. He gave thanks for their blessings and humbly asked for guidance and for what they needed. He then proceeded to individually bless each family member by name. He also prayed for those yet to be born, and that the blessings would be passed on to their children's children's children. Georgia contentedly crawled into bed next to Ioanna, both of them between their grandparents, and quickly fell asleep.

Ioanna, on the other hand, had a lot on her mind from the day's activities and found it difficult to sleep in a different bed. Before long, she started to hear some unfamiliar sounds. From her left where her grandmother was lying, she heard deep blowing punctuated by popping sounds as her lips caught and briefly stuck together as she blew, "*Whooo...pup pup pup, whooo... pup pup pup.*" And from her right towards her grandfather, she heard a rhythmical throaty growl, "*Hhhhhoouaac... hhhhhoouaac.... hhhhhoouaac.*" Ioanna had never heard snoring before and didn't know what to think. She felt uneasy in a strange place with this inexplicable chorus around her, but she also remembered her brave promise to her mother.

Her grandparents and Georgia seemed relaxed and comfortable despite the noise, so maybe everything was all right. That is, until she heard a third sound... From somewhere outside of the bed came a piercing and tremulous, "*Ooo-aaaaahc, ooo-aaaaahc, ooo-aaaaahc!*" During the bedtime prayer Ioanna had noticed her grandfather's boots in a heap at the bottom of the bed, and now she was sure that this terrifying sound was coming from the boots. Unable to contain herself any longer, Ioanna started crying hysterically.

When her grandparents woke up and asked her what was wrong, she explained, "There is a monster! There is a monster in the boots!" Her grandparents were groggy and confused. "What could she mean?" they asked each other. "That sound!" Ioanna expounded, "And you make sounds too!" as she pointed to both of them.

Ioanna's aunts had come into the room at the commotion and caught Ioanna's descriptions and distress. All too familiar with their parents' nocturnal turbulence, stifled giggles escaped surreptitiously from the aunts. Nonetheless in sympathy for the small girl's feelings, they hurried Ioanna out of the room, soothing her saying, "There are no monsters; just an owl in the mulberry tree outside the window." "You can stay with us tonight so that the snoring and the owl don't bother you, but everything is okay." It was quite a while before the girls wanted to stay the night at their grandparents' house again.

Chapter 11

While the weather was still making up its mind whether it was winter or spring, Nikolas dove into action to try to clear what he could of the *Sterna* piece of land. He didn't dare get too close to the unexploded bomb, but there were many sharp metal fragments from other detonated projectiles that could be carefully removed and the large depressions they left leveled out. He did not want Arianna or the girls to help, thinking they could hurt themselves.

Most of the debris was centered within about an eight-meter area, but some had scattered randomly beyond. He decided to start in the outskirts since the dispersed pieces could be extra dangerous if unexpected. Nikolas' mind jumped ahead. He must not only find and extricate all the wreckage but level as much of the area around the big crater that could be safely used, barricade the bomb, re-plant his crops and then re-dig the irrigation trenches strategically from the cistern. Bringing his thoughts around to the task at hand, he smiled to himself that if the rubble had not been sharp, he could imagine the girls making a sport out of trying to find the hidden plunder.

It took weeks of juggling this laborious undertaking with all of his other spring plowing, hoeing and pruning before most of the *Sterna* field was restored enough for some planting. Going back and forth among the crops in Karidia, Prasinos Kampos and Lithos took time away from investing time in his closest large property, but it was important for him to maintain all of the fields, vines and trees to later be able to harvest for food and trade. Day laborers were still hard to find, so the whole family pitched in to help.

Nikolas taught seven-year old Georgia how to oversee the windmill. "When the wind is too strong, we need to protect the windmill by tying up all eight of the cloth sails, but when the wind slows we need to untie them to help pump water to the cistern and then out to the soil," Nikolas explained as he demonstrated to her how to tie and untie the sails.

Using large rocks, he built her some steps up to the cement base of the windmill. Georgia was not crazy about any kind of heights, but not everyone could drop everything and run when the wind changed. She didn't want the windmill to break, so she proudly accepted the responsibility.

Georgia was more excited about the adventure of gathering snails. In the spring after it rained, the snails would come out of hiding. It was fun for the kids to find them, and the adults enjoyed having them combined with boiled crushed wheat or prepared in other ways. The snails in Crete were particularly tasty since they fed on the savory herbs growing on the mountains.

One day while Ioanna stayed home with Barbara, Georgia and Stella joined their mother for a snailing expedition. They each carried a bucket and a long stick and prodded along the sides of the road. Stella squealed and jumped up and down whenever she found a snail.

Along the way, they ran into Arianna's second cousin Stefanos Psomiaki and his wife, who were doing the same thing. They visited together while searching for snails. After they greeted one another and Arianna showed off the girls she asked, "What are you doing in Crete?" Stefanos answered, "Living in Athens during the war was hard, but it seemed even harder after the war. It was very hard to find food. We decided to stay here a little while with my parents and sister."

Arianna sympathized and said, "Well it is really good to have you here. You are welcome to work in our fields and share our crops." Stefanos thanked her, "I may join you every now and then, but we have a lot to keep up with at my parents' property."

When they returned home, they saw that Ioanna already had a caged area with wheat flour and pieces of grape leaves to feed the snails. They had to wait several days for the snails to eat this diet and clean themselves out before boiling or frying them for dinner. Arianna told

Nikolas about meeting her second cousin. He commented, "I hope he takes you up on your offer. I don't like how hard you are working during your pregnancy. Either way, you need to take it easy."

At the end of summer, Nikolas was able to trade enough of his produce to obtain a few extra supplies. He was finally able to get some plaster paint that had been made from burnt limestone for painting over the swastika on the roof. There hadn't been too many planes flying overhead, and often throughout the summer they had laid wheat or raisins on the flat roof to allow them to dry, partially hiding the swastika. But it bothered him greatly to know that his home was stained with this symbol.

Nikolas eagerly applied the paint as liberally as he could without it being too thick to dry thoroughly. He quickly realized that it was going to take several coats to cover the symbol and more paint than he was able to afford right then. He felt some relief to at least dim it slightly with some initial layers.

One day before school began, Arianna came anxiously from Prasinos Kampos. She found Georgia on the balcony and asked, "Have you seen any big ships?" Georgia shook her head and asked, "Why?" Arianna told her, "There are rumors that there may be a large boat filled with Jewish people trying to return home to Israel. They said that another boat may be trying to drown them." Georgia looked again and said, "I don't see them."

Filled with a sense of dread, she didn't want to see them if they were going to drown. Georgia didn't know anything about the Jews, but she was reminded that the awful war was affecting other people in other areas of the world. She was fearful for themselves and for any others where violence was still going on. And she knew how happy it was to make it home after being gone a long time. She prayed that they would arrive home safely. Arianna did too.

Later when Arianna told Nikolas about what she had heard about the Jewish people possibly traveling by ship nearby, she added, "The people in Prasinos Kampos were also discussing theories about the war. Some thought that Greece may have played a big part in the Allies' victory. If Mussolini invaded Greece before Hitler wanted to, it could have delayed Hitler from advancing into Russia. Maybe since the Greeks fought so hard, Hitler had to come bail out Mussolini, delaying the conflict in Russia until the bitterly cold winter they have there." Nikolas agreed, thoughtfully, "I guess that makes sense and could have contributed to the outcome."

At times, now that some time had passed, Nikolas and Arianna were astounded at what all they had experienced first-hand during the war. It almost seemed like a bad nightmare, although its reality tainted too much of their consciousness. They really wanted to put it all behind them.

By the second fall after the war, Arianna was happy that things had stabilized enough for the village of Asprada to attempt a semi-regular school season. It was generally understood that with harvests, extreme weather or sickness that perfect attendance could never be expected. Arianna walked with Georgia and Ioanna the two and a half kilometers east to Asprada for the first day of school.

Although they all were accustomed to a lot of walking, Arianna realized that she would need to send with them some extra water for their journey there and back. But it would be hard for them to carry their books, lunch and a jug of water. They decided to stop at a neighbor's house along the way to ask for a drink. The neighbor graciously offered that the girls could stop in anytime.

Only the first six grades were taught in Asprada and the other nearby villages. One teacher taught all of the children in a one-room schoolhouse. The teacher of the small school in Asprada was a woman from Heraklion.

After meeting Georgia and Ioanna, the teacher explained that she would usually stay with a nearby family during the week but would return to Heraklion on the weekends. As long as the rudimentary bus was able to bring her, she should be in class. The bus was really a temperamental tractor pulling an open-air wooden wagon with benches. Arianna pictured her young girls making the long trek by themselves, sometimes in harsh weather, while not knowing if the teacher would even be there. But she really desired for her girls to be able to read, and this was part of the price to be paid.

Nikolas carefully watched that Arianna would not work too hard while her two helpers were away at school. He was glad when he observed Arianna slowing her work pace until he noticed the worried look on her face. "What's wrong?" he asked her. "I haven't felt the baby move in a couple of days," she answered. Nikolas felt the blood drain from his face. He begged her to lie down and remain in bed as much as possible.

A week later, they faced the reality that the baby had died. They grieved silently, not knowing what to tell the girls. One morning while the older girls were at school, Arianna was washing clothes at the ocean shore behind their house. A sudden, strong, cramping pain came over her. Minutes later she delivered a stillborn baby boy. In overwhelming grief, she collapsed into the shallow ocean waves, clutching her lifeless son. She held his tiny body close, mourning this child and the life that could have been theirs together as a family. She had already begun to love this little one, and now knowing that he was a boy who could help erase some of the cultural shame added a sting to her heartache.

Nikolas, from the hill above, looked down and saw Arianna in the ocean, hunched over with pieces of laundry floating around her. He knew. With a gasp, he grabbed something to warm her with and ran to her. He put his arms around her and led her out of the water, draping a shawl around her shaking form. They sat on the sand as he looked at his son. He thought that he had already grieved, but as he took a turn holding him, he broke down under the weight of sorrow that overwhelmed him. Any life was precious, and he mourned this unique individual, but the memories of his first son's death intruded and intensified Nikolas' desolation with the loss of his second son.

Christmas a few months later was bittersweet. They were filled with anguish knowing that their precious son who should have been born around that time would never celebrate Christmas on earth with them. It brought comfort to perceive the loving Savior now holding their baby in His arms. They made an effort to make the season special for the girls, whom they were so proud of. Arianna was somewhat glad when school started up again so that she could let some of her tears flow privately.

108

In the early part of the next year, Arianna heard a knock at the door. She saw two ladies known to be beggars in the area. Occasionally they had stopped at their door with religious pamphlets that they tried to sell. Arianna greeted them and offered a little bread that she had made. Arianna apologized that they did not have more to give.

One of the ladies asked, "Why don't you have more? Haven't you been to the city to get aid from the government? Other countries have been sending food and clothing after the war, and they are handing it out." Arianna replied with surprise, "We didn't know anything about it." The other woman advised, "Make sure you both go and take all of your children since the amount of aid depends on the number of family members."

That weekend, Nikolas and Arianna decided to take all four girls to Heraklion to see what aid might be there. They got up early in the morning and bundled the girls in blankets in the wagon, where the little ones continued to sleep. Arianna took in the beautiful winding cliffside journey along the ocean. Nikolas, however, noted the tunneled bunkers etched in the mountain caves on the other side of the road. He almost thought he saw some activity in one or two of them. As they neared the city, several ships that hinted ominously of wartime loomed in the sea near the harbor.

They reached a checkpoint close to the city and could go no further without a permit. When Nikolas explained where they were from and why they were there, one officer consulted with another. While the man was occupied, Nikolas chatted with some other local men about the bunkers he had seen and the continued military presence. He learned that there was something of a Greek civil war between government forces and Communist insurgents. Each group had support from other nations.

Nikolas was distressed that the conflicts were not over. With other countries involved, it sounded too reminiscent of the recent world war. At the same time, he may have some of those countries to thank for any aid he might receive. He realized that in this crucial era of instability and rebuilding, several parties probably had an interest in filling any power vacuum. He prayed that order would be restored quickly and that no harm would come to innocent civilians.

The officer waved him over. He asked Nikolas about the number in his household and where he lived. When Nikolas answered, the officer glanced over to another officer who counted Arianna and the girls in the wagon and confirmed the number. "*Endaxi* [Okay]. We have registered your family and will have agents get you some supplies," the officer explained. Nikolas and Arianna were disappointed that they couldn't get the donations right then.

Nikolas asked, "Are we able to go into the city?" The officer replied that in order to get to the main square they would have to pay a duty to collect city taxes, and also that there was a city-wide curfew. Nikolas and Arianna discussed that they didn't have money to buy enough to be worth paying a duty.

Before leaving, Nikolas asked, "Is anyone in the government doing anything to remove unexploded mines or bombs on people's properties?" The officer asked him for more details and made notes on his papers. "We will see what we can do, but I am not sure when we will be able to get to it." Nikolas thanked him and they all departed for home.

Arianna was anxious that they arrive home from the almost two-hour journey before the girls started complaining for lunch. Sure enough, once they arrived home, the girls couldn't wait to eat and tried to drag Nikolas into the house. He told them, "You run ahead and help *Mama*. I have to take care of the horse— she needs to eat and drink before me." Arianna thought that his consistent attending to the horse's needs before his own was why he and the horse had such a special connection and partnership. She appreciated both of them— Nikolas for his unselfish character and the horse for her faithful service in trying circumstances.

It was several weeks later when they were able to obtain the donations from the agents of the government. When Arianna saw the packages of food, she asked, "What about clothing? I heard that others received some clothes, and we have six people in the house." One of the agents found a black wool dress with holes in it. "This is

110

all we have left of the clothing. Nobody else wanted it but you can have it if you wish," the agent offered. Arianna was disappointed but took it thinking there should be something she could do with it. Nikolas asked the agents about any plan to excavate the bomb or mines, but they didn't know anything about it.

Afterwards, Nikolas and Arianna looked at the curious packages of food. They had never seen canned goods before and weren't sure how to open them. All of the packages had labels in foreign languages. The flour and butter made sense to them, although the butter was packaged in small, restaurant-style portions. The chewing gum was a complete mystery. Arianna was also unfamiliar with corn meal.

When they opened the can of grapefruit juice, they couldn't figure out what it was. Ioanna smelled it and said, "It smells like horse pee." Arianna whispered to Nikolas, "You don't think any of the nations competing for influence here would want to poison us, do you?" He didn't think so, but it could have spoiled. He hated to waste anything, but he wasn't sure what to do with it. He had an idea, "Girls, let's take it outside and play a game!" They each dug a little ditch down the road. From the top of the incline, they poured the juice down to see which would go the farthest. The girls clapped their hands and laughed as the grapefruit juice trickled down the road.

Meanwhile, Arianna smelled the powdered milk with skepticism. Although she thought it was okay, she decided to mix it with some water and give it to the horse to make sure it didn't die. But later when the horse lived and she tried to use the powdered milk to make bread, it didn't turn out. The canned milk, however, they used and enjoyed. As she tucked the girls in bed, she told them, "Let's say a prayer to bless the countries that sent us provisions. Even though we may not have known what to do with some of them, the people wanted to help us and we should be thankful."

They were also thankful when they were finally able to get some chickens. Most of the chickens Nikolas occasionally earned during the war were eaten pretty quickly. When Nikolas was able to pull together some crops, he was able to trade them for half a dozen chickens to raise. The eggs they would lay would be valuable for meals, and eventually they might be able to roast a chicken for a special occasion. They let them roam free during the day but kept them in a pen beneath the wood-burning oven under the balcony at night to protect them from predators.

It was several months after Nikolas spoke to the government before a group of trained men showed up at their home to deactivate and extricate the bomb in the *Sterna* field. As he prepared to depart with the men, Nikolas told Arianna and the girls, "Please stay clear of that whole area all day." Arianna looked at him with apprehension and cautioned, "Please be careful and stay clear yourself!" She could imagine Nikolas feeling the responsibility of his field and entrenching himself in the endeavor. She added, "Those guys are trained in this; you are not. Let them take care of it."

Nikolas couldn't help but tease her, "Mmm-hmm, and did my similar warning stop you when you single-handedly assailed the mines on the beach?" Shocked, she stammered, "But I had a long rope… and this bomb is a lot more powerful." Nikolas chuckled and kissed her on the cheek, "I will steer clear."

Nikolas stayed true to his word and the bomb was disengaged with no incident. Although the men contracted by the government defused and removed the explosive, they left it for Nikolas to fill in the crater left behind. Nikolas asked the men about the mines along the beach. The foreman answered, "That will be a different team. There are mines all along the beaches from the city and beyond, so it will take a long time to do." Nikolas thanked them profusely and offered them a meal back at the house in appreciation.

Nikolas was relieved to have that menace off of his property. But he still had the arduous chore of filling in and leveling the large hole in the ground. Fortunately, day laborers were becoming more obtainable, and even Arianna's second cousin Stefanos Psomiaki helped some before his family returned to Athens. Stefanos had stayed in Karidia several months, working mostly with his parents but also occasionally in the vegetable gardens with Nikolas. Stefanos' wife, a lady of sophistication, was anxious to go home to

112

Athens, and Stefanos felt that the capital city probably had recovered enough from the war to have food available.

It took weeks of leveling the land, planting the vegetable crops and irrigating the soil before Nikolas felt a sense of accomplishment. He had taken one step closer to normalcy. Over time, he watched his newly planted crops to make sure they were being watered. He realized that the windmill was too inconsistent to rely on. With their location between the mountain and sea, the winds were often too strong to allow the windmill to function and the sails had to be tied back. Yet other times, if there were no winds, there was also no water. He had a lot at stake to get things up and running after the war.

After discussing it with Arianna, Nikolas decided to take a chance and purchase a motorized pump. The paper currency they had kept since before the war was not usable anymore, even after the war. But they had some gold coins to spend for this investment in that piece of property.

Nikolas got some help disassembling the windmill, re-routing several of the pipes and installing the new pump. Arianna was worried about spending the little money they had on a new-fangled contraption that they knew very little about. But Nikolas was always enterprising and most of his ideas were successful and often before their time. Pioneering often brought bumps in the road, though, and although for the most part the pump worked very well, it also occasionally broke down or overheated.

On one occasion, Nikolas inspected the well and realized that he needed to do some repairs on the pump. The next day, he was gathering his tools to go work on the well when Arianna decided that she and Ioanna and Stella would go along in order to help him and also prune the tops of the grape blooms in the field nearby. Since the hazards had been removed, there should be little danger in having a couple of the girls along.

The well had a small roof on top and dirt steps leading down below ground to a platformed area surrounding the well that ran deeper still. While Nikolas was doing his work in this little earthen room below, four-year old Stella became curious and begged to join him. "Please, *Mama*, I want to see how it works and help *Baba*." Nikolas shouted up to Arianna, "It's okay with me if she comes down for a little while." Arianna reluctantly consented and helped Stella down the steep, narrow steps from above, and then Nikolas helped her from below. She sat on her daddy's lap as he pointed and explained how everything worked.

Nikolas and Stella were down in the underground room near the well for a few minutes when Arianna started tidying above where they were sitting. Suddenly she accidentally dropped a piece of metal. "Look out!" she yelled. Immediately she heard screams from below and her heart was gripped with fear. Stella kept screaming as Nikolas carried her up the steps in his arms. Arianna turned white when she saw blood pouring from Stella's head. Arianna shrieked in panic, "I killed my daughter!" Day laborers came running at the commotion to see if there was anything they could do to help. Ioanna was immobilized in fear.

When Nikolas reached the top of the steps, Arianna grabbed Stella from him and started racing towards home. Blood was flowing down Stella's face and onto Arianna's dress as everyone in the area ran after them. One kind man caught up with Arianna and yelled, "Do you want me to take her?" But Arianna didn't want to let go of her. She frantically prayed, "Dear Jesus, please save my daughter."

Georgia heard a disturbance outside and opened the door as everyone burst into the house. She was horrified to see Stella and her mother covered in blood. Ioanna staggered inside, her heart pounding with adrenaline and fear, but Georgia felt dizzy with the shock of trying to comprehend what of all the blood meant. When Stella stopped screaming, Georgia was overcome with a sudden dread that she had died. Both girls clung to one another until they heard someone say that she had passed out.

People were running everywhere trying to find a cloth to use to stop the bleeding. Someone ripped a sheet and pressed it against Stella's head. When Stella woke up several minutes later, she was confused by the bandage on her head and so many people standing around her. When they asked her questions about how she felt and what she remembered from the accident, she couldn't remember what had happened. Since the bleeding had stopped and Stella seemed fine, they didn't think it was crucial to try to hunt down the only overworked doctor in the region.

The family watched Stella closely for the next several days. Miraculously, she did not seem to have any serious effects from her head injury. Arianna whispered prayers of thanks every time she changed Stella's bandage and witnessed the progress in her healing. Finally after a couple of weeks of imploring her mother to let her go outside, Stella was allowed to go play on the rope swing across the road near the flattened villa. "Don't let her swing too high," Arianna cautioned Ioanna who went with her.

Meanwhile, Nikolas was preparing to put another coat of paint over the swastika on the roof and asked Georgia to climb the wooden ladder to sweep the area first. When Nikolas followed her up several minutes later, he found her trembling. "What's wrong?" he asked her. "I am dizzy and afraid of falling. We are so high up." Nikolas tried to reassure her that she was safe and told her not to look down. But Georgia was so frightened that she was flustered and inconsolable.

Nikolas saw that Georgia was miserable and wasn't going to be able to do anything to help. He reassured her that it was okay and tried to gently coax her down the ladder, but he soon realized that she was too agitated to navigate safely. He tried to go ahead of her and hold her around her waist, but she cried, "I can't do it, I'm going to fall. The earth is spinning." So Nikolas sat her down in a safe place on the roof and assured her, "I will be right back."

Nikolas found Arianna and detailed Georgia's predicament. At first Arianna was irritated. But when Nikolas explained that her fear was real and described all of the attempts he made, she realized the peril and asked him what they should do. At eight-years old, she was too big for him to try to carry down an unstable ladder.

Nikolas finally decided to try to lower her in a large basket by rope. He carefully secured the rope to the handles of the basket then flung the rope over his shoulder as he climbed up the ladder. As he pulled the basket to the roof, he explained the plan to Georgia. She wasn't too sure about the idea, but Nikolas encouraged her to get in and cover her eyes. Resolving to trust her father, Georgia got into the basket. Nikolas steadily lowered her from the roof to Arianna below, who steadied the basket and then helped Georgia out. They all breathed a sigh of relief when she was safely on the ground.

After things settled down a little later, Nikolas admitted to Arianna, "I guess I should have known about Georgia's fear of heights. She used to have enough trouble climbing up the few steps to adjust the sails of the windmill when we had it in *Sterna*." Arianna paused a second, letting the full realization hit her and looked at Nikolas skeptically, "Did you just lower our eight-year old daughter from the roof in a basket?" He smiled at her and winked. Arianna returned a dazed smile and pondered if there might be a little wisdom in not dwelling on some things too much.

Chapter 12

It wasn't long until school started again in the fall. Georgia and Ioanna did not complain much since they knew that schooling was important to their mother, and they saw that most of the other kids had the same difficulties that they did. The journey to Asprada was about an hour long and tiring. Although they brought with them a jug of water, they soon ran out and walked the rest of the way thirsty. They often stopped at someone's house along the way, but since the people had to walk up to three kilometers to the nearest well and carry their water back in a heavy clay jug, sometimes they had no water to give them.

Frequently, the girls made the journey to the school but the teacher wasn't there. They would ask someone if they heard the church bell announcing that classes were intended for that morning, but usually the person could not recollect. They waited until the second bus from town came much later in case she would show up, otherwise they walked home futilely.

During the various harvests, which was much of the school year, they switched back and forth among the schools in Asprada, Prasinos Kampos and Lithos, depending on which field or orchard they were working with their parents. They didn't have many books, usually just Greek history and religion, but sometimes the schools used different versions. In addition, two grades were taught together, so the coursework could vary considerably. These inopportune circumstances led to disjointed lessons. Combined with the occasional need to miss classes, the girls were often confused or behind, and their learning suffered. They didn't understand why the teacher would use a tree branch to slap their already work-torn hands when they did not know their lessons.

Georgia was the one most called upon to stay home and help when Stella, Barbara or her mother was sick, so she was not able to learn much beyond the alphabet and basic phonetics. Ioanna fared a little better with basic math, but she dreaded spelling. Classes such as history, grammar and geography were puzzling, but she loved Bible stories, especially from the Old Testament.

Walking home one day Ioanna asked Georgia, "What do you think about all of our classes?" Georgia answered, "I am having trouble with all of the things that we are supposed to be learning." Ioanna agreed. As hard as they tried, the lessons often didn't make sense. She reflected to Georgia, "I wonder why no one realizes we aren't really learning anything."

One Sunday, Georgia dreaded the thought of school the next day. Her thoughts swirled with the perplexities surrounding the purpose and challenges in learning until she felt restless for an escape. The winds of late fall were stirring up, and it wouldn't be long until it would be too cold to take long walks unless she had to. She knew that if she asked her mother, more than likely she would be given a chore to do, but she wanted some time to herself.

Georgia slipped down to the lower part of the house and heard the horse whinny at her from the barn area. She walked over and stroked her nose, "Are you fidgety too? I guess you can come with me." She attached a rope to her bridle and led her on a slow walk along the beach. Georgia knew to stay very close to the water's edge to avoid any remaining landmines that could still be active. They took their time, walking side by side enjoying the beautiful scenery— they themselves making a pretty picture along the northern island coast. The waves were calm and soothing.

Before long, Georgia felt invigorated and turned around to head back home. While still at some distance but within view of her house, the horse suddenly pulled away and ran toward some shrubs further inland. Too late, Georgia reached for the rope and yelled, "No! Come back!" The horse was intent on grazing and wasn't to be deterred. Georgia panicked. She knew the horse was in a dangerous area. But what was she to do? The horse was beloved and valuable to her family. She must go rescue her. She took some steps, cautiously following in the horse's hoof prints. As she neared the

118

horse and grabbed the rope, she froze as she felt three metal prongs come through her sandal.

Georgia's heart was pounding. She had never been more scared in her life. It was terrifying to see bombs dropping from the sky, but even more so to be standing on a bomb. Any second she was probably going to die. She waited. Nothing happened. Now what? She was afraid to move, but she hadn't told anyone where she was going, so it would probably be a long time before someone would find her. The horse seemed to be finishing up her grazing and soon may start to get antsy. She said a simple but earnest prayer, "Jesus, please save the horse and me."

Shaking like a leaf, Georgia slowly eased her foot out from her sandal. When her foot was clear, she firmly grabbed the horse and said, "Come on!" Not knowing if the mine might still go off, at first they walked away gingerly, then they ran quickly, following the path that they had taken. When they made it several meters away, Georgia's heart flooded with relief. She thanked God. They took a few more steps and then she panicked again. How was she going to tell *Mama* that she was in a place she wasn't supposed to be, lost one of the shoes of her only pair of sandals and almost killed the horse and herself?

Arianna was preparing dinner when Georgia walked in. "Where have you been? And where is your sandal?" Georgia heard the frustration in her mother's voice. She knew that as the oldest, she was expected to be responsible as the primary help in running the household. Georgia lowered her head, knowing the disappointment her mother would feel when she heard the story. Arianna could sense that she wasn't going to like the confession, but she wasn't prepared for the fear that enveloped her at nearly losing her oldest daughter.

Before Arianna could reply to Georgia's narrative, she ran to grab a bucket to vomit into. Georgia was alarmed and lamented, "I'm so sorry, *Mama*. I have made you sick!" Arianna consoled her, "No, it wasn't you. I think... Anyway, why did you walk so far? You know that we don't allow you girls to go swimming. What made you think that you could take the horse so far along the beach, and without telling anyone?" Georgia answered, "I know. I'm sorry and won't do it again— I was so scared." Arianna believed her. "You know we only make rules to keep you safe. God miraculously protected you today. Thank you, Jesus," Arianna said as she made the sign of the cross by briefly touching her head, stomach and each shoulder.

A little later while they were cutting up some broccoli, Arianna asked Georgia, "Was there any particular reason why you were walking the horse instead of riding her?" Arianna imagined a gallop on the beach with the wind blowing back her hair would be the most revitalizing aspiration. Georgia told her, "I thought I might see better to avoid any mines if I walked, and plus it hurts my stomach if I ride the horse too long or lift anything heavy."

Arianna considered the small bulge on Georgia's stomach that she had been born with. A doctor had looked at it one time and said that it was probably a hernia. But with the war and shortage of doctors, it wasn't a priority to do anything about. Now that it had grown to the size of an egg and was bothering her, maybe they should consider having it checked out again. When it seemed like a good time, she would discuss it with Nikolas.

Nikolas worked many hours in the fields, often getting home after dark. Little Barbara constantly ran to the door to look out for his return. Arianna tried to put her to bed after they cleaned up after dinner. The four girls shared a double bed, so she tried to calm her so the others could sleep. She told her, "You know he has had a busy day and is tired," but Barbara couldn't sleep until her *baba* came home. She sat quietly in the dark at the foot of the bed. Sometimes when she was extra tired, she would think to herself, "Come on, Daddy, let's go to sleep!"

Nikolas finally arrived, exhausted. He immediately gave his horse some water and oats, and knowing Barbara would be waiting, he ran inside the house before the horse was done eating. Barbara squealed and jumped up and ran to him when she heard him come. He scooped her up and gave her a big hug. Barbara's entire body shook with excitement that her daddy was home. When she settled down a little, Nikolas put her to bed and then returned to care for his horse. Arianna shook her head at the nightly ritual and was glad when the winter season eased his workload.

120

Christmas day arrived, and Arianna and Nikolas announced to their daughters that they would have a little brother or sister the following summer. The four girls were thrilled. Over the next few months Arianna had some nausea and vomiting, but she didn't let that stop her from her activities. Ranging in age from three to eight years, the girls were able to help with many of the household duties.

Arianna noticed that Georgia continued to have pain when she tried to lift things that were even moderately heavy. One day, she was doubled over in pain. Arianna asked, "Did you just carry something?" Georgia moaned, "No, this is different. The pain is over here." She pointed to her right side. Arianna felt her forehead and it was very hot. "Go lie down and I will have *Baba* fetch the doctor."

When the doctor examined Georgia, he determined that she had appendicitis. "You will need to take her to the hospital in Heraklion for an operation to take out her appendix," he urged. Arianna packed an overnight bag for Nikolas and Georgia while Nikolas hitched up the wagon. Nikolas knew Arianna really wanted to go along, "Don't worry, she will be fine, and I will come and get you for a quick visit if I can." Arianna reminded him, "Don't forget to tell them about the hernia too."

It was a very long two-hour ride for Georgia. With every bump of the wagon, she winced in pain. She had never been to a hospital, and it was frightening. She was assessed, and the diagnosis was confirmed. They decided to go ahead and remove the appendix and fix the hernia during the same operation. Nikolas assured her that he would stay at the hospital through the whole procedure.

In spite of reassurances from her father and the medical staff, Georgia was agitated. She apprehensively watched as a large mask came towards her face. Then she was out. Nikolas anxiously paced the hospital corridor as he waited and prayed through the long surgeries. At home and without word, Arianna worried even more, remembering her brother Konstantine's abdominal surgeries. She prayed that nothing would go wrong with her young daughter.

The procedures went well, and finally she awoke to see her *baba* sitting at her side. He smiled and told her that she was all right. "I'm so sleepy…" Georgia drifted off to sleep. The next morning when Nikolas was assured that she was stable, he decided to go get Arianna for a visit. Arianna was glad to be able to go and left the care of the two youngest girls to seven-year old Ioanna. "Don't worry about the house too much," she admonished, "Just see that Stella and Barbara are okay. I will be back tonight."

Ioanna was proud to be trusted with such a responsibility and decided to clean the house to surprise her mother. She polished the small house from top to bottom while taking care of her sisters, as well as the chickens and the goat. After the sisters ate the lunch she prepared, Ioanna cleaned the kitchen and put all of the dishes away. When Arianna returned later that day she exclaimed, "My, you have been working so hard. It looks perfect! And your sisters look happy and well. Bless you, Ioanna!" Ioanna beamed at the praise. "How is Georgia?" she asked. Arianna answered thankfully, "She is doing great and should come home soon."

Her younger sisters were so excited when Georgia came home. They all asked her questions at once, wondering what it was like. Ioanna told her, "All of the other kids in school will be so jealous that you had an important operation." Georgia thought that she could forgo those kinds of accolades. Nikolas chimed in, "She needs to rest quite a while before she can be up and around."

Over the next several weeks, Georgia healed and got her strength back. At the same time, Arianna's nausea and vomiting kept getting worse. When Georgia was back on her feet, Nikolas sat down with her and asked, "How do you feel about school?" She thought a minute, "I have missed so much, I am not sure I want to go back. But whatever you want me to do." Nikolas had some misgivings but admitted, "We could really use you at home. *Mama* has not been feeling well and can really use your help." They discussed it a little further and decided to take Georgia out of school. Ioanna was sad to lose her school buddy, but she understood that the family's needs come first. And next fall, Stella would join her on the trek to the schoolhouse.

122

Spring was a miserable time for Arianna. She could not retain very much of her food or liquids. She had no energy. She relied on Georgia, with Ioanna helping when she was home, to do everything around the house. Arianna sampled different foods and herbs, but there was no improvement with anything she tried. Nikolas summoned the doctor, who said he couldn't do anything but advised her to eat anything she could keep down.

A few weeks later, Arianna was in crisis. She retched so much that it eroded her esophagus and she vomited blood. She was so weak that she was delirious, and her blood pressure and heart rate were erratic. When the doctor was summoned again, he was exceedingly grim. He pulled Nikolas aside and made him sit down. "I am afraid it is very serious. I have never seen this condition so bad. And I don't know what to do." Nikolas felt a lump in his throat at the sound of the doctor's words. He managed to ask, "If I took her to the hospital in the city, could they do anything?" The doctor shook his head, "You know that the hospital in Heraklion is pretty much set up just for surgeries. She needs nutrition, and she needs to stop vomiting. She's tried various herbs, and there is no medicine that can help her."

Nikolas braced himself as he asked, "What do you recommend?" The doctor looked sad and took a while to answer, "You have a very tough decision to make. It is my opinion that if you don't end the pregnancy, they both will die." Nikolas felt like he was crushed by an avalanche, "You can't be saying..." The doctor put his hand on Nikolas' shoulder, "Only you can make that decision, but you should consider the rest of your family. I really can't give you any other hope."

Nikolas sat motionless in shock for several minutes after the doctor left. Then as the gravity of the choice he must make sank in, he held his head in his hands and wept, "God, You have been with us from the beginning, holding our hands and delivering us through all of the ups and downs. What do I do? This is too much for me to make this decision. Please help me."

After taking some time to compose himself, he went inside to Arianna. He wasn't sure if she was very coherent. He whispered to her, "I can't lose you. I don't know what to do, but I need you more than you know. And your four young daughters need you. Could you ever forgive me if we did everything we have to do to save you…?" Arianna squeezed his hand but couldn't say anything. A tear slipped down her cheek. Nikolas bowed his head and sobbed.

Nikolas felt the burden of the decision so heavily that he swallowed any pride that he had and sought counsel of Arianna's family in Prasinos Kampos. Petros, with his father's advancing years, was thought of as a leader in the family. He was in town from the city and heard Nikolas' report with great concern. He traveled back with Nikolas to see Arianna. Seeing her emaciated and delirious condition, he reluctantly agreed with the doctor that she might not make it and supported any choice Nikolas had to make. The next day, arrangements were made for Arianna to have a procedure. The decision tore Nikolas up, but he supposed that the endeavor to save one life was better than losing two lives.

The night before the procedure, Nikolas packed a bag for Arianna. He didn't know how he would be able to sleep, but he knew that he needed to be strong for his wife. In the middle of the night, Nikolas had a vivid dream. He dreamt that he was cutting up Barbara into little pieces. His beloved youngest child— funny, playful and affectionate, and the one who looked most like himself— by his own hand, he was killing her. In the dream, Nikolas was very upset. He then heard a voice ask him, "If you feel this way about doing this to the child whom you have seen, how can you think about doing this to the one you haven't seen?"

Nikolas awoke with a start, distraught at the dramatic portrayal. It so shook him that he had to make sure that Barbara was okay. When he found that she was safe, Nikolas made up his mind then and there that he could not go through with the procedure. He suddenly felt that the baby in Arianna's womb was real and his, just as much as Barbara was, who was sleeping calmly before him.

When Nikolas returned to bed, Arianna awakened. She asked him, "What's wrong?" Nikolas told her his dream and then said resolutely, "I really don't want to see you die, but if I have to, I will bury you with our baby. This is killing, and I am not going to do that. I am not going to kill our baby to save you." Arianna was

124

moved by the dream and his fervent vow. She agreed with him and said, "We will commit our lives to the Lord and leave our future in His hands." They slept the rest of the night at peace.

Arianna's family and neighbors heard of the situation and the Stavrolakis' latest resolve. They expected that at any moment they would hear bad news. So when Nikolas showed up at the small café near Asprada, the local people anxiously asked him how Arianna was doing. As they were discussing her continued struggles, some strangers who had been looking for herbs in the mountains overheard and asked what they were talking about. The visitors seemed to exhibit genuine concern rather than an interest in gossip. When Nikolas nodded giving permission, the people told them the dire account of his wife, a mother of four who was helplessly fighting for her life and the life of their unborn baby. One of the outsiders turned to Nikolas and said, "We have studied herbs extensively. Can we see her?" Nikolas was surprised and a little unsure. The trained doctor offered no hope— and who were these strangers? But he decided to take the chance and led them to their home.

When they arrived, the visitors introduced themselves to Arianna and reviewed her symptoms. One of them comforted her, "We have some special herbs that should bring you some relief." Another asked, "Can we use your kitchen?" They prepared a mixture of medicine in a palatable base of goat's milk and honey. She was able to take the combination with no problem, so they left Nikolas a bag of the herbs and shared the recipe and instructions. One added, "You may want to boil a chicken and feed her the broth." The strangers then disappeared, never again to be seen by anyone in the area. From that moment on, Arianna began to improve. Nikolas followed their instructions to the letter and made sure that she continued to rest.

Before long, Arianna regained her strength and was able to resume most of her daily duties. When everyone heard about her miraculous recovery, they marveled and wondered, "Could the strangers have been angels?" Nikolas firmly believed they were a direct answer to his prayers and sent by God, whether they were literal or figurative angels.

Chapter 13

One day in June, Nikolas and Ioanna were working in one of the vineyards. Arianna walked up, looking for Nikolas, and found Ioanna first. Glowing with a beautiful smile, Arianna told her, "Today is the day!" Ioanna was confused, "What day, *Mama*?" Arianna beamed, "Today is the day that our baby is coming!" To Ioanna it was like they were going to receive the greatest blessing. She jumped up and down with excitement as Arianna continued on to find Nikolas.

Ioanna was so excited and already loved the new baby. But at the same time, she acutely felt the cultural disapproval of their having four girls. She had heard idle talk among the local people saying things like, "What are you going to do with that many daughters? If it is a boy you all will make it, but if it's a girl maybe we are just going to put a stone around her neck and drown her."

As a young girl, Ioanna believed their jests and dreaded what might happen if it were a girl. The joy that was about to fill their house was fantastic, but at the same time she prepared herself to kidnap a baby girl and hide her like Moses if she had to. "What can I do as an eight-year old girl?" she pondered, "But I will be prepared for whatever I need to do!"

Nikolas rode off to get the midwife while Arianna and Ioanna returned to the house. While Stella and Barbara were playing, Georgia was cleaning some wheat kernels, sorting out the rocks and other impurities. Arianna's pain increased quickly. She yelled to Georgia to heat some water. "This baby is not waiting for the midwife," Arianna bemoaned. The older girls tried to distract the younger ones while Arianna was yelling in pain.

The baby came just as Nikolas and the midwife ran in the door. The midwife saw so much bleeding that she was more worried about

Arianna than the baby. "A girl," she said as she grabbed the baby and put her on a blanket on the floor. She turned her attention to Arianna, who was bleeding so much that the blood was seeping through the towels and the basket she had near her.

While the midwife and Nikolas were occupied with Arianna, Georgia warmed some water, and Ioanna covered the baby with the blanket and paced close by. "No one's going to throw her into the sea or harm my baby. She's my baby to protect!" Ioanna anxiously thought to herself.

The baby was born with sharp nails and was scratching her face with them. The more she scratched, the more she cried. When Arianna was stable enough for Nikolas to leave her side to check on the baby, he saw the scratches on her face as well as a small, dark birthmark near her eyebrow. Immediately he came to the baby's defense, thinking Ioanna didn't want another sister. It seemed apparent to him that Ioanna had scratched her and marred her skin with a piece of coal from the fire, so he gave her a spanking. Ioanna had so much love for her little sister that she almost didn't mind. She reassured herself, "Maybe the baby was safe after all if *Baba* felt that protective also."

Things in the home calmed down enough to send for Arianna's mother to come stay for a couple of days and also for a priest from a neighboring village to come baptize the baby. Because Arianna had so many difficulties during the pregnancy and delivery, they weren't sure if the baby would live. So they decided to baptize the baby at their house the day after she was born.

A cousin of the caretaker of the nearby Minoan ruins was in town and agreed to serve as godmother for the baby. She chose the name Sousanna after herself, and since Arianna's mother had the same name, the family was very happy to call her by that name. They wrote out the name of the baby for the priest to officially declare and remember throughout the ceremony. They got a bowl that had never been used, since it needed to be reserved for holy use. Afterwards they would break it and bury it in the ground in order to not take lightly its religious purpose.

Because the ceremony was so soon after the birth, there wasn't much time for word to get around, so only a few people knew when and where they were going to baptize the baby. But when the time came, many people, including strangers from other areas, appeared at the house. The family looked around in amazement, "Where did everyone come from? How did they know, and why would they make the effort to come?" Stella was fascinated with all the candles. It seemed like everyone held a candle. She wondered, "Did the priest bring all of those candles? If not, where did they all come from?"

The priest began the service. In time, he came to the question, "What name shall this child be called?" Before the godmother could say anything, somewhere from out of the depths of her being, Ioanna blurted out in a loud voice, "Evangelea!" As soon as she spoke, Ioanna was scared to death that she would get in trouble. She didn't know where the name or boldness came from, but she couldn't help it. Her parents and godmother looked at each other in surprise, but the name had been spoken and by custom must remain.

As the baby was anointed with oil, the extra oil dripped into the bowl of water and astonishingly made the unquestionable, well-defined symbol of the cross. At the same time, a sweet fragrance filled the room. All who were present noticed it and wondered where it came from, since it did not smell of oil or anything used in the ceremony or from outdoors. It was as if someone opened an expensive bottle of perfume and spread the lovely aroma through the entire place. Some looked at each other and remarked, "What kind of special child is this?"

After everyone left, Nikolas and Arianna marveled. How it all came to be and what it all meant did not make sense to them, but they took every aspect of the event as a special blessing from God. The family decided to call Evangelea by the nickname Lea. Nikolas was teased about having five girls, but he didn't care. He was a proud papa and loved each and every one of his girls individually. He added in faith, "God gave them to me, and He will provide."

Arianna's parents thought that it might be a good time for a sleepover. Georgia stayed home to help her mother, but Ioanna, Stella and Barbara went to Prasinos Kampos for a few days.

The girls greeted their grandfather as their mother had taught them to, according to proper custom for the respected men of the family or for priests. They held out their right hands. When their grandfather placed his right hand in theirs, they kissed the top of his hand. With most other men, except for occasionally some priests, that was the extent of the greeting. But their grandfather always placed his left hand on the child's head and pronounced a blessing on them. Although this was a formal tradition, the girls appreciated the mutual honor bestowed.

The girls liked playing outside with the children, including their cousins, in the more populated village. There was a lot of activity in their grandparents' household, but they didn't have to help with a lot of the work, so they enjoyed themselves.

The weather was good, so some decided to sleep outside on the upstairs veranda. Ioanna and Stella slept out there while Barbara slept in between her grandparents inside. Ioanna remembered back to her frightening experience with hearing her grandparents snore, so she wasn't sure how long Barbara would stay in their bed. Sure enough, it didn't take long to hear Barbara screaming, "I want my mommy!" She was comforted by being taken out to sleep with her older sisters on the veranda.

In the fall, two of the girls went to school— this time Stella and Ioanna. Stella was especially excited and felt grown up to be attending school for the first time. Arianna had admonished her to be good, so she sat attentively on her bench, all prim and proper. She soon grew to love learning, finding almost every subject interesting.

Several weeks after school started, the teacher announced that they would have an important special guest the next day. They all spent some time cleaning the one-room schoolhouse and even the school yard. She told them to make sure to wear clean clothes, cut their fingernails and be on their best behavior. They were instructed that when the dignitary arrived and the teacher gave the signal, they should all stand up quietly in respect for him. Some children were assigned to offer him some refreshments after he greeted the class.

Ioanna and Stella talked about the special visitor all the way home. They wondered who he was and felt honored that their little schoolhouse would be so graced with his presence. They passed along all of the teacher's instructions to their mother, and they could hardly sleep from all of the anticipation.

The next day, the students found it difficult to concentrate on their classes before the guest of honor arrived. Everyone was nervous and excited— no one could remember anyone of distinction ever visiting the school before. When they were dismissed for lunch, the teacher reminded them to not get dirty.

In the afternoon, Ioanna and Stella glanced out of the schoolhouse window and saw a beautiful chestnut-colored horse and a rider with shiny, distinguished boots. The horse came a couple of steps into the courtyard and the rider secured it to a tree. Ioanna looked further and was shocked to see her grandfather! She was confused with so many tumbling thoughts, "What is he doing here? Of all times for him to come— he is going to interrupt the proceedings! Did something happen, does he need help? I hope my grandmother is okay. I have to pee."

Ioanna was expecting a royal procession and chariots, and much as she loved her grandfather, she was a little disappointed to see him at that moment. Stella was in awe of his splendid appearance. She was used to seeing him in full Greek costume, but he had outdone himself with his impeccable ornamental attire and commanding posture.

The mayor walked up the school steps and the teacher gave the students the signal to rise for the dignitary. Ioanna and Stella were flabbergasted. Could their grandpa be the eminent celebrity? He couldn't be! The teacher had led them to believe they were expecting someone next to God. Over the years Arianna had told the girls that he was a mayor, built churches and helped orphans, but they only really knew him as Grandpa. Ioanna stole a glance at the teacher and almost fell down in her chair when she realized he was indeed their esteemed guest.

130

When the mayor reached Ioanna and Stella's bench, he stopped and smiled at them. Ioanna was almost too flustered to react, but when her grandfather started to extend his hand, she automatically took his hand and kissed the top of it. Lovingly and sincerely, he placed his other hand on her head and said, "Receive my blessing." All the other students and even the teacher stared in disbelief, "Do they know this renowned leader?" All eyes were glued to the interaction between this personage and their two classmates as he repeated this greeting with Stella.

The mayor then continued to the front of the room and the class saluted him. He thanked them and told them to be seated. He addressed the class briefly, encouraging them to study and make the most of their education to better themselves and make their school and country proud. He was presented some refreshments and then classes were dismissed early so the mayor and teacher could discuss school business.

Ioanna and Stella walked out of the schoolhouse bewildered but a little proud. The other students pounced, "Who do you think you are!" "You don't know him!" Ioanna answered, "He is our grandfather, my mother's father." They kept badgering them, "No he's not!" "We don't believe you." "You're lying!" "You're not any more special than the rest of us." Ioanna grabbed Stella's hand and they hurriedly walked towards home. When they were out of earshot, Ioanna told Stella, "They're just jealous." Stella mused, "Did you see how perfectly he was dressed? And the pretty horse…"

Arianna and Nikolas smiled when they heard the tale from the perspective of an eight and a five-year old. They could picture the pomp and circumstance and the girls' incredulity. Arianna encouraged them, "Be kind to your classmates, even if they aren't kind to you. You know that your grandfather cares for all of the children in the school, and that's why he was there, to help everyone."

Although their schoolmates continued to pester Ioanna and Stella, when they did not provoke them back, eventually the children left them alone. After their grandfather's visit, the teacher realized they must be family and the discipline for imperfect recitations lessened.

Stella wondered if the teacher told their classmates to straighten up and not cause problems.

With two girls away at school, the rest of the family worked hard to keep the fields, vines and orchards going. But even the schoolgirls helped in the pruning or the harvests when they got home from school. Arianna would tell them, "You were sitting all day at school. Go do some work now." Throughout the day, Georgia helped some outdoors but was mostly busy with the housecleaning, cooking and watching the baby. Throughout the years of caring for all her sisters, she couldn't believe how many diapers she had to wash.

Even four-year old Barbara was given tasks, especially running various errands. She was full of energy and liked to be active and helpful. One day she darted to some bushes on the far side of the house in order to empty a compost bucket, and she felt something poke at her sandal. Before she even had time to panic, she was off and running back to the house to tell her mother.

Arianna walked with her carefully to find the spot and, sure enough, discovered a landmine. She barricaded it with some rocks until Nikolas could dig it up and put it with the others that had been safeguarded. Arianna, realizing yet another close call that could have taken the life of one of her children, thanked the Lord for protection and then told Barbara, "Please be careful. Let's empty the bucket over here closer to the house and stay away from this area, okay?"

Barbara was also the one in charge of running over to *Sterna* every now and then to make sure the water was flowing as it should from the cistern to the plants. If the motorized pump stopped, she would run and tell her daddy to re-start the machine. On one occasion, she approached the cistern and jumped back in fright. She ran with all her might back home and yelled, "*Baba, Baba, ella, ella* [come, come], there is a monster and it goes like this!" She made rapid paddling motions with both hands. "Come quick 'cause there is a monstrous beast and it may eat us up!"

Nikolas grabbed a hoe and ran towards the cistern. He found a porcupine stuck and swimming for its life in the cistern. He chuckled and carefully rescued it. Nikolas later reassured Barbara that it was harmless, but she wasn't so sure. It looked pretty ferocious to her. For years she was teased by Nikolas and anyone who had heard the story of the man-eating porcupine. With a twinkle in his eye, he would ask her, "Now how did the huge monster go?"

The fieldwork lessened as the season turned colder. It was a rainy and cold autumn. The house was not sealed or insulated well, so it could be drafty inside, especially when windy outside. Baby Lea very suddenly came down with a critical case of pneumonia. One rainy night, the symptoms were so severe that Arianna panicked. Nikolas was away with the horse and wagon, so she had no way to send for the doctor.

Arianna gathered the children and urged them to pray for their baby sister, "Baby Lea is very, very sick. Pray, come and pray. If you want this baby to live, call upon Jesus that He may come. Only Jesus can save her. Pray to Jesus to save her." The girls were frightened by their mother's tone and dropped to their knees to cry out to God. They had such a love for their sister. Their hearts were broken. So broken before God, they asked Jesus for help.

In her anguish, many thoughts ran through Arianna's mind. She loved all of her children, but perhaps with all that she went through during the pregnancy and delivery, she had a special love for this little miracle. And knowing that they hadn't really planned on having a large family, she realized her baby girl might never have been born had either of Lea's older brothers lived, and Lea became even more precious.

When she looked at the frail, four-month old baby, Arianna saw the glazed eyes of a dead person. She wailed and screamed, literally pulling the hair out of her head in desperation. She knew that she was going to lose this baby for sure, and she felt so helpless that there was nothing she could do. As she continued to cry out, she stumbled around to see what she could find for burial clothes. After settling upon something usable, she dropped to the floor in agony.

Georgia saw her mother all shaken up and all of her sisters crying. She knew they did not have any close neighbors, but she thought that she should run to get someone. Even if they couldn't do anything, someone should be there. So she grabbed her shawl and ran out the door. She ran in the direction of the school. There was an older lady who lived along the way at a little distance off the road who occasionally gave the girls bread with a little honey on it, which was a rare treat. Georgia was so relieved that the lady was home. In gasping breaths, she told the lady what was happening. She and another woman hurried over to their place that evening. They gave instructions to the girls to stay in another area of the house.

They decided to do a cupping treatment to try to improve the circulation and get the toxins out. They undressed the baby and laid her face down on the bed. Taking a piece of material, they soaked it in alcohol and made a wick. They took a tiny glass, lit the wick with a flame, held it in the upside-down glass, quickly withdrew the wick and pressed the glass upside down on Lea's back. The heat sucked up the air and made a vacuum, causing the glass to stick to the skin. They left that one there and repeated the process with another glass in another area of her back. When it had cooled a little, they removed the glass and made a small incision on the blistered skin and repeated the heated glass procedure on the same area to draw the blood out.

All of the sisters were supposed to stay away, but Stella peeked to see what they were doing. She thought to herself, "If the pneumonia doesn't kill her, maybe that will." They bandaged up the baby, and since it was very late, they told everyone to get some rest.

Arianna and the girls had a difficult time sleeping but continued to pray as they tossed and turned. In the morning, they awoke from their fitful sleep to see Nikolas dozing in a chair next to Lea's crib. He roused when he heard them running over to check on Lea. Her eyes were open and she was hungry. Joy and relief filled all of their hearts— they knew she was going to be all right. Arianna spent a minute crying on the floor thanking Jesus for his mercy before feeding the baby. Once the baby was content and stable, Arianna, physically and emotionally drained, passed out on her bed.

Chapter 14

The next year sped by with comparative tranquility. The family, with the help of some day laborers, worked hard in an effort to get the land and crops restored to pre-war productivity. Nikolas was able to purchase and apply another coat of paint to the swastika on the roof, and he was glad to see it mostly diminished. Barbara started school along with Ioanna and Stella in the fall. Shortly after that, they heard that the Greek civil war had ceased, with Communist influences held back. At some point several years after the world war, the Stavrolakis realized the crosses marking the German graves in their area weren't there anymore. There had been many not far from their house, so they were surprised at how they all could have been moved without their noticing.

The following spring, their horse had a beautiful foal. Nikolas kept it to raise and probably sell when fully grown. He tried to tell the girls not to get too attached to it, but it was hard for them not to be fond of the adorable thing.

About a month later, Nikolas noticed a frenzy of activity along the beach to the west. Curious, he crept furtively in that direction to see what they were up to. When he saw that they appeared to be his countrymen, organized and held to some task, Nikolas introduced himself to a man who seemed to be in charge. "The Greek military sent us here to remove the landmines," the man told him.

Nikolas could barely contain his excitement and asked how they were doing it. The foreman answered, "We have several teams. The first has a metal detector to find and mark them. Another group deactivates them, and the final team removes them. It's a painstaking process, but we are making our way slowly across the northern coast." Nikolas offered, "Anything we can do for you, just ask. We are so happy you are here. We also have a few mines that may still be active barricaded in our yard that I need to show you when you reach our place." The foreman told him that they would be in contact with him and to try to keep everyone out of the area for the time being. With a parting admonition that there were mines also in the grasses further inland as well as on the beach, Nikolas waved and left them.

The men were in their area for many days. Nikolas was impressed that they were able to successfully neutralize all of the different types of landmines— the tall skinny ones, the wider shorter ones and any other kinds they found. Arianna was so happy they were there that she kept offering them food and water. The girls, watching from the balcony, were intrigued with the machinery and how the different teams worked together.

When Nikolas showed the men the mines that they had sequestered, the foreman was shocked, "I thought you had just marked them in the ground. I don't think anyone else has dared to remove them— you were crazy and very lucky!" Before they left the area, the foreman gave Nikolas some of the yellow inner contents that they had removed from some of the mines and explained how to carefully use it for heating the fireplace. He also warned them that it was possible that they hadn't found all of the mines, especially those that the sand had buried deeper than the metal detector's range.

The girls were finally allowed to go swimming in the ocean, with the caution to still be careful in case some mines became uncovered. The older girls liked when there were some stronger waves. They challenged each other to try to stay standing when the waves would surge to knock them down. The younger girls liked it calmer and enjoyed playing in the sand. Nikolas, who had always loved the ocean, took breaks from his work whenever he could to go fishing or swim along with them. He played games of chase with the girls and threw them up into the air, sometimes catching them and sometimes dropping them in the water. The girls would get an extra thrill when Nikolas would go swimming with the horse. Many times they would show up out of nowhere to take a quick dip. Nikolas and the horse made a splendid scene of beauty, grace and power, together swimming as one.

136

Other special times for the girls that summer were visits from Uncle Elias and his flock of sheep. The girls were excited to tell him that most of the mines had been removed. "Wonderful! I can come a lot more often to rest the sheep and see all of you," Uncle Elias said. "I can safely take the sheep down to the rainwater cistern by the side of the house to give them some water." After he did that, he let the sheep rest under the shade tree as he gently bounced the younger girls on his knees and told the older girls stories from his travels.

The girls were amazed that he had been able to work various jobs in America. Georgia thought that it must have been a little difficult though, and maybe he was glad to be home. When she had been in school, one day she asked a classmate where America was, and he pointed straight down. Georgia knew that the earth was round, so she thought that it must be on the other side of the world. So while her uncle was telling them stories, she sat on the ground and thought, "If anybody wants to go to America, they better start making a big hole and go deep and deep and deep, and eventually they will get to America." The girls asked him to tell them some English words and visited with him until Arianna came out and told them to get to their chores.

Often the girls would either take the horse or walk the hour or hour and a half over the mountain to Lithos and then back after picking various summer fruits and vegetables from the *Lemoni* field. Once, Ioanna walked this path barefoot and a sharp rock gashed her toe. She cried out in pain and soon realized she needed to stop the bleeding. She spat on the ground to make a paste and pressed it on her throbbing toe. She continued on her journey, knowing there was work to be done. When Nikolas heard about the accident, he took a stick to measure her foot to take to her grandfather's cobbler shop to get her a pair of shoes. He made sure the other girls had shoes too.

Stella loved climbing trees, so she enjoyed fruit-picking season. They sometimes played games to see who could climb the highest and pick the most. At the house one day, Stella and Barbara started to load the horse with big baskets to try to go collect some pears. Stella put the saddle on the horse and Barbara started to mount when all of a sudden the horse jumped up, knocking Barbara down. Barbara was more surprised than hurt, so she ran into the house yelling, "*Mama*, the horse jumped and I fell off!" Arianna asked, "Are you hurt?" Barbara told her, "No, but it scared me. Why did she do that?" Arianna went outside and took off the saddle, "She's sunburned," she told the girls. "Let's give her the day off and you can get the pears in a day or two."

Another day Stella was sick with a sore throat and fever, so she stayed home while the rest of the family went to Lithos. Later in the day as she was resting in bed, from out of complete stillness came rapid gunfire and yelling. She jumped out of bed and ran to the balcony. She couldn't believe it when she saw men with guns crawling on their bellies along the beach. Suddenly she heard and then saw airplanes in the sky and paratroopers jumping out of the planes. She had heard all of the stories of the war and was terrified.

Stella ran out the front door and right into the arms of a dumbfounded soldier. She looked around and saw many stunned military men looking at her. An officer, seeing the seven-year old girl, yelled, "Cease fire!" as Stella pushed her way out of the soldier's arms and ran towards the mountain to try to find her family. She thought to herself, "What are we going to do? The war has come back!" Exhausted, anxious and still not feeling well, she decided not to try to make it all the way to Lithos but stopped at a distant relative's house along the way.

Stella arrived, agitated and breathless. She had lost her voice, so she could hardly talk. At their confused looks, Stella turned and frantically pointed to the parachutes in the sky. Her relatives explained, "Yeah, the Greek military is doing exercises today. Didn't you hear about it? They warned us several days ago." The experience was so real before her very eyes that it took a while for Stella to really comprehend that the world wasn't coming to an end. The family took her in and let her rest until her parents came by.

From a distant field, Ioanna looked up and saw the parachutes. "How pretty!" she admired. Later as the Stavrolakis walked home, Stella ran to meet them. Nikolas was surprised to see her and asked, "What's wrong?" Her aunt explained for her, "She had quite a fright. The military was doing some exercises in the area and I think she thought it was real. Didn't they tell your family about it?"

138

Realization dawned on Nikolas as he remembered seeing the parachutes earlier, "No, we hadn't heard. Stella, I'm sorry if they scared you." He hugged Stella as he thanked her hosts and took off with his family towards home.

Later Stella conveyed to her mother that there were people at the house with guns shooting. "You poor thing," Arianna sympathized, herself flashing back to her experience in the war, "I can't imagine seeing that by yourself as a young girl. I am so sorry!"

When they returned to Karidia, laden with fresh fruits and vegetables, Nikolas had an idea. He loaded the wagon and went in search of the temporary Greek military outpost. It wasn't long until he found them. He spoke to the officer in charge and asked permission to sell his produce to any of the men who wanted some fresh food. Having a strong sense of duty and service, Nikolas almost felt bad charging them anything, so he priced things cheaply, and the men seemed happy to pay to have something fresh to eat. He didn't have very much left in the wagon when he departed. He also found out that they would likely be in the area yearly for training exercises and to come back and sell to them in the future.

On his way back, Nikolas rode near the Minoan ruins and saw a new family at the caretaker's residence. He stopped to introduce himself and gave them some fresh pears, squash and tomatoes from his wagon. As he welcomed them, he said, "I think you will like this area. It is beautiful and quiet— only about a dozen homes all spread out, which is more than there were when we first moved here. There is a small café between here and Asprada, where I sometimes take a few goods like these to sell, but if you need supplies, Heraklion is the closest place." When he found out that they had a young daughter, Violetta, he invited her to play with his girls and pointed to their home down the road.

The girls were so excited to have a girl their age within a short walking distance. Violetta was closer to the younger girls' ages but was friends with all of the girls. They didn't have many toys. As a young child, Georgia had been given a doll made out of thin plastic by her godparents, but during the war it was accidentally left in one of the hidden caves and only a few remnants of it remained when they went back for it. When she grew older and more sisters came along, Georgia's childhood evaporated as she had the real "dolls" to take care of.

The other girls didn't need fancy playthings. One of Arianna's sisters had made them a couple of cloth dolls, so simple that it took imagination to see them as dolls. Happily, the girls had plenty of inventiveness. Barbara liked to pretend she was a schoolteacher with a leaf and stick representing paper and a pencil, and they sometimes played school together.

One day Stella, Barbara and Violetta were playing on the beach near the rock breakwater at a little distance west of the house. Stella was digging in the sand and found some broken pieces of pottery. "Hey, we can play tea party!" she said excitedly. Some pieces were so old that as soon as she lifted them into daylight, they crumbled in her hands. "Some of these look like what you would imagine to find at the ruins that my dad works at," remarked Violetta. They had fun playing with a few of the stronger pieces that had been buried deeper and kept them to play with later.

For other games, they played hide and seek, jump rope, hopscotch and something like a jacks game played with rocks. They especially liked to play hide and seek within the archeological ruins down the road. With the waist-high walls and various sections, almost like a maze, it was perfect to hide in and also run around, while being careful not to disturb anything. Down the road in the other direction toward the flattened villa was the tree rope. Arianna would sometimes let them bring a pillow to sit on while swinging. At the beach, besides swimming, they would build sandcastles or collect shells, interesting rocks or whatever else washed up on the shore.

Having a playmate near their age also made their name days more special. Instead of birthdays, many of which were not known for certain, the Greek people celebrated the saints' days corresponding to their names. Arianna would make some sweets and sometimes family members and friends would come over to the house. If gifts were given, they were simple, like flowers or a hand-written card, but it was more important to get together to have fun.

140

Adding to the outdoor fun was a newly adopted stray dog. At first Arianna was reluctant to take care of it, but Nikolas looked it over and thought she seemed healthy and friendly and could be good protection. "Please can we keep it?" the girls begged. Arianna consented on the condition that she would be an outdoor pet.

The Stavrolaki girls really didn't have too much time for playing because of the housework and babysitting at home as well as all the fieldwork at great distances away. Nikolas wanted to decrease their workload. He was in a little better position than he was right after the war. And now that he had five daughters and probably would never have a son, he had a strong desire to acquire more land for dowries or to support the girls if they didn't want to marry. His goal was to eventually obtain a thousand grapevines for each daughter.

In the meantime, he thought about trying to find a hired hand. He would still use day laborers for peak season activities, but a hired hand could be his right-hand man for a one or two-year contract. Legally, a hired hand could even represent him in business dealings. This man could hire the day laborers and manage the fields and the olive and other fruit trees. Nikolas could then help out but also restart his hauling and fishing businesses and any other entrepreneurial ideas that he might come up with.

Nikolas tried out several hired hands and didn't have much luck. One was dishonest and took off with the profits of a sale, and another was too lazy to be of much value. Arianna was about ready to give up and told Nikolas, "I know you want to spare us from working so hard, but at least when we are doing the work, things get done properly and you can trust us. We don't want to be worse off than when we started, now that we're finally back on our feet." Nikolas continued to ask around but with a much more cautious approach as to whom he would trust.

One hot summer day, ten-year old Ioanna loaded the horse with a couple of burlap bags of broad beans and rode from *Lemoni* back home to Karidia. It was proper for females to ride sidesaddle unless two rode at once— the one in front rode sidesaddle and the one behind sat astride in order to not fall off. Ioanna was by herself so she rode sidesaddle. She was startled when the horse suddenly reared. Ioanna struggled to hold on and tried to calm the horse.

Behind her, Ioanna saw a mule loaded with wheat charging in their direction, with a man chasing after it. Both animals ran uncontrollably, bounding over large rocks and uneven terrain. Ioanna hung on, terrified. She knew that her Uncle Kosta was killed by a runaway mule. The animals slowed down but then started confronting each other, jumping and fighting. Ioanna's legs got battered in the fray, and wheat went flying out of the mule's sacks.

Finally the mule ran off and Ioanna could control the horse. Her heart was still beating fast when she made it home and told her mother what happened. Arianna looked her over and bruises were already starting to appear, "I am so glad you were able to stay on the horse. It's a miracle you weren't hurt worse. Here, sit and rest for a while."

Shortly after that, Nikolas brought a teenage young man to meet Arianna. Right away she could tell that he was different than other hired hands. His appearance was well kept and he seemed educated. With polite sincerity, he said that he was eager to work. Arianna liked him but later asked Nikolas, "Where is he from and what do you know about him? He is just a kid and almost seems a little scared. Where is his family?" Nikolas replied, "He doesn't talk much about himself. But he is old enough to make his own way and he is a hard worker. We can ask around if it makes you feel better." After a brief trial period and a sincere inquiry if he really wanted to do this job, Nikolas employed the lad for a two-year contract.

Below the balcony of the house between the wood-burning stove and the barn area was an open space. Nikolas and the lad constructed a makeshift room in that area. They tied many thick bamboo stakes together for two side walls and hung a sturdy cloth for a door. They covered the hut with a particular weed that rain wouldn't go through. The hired hand was very happy with that living arrangement, and Arianna fed him well. They had barely settled into the new routine of things when one day they heard a pounding at the door. Arianna's nephew was at the door and urged her, "You'd better come quick."

142

Chapter 15

Arianna gasped, "What is it?" Her nephew replied, "It's *Pappou*, your father. He is not well and they sent me to get you." Arianna gave some quick instructions to the girls and left with her nephew for Prasinos Kampos. When they arrived at her parents' house, many of the family members had already gathered and everyone looked sad. Arianna hugged her mother but saw that she was emotional and unable to talk. She found her oldest brother Petros, who told her that the doctor said that their father was dying and there was nothing that could be done. They were trying to keep him as comfortable as they could. Arianna asked to see him. "He is making his will right now, but you can probably sneak into his room," Petros told her.

Arianna's father was in bed. She had never seen him look so weak. She sat with him for a while and then left the room to let him finish getting his affairs in order. She decided to bring the rest of her family to see him. Later as the girls visited with him, Arianna reflected that even on his deathbed he still had a commanding presence and displayed a love for his gathered family.

It was not long before Arianna's father passed away. The family knew that he was well respected, but they had no idea of the reaction that his death would generate. People came from far and wide to honor him. The family quickly realized that they must plan a tremendous funeral. The family itself was large, with his ten remaining children and all of their children and in-laws, but the devoted people of Prasinos Kampos and the surrounding villages added greatly to their number.

To lessen the burden on the grieving family and make sure the guests were well taken care of, they decided to hire professional cooks. They planned a huge meal. They killed several sheep and managed to purchase beef, although cows were very rare on the island. The baking of bread and desserts began with a fury, and fruits and vegetables were quickly gathered.

Since the economy had improved somewhat since the war, they were able to get a wooden casket. They followed the usual practice of standing the lid of the casket outside the door of the home, so people knew which house to call on. That evening they had a service at the church on the outskirts of town, near the cemetery.

The next day, they had an enormous funeral procession to the burial site, with everyone wearing black and the women crying out in sorrow. The Kazandakis had their own area of the cemetery. As was the custom in many parts of Europe at the time, room was continually made in the burial plots by later digging up the bones, washing them with wine, placing them in a wooden box and stacking them in a "sleep forever" room in order for the graves to be re-used.

The tributes to this honorable man surprised even his immediate family. The tales the guests told, along with documents his daughters later found as they helped sort through his things, continued to tell of the great deeds he had done for people. The stories reached back to the early part of the century during the Turkish conflict when many were killed. The mayor had provided aid to many widows, orphans and the poor even back then. The acknowledgments of his putting others first continued through the World Wars and until his death.

The family lamented that they were going to miss their beloved patriarch and his caring and steady leadership. He always tried to walk uprightly in public and in private, even through harrowing political and personal circumstances. He was devoted to God and regularly prayed for His blessings on his children and grandchildren and those to come after. He was so beloved and relied upon that they didn't know what they were going to do without him.

Nikolas paid his respects to his father-in-law, whom he admired greatly, and helped the family wherever he could. He also used the opportunity to visit among the many outsiders who had come to the area. He enjoyed meeting new people, but he also hadn't forgotten his promise to Arianna to try to find the parents of his hired hand. In a friendly, dignified way, he subtly tried to piece together any

144

information he could about his young helper. After mingling with many of the guests, he was fairly sure when he found the youth's parents. He invited them out to their home so that he could delicately probe further at a more appropriate time.

After the funeral, there were periodic memorial services. The custom was to prepare a special dish called *koliva*. Wheat was boiled and drained as a reminder of resurrection, since wheat is planted in the ground and rises as a new crop. Cinnamon, sugar, nuts and other ingredients were added, and the wheat mixture was pressed into a large mound, symbolizing the grave. The initials of the deceased were spelled out on the mound using almonds or raisins, and a cross also adorned the center. Guests were served *koliva* in remembrance of the departed.

The week after the funeral, Arianna helped her mother and family with things they needed to take care of. In the past, the mayor had relinquished his official duties, so at least they did not have to worry about gaps in transitioning any immediate needs of the village. He had been so popular and philanthropic that it took his wife to finally insist to the townspeople that she needed her husband back— they had had him long enough. But it took time and was difficult to sort through all of the papers and belongings of a man they revered so much personally and professionally.

Nikolas encouraged Arianna to take time to grieve as well as assist her family. Arianna dyed many of her clothes black in order to have enough to wear during the customary three-year mourning period. Nikolas tried to be sensitive to the girls' feelings, allowing them freedom to talk or be sad, in whatever way they needed. He was glad that the fall school term hadn't started yet so the girls wouldn't be bothered by any insensitive prying of classmates.

A few weeks later, the family that Nikolas had met at the funeral came by their house in Karidia. Arianna welcomed them and offered them some refreshments. Nikolas and Arianna visited casually with them for a while before Nikolas steered the conversation towards their son. The story eventually came out that their son ran away from home after he accidentally broke a small family heirloom. The parents seemed more upset that they didn't know where he was than they were about the heirloom. Nikolas expressed sympathy and then excused himself from the room.

Minutes later, he returned with his hired hand, who was immediately greeted with exclamations of surprise, relief and love. Arianna and Nikolas looked at each other and smiled. They gave the family time to reconcile any misunderstanding and extend apologies and forgiveness over the accident and running away. Nikolas then offered to the parents, "Your son has been a dedicated, hard worker. He agreed to a two-year commitment, but under the circumstances, I can release him." His father said, "I appreciate that. And we are indebted to you for reuniting us with our son. But we have taught him to honor his obligations." Before they left, Nikolas showed the parents around. He assured them that they would take good care of him and invited them to visit anytime.

Nikolas was happy for his part in reconciling a family through a simple misunderstanding, not knowing that he would soon be a part of one in his own family. One day Nikolas ran into the father of Arianna's second cousin Stefanos Psomiaki. The father greeted Nikolas and asked if he had a moment to discuss something. "You know my son, Stefanos..." Nikolas nodded and asked, "Yes, how is he?" The man answered, "He is well, but his wife had to have one of her kidneys removed, and they want a girl to come live with them in Athens. They were thinking that this girl could reduce the workload of my daughter-in-law by helping my young granddaughter... escorting her places, maybe doing some light lifting..."

Nikolas nodded but wondered what the man was leading up to, when unexpectedly he heard the man mention four-hundred drachmas (at the time less than twenty dollars) a year. The man was continuing, "...all of her room and board would be taken care of. Would any of your girls be interested?"

Nikolas thought quickly. Athens was a long distance away, but they could really use the money. The duties would require less physical labor than working in the fields, and his daughter would be with family. Georgia as the oldest was needed at home, so Ioanna might be the most appropriate choice. Ioanna already completed about half of the local grades of school, which was more years than Georgia, so they could discontinue her coursework. Plus it would be a great cultural opportunity. Nikolas finally consented, "I think Ioanna might be well suited for this. Thank you for thinking of us!"

When Nikolas told Ioanna about the arrangement, he used the name of the family, not realizing that Ioanna had never met them as Georgia had in delivering food to the fields or collecting snails. Ioanna did not know that they were family but thought that she was being consigned as a servant girl to a stranger in a faraway land. In her ten years, Ioanna had never left the island or her family before, other than staying with her grandparents. But she understood that her family would get four-hundred drachmas a year— which seemed like a fantastic amount of money— and she would do what she needed to do to help.

One afternoon, Ioanna was home with Lea when all the others were out working. The weather suddenly changed and Ioanna ran out onto the balcony. She couldn't believe her eyes when she saw a huge waterspout develop in the ocean. She stood frozen in fear for a few minutes as it swirled violently, coming towards her. For a moment she wondered if what she saw was real or merely a reflection of the upheaval in her heart. With her grandfather's passing and her life about to dramatically change, Ioanna felt disconcerted. Maybe she would never see her family again. She snapped out of her reverie when she felt a blast of wind and heard the doors slam and windows rattle. The spout had lost its formation but the wind swept onto the land and into the trees. After it very quickly calmed, she consoled herself that turmoil in life could be fleeting.

The day came when it was time for Ioanna to leave. She struggled not to cry as she grabbed her few belongings. Tears slipped out of all the girls' eyes as Ioanna said goodbye to her mother and sisters. Arianna started to have some misgivings but tried to reassure herself and all of them by encouraging Ioanna to have fun on her adventures. "You are going to be a city girl now. You are going to have so much fun! Did you know I lived in the city of Heraklion for a while and loved it, but you are lucky to be in the even grander city of Athens!" Arianna knew that Ioanna was plucky and resourceful and that she would be fine once she got settled.

As Arianna rode off with Nikolas and Ioanna towards Heraklion, she continued to reflect how blessed she was with each of her special daughters. They all loved God, cared for others and worked so hard to help the family. Georgia was very friendly, generous, capable and dependable. In addition to being confident and resourceful, Ioanna was innovative in caring ways. Stella was easygoing, self-sufficient and loved to learn things, both by reading and by curiosity. Barbara liked hostessing, doing creative needlework and with her fun personality was always making people laugh. And Lea... Arianna could already tell that her youngest liked to talk and laugh, share with others and be a part of family. Arianna loved them all and said a quick prayer for God to be with Ioanna.

Ioanna gazed out at the crashing ocean on the long ride to Heraklion. She thought of the Bible story of Joseph being sold into slavery away from his family. But good came out of it, since he was able to help them out of famine later, and she hoped for the same in her situation.

When they reached the port, Nikolas and Arianna led Ioanna to the ship and waved to Arianna's friend, who they had discovered could travel with Ioanna. Ioanna didn't know this friend but knew that she was in safe hands with her. Nikolas thanked the lady and told Ioanna to send word if she needed anything. Arianna hugged her, "We will miss you." Ioanna swallowed hard as she said goodbye to her parents.

It was about a twelve-hour passage from Heraklion to Athens, so Ioanna and her escort got settled in the large ship. Ioanna was so thankful to have someone to travel with. When they finally reached the port near Athens, Ioanna looked out over the railing apprehensively. How would she know whom she was supposed to meet? But her mother's friend assured her, "Don't worry. I will make sure you find Mr. Psomiaki." Ioanna thanked her and scanned the waiting crowd. She saw a good-looking gentleman who looked very nervous and was looking quickly here and there. This gentleman approached them as they disembarked. He hugged Ioanna as family and welcomed her. He thanked her escort and told Ioanna, "Come, your aunt is waiting." Ioanna was confused, thinking, "I am here to be a maid. Who is my aunt?"

148

Stefanos' wife embraced Ioanna as if she was one of her own children and ushered her into their lavish home. She gave her a snack and asked all about her mother and sisters and Karidia. She told Ioanna, "With my family's help, I have planned a party to welcome you. What other clothes did you bring?" Suddenly, Ioanna felt very shabby and embarrassed that she really didn't bring much else. Her hostess put her at ease and said, "Never mind, let me see if I have something that will fit you." But her dresses were too big, so she took Ioanna over to a neighbor who was a seamstress to whip her up a dress in a hurry. Then she was taken to a hairdresser to get her hair cut.

This attention became very dramatic for Ioanna. Being suddenly all dolled up was not what she was used to. She thought that she was there to be a servant, and she didn't know these people, lovely as they seemed. She had a glancing thought, "There goes my hair, am I headed to the auction block?" Although she was skeptical at first, everything about the party amazed her, and she enjoyed herself. But as she prepared for bed, she couldn't help but gaze out the window at the moon and stars and wonder if her family was also looking at the same sky.

Any trepidations Ioanna had soon vanished. The family regarded her with respect and kindness, providing her with the best of everything as she helped take care of their daughter. They treated her as family and never as a maid, and she became very fond of them. Ioanna quickly acclimated to city life and as time went on, she grew to revel in it. She had left the heavy work for a really good, rich life.

Ioanna had to figure out a way to get her family here! They should all move to the city— everyone is better off. Her thoughts began to churn as she took note of everything. When she saw a vendor with a produce cart, she thought her father could do that. They could open a small café and grow the vegetables for it. Her sisters could go to a much better school. She enjoyed musical performances and all of the finer things that she had never experienced before and thought that her family would enjoy them also.

***

Meanwhile her family tried to adjust to Ioanna's absence. Stella and Barbara started another school year without her. By this time, a small room adjoining the schoolhouse had been built for the teacher. She didn't always have everything that she would have liked though. The girls giggled when they heard a story about how one day when the teacher was craving a boiled egg but had no water, she boiled the egg in wine. With Ioanna in Athens and Stella and Barbara in regular school, it always seemed like there were more chores to be done, although the hired hand helped enormously. Mostly they just missed Ioanna. Christmas wasn't the same without her. But they were happy when they got a letter from her saying that she was having a wonderful time but missed them.

In the spring, Nikolas looked for simple ways to supplement their income as they continued to rebuild after the war. One day he surprised Arianna by showing up with thirty turkey eggs. Arianna challenged him, "What do we know about raising turkeys?" Nikolas replied, "Well, not much, but it seems like a pretty straightforward experiment. We have to keep the eggs and small turkeys warm. And I got instructions on different things to feed them as they grow. Once they are grown, I can sell them for a good price."

Nikolas created a warm spot underneath the balcony for the turkey eggs. The girls checked on them every day, even though Nikolas told them that it should take about a month for them to hatch. When the day came, not all of the eggs hatched and a few of the young turkeys died, but most of them were healthy poults. The girls thought they were the cutest things. There was a certain spinach-like weed that they boiled and fed them, along with bran and boiled eggs chopped up for protein. Over the weeks as they grew, they also gave them some wheat and barley.

Later in the summer when the girls were out of school and the turkeys were old enough to forage for their own worms, snails, grasshoppers, and so forth, Stella and Barbara took them for walks twice a day. Usually they walked around to the front of the house and down the road to the west where there was a large ravine. Barbara was used to walking barefoot, despite the stickers in the grass. The turkeys came to know their way to their spot, but Stella and Barbara carried bamboo sticks to prod them along if needed.

150

One morning as they walked towards the ravine with the turkeys, Stella and Barbara came around a corner and instantly stopped in amazement. The hill facing out towards the ocean was covered with small olive-green tents. The family wasn't used to seeing many people in the area, yet suddenly the girls came upon what seemed like hundreds of men and tents.

Some of the men were walking around and looked very surprised to see two young girls and over twenty turkeys. The men looked like they were in the military but didn't look Greek. While the men and the girls looked at one another, trying to figure each other out, the turkeys made their way to their usual eating place, not caring that there were tents or other people around. The turkeys made themselves at home as they infiltrated their camp. The audacity of the turkeys broke the ice. The men smiled, said a few words and helped the girls round up their feathered friends from in between the tents. One of the men said, "American." The girls smiled and nodded, remembering the kind Americans that their Uncle Elias always spoke about.

These American men on their island were so friendly and intriguing that Stella was looking forward to seeing what they were up to the next day. But when they got to the same area the following day, the men had vanished. Stella was a little disappointed. The girls let the turkeys forage while they walked around the area. They knew every hill and rock, so when Stella saw a little mound of dirt in one area, she said to Barbara, "Hmm, there's something different here." They poked around, and buried shallow in the mound were many kinds of canned foods, chewing gum and chocolate candies. Barbara asked, "Do you think the Americans left these for us?" Stella looked around and answered, "I think they have gone, so they must be for us. How nice of them!" The girls happily brought the plunder back home. They had never tasted sweetened beans, canned meat or chocolate before. The girls especially raved about the chocolate. Arianna said aloud, "Bless the Americans for sharing with us!" God not only kept providing for them, but He occasionally blessed them with a special surprise, and they were grateful.

Chapter 16

At the end of July, the mother-in-law of one of Arianna's sisters came from Heraklion to stay with the Stavrolakis for a couple of weeks. She had arthritis and thought that burying herself in the hot sand for some time each day might help her symptoms. One afternoon, she and Arianna had some coffee with a couple of neighbors who had stopped by. Georgia sat with them, knitting and keeping her eyes out for the bus in case it stopped at their house. Often the visiting lady's family would send a basket of meats, breads, cheeses or sweets from Heraklion, and the bus driver knew where to stop to deliver it. After a bit, Arianna excused herself to go down to the lower barn area to feed the chickens. Georgia continued to knit the wool sweater she was making for her father while the adults visited.

In a little while, they heard the bus pull up and stop across from the house. Wanting to be polite as the youngest person present and to save the older woman pain from getting up and walking across the road, Georgia started to rise to get the basket for her. As she started to get up, the yarn, which had been in a tightly-wound ball in her lap, fell to the ground and wrapped around and around her ankles and even under her feet. Georgia could not move, all tangled up tightly with no way to escape. She bent down, trying her hardest to untangle herself since she knew that the bus driver couldn't wait forever.

In the meantime, the mother-in-law saw that Georgia couldn't move, so she went to pick up her basket. As she hurriedly crossed the road, a truck was coming from the opposite direction. The driver couldn't stop in time and hit the lady. Even though she was only about seven meters away, Georgia was hunched over and concentrating on her yarn, so she did not actually see the accident. But a neighbor who had been there drinking coffee yelled, "She got hit! She got hit!" Arianna came running and the people got out of the bus in alarm.

The driver and passenger of the truck stopped and were deeply shaken, "Are you okay?" But the lady lay motionless in the road. The truck driver started crying.

When Georgia looked up to see what was happening, suddenly her feet became completely free. She stood up to see some men bringing the lady inside the house. Georgia thought that surely she had died. She was limp and her head was tilted to the side towards her shoulder. When they laid her on the floor of the house and a piece of bone fell from her skull, they knew they needed to take her to the hospital in Heraklion. The men lifted her into the truck and they drove away quickly. All who had been in the area were very upset. Arianna sent Stella to find Nikolas so that he could send word to Arianna's sister. It wasn't long afterwards that they found out that the lady had died on the way to the hospital.

The Stavrolakis were completely devastated. They had known her well. The family unit was treasured in their hearts and culture, often with many generations living together to help one another, in-laws included. Late in the evening, Arianna noticed that Georgia hadn't said much and asked if she was okay. Georgia told her, "It could have been me, *Mama*." She told her what had happened with the yarn. "I am not lying. As God is my witness, I couldn't have gotten that tangled up and then suddenly untangled all by myself." Arianna was so astonished she couldn't reply. All she could do was hug Georgia tightly.

A few weeks later, Georgia was required to testify in court, along with the other witnesses. She had never seen a courtroom, much less had any responsibility in one. It was difficult to relive the experience by hearing it described in detail. The driver was crying as he testified. Georgia was called forward, but all she could testify was that she didn't see anything. After all of the testimony was heard, the death was ruled an accident.

Arianna spoke to the girls about the importance of being careful near the front of the house since it was very close to the road. Most people in the villages still used horses and wagons, but motorized vehicles also sometimes used the same road. They needed to be cautious about anything coming their way from either direction.

Multiple vehicles of the Greek military came back again for exercises. And now that things were stabilizing after the war, more tourists were coming to the area, bringing more traffic.

One group of tourists who came along were some French actors who were filming a movie in another part of the island. Arianna and the family didn't know much about movies, but they always welcomed anyone passing through. There were no inns, restaurants or shops in the immediate area. For those visiting the nearby Minoan ruins, the seaside Stavrolaki house was an attractive location for anyone wanting to swim and lounge on the beach. If vacationers needed a place to change into their bathing suits or wanted a bite to eat or something to drink, the family shared whatever they had. The Stavrolakis treated everyone the same and often didn't know if someone was famous or not.

One other time, a chauffeur brought a couple to spend a few days in their area. Arianna caught bits and pieces of conversation implying that one set of visitors was an American actress with some kind of eastern prince. They welcomed them as they would anyone else but were curious and especially fascinated with the different lives of foreign visitors. They tried to visit as much as any language disparities would allow and yet give anyone privacy if they preferred.

Many tourists exclaimed over some of Arianna's handiwork, especially a basket that she had hanging on a wall. She had dyed the straw different colors and woven the strands in a unique pattern. She had many offers to purchase it, but because of all the hard work that she had put into it (and no time to try to re-create it), Arianna was proud of it and politely declined. In addition to those wanting to vacation in their area of Crete, some hung around not by choice when the temperamental rudimentary bus broke down near their house. Whatever the circumstances, they tried to welcome everyone without asking for anything in return and yet still complete their daily work.

In August, the whole family, with the hired hand and a few day laborers, headed out to the grapevines to pick seedless green grapes for making raisins. Nikolas knew exactly how to make the solution

154

with water, potassium and a little olive oil. He had a large aluminum container with the solution and another smaller container with holes in it, facilitating the easy dipping and draining of a large batch of grapes. He had a meter to measure acidity and would adjust the mixture as needed.

One team picked the grapes, while a few people broke apart the large clusters to allow better solution saturation. Nikolas dipped the grapes twice, and Georgia oversaw a team placing them out in the sun to dry. Rolls of white paper one-meter wide were rolled out in a smooth area in the direct sunlight, and the grapes were laid flat on top of the paper. Many rows of paper were laid side by side, leaving enough room to walk between them, and the grapes were left there for several days to a week to dry.

Arianna and the girls checked the grapes carefully to make sure they were drying well enough so they wouldn't rot. They would rotate them on the paper if needed to dry more evenly. If they got too dry, the girls would spray the grapes with the solution. They always hoped there wouldn't be a heavy dew or rain, otherwise they may need to re-spray them thoroughly or even start over. Georgia became skilled at monitoring and adjusting things so perfectly that others wanted to hire her to supervise the making of their raisins. When they had dried, it was easy to quickly brush the raisins off the stems. With excellent quality grapes, Nikolas' perfect mixing of the solution and Georgia's and the other girls' careful fine-tuning, the Stavrolakis always had the best raisins.

The grapes for making wine were different than the ones used to make raisins and were picked after the raisins were made to allow them to sweeten longer on the vine. In addition to helping pick the grapes, Arianna prepared a large lunch for all of the workers. Since they worked from sunup to sundown during the harvest season, there was an afternoon rest, and then about four in the afternoon, she would fix another snack such as bean soup, bread, vegetables, olives, or sardines. Nikolas would always pay the day laborers, usually in produce, every day and not just at the end of the harvesting. He said, "A laborer is worth his pay, and he needs it to take care of his family."

On Saturday evenings, the church bells would ring and they would have to stop working until Monday in observance of the Sabbath. Wanting to get as much work done as possible, Arianna always hustled everyone along on Saturdays, "Hurry up! Hurry before the bells ring!" If they happened to be in Prasinos Kampos or Lithos, they might attend church on Saturday evening, but regardless, they always tried to attend a Sunday morning service.

Everyone had to be clean for church. They used bar soap for everything— cleaning themselves, their hair, their clothes and the dishes. The older girls wore their long hair in a single braid. When it came to washing clothes, Arianna insisted that everything be *white*, white. "As we hang things out to dry, you never know who from up on the hill can see them and they need to be pure white!"

After doing an initial washing, they saturated the clothes in an ash solution in a tall, light-colored basket. First, they layered the clothes, with the darkest at the bottom. After completely covering the stack of clothes with a thick cloth, on top of this they layered leaves from the lemon tree and then white ashes from a clean wood, like from the grapevines. They poured hot water over the layers and left the clothes to sit overnight. After this process, it was easier to wash the clothes with the bar soap the next day.

Even after pre-washing and then washing the clothes, Arianna would often have the girls *re-wash* the clothes because they were not white enough. The girls sometimes jokingly sang a traditional song to themselves during the ritual: "Monday I begin the laundry, Tuesday I wring it out, Wednesday I hang it up, Thursday I take it down, Friday I mend it, Saturday I iron it, Sunday I change my clothes, and Monday I start all over again!" Nikolas was usually able to purchase soap, but Arianna was also able to make it out of the thick sediment that formed after olive oil had settled for many months.

Later, once the grapes were picked, the family made their own wine. They prepared it mostly for their own or extended family's use, although they could use wineskins to transport some to sell or others could bring their own containers to purchase some. There were a few times when older wineskins burst or got a hole, and if a lot of the wine was wasted, they were sad to lose the product of their hard labor.

The Stavrolakis had their own large, round wooden basin that they used as a winepress for stomping the grapes, although theirs wasn't as big as the ones used to produce wine commercially. Before they stomped the grapes, they let them sit for several days to make them easier to crush. Since bees were attracted to the sweet fruit, the girls usually waited until dark when the bees were less active, but they were often still stung, especially on their feet. Other than that, the girls had fun stomping the slippery grapes with their clean, bare feet.

The grape juice flowed out of a spout, through a filter to catch any stems, seeds or skins, and then through a pipe into a wooden barrel. When they thought they had gotten most of the juice from the crushed grapes, they put a clean wooden board on top of the residue and stomped on that some more to get every last drop.

The wooden barrel had a hole at the top that could be closed with a wooden stopper at the proper time. In the meantime, Nikolas would measure the sugar and the acidity of the grape juice. If it was too acidic, he would add sugar, but if it was too sweet— as it was most of the time from their sweet grapes— he would add water. Once the consistency was just right, he left the stopper off and didn't overfill the barrel in order to allow some air to escape during fermentation.

The girls were fascinated that all by itself in a day or two, the liquid would start to bubble and sound like it was boiling. At the right time, Nikolas would plug the barrel with the wooden stopper but could check the consistency or taste either through the stopper opening at the top or from the wooden spigot near the bottom of the barrel. He checked it often for the next three months and then left it for some time. It would be ready to pour from the spigot into a smaller bottle or wineskin in six months to a year. At times, the girls brushed their teeth with wine as an antiseptic. When they got a little older, at the dinner table, Arianna would give them a little wine that had been watered down. She would say, "For your blood..."

For their meals they prepared mostly vegetables, including salad, and they always had bread. Each time Arianna made bread, she used oil and salt to preserve a portion of bread dough to save and multiply the yeast. Before baking it, she would make the sign of the cross over the dough to bless it. Often, to make the baked bread last longer, Arianna would slice it thinly and bake it using low heat in the oven overnight. Since this toast was completely dried out, when stored in an airtight container, it could last for over a week. Arianna sometimes liked to cook vegetables together, like green beans mixed with potatoes and tomatoes. They could dip their *paximathi* [dried toast] in the sauce or in olive oil to soften it. Arianna also knew how to make her own butter and cheese out of goat's milk.

Nikolas was a pretty good cook, too, having learned from his grandmother. They sometimes had scrambled eggs mixed with sliced potatoes or other vegetables. If they had meat, it was only about twice a week (usually Thursdays and Sundays), on days they weren't fasting. In addition to fasting before certain holy days, they usually fasted on Wednesdays and Fridays. Their main meat was usually fish that Nikolas caught straight from the sea behind their house. The fish was so fresh that occasionally it would almost jump out of the pan when they were trying to fry it. Ioanna enjoyed the tender meat in the fish heads.

Nikolas loved *stifatho*, a meat stew with tomatoes, garlic and onions. It was also a rule that they couldn't put any meat on the table until their father got home. Barbara loved to eat and could usually get away with stealing a bite… maybe two, before they sat down to dinner but was scolded with the third bite.

One day, Nikolas brought home some rabbits that he decided to raise for food or for sale. He built a cage for them in the barn and told the girls how to keep the cage clean. If they butchered rabbit, goat or lamb, they would need to skin it before cooking it over the fire. Nikolas or Arianna would insert a knife, usually in the leg, and then insert a straw and blow to lift up the skin, making it easier to remove.

After witnessing some of her pets killed and skinned as well as seeing the unappetizing skinned animals hanging in the markets, Stella decided that she couldn't eat meat anymore. Barbara, on the other hand, was happy to eat anything, including food from someone

158

else's plate. A favorite trick of hers was to make other people laugh, and while they were distracted, she would sneak some food off their plate, or sometimes even out of their hand.

November was olive picking season again. Barbara tried to eat one straight from the tree but spat it out, making a face. Arianna chuckled, "You can't eat them off the tree. For our table olives, we have to soak them a long time in salt water and sometimes a little oil or vinegar to take the bitterness away."

When they were leaving, Georgia pointed, "*Mama*, there are a lot more olives over there that we can collect." Arianna taught her, "No those aren't ours. They are for the poor. Just like we left the grapes that weren't quite ripe, we will leave them for those less fortunate than us. It is a way we can give thanks to God by helping others. He said whatever we have done for the least of these, we have done for Him." In addition, to give an offering to the church, they brought a portion of their olive oil for the priest to use in holy ceremonies.

Christmas reminded them all of Ioanna and how much they missed her. She sent a letter saying that she was doing well and wished they all were with her in Athens. Nikolas wondered when he might see the four-hundred drachmas for the previous year, but he never liked to pressure anyone for money.

In January, the almond trees in *Lemoni* blossomed. Each tree was completely covered with beautiful white flowers with a little pink and yellow in the center. The girls admired how pretty they were and loved the honey-butter fragrance. They knew from then on to watch the almond start to form in anticipation of a special treat. When the almond was still soft, the girls picked a few early but in their minds, just in time. They ate the whole thing, which was at this point a soft and chewy sour morsel which they enjoyed like candy every year at that time. The customary hard almond wouldn't be ready to pick for several months.

Out of the blue one early morning while it was still dark, most of the family was awakened to the sound of heavy stomping in front of their house. Nikolas and Stella ran to the window and saw a massive number of Greek troops marching in formation. By then, they were used to having military exercises in their area about once a year, but their presence that early in the morning with so many men in loud boots shook them up. They had no idea about a Korean War or a Cold War, with other powers flexing their military muscles in the Mediterranean but were somewhat comforted by seeing only their own forces in strength. They were on edge for a while, not knowing if the soldiers would suddenly show up again, but they did not see any more activity for some time.

In the summer when the two-year term of the hired hand was up, he thanked Nikolas, "I am going to miss you, boss. You taught me a lot and treated me better than I could have ever expected." Nikolas was sorry to see him go, "I can guarantee that I am going to miss you more than you will miss me. You were a very hard worker. I wish you the very best and say hello to your family for us."

After he left, Nikolas considered whether he wanted to try to find a replacement for him. Although he liked having steady, reliable help in his work endeavors, he knew that it would be a challenge to find someone hard working and trustworthy. He was also very protective of his daughters who were growing up. So he decided to just use day laborers as needed.

Nikolas thought about his daughters and smiled. Many times he was teased, "How can you handle five girls?" Nikolas would always answer, "It's very easy. Each one is different and I love each one differently." He sometimes also added, "I'd rather have five daughters than one lazy son."

After seeing his worker go, Nikolas decided to take a swim to clear his head and to cool off from the summer heat. He was an excellent swimmer and loved to dive underwater without coming up for air for a long distance. But he knew the girls got scared when he did that. Stella would always tell him later, "Don't *do* that!" So he decided not to pull any stunts since he knew Georgia and Arianna were out on the balcony. He also consciously stayed away from the region towards the east that he had warned the others to avoid. He knew every area of the ocean near their house— every dip and current. Over to the east, a little before a rock wall formation jutted out from

160

the shore, was a turbulent current that others had found very dangerous. He decided to relax and just float in the water.

He was still very clear of the dangerous section, but the ocean became unpredictable. Suddenly he felt a strong undercurrent. He tried to swim out of it, but a spiraling tide held him stuck, slowly drawing him eastward. He waved at Arianna and Georgia frantically. They saw him, but they thought that he was just waving to them, so they waved back. Nikolas saw that they didn't realize he was in trouble and his heart started pounding fast. He had never felt so helpless in the water.

There was nothing Nikolas could do but save his strength until he could try to pull out at the right moment. He tried not to think of the others who had drowned in the area. He started praying, "Lord, loosen this current or send another one to get me out of this one. Give me strength to hold on." Instantly he felt the current loosen and he swam over to the rocks to hold on a few minutes to catch his breath. Once he rested a bit, he swam to the shore.

When he walked into the house, Arianna could see that he was shaken. "What's wrong?" she asked. Nikolas was still breathing a little hard, "I got stuck in an undercurrent and couldn't get out of it. I was waving to you for help." Arianna suddenly felt the fear almost as if it were happening right then, "Oh no, I am so sorry! If something had happened to you, I could never have forgiven myself! How did you get out of it?" Nikolas reassured her, "God took care of me as always."

Another time, the whole family went swimming since the sea was so beautiful. Georgia thought she saw something unusual not very far away and yelled, "There's something here!" Nikolas was a little further away but didn't see anything. One of the other girls saw it coming closer and screamed. Arianna said, "Let's get out of here." Later they found out that two sharks had been spotted in their area. Arianna thought about the recent near misses and thanked God for rescuing them from harm, known and unknown.

Chapter 17

One Wednesday in the summer, a well-to-do attorney was driving by their house and stopped around lunch time. Arianna was home with Lea, so she went out to greet him. He got out of the car and stretched, as if he had just driven a long way. "Such a beautiful place you have here," he told Arianna. "Thank you. Is there anything I can help you with?" she asked politely. "Is there a restaurant around here? I would pay very well for a substantial meal," he queried.

"No, there isn't anything except for a small café several kilometers up the road. We used to run a restaurant years ago, but we don't really have one now. But I can cook some chicken for you if you have some time," Arianna offered. "That would be delightful. Take your time. I will enjoy your beautiful view, if that is okay," he said with satisfaction. "Please make yourself at home. There are some chairs out on the balcony and in the living room," she invited.

After setting some water on the fire to boil, Arianna brought the man a glass of water and some bread. When she saw that he was happily settled, she ran down to the lower level. Since they fasted from meats and sweets on Wednesdays and Fridays, she didn't already have a fire burning or desserts made. She lit the wood-burning oven and then walked over to the barn area and grabbed a chicken. Stepping on its feet and stretching its head, she struggled to hold it still as she slit its throat with a knife. She cut off the feet, and then took it upstairs and inside to prepare it. In order to make pulling out the feathers easier, Arianna dipped the chicken in the hot water. She worked quickly, plucking the feathers as many as she could at a time. She cleaned it, cut it into pieces and put it in a roasting pan with lemon and oregano. She cut some potatoes and zucchini and added them to the roasting pan. Finally, she took the pan down to the oven and placed it inside to roast.

Arianna breathed a quick sigh of relief and thought to herself as she walked upstairs again. It would be a while before the chicken would be ready. Earlier that morning she had picked some fresh grape leaves to make *dolmathes* for her family. She decided she would go ahead and make them now. She heated more water and then summoned four-year old Lea to break the stems off the grape leaves and help wash them. Arianna started sautéing some onion in olive oil and then added rice, water, salt, pepper, parsley and dill. While that was simmering, she dipped the grape leaves into the hot water to soften them.

When the rice had softened but not fully cooked, she began to spoon the mixture into the leaves and roll them tightly. Fascinated, Lea begged, "I want to do some!" So Arianna gave her some leaves and a spoon. She told her young daughter how to do it but didn't slow her own pace. Arianna packed the rolled *dolmathes* snugly in a pan in layers and topped them with water, lemon juice and the remaining grape leaves to keep them tender. She covered the pan, allowing the *dolmathes* to steam cook.

Knowing that she had about a half hour before the *dolmathes* would be ready, Arianna was able to relax a little. She was used to working quickly and doing many things at one time, but couldn't help thinking to herself, "What a day to have the three girls out in the fields…" As she started to prepare a large salad, she smiled at Lea, "Thank you for being *Mama's* helper!" When she brought the salad to the man, he asked her a few questions about the area. They visited a while before she excused herself to go check on the food. Finding the *dolmathes* nice and tender, she served them with lemon wedges. "I will bring you the chicken in a moment," she told him.

When all had been served, the visitor was very pleased with the meal. In the absence of dessert, Arianna prepared a mixture of fresh fruits. He gave her a generous payment and asked if he could come around every Wednesday for the next few weeks when he would be in the area. "I may even be able to bring some colleagues with me, if that is okay," he inquired. She agreed and said, "I will try to have things more prepared when you come." She thought to herself that she must have some desserts ready next time.

Later, she proudly gave Nikolas the money and told him that the lawyer would be back next Wednesday. Nikolas knew that she was already busy almost nonstop from five in the morning until sometimes midnight. He hesitated, "That's good money if you think it is worth all of that work for one person." Arianna replied, "We can have the leftover vegetables and *dolmathes* tonight, and he mentioned that he may bring some other people with him next time, so I think it is worth it."

The attorney and some of his associates came every Wednesday for several weeks. Each time they complimented Arianna on her cooking. Then the lawyer told her that their work in the area was done and they wouldn't be back. Their substantial compensation was a great blessing to her family, and she thanked them and wished them well as they left.

***

Somehow in the past two years that Ioanna was in Athens, she figured out that she was distantly related to the family that she was staying with. The situation made more sense to her. One day a cousin of Stefanos, whom Ioanna knew from Karidia, came for a brief visit. When Stefanos presented Ioanna to her, she was amazed at the change in Ioanna but greeted her politely. Ioanna excused herself to do a little hand sewing in the next room.

Ioanna didn't mean to overhear their conversation as the visitor exclaimed, "How did it come about that you took that girl, who was tilling in the fields with the horse, and now look what happened to her— look at her beauty now! Why did you welcome her and not my sister's daughter?" Stefanos was a little surprised but he answered her, "I had nothing to do with the deal. I only asked my father to choose an appropriate young lady for some very light work to help my wife and daughter. I told him to tell her father that if he were to send a daughter to the city for an education or training of any kind, it would typically cost him four-hundred drachmas a year for room and board. She could live with us in a fine city and he would save all of that money for the experience. I guess technically Arianna is a second cousin where you and your sister are my first cousins, but we have all loved having Ioanna here and are pleased with his choice."

164

Ioanna heard the discussion and was astonished. That was the first time that she understood the deal directly from the source. There had been a huge mistake. Either her uncle's father misunderstood her uncle's instructions, or her own father misinterpreted the expectation of four-hundred drachmas a year. And with the way her uncle was treating her and the lifestyle she led, she was costing him much more than that anyway. Furthermore, although she had taken a few casual sewing lessons, she wasn't using her time in Athens to formally learn anything.

Ioanna had to fix the situation before things got out of hand. Her father really needed her in the fields since she was not earning money. She thought to herself, "My father cannot stand another defeat. I need to break this agreement and return before he feels dishonored by the deal he made and tries to demand money or sue my uncle." She had to preserve the peace at all costs.

She had all kinds of grandiose plans for her family to move to Athens, but she had to extricate herself first and then persuade them all later in person. But even if it meant she had to sacrifice by leaving the people she had grown to love and trading the good life for the poverty life, she knew that was the honorable thing to do. Now how was she going to convince this family to let her go? She must think fast so that she could go with her uncle's cousin back to Karidia. She could think of no other way but to pray, "God forgive me, I have to lie to them and tell them that I am homesick."

Sure enough, when she told her uncle that she missed her family too much and wanted to go home, he implored her to change her mind. "But we all love you. You are going to break the hearts of my wife and daughter. What if you went back for a quick visit?" he suggested. Ioanna replied, "You have been so good to me. I can't thank you enough. But I miss my mother and my sisters." He tried again, "You are crazy to leave this life for the one back home. Are you sure that's what you want to do?" She nodded, choking back tears.

When they told her aunt, she cried and tried to change her mind, "You have been like my own daughter. Please don't leave!" But she knew that she couldn't come between a mother and a daughter, so she had to let her go. When Ioanna hugged the young girl, it was like she was saying goodbye to her own sister.

They sent word to her family that she would be returning in a couple of days, and she started packing her things. Her uncle gave her twenty-nine drachmas (about a dollar) to get a drink or whatever she needed on the ship going home. But Ioanna snuck out to the market to buy her family some small presents with the money.

At the pier they said goodbye, and Ioanna tearfully thanked them for everything. She boarded the ship with Stefanos' cousin. Along the calm seas, she tried to adjust her thoughts to her hastily-made plan. She hoped she had made the right decision. She hated to lie to those precious people. Would her father be mad when she told him the whole story? Pushing her worries aside, she started to really look forward to seeing her sisters again.

***

At home in Crete, Georgia, Stella, Barbara and Lea were all excited in anticipation of Ioanna's return. Their parents had told them she would be returning by ship and then by bus. Twice a day, they heard the bus and jumped up and down yelling, "It's coming! It's coming!" They ran out to meet it, hoping she would be there. They couldn't wait to see her.

One bus came and a beautiful young lady got out and walked towards them. Stella thought that she was the most beautiful person that she had ever seen. None of them recognized Ioanna until she started calling their names and hugging them. Georgia couldn't believe how much she had changed. Lea ran inside to get *Mama*. Arianna came out and exclaimed, "Look at you! Look how much you've changed. Welcome home!" She hugged her and led her inside after her long trip. As she was enjoying some refreshments, her sisters marveled at her smooth, white skin, styled shiny hair and perfect nails. They thought she looked like a model.

When Nikolas came home, Ioanna ran to hug him. It wasn't long before she burst out, "We have to move to Athens, *Baba*. You should see how much business we could do there. And *Mama*, you should see how perfect and clean it is there. Everything is so run down here. We can sell some property here and buy some there to raise fresh produce to sell to the markets. *Mama* and Georgia can run a café, and Stella and Barbara can go to a much better school. We can all learn music or other skills, see the concerts and shows and live a good life with lighter labor. Everyone seems much better off there." Nikolas chuckled, "Whoa, slow down there. We are glad you had a good time."

Later she explained to Nikolas the misunderstanding with her uncle, and although he was disappointed, he appreciated her concern for her family. Relieved, Ioanna continued to press her case for the family to relocate. But in the meantime, she rolled up her sleeves and with whatever soap she found, tried to start cleaning everything. She wanted everything to be as polished as it was in Athens. Nikolas and Arianna thought that it might be best to gradually ease her back into her chores, so they left her to care for the house and any tourists that might come by.

Word of Ioanna's return and transformation got out, and before long, interested young men kept coming up with excuses to go see her. Although they didn't have a formal café or shop, townspeople knew that they could purchase some goods that they needed from the Stavrolakis. So young men kept visiting every day, until Ioanna got wise to their schemes and insisted to her *baba* that they shut this down. "I will go to the fields. I am only twelve and am no one's female companion." So she returned to the field work, her smooth hands soon becoming rough with hard labor. But she felt satisfied that she was helping her family.

Gradually her appeals for them to become Athenians lessened. She appreciated the tranquility and beauty of the island, but a part of her always wished for something more. Arianna, remembering her own brief time living in Heraklion, could relate to Ioanna's feelings and was very patient with her. At the same time, Ioanna recognized the improvements Nikolas and the family had worked hard for— the new motor for the well, the painted roof, the rabbits and turkeys… And also the fields, vines and fruit trees were well maintained and producing at capacity.

Not long after Ioanna returned, Arianna's relatives came to their house to welcome her back. One of the uncles brought over the biggest apricots they had ever seen. Another uncle brought some drinks. They sat out on the balcony and asked Ioanna to tell them about Athens. Uncle Demetrios teased young Barbara as he poured the last of his beer into a glass. He held the glass beer bottle upside down and squeezed it, pretending to squeeze out every last drop. Barbara watched, fascinated, wondering if that really worked, but she saw drops coming out!

The extended family stayed late into the evening, some deciding to stay overnight, while others went home. The girls always loved it when the extended family got together. It didn't matter if it got a little crowded; people slept on the floor or outside if they stayed over or took naps. It was always a little sad to see them leave.

The next month, Georgia, Ioanna and Stella started up the mountain to pick grapes at their furthest grapevines near Topos. Nikolas took the horse the longer winding way that was less steep. The girls reached the top and, as was their typical routine, sat on a large rock to rest and wait for him. They glanced down the mountain and saw that he had stopped, but they didn't think much about it. A little later, he joined them and they continued on their long journey. Hours later, they reached the vineyard and started picking grapes as fast as they could so they could make the long trip back home before dark.

After a while, they took a break for lunch. Nikolas, in mock seriousness, asked them, "Did you notice that I stopped on the way up the mountain? Did you wonder why?" Ioanna replied, "Yeah, we saw you stop but didn't think much about it." With a glint in his eye, he began, "Well, I need to tell you a story…"

The girls listened with anticipation as Nikolas regaled, "There was a man who had an *episode* around the midnight hour and he wondered what he was going to tell his wife. His wife woke up, sensed that he was troubled and asked what was wrong. He thought quickly and claimed that he had just had a very dramatic dream. She asked him what it was about, but he said he couldn't divulge it to her, it was too dramatic. She said that she could handle it and to tell her. He

168

unfolded that in the dream he was outside on top of a tall tower, and on top of the tower was a chair. On top of the chair was a table and on top of the table was a stool. On top of the stool was a needle and balanced on this needle was another chair. He told her that he was supposed to sit on that chair to shout an announcement to the whole village. He asked her what she would think if that were her, if *she* had to sit on that chair. She had been following along carefully and declared in dismay that she would soil her pants. He told her, 'Well, that's exactly what just happened to me!'" The girls pictured the whole story and laughed.

Then Nikolas confessed, "I'm afraid I had just that kind of situation on my way up the mountain. As I was riding, I felt what I thought was just a little air, but as I let it out, there was a lump in it." The girls' laughter escalated even more at his revelation. Nikolas expounded, "It wasn't much, but it was uncomfortable, so I dismounted and cleaned up with some soft sage that was growing there." With twinges of pity, the girls tried to restrain their laughter but were unsuccessful. Nikolas concluded, "I wasn't sure how to tell you…" Another burst of laughter erupted as their father punctuated his tale within a tale by cunningly redirecting attention back to the unfortunate but creative husband.

The girls finally began to regain their composure and in between bouts of giggling uttered tokens of sympathy for their father's plight. Stella appreciated that her father had a fun sense of humor. If he hadn't told them the story, they would have never known. And what a comical way to tell them what happened!

Weeks later, Nikolas was able to sell the grown turkeys for a favorable price. Soon after that, he came home with his latest business idea. The girls were curious when they saw him holding a burlap bag that was wriggling. He let them open it to find a baby pig. Arianna was disgusted, "I don't want my daughters to raise pigs!" He answered, "Don't worry, I will take care of her." Arianna grunted, "Hmm, don't say that. You know that I will end up taking care of it."

The girls immediately loved the one-month old piglet. "She is so cute!" they exclaimed. Nikolas let them play with it while he constructed a pen near the barn area. They fed it leftovers sprinkled with wheat flour. It began to grow quickly and became almost like a pet. It seemed to get excited when Stella and Barbara came home from school and took it swimming with them.

That fall, Georgia visited Nikolas' mother in Lithos. Georgia knew that her father and his mother weren't really close, but she had always been very good to Georgia. She felt extra beloved as her first grandchild. The teenager encouraged her grandmother, "You have been talking about picking your figs for weeks. Why don't we go get them now? You can ride your donkey and I can walk alongside."

Her grandmother thought that was a good idea, so they headed that way. They picked a few that they could reach, and then Georgia climbed the tree to get the higher ones. She had the best intentions but forgot how dizzy she got with heights. Her grandmother kept telling her to pull this branch or that one or to climb higher, but she couldn't do anything because she was shaking, thinking she was going to fall.

In the meantime, her grandmother, while she was barking orders, tripped on a stone and fell down. Georgia knew that she couldn't have been badly hurt, and seeing her grandmother's rare undignified state after primly ordering her around, she couldn't help but laugh. Her grandmother was insulted and cynically snapped, "You think I am going to die, is that why you are laughing? Is that what you would do at my funeral, laugh at me?"

Georgia at first thought she was teasing her back but then realized she was serious. She tried to reassure her that she didn't mean anything by laughing, but her grandmother packed up their few figs and was mad all the way home. Georgia made a mental note to be extra considerate with her from then on.

A couple of months later, Nikolas decided to start working on a special Christmas surprise for Arianna. He cut several large and small pieces of wood, and on his next trip to Heraklion he would see if Arianna's brothers could help him find someone to fashion a loom for her. She had used one often while in her mother's house, but she

170

never had one in their home. A large loom would allow her to make almost any kind of fabric from different threads or yarns.

When Christmas came, Nikolas kept hinting about a surprise gift all throughout their special lunch. After they cleaned up the kitchen, he finally revealed his present to Arianna and the girls. Arianna was thrilled when she saw the loom. Nikolas also got her some different threads, so she was able to demonstrate it for Georgia and the other girls.

The loom was mostly manual, with Arianna initially threading across and through other threads that went in the opposite direction. The threads were held in place by posts and weighted pulleys operated by her feet. The girls watched as she sat and moved things back and forth, and mysteriously a fabric slowly appeared. She could change the colors to create unique patterns and use different kinds of threads to vary the thickness and density of the weave. She could make anything from tapestries, table or bed linens and aprons to blankets or towels.

Arianna even had the skills to make her own threads from twisting and dyeing wool or cotton. She asked Nikolas, "Can we plant some cotton next spring, just enough for us to use?" Nikolas answered, "Yes, I think we can manage that." Arianna happily replied, "Thank you, and thank you so much for this thoughtful gift!" During the Christmas and New Year's holidays, they thanked God for His protection and many blessings. They were so glad to be together as a family again.

Chapter 18

Early the next year, Nikolas took the pig to another farm, hoping she would soon have piglets. He brought her back home to her pen and before long it became obvious that she was going to be a mother. The girls were delighted and couldn't wait for her piglets to be born.

That spring was unusually cold. There was a north wind that put the small plants in *Sterna* at risk. Nikolas had a lot of extra bamboo growing in the *Lemoni* field. Sometimes he sold it to others wanting to use it to construct their roof or other projects. With the cold, Nikolas decided to use some bamboo to build a short temporary fence on the north side of *Sterna*. He cut the stalks in equal pieces and dried them so there would be no new shoots. After they had dried, he dug a deep trench in the ground. The girls stood the bamboo stalks upright, side by side, and filled in and stomped on the dirt around them to hold them up.

Everyone always looked forward to Easter. They had begun a partial fast forty-eight days before the holiday, as was the custom. There were many church services throughout the week leading up to Resurrection Sunday.

On Good Friday, Jesus' burial was symbolically re-enacted using an *epitaphios*, an intricately-carved wooden canopy covering a platform with long handles. It was extravagantly adorned with fresh flowers that church members had specially grown at their homes. During the liturgy, the priest took a representation of the body of Christ, wrapped it in a burial sheet and placed it inside the *epitaphios*, symbolizing His burial. While hymns were sung, the priest led men carrying the *epitaphios* in a procession inside and outside the church. The congregation followed behind, mourning the death of Christ, who lived a perfect life and sacrificed all to atone for their sins.

Saturday, Arianna and the girls boiled eggs and dyed them all a bright red, symbolic of the blood of Jesus and also the joy of His victorious resurrection. They made everything they could make in advance for their Easter meal, including the *tsourekakia* [butter cookies twisted into various shapes]. Arianna baked the Easter bread, one of the few breads they made with sugar.

Almost five-year old Lea was most looking forward to the late Saturday night service. She loved to go to church anyway, but the moment near midnight when they waited in the darkness for the Easter announcement "Christ is risen" and they lit all the candles was thrilling. The girls took an evening nap so that they could stay up late.

When it was time to get up, Arianna looked at sleeping Lea and told Nikolas, "Let's not wake Lea. I think she is too little to be out in this cold at midnight." She was still protective of her youngest, who almost didn't survive her bad case of pneumonia years earlier. Nikolas replied, "I will stay home with her and make the Easter soup while you all go."

Around ten o'clock in the evening, Arianna, Georgia, Ioanna, Stella and Barbara grabbed the large white candles they had purchased, and they bundled up to walk to the church. Along the way, they met other groups who joined them to walk together. At that time, Lea had a dream. It was so vivid that it was as if she walked alongside them. She saw who they met along the way and heard all of their conversations all the way to the church. When there, everyone gathered to stand in the middle of the church since there were only a few seats along the outer edges for the elderly or disabled. They knew that "*orthos*" in Orthodox meant to stand up as well as correct or right.

Although physically far away, Lea heard the hymns being sung and the resurrection story being read in the liturgy. And soon came the moment when they extinguished all the lights. At midnight, the priest exclaimed, "*Christos anesti* [Christ has risen]!" and with a candle that had been blessed and was considered "holy" began lighting the candles of the others. The congregation replied, "*Alithos anesti* [Indeed He has risen]!" as they lit one another's candles. The

173

new light after darkness symbolized new life after the dark of death. Then they sang the traditional "Christ is Risen" hymn.

Afterwards, they all gathered outside the church for a bonfire and celebration. Lea saw it all, including when a woman's hair accidentally caught fire from a spark from the bonfire. As they dispersed to go home, everyone tried to keep their candles lit in order to bless their homes with the holy light.

When Arianna and the four girls were a few minutes from arriving home, Lea woke up. She ran to Nikolas, who was stirring the soup. Lea jumped up and down, all excited, "*Baba*, they're coming! Jesus has risen from the dead! They are almost here with the holy light. They are by the turn in the road over there." As Lea pointed in the direction her mother and sisters were coming from, Nikolas was baffled and asked her, "What are you talking about?" Lea continued excitedly, "I was at the church and saw everything."

Arianna stopped outside their door and using the smoke from the burning candle, she marked the sign of cross on the doorframe to bless the home. When they came in, Lea ran up and said, "That was really fun! I was right there with you and saw you walking... and the service... and the bonfire!" Arianna looked at her skeptically and Georgia said, "No you weren't. You know you shouldn't lie." Lea said, "But I was there, didn't you see me?" The girls looked at each other and replied, "No." Arianna asked her, "What did you see?"

Lea described, "I walked with you— Mrs. Spiriaki didn't walk with you because her mother was sick, her husband said. And her sister had a new dress that was light green with a blue collar. I heard the priest say 'Christ is risen' and saw all of the candles light up after it was all dark. The boy in front of us almost dropped his candle. And I was scared when Mrs. Metasaki's hair caught on fire from the bonfire."

They all looked at each other amazed, realizing she was telling them details that she couldn't have known unless she had been there. But she wasn't physically with them. Nikolas dabbed a tear from his eye as Arianna grabbed Lea's cheeks and said, "Oh, *koukla mou* [doll of

174

mine], the Lord knew how much you wanted to go, and He miraculously showed it to you!"

The Stavrolakis slowly eased out of their fast that night by eating some Easter soup and then went to bed. The church service on Sunday wasn't until midday, so the family slept a little later than usual. After they all came back from church, they enjoyed an Easter meal of roasted seasoned lamb. With their red eggs, they played a game in which they hit each other's eggs, and the one who had the egg that didn't crack was the winner. After seven weeks of fasting, the family really enjoyed celebrating the meaningful day with the elaborate meal and desserts.

By the middle of April, the pig had gotten so big that they all thought that she would have the piglets at any moment. Nikolas checked on her every day, but one night he was late in coming home. That night the pig had eleven piglets, and she started killing them. When Nikolas was finally able to get there, he found one piglet hiding. He brought it inside and coaxed Arianna into bottle feeding it. Unfortunately, it had a hard time adjusting to the goat's milk and had diarrhea. Nikolas thought that to ease Arianna's burden, he would sell the mother pig. She would not be a good investment if she kept killing her young anyway.

The girls were sorry to see the mother pig go, but they liked playing with the little pig who basically lived in the house with them. They were also thrilled when their beloved horse had a beautiful chestnut-colored foal. Nikolas knew that its mother was getting older, and he planned to sell the other young horse, so he decided to keep this foal. The girls were elated that they could bond with this exquisite creature.

True to the promise he had given Arianna over Christmas, when it was warm enough, Nikolas planted several rows of cotton in the *Sterna* field in Karidia. In the same field, he decided to try some flax as well, in case Arianna wanted to make some things with linen.

Soon after that, a south wind began to blow. Every few years there were winds that brought sandstorms from the African desert. These winds could last up to a week, and they had to cover the doors and

175

windows with sheets. Dust got on all of the vegetables, the fruits on the trees, the grapes, everywhere. If it rained a little, everything turned to mud, but if it rained a lot it would wash it all off. When the wind whipped up the sand that year, Nikolas tried to make a bamboo awning that they had to duck under to get into the house.

The next day, Ioanna, Stella and Barbara were walking along the beach. A little sandy wind wasn't going to stop their usual practice of looking for washed up treasures along the beach. A bottle, pencil, special shell— anything they could find was a treat. They also liked to see what kind of ships might sail by. The girls' whole world was their house, the fields and their beach, and they were happy. But at times they wondered what was beyond the sea. Ioanna had been enthralled by Athens, but she knew there were countries beyond Greece, and one of those might be a "promised land."

As Ioanna looked out towards the island of Dia in the distance, she saw some different ships coming their way. In her mind's eye, she saw a vision of a canopy over these ships, like a blessing and a protection. She had a feeling, "They are coming here for us. Our destinies are somehow going to be affected by these people." She flashed back to a dream she had when she was a young child of many ships and another country coming to hers and wondered if these were the same people.

The girls watched as the five or six boats came closer. They saw that there were many men sitting in each open-air troop carrier. The sisters had seen many kinds of boats, but they were bewildered when these all of a sudden appeared to have many wheels and started driving onto the west side of their beach. While Stella was thinking to herself, "How did they do that?" Ioanna continued her reverie thinking, "They walk on water like Jesus; these people must be blessed of God." The men didn't appear to be Greek and they were driving the strangest vessel, yet none of the girls felt afraid.

Arianna saw the boats coming ashore and came running. She had a fleeting thought that maybe she should have picked up a shovel in case, like some women had during the war. But a couple of the men who got out of a boat acted very friendly saying, "American!" Stella thought to herself how much taller these men seemed than the Greek

176

people. They were just like the men she and Barbara had seen with the turkeys years before. As the sandy wind stirred up, Arianna nodded and blew out of her mouth and pointed to try to communicate with them about the south wind storm.

Everything seemed amiable until one of the officers gestured to try to communicate that there may be bullets in the region and they should stay inside. When Arianna saw the hand motions, she misunderstood that they were there for the women. She called to the girls, "Come quickly, let's get in the house!" As they ran to the front door, a gust of wind blew off the bamboo awning that Nikolas had constructed. Arianna yelled to Nikolas what she thought was happening.

Hurriedly they packed a couple of things, and Arianna took off to one of the villages with Georgia and Ioanna for the night. As she ran, Arianna spread the word to the local people to hide the women. Nikolas kept the younger girls inside but tried to peer out every now and then.

The next day, the men left the same way that they had come. Nikolas told the girls to stay inside while he checked out the area. He found a small mound of buried food not too far away, but no sign of soldiers. Word got out about the food, so other people came trying to find the buried treasures, but there was only the one spot.

When Arianna and the older girls came back, she asked Nikolas what had happened. He mused, "As I was walking around afterwards, I found an empty strip that probably had bullets. I think we misunderstood and they were signaling that they were doing military exercises with bullets." Arianna was somewhat relieved, but bullets were pretty scary too. She asked, "Did you hear or see them shoot?" Nikolas answered, "No, they must have been in one of the remote areas. Or maybe there is a war going on somewhere and they were here just in case."

Soon afterwards, they saw an airplane swoop low near the ocean and land on the water. The girls were incredulous again at the extraordinary new inventions they kept seeing. Nikolas and Arianna were suspicious at what they might be up to. As it floated closer towards their beach, other people from the area came running towards them carrying their work tools. One yelled, "Is it the Germans?" Another asked, "Is it another war?" Someone exclaimed, "I've never seen such a thing. What could they want?"

A couple of men got out of the plane with their hands raised to indicate that they came in peace. They seemed to be asking them a question in English but no one understood them. They looked around and didn't see what they were looking for, so they waved kindly to the people and took off in the plane. The Greek people didn't hear anything more about it but wondered what it meant.

After those occurrences, Nikolas decided to invest the profits from selling the pig into buying a radio. When he had purchased this isolated piece of land many years ago, he had no idea of the kinds of activity the area would have. He thought that they should be better informed about world events and maybe catch some warnings that might affect them. Not many people had radios since they had to register for a license, pay regularly for its use and operate it with a big car battery.

Arianna couldn't believe that he had spent good money on that contraption. "Why did you get that thing when we had never heard of it or needed one before?" Nikolas didn't want to worry her with his concerns, so he explained the differences between the radio and phonograph, which they had owned when they were first married, before it was taken during the war.

Nikolas added, "I think you can pick up the full church liturgies. Just think, if someone were sick or not able to walk almost an hour to church, we could listen from here, and even invite others." Arianna wasn't sure if that was sacrilegious. But then again, she had meaningful times of reading Bible stories under their tree, which was unconventional but uplifting, and radio services could be better than going without. So she reconciled herself to the idea of having a radio, and later they were able to hear services or music from Athens, Germany, Italy or other nearby countries. Arianna was happy when church services were on and encouraged others to come and listen. They reverentially participated by singing, kneeling or crossing themselves at the appropriate times.

Before the cotton formed, the girls admired the beautiful flowering blossoms. When the cotton was finally harvested, Arianna showed the girls how to remove the seeds and stickers and then twist it finely into a thread and wind it around a spindle. To get the linen fibers out of the flax, they had to soak the stiff straws in the sea. Then they dried them in the sun and beat them to break the outer stems. The girls exclaimed at the soft fibers. Arianna told them, "Your grandmother had silkworms which made even more luxurious threads from their cocoons." Arianna showed them how to dye the different threads and incorporate them into the loom.

Around that time, Arianna started allowing the girls to wear short-sleeved dresses, which they were glad about, especially during the hot summers. For practicality, almost all the dresses they made had to have pockets. Usually the girls went to their aunt in Prasinos Kampos to help sew their dresses, since Arianna wasn't too confident and they didn't have a sewing machine.

That year when the Greek military came, they stayed longer than usual and camped out in tents not far away from the Stavrolaki home. Nikolas again sold some of his fresh produce to the men. A few soldiers came to the house asking Arianna to cook a meal for them. Nikolas arranged some tables outside, turned on some music from the radio and sold them whatever meal they could scrounge together. He told Arianna to keep the girls out of sight.

One young man caught a glimpse of Georgia and became very enamored with her. He came to the house as often as he could. Before long, the young soldier couldn't wait any longer and asked Nikolas for her hand in marriage. Nikolas was shocked, "She is only fourteen years old! No, she is too young."

The young man was not good with taking no for an answer. On a Friday night, he got three of his comrades drunk and led them to the Stavrolaki house. One of the men said, "Give us a drink!" Nikolas replied, "We are closed." Another one of the guys hand cranked a record player to play a song with words like, "Stop you who run the café, you are out of your mind and soon will be in the ground."

Nikolas tried to calm them down, but they started breaking dishes and physically confronting him. Arianna screamed. Some nearby officers heard the commotion and came to take the men back to their camp. The next day Nikolas approached the man in charge to file a complaint. The officer was sympathetic but couldn't cancel their mission. "We will punish him. Try to keep your daughter out of sight as much as you can," he advised.

Arianna kept Georgia busy with work inside the house. Georgia was puzzled when her mother told her to clean out any rocks or dirt from the lentils. "We did that yesterday," she said. Arianna answered, "Do it again." Nikolas escorted each of his daughters to the bathroom, and Arianna stopped hanging out some of the girls' garments on the clothes line.

After a few weeks, Georgia begged to get out of the house. Finally Arianna agreed but went with her to fetch some water from their well. After a few trips with Arianna accompanying her, Georgia convinced her mother to let her go fetch some water on her own.

Some local people saw the young man creep behind an oleander bush near their well, so they watched to see if Georgia had arranged a secret meeting with him. He approached her saying, "Your beauty is making me crazy!" She told him loudly and firmly, "Leave me alone, stay away from me!" The neighbors saw that she wanted nothing to do with him and came to her rescue. When Arianna found out about the incident, she panicked. After questioning Georgia on everything that happened, she calmed down some but discussed with Nikolas what they could do since the man seemed persistent.

One day, Georgia's uncle Antonios came to the house. Arianna brought Georgia out to greet him and told her to go with him. He took her to a distant relative's house in Prasinos Kampos and told her to stay there a while for a vacation. Georgia plagued them daily, "My family needs me at home. I need to go. They have so much work to do." But the family found things for her to keep occupied indoors.

Finally Georgia reconciled herself to staying there, but she missed her freedom and also missed seeing the ocean. Often when the

180

family had visitors, she yearned to talk to them until she overheard bits of conversations, "Have you seen the Stavrolaki girl?" "She moved to Athens." "She's in love with him." "No, he's trying to kill her family." Georgia realized they were talking about her and didn't like being the subject of their speculations. Finally near the end of the summer, her uncle came to take her home.

Georgia was so glad to be home with her family, but she also wanted to be useful for whatever they needed. For weeks they didn't let her out of the house. One day, Nikolas was discussing with his sister Zoe's father-in-law something they needed to do in Lithos. Georgia begged her father to let her go with him to help. Nikolas said, "No, we need you here." The father-in-law said, "I can escort her. She'll be safe." Georgia added, "Please *Baba*, I haven't ridden a horse all summer." Nikolas protested, not feeling right about it, but he finally relented. The father-in-law and Georgia proceeded up the mountain, each on horseback. Georgia was happy to be out riding the horse in the beautiful sunshine.

After they had made it about half way, Georgia's escort suddenly became agitated and said, "That guy, that soldier..." Georgia looked around, "I don't see anyone." He told her, "On the ground." Georgia then saw a figure skulking around the brush near them. The father-in-law gave her hasty instructions, "Ride as fast as you can to Lithos. Don't stop to tie the horse when you get there. You know every hiding place." He then kicked his horse and took off at a fast gallop. Georgia did the same, but could hardly keep up. "You are going too fast for me!" she yelled.

As she galloped, out of the corner of her eye, Georgia thought she saw her mother, but that didn't make sense. She wasn't sure where her escort went, but she finally made it to the village. She thought about his instructions but she couldn't bring herself to part with the horse. She thought to herself, "I need it to get back home." She stood there paralyzed on the road.

Before long Georgia turned to see her mother running at high speed. She looked winded and red faced. Arianna reached her but before she could say anything, she fainted. Georgia was confused and worried as she tried to revive her. Finally, Arianna regained consciousness and told Georgia, "Don't be afraid. I saw you and followed behind. The guards detained the man and kept your dad away so there wouldn't be a fight."

Arianna took her to a friend's house in Lithos, where she told her to stay for a while. Georgia was beginning to realize she wasn't in a good situation, but she couldn't figure out why it was involving her. As she was mostly kept hidden in that village, she again sometimes caught remarks like, "Is that the girl?" "No, that's her sister."

But this place had other drama since her hosts had a son who loved the girl next door but his mother didn't approve. It caused so much conflict that Georgia thought to herself, "I am glad we don't have any boys." Georgia adjusted to her temporary life and tried to be a help to the nice family who took her in.

Georgia's sisters didn't understand what was going on and missed her. Their parents assured them that she was well and was away visiting friends and family. That year Lea started school, and Arianna cried as her youngest walked off with Stella and Barbara. She kept worrying about her becoming exhausted on the long walk and gave them extra water.

Over the next few months, the pig continued to grow up in the house. They were convinced that he never thought of himself as a pig but as a person. One cold fall day when he had gotten quite big, they had a charcoal bucket on the floor to warm the room and the pig accidentally burned himself on the hot bucket. It whined in pain. Arianna saw that his hair and skin had singed off and blisters were starting to form. She could tell it was hurting and felt sorry for it.

She made a compress with gauze, olive oil and a few other ingredients. The pig recovered under their loving care and grew very large. Later Arianna reflected that they probably should have started to prepare the girls for thinking of him as Christmas dinner a little sooner than they did.

In December, Georgia helped collect the last of her uncle's olives in Lithos. She thought her uncle was a comedian and was having a good time until she overheard more talk about her. Some said that the military had left the area, but the young man had become a civilian and had offered townspeople big money for any information about her. Her uncle declared, "Let him try anything. There are so many of us, we will tear him to pieces." Another remarked, "Well, unless he has a gun."

A few days before Christmas, Nikolas came to Lithos for Georgia. On their journey home Georgia asked, "Why didn't you come and get me sooner?" He answered her, "You needed a vacation. We knew you would have a good time." She admitted, "Yes, they were good to me and my uncle was funny, but you needed my help with your olives." Nikolas said, "Next year."

When they got to the top of the mountain and looked down at their house and the ocean, and saw no military tents along the hill, Georgia said, "Look at how beautiful the sea is. This is how it used to be." Nikolas went further, "This is how it *is*." After a moment to let that sink in, he expounded, "For Christmas dinner I will kill the pig that we have raised. You girls will make cookies and all kinds of great food, and then we will go to church for Christmas service."

Georgia and her sisters were so happy to be reunited. But Georgia was not quite at peace and told her mother, "I heard people in the village say that the man offered a lot of money for information." Arianna was completely convinced, "We have good family and friends and they won't give you up. He's gone now and you are safe." Georgia was relieved and grateful. She finally felt free to enjoy the holiday.

Nikolas coordinated with other men in the area who were planning to slaughter their pigs. Together, they would go from place to place to help each other, mainly with the killing and lifting since the women did most of the cleaning and sectioning. There wasn't a very big team that year, so the girls needed to help where they could. They made sure not to feed the pig for a day before their scheduled time to slaughter. Ioanna helped hold two of the feet as Nikolas cut the pig's jugular vein. He made another incision and the men turned it to allow the blood to drain.

Then they dipped the pig in scalding water to be able to scrape the hair and outer membrane off easier. Once it was scraped, they hung it by its feet, cut off the head and carefully took out the insides. They used every part of the pig that they could. Fat from around the kidneys was collected to make lard. They washed out and soaked the small intestines for sausage casings. After burying the waste in a field, they left the pig hanging to cool in the winter air for a day before cutting it into sections.

Nikolas' mother was the family expert in making sausage, so she helped Arianna and the girls with the preparation. After marinating a portion of pork, the girls chopped it finely. They looked to their grandmother to add her perfect secret blend of spices and supervise their stuffing the casings just right. Barbara was fascinated, peeking inside the fireplace to see the long sausage links hanging to smoke while the family did their daily cooking.

Arianna did a fine job of preparing the pork roast for Christmas dinner. But after seeing their pet pig slaughtered first hand, Ioanna joined Stella in not eating any meat. She never thought of fish as having life though, so she continued to eat the various fish varieties with her breads and vegetables. Arianna was glad to be able to store some smoked and salted pork buried in some lard in a cool place for a couple of months.

At the end of the day, Georgia reflected that that was her favorite Christmas. She was so grateful for the lengths that her parents had gone to in order to keep her safe. And even the local people were more loyal to her than they were interested in their own pocketbooks. And most of all she was thankful for God's protection— how many times had she and her sisters traveled alone or small groups over great distances... He ultimately kept them from harm. A peace settled in her heart as she snuggled up in bed with her sisters. It was so good to be home.

184

Chapter 19

The next year was filled with their usual routine with the exception that the family heard that the Americans had built a military base near Asprada. Nikolas wasn't very surprised, considering their past encounters with the Americans and the increased activity in their area. The local Greek citizens were a little wary of the foreigners' intentions, opting to watch their activities with distant caution. The Stavrolakis remembered the Americans' kindness in speaking to them and leaving presents behind, so they did not fear them but did not expect to interact with them much either. The base officially opened in the fall.

The following spring, Nikolas noticed that the well didn't seem to have much water. He arranged for some experienced men to use dynamite to dig deeper. After they had done their part and reached more water, Nikolas needed to clean out the extra debris from the well. He waited a couple of days to allow the fumes to dissipate before going down there. Arianna and all of the girls except for Georgia went along to help him.

Nikolas went all the way down into the well and started to fill buckets with rocks and other debris. Arianna stayed above him in the earthen room so she could pull the buckets up by rope. The girls took turns bringing some bucketloads from the underground room up the dirt steps to the surface.

Pretty soon, Nikolas started to wobble and yelled up that he was losing it. The lingering fumes suddenly overpowered him and he passed out. Arianna screamed, "Run! Go get help! Hurry! Hurry! Run!" The girls ran up the steps and then began running in different directions, screaming for help at the top of their lungs. The more they grappled with his predicament, the more dread overcame them. He could die from the gases or he could fall and drown in the well. How could anyone get him out without fainting themselves?

Six-year old Lea feared that he might have already died. She dropped to her knees, facing towards the east. She wasn't sure if that Orthodox custom was based on Scripture or because Jerusalem was that direction, but her church was also east. She thought she would do everything she possibly could to call on the name and power of Jesus. Lea cried out to Him and begged with all of her heart, "Jesus, please save my daddy!"

Before long, a few men heard the screams for help and came running. One young man went into the well below and the others lowered a rope to him. The young man tied Nikolas securely to the rope and helped lift him while the other men pulled him from above. As they steadily lifted him, Arianna prayed that the rope would hold and that they would bring him up in time.

They lifted him to the platform but then had to carry him up the precarious steps. Arianna held her breath since the narrow steps had no railing and if they lost their balance, they could fall into the well. Finally the men reached reach the surface, and Arianna helped lay Nikolas on the ground. He was unconscious and his skin was a pale yellow.

Stella dropped to her knees and made a promise to God. She knew of a special monastery that was hours away near the center of the island. "If you save my daddy, I will go to that church and give You thanks," she prayed earnestly.

While Ioanna and Barbara also prayed, Arianna knelt by Nikolas' side and buried her face in his chest, clutching his shirt, "God, give Him breath. Give him back to me. We need him. Please revive him." She shook him gently and fanned him with fresh air, "Breathe, *Agape* [Love]!" Soon Nikolas started to barely move and then began coughing. Arianna gasped, "Thank You, Jesus!" The relief that they all felt was indescribable.

They sat with Nikolas in the field for some time before they would let him exert himself to stand up and walk towards home. Nikolas sincerely thanked the men and promised that he wouldn't come back to work on the well for a long time to give it plenty more time to air out. He realized that since he had replaced the old roof over the well with a flat cover, the well became more enclosed, which may have prevented faster clearing of the fumes. The girls and Arianna tended to his every need for several days before allowing him to return to any kind of work.

After Nikolas was up and around again, he brought to Arianna an experimental idea that he had discussed with the government. "Tobacco?" Arianna questioned after Nikolas told her what was on his mind. He hastily added, "They promised a lot of money. We can use it to send Stella to school in Heraklion when she finishes the sixth grade in a year. She can become a teacher." Some community leaders in Asprada and Lithos had introduced that idea since they didn't have any candidates to take over their schools when the current teachers retired. They had suggested that Stella might be suited to take over either school.

Arianna liked the idea of one of her daughters becoming a teacher, but she still wasn't sure about this proposal, "Doesn't tobacco make a mess? And do we know if it even grows well here?" Nikolas assented, "That's part of the experiment. They want to see if it thrives in this area. There will be a lot of regulations and it may make a little mess, but for the amount of money, I think it is worth trying."

Nikolas was always careful to rotate his crops and left some areas dormant in turn, so he had to consider in which field to take his new risk. Even though the field in Topos was the furthest away, Nikolas decided it was best since it had been freshly plowed, was the right size and wouldn't take away space from his other valuable more certain crops.

The whole family helped plant the tobacco in the cultivated ground near their grapevines. The girls were cautioned that they had to account for every seed and couldn't lose any. They each had a stick that helped them measure the exact distance between each seed that they planted. A strict watering schedule had to be followed. They carried the water from the well by horseback and measured out a precise amount for each plant. Once the plants were fairly

187

established, they could mostly leave them alone until ready to harvest, but every plant had to be counted.

Arianna asked Nikolas, "Do you think there will be enough leftover money from the tobacco to finally buy a sewing machine?" Arianna had complained many times over the years how she needed a sewing machine for their large family. The girls usually got new dresses around Easter each year, and they wore them out, so there were no hand-me-downs. The clothes for the whole family as well as the other household sewing were a lot to do by hand, and she didn't want to keep bothering her sister to help. Nikolas recognized that in many ways Arianna worked harder than he did but admitted, "A sewing machine costs closer to the price of a horse or a piece of property."

A few days later, Nikolas presented Arianna with a sewing machine. Arianna shrieked in amazement, momentarily speechless. Nikolas explained, "It is used, but it is in great condition and powered by foot." Arianna asked, "How did you do it?" Nikolas answered, "I sold the next-to-youngest horse." He had sold the first foal to his father-in-law and kept the chestnut-colored foal, but he had always planned to sell the one in between.

Arianna was so excited and wanted to make plans to train at least one of her daughters to become really proficient at sewing. Georgia said, "No way! I have too many other things to manage." And Stella planned to be a teacher. Barbara and Lea were too young. Ioanna didn't want to do it but said, "If you really need me to learn, I will try it."

A lady in the area offered embroidery lessons and had been pressuring Arianna for one of her girls to learn. Now having a machine and wanting her girls to have some finer things, Arianna agreed to start Ioanna's lessons with embroidery. She could learn traditional sewing afterwards.

To pay for the embroidery hoop and the lessons, Ioanna took a job working for other farmers for the month of June. She was hired to group onions together in bunches by braiding their stalks. She earned ten drachmas a day to get the three-hundred drachmas (about ten dollars) that she needed. When she had earned the full amount, she stayed with the lady for a week and a half to learn this skill on the instructor's embroidery machine.

One day while Ioanna was away, Georgia was baking bread and Stella and Barbara were out walking the goats, Lea went for a walk along the beach. She always hoped to find something unique or special, but her mother wanted her to be on the lookout for wood that they could use for the fire. She walked quite a bit west but didn't find too much that day. She was starting to get hot, so she waded with her flip-flops in the ocean to cool off a little and then turned backed to go home. She decided to take the short cut through a field, at a little distance from the house.

While she was walking back, all of a sudden Lea felt something sharp poking the arch of her foot. "What is this?" she thought. She lifted up her foot, but the sandal didn't come with it. She looked down and saw that something wiry was holding her flip-flop. She didn't know what it was, but she wasn't about to go home without her shoe. She knew how hard the family worked for the things they had, and they were expected to care for their few possessions. She bent over and pulled the sandal straight up. She was disappointed to see a small hole at the bottom of the flip-flop, but she knew that she could still wear it.

When she got home, Arianna saw Lea walking a little funny and asked her, "What happened? Did you hurt your foot?" Lea answered, "I stepped on some kind of pointed metal thing. I got a hole in my shoe, but I can still wear it." Arianna's heart almost stopped, "Did you step on a landmine? Do you know what that is? Oh, my dear girl, those are so dangerous. We haven't warned you enough about them since the government came to remove them, but I guess there are some still around. Oh thank you, Jesus, for protecting my baby!" Arianna hugged and kissed her youngest, who had just turned seven. She just couldn't stand it if she lost her.

Arianna cared for the bottom of Lea's foot and gave her a thorough education about landmines. Later, she sent Nikolas out to examine that field meticulously. For days Arianna kept praising God for His protection. First Nikolas in the well and now Lea... and all of the many times before... She acknowledged gratefully, "We wouldn't be here but for You."

Later that summer, the tobacco started to become ready to harvest. The plants had grown about two meters high, and the ones that had a little yellow or had a certain texture were ready to pick. Day after day, the girls had to walk almost three hours each way, starting at a very early three or four in the morning to pick the leaves. If it got too hot, the leaves would get too sticky.

They had to identify which of the leaves were ready to pick and then not just throw them but carefully lay each leaf smoothly in a basket. Everything had to be weighed for the government, so they had to be careful not to lose or damage any parts of the plant. None of them liked the stinky smell or having a black gummy coating all over their hands and clothes after hours of backbreaking, tedious picking. Often they were hungry or thirsty but didn't want to touch anything.

The girls returned home with their baskets and sat under their shade tree. Taking a long flat needle and a long piece of string, they carefully strung up the leaves to dry. They had to make sure to stick the large leaves exactly in the center as they threaded them with the string. It was important to dry out the leaves so they wouldn't mold, but direct sunlight had to be avoided in order to not overdry or damage the leaves. The girls returned every day to pick the leaves that were ready and repeated the drying process.

Although they didn't want to complain, the sisters were very sleepy from getting up so early, and they got many small blisters on their hands from all of the toil. Once the leaves had dried, the family stacked the piles carefully in the storage area downstairs to protect them.

When the government inspected their results, they were very impressed, saying that their crop was the best quality in color and texture. The officials told Nikolas to store the leaves while they negotiated the best deal, either within the country or in competition with other countries.

190

In many ways, school was easier than the tobacco project, so Stella, Barbara and Lea were almost glad when classes began in the fall. Around this time there were more families in the area, so they met several groups of students as they walked along the way.

Stella, as the oldest and tallest, became the leader of the group, and many mothers were glad that she accompanied their children. One worried mother in particular, who lived about halfway to the school, trusted Stella to watch over her young boy who was very small for his age. She knew how far they had to walk each day, so she tried to have water and maybe a small snack ready when the group stopped by to walk with him.

Even though much of their day was occupied with school, the younger girls were still expected to help with the harvests and chores in addition to walking many kilometers to and from all of those tasks and to and from school. One day, Lea was particularly tired and fell asleep on a bench in the school courtyard during the lunch break. The teacher had an older son who sometimes stopped by. He noticed Lea sleeping, and he took a cigarette from his pocket and put it in her mouth. She had been sound asleep but eventually heard people laughing hysterically and woke up. She was confused, finding the cigarette in her mouth. Then she realized they were playing a joke on her. Guessing where the cigarette had come from, Lea tried to give the young man a stern look, but she ended up laughing at the unexpectedly funny scenario.

On the rare occasion that the timing worked out and there was space on the rudimentary bus that went in their direction in the morning, the bus driver took pity on the children and stopped to pick them up. The girls were glad, since they had so far to walk, but they also made sure that the driver stopped for all the other kids along the way. It wasn't too often that this happened, but they were thankful when it did.

In addition to their regular studies, they learned some Greek history, such as stories about Alexander the Great. They heard a little about Greek mythology, which wasn't usually a part of the islanders' day-to-day conversations. Stella was mostly curious about the unusual creatures like cyclops and the one that if you cut off his head, more heads would grow.

They were glad to find out about the Minoans who lived in their area thousands of years before Christ. Stella, appreciating the history more, reflected that they probably should have been a little more careful with some of the pottery they had found on their beach years before. She was glad they had always been conscientious while playing in the ruins. Playtime at recess was even more fun now that they were older and stronger from all of their hard labor. Stella was tall and Barbara was fast, and with no problem they could beat the boys at the games.

Georgia, with all of her work at home doing laundry, cleaning and cooking for the family and the day laborers— sometimes baking dozens of loaves of bread at a time— rarely had time for leisure. But one day a friend of theirs came over and begged Georgia to go swimming with her. Arianna agreed, so the two went swimming while most of the younger girls were at school.

Georgia wasn't much of a swimmer, so she mostly stood fairly near the shore. As she watched the waves, she got a little disoriented and ended up walking into a hole that put her under water. The waves kept overtaking her. She tried to call out to her friend, but she was having fun and wasn't paying attention. Arianna looked out of the window occasionally, but Georgia couldn't even lift her arm to signal her.

She was saved by a swimmer who happened to be in the area. He had seen her struggling and pulled her by the hair to shallow water. Her heart was beating fast as she thanked him. When her friend realized what had happened, she was very sorry. Georgia told her, "That's okay, but I think I have had enough swimming for today." Together they went inside and had a snack. Eventually, Georgia was able to calm herself.

As the school year progressed, the weather started to get cooler. One day as Stella, Barbara, Lea and their friend Violetta had just started off to school, an automobile pulled up beside them. The girls recognized the type as one from the American base. The man

192

signaled for them to jump into the vehicle. As they drove along, the girls told him to stop for the other kids to pile in. He came to understand, "*Etho* [Here]!" to mean stop for more kids, until the vehicle was crammed with children. The shining faces of the youngsters saying, "*Efharisto* [Thank you]!" as he dropped them near the school touched him, and he sought to repeat the kindness. He timed his trip back to Heraklion to catch them going back.

The children knew to not necessarily expect the ride every day, but it turned into almost a twice a day occurrence. The kids even made a crude "school stop" sign in Greek near the schoolhouse to mark the pick-up point in the afternoon. The American might not have been able to read it, but he came to recognize the spot.

Not long after that, another American officer came to their school to teach the children English. He pointed out things like a pencil, table, chair and told them the English word for each. Stella was so excited. She took careful notes of about fifty words and took them home to study. In no time, she knew them.

For another special treat, the Americans came one day with a large open-air truck to take the children into Heraklion. They had obtained permission from the families beforehand to take the children to buy each of them a pair of new shoes. When the children got to Heraklion, the city streets became a flurry of activity. The merchants quickly got together to find shoes that would fit everyone. The children felt like they were in a dream. Lea couldn't remember ever going to a store to buy shoes.

All of the kids were so proud, showing off their new shoes, but the shopkeepers couldn't find a pair large and narrow enough for Stella. She was so disappointed. The vendors continued to look, the word spreading with the last shoe size that they were looking for.

Finally, they found a pair of ladies' shoes that had a little heel. Stella didn't want to have different shoes from the others and also didn't want to be any taller, but she knew that was all they could find and she was grateful. Arianna wasn't happy that her twelve-year old was dressed up beyond her age, but when Stella explained how hard they had tried to find shoes that fit her, she understood.

The weather continued to get colder, and a rainstorm gusted through. When it rained, Arianna liked to take the opportunity to use the soft water collected from the cistern to wash their clothes. So she and Georgia gathered their laundry to soak overnight to wash the next day. They had very few pieces of clothing, consequently almost all they had was soaking in the wash. Around the time they went to bed, the rain stopped but the ocean waves were still crashing and it was extremely cold.

About three in the morning, Nikolas sat straight up in bed. He suddenly knew that there were people in danger on the water. He quietly snuck out of the house and walked quite a distance along the beach towards the west. He spotted three helpless men. One was in the water clinging to the rock breakwater to rest while another was staggering to the shore. The third was huddled, shivering on the sand.

As he rushed to help them, Nikolas realized that the sea had taken every stitch of their clothing. He yelled to them, "Are you okay?" They were shaking from exhaustion and the ice-cold water and couldn't speak. He urged them, "Come with me. We will take care of you." The men could barely walk and leaned heavily on Nikolas' shoulders. As they stumbled along, Nikolas coaxed them with each step, encouraging them that they were almost there.

Finally, Nikolas helped the men into the house, gave them a sheet to cover up with and yelled to Arianna, "Light the fire! Light the fire so we can warm these people up!" As she struggled to realize what he was saying and comply, Nikolas guided the freezing men into bed and covered them with blankets. The men continued to shiver, even after being warmed for half an hour and given hot tea.

At last, the men were able to explain what had happened. They were from a distant northern island. "We were on our fishing boat when a huge storm, almost like a hurricane, came upon us suddenly. We were tossed about in the ocean for hours before the boat broke apart." Another added, "We could barely swim to shore in the violent, frigid waves."

194

Nikolas and Arianna shook their heads in sympathy but marveled that they made it to their shore. The third man acknowledged, "We had no more strength and might have perished down there on the cold beach if God hadn't sent you to us." Nikolas assured them that they were safe now and told them where they were.

As Arianna and Nikolas looked for some clothes for them to wear, they realized that their clothes were all wet in the laundry. They looked at the men with embarrassment as they offered Arianna's underwear (really like pantalets) as the only dry clothing they could find. Although the men looked slightly comical, they were grateful for anything. Arianna grabbed some of Nikolas' wet clothes, cleaned and wrung them out and hung them by the fire to dry for the morning.

The next day, the Stavrolakis gave the shipwrecked survivors a good meal, clothing and some money for their journey home. Nikolas escorted the men to the authorities to send word to their families and arrange for their travel back. The men were so overcome, they could hardly express their thanks. They all recognized that it was a miracle that the fishermen were alive and that Nikolas had been awakened in the middle of the night to go help them.

Chapter 20

All of the local children were invited to a Christmas party at the American base. Some of the adults were still skeptical about the motives of these strangers on their island. But the acts of kindness that they had shown won some guarded respect. The parents decided to take the chance, mostly out of curiosity, and accompanied the kids to the party. But they watched over the children carefully. A very jolly Santa Claus gave each child a small gift, like a book or toy. The adults and children enjoyed various unique and tasty foods and drinks that had been prepared for all of the guests. The occasion created some special memories for the children, and even the adults found themselves having fun.

Shortly after that, a few of the Americans visited the school and noticed how cold it was inside the old building. Most of the children did not wear heavy clothing. As a part of their lesson, the children were supposed to copy what the teacher had written on the chalkboard. But Barbara had trouble holding her pencil, her fingers were so cold. The Americans quickly got together to make some repairs to the schoolhouse. They sealed the windows and made some other basic improvements.

The next year, another group of American soldiers went to the school and measured the kids. They came back with boxes of clothes. The children had never seen anything like them. Barbara and Lea couldn't believe all of the ruffles and bows on their dresses. And the fabric was so delicate and shimmery. Stella was glad to see the others delight in their presents but was disappointed that there wasn't a dress to fit her.

One morning as the American officer with his vehicle full of children got close to the school, he pulled over for a minute outside of the base. A woman and a girl were standing outside. The man seemed to be introducing them to the kids, and the woman and girl looked happy to see them. The children guessed they were his wife and daughter and smiled and nodded politely to them. Stella thought that it was an honor that he would think highly enough of the young people to introduce them to his family.

Early in the spring, several gypsy families passed through Karidia. When they came by the Stavrolaki house and offered some items for sale, Arianna was skeptical about doing business that way. But Nikolas was drawn to a striking donkey that they were selling. He had worked with a similar animal in the past and wanted one again. This donkey had no teeth, but it stood regally tall and was a beautiful, shiny black color. Nikolas studied how alert and strong she was by her large ears that stood straight up. After Nikolas proudly bought his donkey, Arianna shook her head at him and then turned the gypsies away.

The girls ran to see the new animal and exclaimed how beautiful she was. They had never seen such a good-looking donkey. They gave her some food and water and left her to get used to her new barn.

Later, Nikolas loaded her with seed for the spring and summer vegetables and led her to the *Sterna* property. After she worked up a sweat, Nikolas proudly reached out to pet her, and black came off on his hands. Perplexed, he looked at his hand and then at the donkey. He rubbed her further and realized she had been painted with shoe polish. Underneath, she was white! He couldn't believe it. Why would anyone do that? Would it harm her? It couldn't be good for her. How could he have been so duped, and yet it was so unthinkable.

Nikolas had quite a job removing the dark shoe polish from all over the donkey's body. Arianna couldn't help it, she laughed until tears streamed from her eyes. Stella was shocked at first, but then chuckled at the humor of the situation. But more so, she mourned the loss of the donkey's proud façade— she had been so pretty.

Worse yet, they discovered that there was something wrong with her hip. Whenever she was loaded down too much or got too tired, she summarily wriggled her rear end to the ground, while keeping her

197

front legs extended. The gypsies had long gone, so the family was stuck with her.

The time came again for Nikolas and the girls to go back to Topos to plant another crop of tobacco. They didn't trust the new donkey for a journey that far away, so they took the horse. They were all a little frustrated because the crop from the previous year was still being stored in their house. Nikolas had tried several times to convince the government to sell it for them, but it was tied up in negotiations. He had already committed to a second crop, so they carefully planted and watered another round of seeds in the same area. At least they had the consolation of knowing that the crop from last year had been top quality, so this one probably would be also.

Before school let out for the summer each year, they always planned a graduation party. Stella was one of the ones finishing the six grades of schooling in Asprada. She went to school longer than her older sisters had and was hoping to continue her education to become a teacher.

That year in addition to the usual proceedings, the whole school planned a big thank you to the Americans who had been their benefactors in so many ways. The teacher chose Stella, Barbara and two boys to go to the base to extend the invitation to their special guests. She wrote a note in Greek with the phonetic English sounds to read to the security guard and to the man who taught them some English words, if they could find him.

The four young people picked some flowers and departed as emissaries. When they got to the gate, a soldier was positioned there and wondered what they wanted. Stella read the note with the date, time and that the pupils wish to thank you. She realized it probably didn't sound like English to him— pupil came out more like poopyil. He looked confused and shrugged his shoulders.

Finally the guard called someone to escort the children to the temporary building near the middle of the base. The kids' faces lit up when they recognized their man. They presented the flowers to him and instead of trying to read the note, Stella handed it to him. He read it and smiled and nodded that he understood. Some men

198

surprised the kids with bars of chocolate, and then somehow they knew it was time to leave. They were guided to the gate where they were on their own and proud to have accomplished their mission.

The teacher planned everything for the ceremony carefully, and the children practiced their roles. Barbara was chosen to recite the special poem. The teacher told her to wear her new white dress and shoes that the Americans had given her. That night Barbara practiced the poem over and over. Usually quite an entertainer anyway, she wasn't really nervous, but she wanted to do a good job. The next day, all of the officers and anyone who had a part in helping the children gathered outside the school. The teacher and students had decorated the platform with hand-picked flowers.

At the right time, Barbara was given the signal to stand before them. In her white dress and with the sun shining on her lighter, waist-length, curly hair, she almost looked angelic. With sincerity, poise and animated gestures, she delivered her thank you address (which rhymed in Greek). The interpreter rendered in English: "Behold our school, does it impress you, does it surprise you? It is because our American friends have helped us. Which one of these Americans do I dare greet or wish to thank, for all of them are a miracle. I wish I could be a rich person to present to each of them a great reward. If I were rich I would give them gold or silver to match their hearts. First to the commander and then to all of his nation and also to his interpreter, one very great thank you from all the pupils. All of the school is extending a thank you with a pure heart."

The audience clapped as she finished her poem and curtsied gracefully. The Americans were deeply moved by the honor from the students. The students, in turn, were grateful to be allowed to express their thanks in such a significant way.

After school let out for the summer, the family got busy again with harvesting. Stella and Barbara took the donkey to Lithos to pick vegetables. They knew they couldn't ride her, but they figured that if they could load her with baskets of produce, it would be worth their while. They got her up and over the mountain and to the field with little problem, other than a rest or two.

When they loaded the donkey with the vegetables and started back up the mountain, however, she decided to quit and sat on her hindquarters. "Oh no," they moaned to each other. The girls coaxed her— one talking to her while pulling at her bridle and the other standing behind her and trying to push up her rear end.

Barbara reasoned with the animal, "Stella here, is a graduate now. You are supposed to do what she says!" Stella, pushing from behind, laughed and only succeeded in sliding backwards herself. The donkey looked back at her and brayed mockingly.

Finally they gave up this approach, and both of them stood behind her, pushing her up and muttering, "*Galvanismeni marka* [You stinker]!" They got her to take some steps, but it wasn't long before she sat back down again. The girls looked at each other, throwing their hands up in helplessness, while Stella scoffed, "*Pali ta eethia mas* [Here we go again]!" They wiped their sweaty brows and continued trying to push her from behind whenever she stopped, all the way up the mountain. On the way down, she fared a little better.

When they finally arrived home, a frustrated Stella told her mother, "Wait until the gypsies come again and sell her back to them!" The donkey's antics became famous in the area. Nikolas went from being envied by people who asked him, "Where did you get that beautiful donkey?" to being a laughingstock. Nikolas felt foolish but took it in stride and tried to use her for smaller jobs when he could. He also very wisely refrained from making any jokes about working with cantankerous females.

Arianna was able to teach Georgia how to work the loom until she was able to weave very well. Sewing she was not so good at, but she taught her daughters what she could. As with most of her endeavors, Arianna would ask for God's blessing by making the sign of the cross over the material before she cut it.

Ioanna had learned embroidery and some basic stitching but wasn't able to make clothing. Arianna's sister in Prasinos Kampos sewed well but didn't feel that she could teach it. She suggested that Ioanna go to Heraklion for training, and maybe her Aunt Dorothea who lived there would know of places to stay and to learn. Nikolas and Arianna discussed sending Ioanna to the city for sewing instruction.

One morning, Nikolas told Arianna, "I have to sell a load of wheat in Heraklion. While I am there, I can try to make some arrangements for Ioanna and also check on the status of selling the tobacco. Do you need anything?" Arianna gave him a list of things and told him to be careful.

That night, Arianna and the girls prepared dinner and waited for Nikolas to come home. It was getting late, and they tried not to get worried. Arianna looked out the window and the girls each snuck a bite of food. "I guess we should go ahead and eat," Arianna conceded. "Your daddy did have a lot that he wanted to do in town today." They ate uneasily.

Abruptly, there was a loud knock at the door. Arianna jumped up. Panic came over her as she saw their own horse and wagon but with a distant neighbor. Nikolas was nowhere in sight. The girls joined her at the door and immediately despaired, thinking the worst. It was traumatic to see their horse and wagon but not their daddy.

"What happened?" Arianna's voice cracked and she was shaking. The man tried to reassure her, "He's alive, but there was an accident." His words echoed distantly in her mind as she struggled to comprehend that Nikolas was alive.

The man continued, "After Nikolas went around a curve on *Kako Oros* [Bad Mountain], he was hit from behind by a Greek military vehicle." When she heard the words "*Kako Oros,*" Arianna felt she was living her worst nightmare. That beautiful coastal portion of the road was also treacherous with its blind curves and unprotected steep cliff down to the ocean.

The neighbor went on, "The man was a new driver and he was with a convoy of trucks with soldiers coming from their military exercises. They've taken Nikolas to a hospital in Heraklion. I happened to pass by..." The man led her out to the horse and wagon and started to unhitch them. "The horse has some minor injuries here to her backside and legs but should be okay."

With the pulsing of her heartbeats reverberating in her ears and throat, Arianna was not even sure if she thanked the man as he left. Ioanna urged her mother, "Let's hurry to Prasinos Kampos. One of our relatives can take us to Heraklion." Arianna agreed but couldn't think straight to give the other girls any instructions but tearfully assured them, "We will send word or come for you. Pray. Just pray."

When Arianna and Ioanna left, the other girls took care of the horse. As they removed from the wagon the goods that Arianna had asked Nikolas to buy, they saw some wrapped goodies from a bakery in Heraklion and started crying. It never failed— despite all that he had to do, their *baba* always thought of them and wanted to bring them something special when he returned home from a trip. They pleaded, "Jesus, please don't let him die. We can't make it without him."

The girls continued praying unceasingly in their hearts to God. They couldn't focus on anything else. The man said he was alive, but what if he was dying or had died since then? They knew that mountain road was very dangerous. They couldn't help but think of the horrible stories of accidents and death. There was a time that a man from their area had been checking on his grapevines that were beyond that road, and on his way home he lost control of his bike and fell down the mountain. They found his body the next day. In their *baba*'s situation, they couldn't imagine his slow, frail rig withstanding a huge motorized vehicle. It was a miserable day while they waited and prayed.

Arianna and Ioanna arrived at the hospital to find out that Nikolas was alive and had already had x-rays. Miraculously the only thing broken was the index finger on his right hand. They were putting a cast on it. Arianna went to his side, "How are you feeling? Are you okay? We were so scared!" Nikolas answered, "I feel okay, just a little sore. How's the horse?" Although the horse was furthest from her mind at that moment, she knew that it was important too and reassured him, "A little bruised but okay. The girls are taking care of her. We were all so worried about you. We didn't know if…" Nikolas squeezed her hand.

202

Arianna turned to the medical team, "How is he?" The doctor cautiously comforted her, "He seems to be okay. He was very lucky. We want to keep him here for a few days to make sure there are no internal injuries or damage to his neck and back." For the first time, Arianna allowed herself to feel relieved, although she knew from her brother's accident that internal injuries could be serious.

Some of Arianna's relatives that had come with her to the hospital left to go reassure the girls. Eventually, Georgia heard a wagon coming and yelled to the others, "Come quick, someone's here." They ran to the door, not knowing whether to feel hope or dread. Innocently, they looked up to their uncle's face. He was smiling, "He's okay..." They exhaled as they each felt the release of a heavy burden. He continued explaining, "...just a broken finger. But he's going to stay there a few days to make sure there are no other problems. Tomorrow we can take you to see him." The girls smiled and clasped each other's arms in jubilant relief.

The girls kept their hopes up as they rode to the hospital with their uncle the next day. The hospital was a little intimidating, but when they saw their father, they knew that he was okay. He said that he felt great and joked and laughed with them. They couldn't stay long since it took so long to journey back, but he assured them that he would be home soon.

After a few days, the doctor did not see any signs of internal injuries so he sent Nikolas home, cautioning him to take it easy for a while. Arianna and the girls saw to it that Nikolas didn't exert himself when he got home— so much so that he joked with them about the luxury of being waited on hand and foot. At their first meal back home, they joined hands around the table and gave sincere and fervent thanks for God's miraculous protection and never-ending care of their family. They all knew the accident could have been much worse.

Chapter 21

Ioanna moved to Heraklion to learn how to sew. Her sisters were sorry to see her go away again, but this time it was closer and they knew it would be temporary. Ioanna was sad to leave and was still not certain that she would like sewing. But she was glad to help her family and knew that she had liked city life in Athens, so she looked forward to this new adventure.

Uncle Demetrios and Aunt Dorothea had a friend that she was able to stay with. Mrs. Delouraki was a nice lady who had just lost her husband. She welcomed Ioanna and gave her attention that she could no longer give her husband. Nikolas arranged for Ioanna to train at a place that advertised for girls from the villages to go to learn to sew. Ioanna's first few days seemed like very slow learning, but she realized that it would take time. She didn't know how these apprenticeships were supposed to work, so she would have patience.

***

One early morning in July, Stella, Barbara and Lea took the donkey to Lithos to pick some fruits and vegetables. With the three of them, they were able to pick the produce quickly. They loaded the donkey and headed back. As what was becoming typical, along the way the donkey decided to take a break and sat down. Stella and Barbara pushed her up from behind while Lea pulled her forward. They had quite a time trying to get the donkey to cooperate. They were frustrated but knew that getting angry wouldn't help, so they tried to maintain their humor as they struggled to shove the arthritic donkey up the mountain.

Meanwhile, Arianna and Georgia were below the balcony of the house packing kernels of wheat into a large barrel to store. In order to seal it well to protect the wheat, they put a cloth on top of the grains and topped that with about six centimeters of cool morning dirt before putting the lid on the barrel. While Arianna was pressing everything down evenly, Georgia had a bucket and was digging for more dirt from the east side of the yard behind the house.

When Georgia stood up, she thought that she was seeing things. The ocean was pulling back and forth in huge waves. She stood wide-eyed in amazement. Finally she found her voice and screamed, "*Mama*, come here! Hurry! Hurry!" Arianna came out from the storage area near the barn. She couldn't believe her eyes either. When she realized their danger, she hesitated a second to see if there was a way to save the chickens and their year's worth of wheat for making bread but then yelled, "Let's go upstairs. Upstairs, hurry!"

They left everything and ran up to the balcony to see what was happening to the ocean. They couldn't believe how big the waves got— almost like one big wave going back and forth. Since their house was on a small bluff, the second-story balcony was about six meters above the sea. The waves when they pulled away seemed about as high as the balcony. But when the water was coming back towards the house, it stayed almost to its usual place. At one point, the water receded for a very long time. It was surreal to see a tall wall of water way out in the distance. Everywhere they could see that used to be ocean was sand and a few rocks. They looked to their left and right and saw a whole new terrain that they had never seen before.

People started running from the surrounding farm lands towards their house to see what was happening. Georgia thought that the time that God parted the Red Sea for Moses and the Israelites must have looked something like this. It was the most awe-inspiring act of nature that they could ever imagine.

Stella, Barbara and Lea made it to the top of the mountain on their way home. The first thing they would always do was look towards the ocean. First, they would see the island of Dia off in the horizon, almost straight ahead of their house. Since it was shaped like a sleeping dragon and it "welcomed them back" after a long day's work, they called it their pet. When they were a little younger, Arianna would point to it and say, "There's our pet! We're almost home now, and it's downhill from here!" to encourage the tired youngsters. Then they would take a few more steps and gaze at the ocean, their next beautiful and comforting milestone on their way home.

But this time, the ocean wasn't there! Lea was momentarily disoriented and then flustered. She pointed and yelled, "Look!" The three of them stood with their mouths open, looking at dry land where the ocean used to be. They saw Dia and the familiar fields around them, so they had to be at the right place, but everything seemed wrong. How can something so "constant" no longer be there?

Barbara saw where the ocean stopped, quite a distance back, and couldn't believe how tall the wave stood. What on earth could cause it to stand up like that? From high up, they looked in both directions and couldn't believe how much land they saw. They were discombobulated and alarmed, but they didn't know what else to do but continue towards home.

Standing on the balcony, Arianna had a flash of realization. Here they were gaping at something that at any moment could let loose and swallow them up. She pleaded in faith, "Jesus, please save us! Bring the waters right back where they belong by the great power of Your hand! We ask You to save us and our house in Jesus' mighty name!"

After what seemed like hours, a violent rumbling noise intensified as the waves came towards them in one smooth motion. Arianna and Georgia stood on the balcony and watched as the water stopped exactly where it was supposed to. The waves normalized almost instantly. The people who had gathered let out a triumphant cheer while Arianna looked heavenward and exclaimed, "Thank You, my Savior!"

The local neighbors remained a while and kept talking about the phenomenon. Everyone marveled at the extent of the potential danger and then their sudden, perfect liberation. Some recognized that they probably did the wrong thing by gravitating towards the threat, while others thought that the waves were so high that they might not have been able to outrun them anyway.

206

When the girls made it home with the donkey and produce, Arianna's faith met her humanity, "It's a good thing you were away in case we drowned. We almost lost a year's worth of wheat too." While Arianna continued to visit with the other people, the girls who had returned asked Georgia to tell them all that she had seen. After she told them everything, the girls looked out to the ocean and couldn't believe how calm it had become.

In Heraklion, Ioanna heard people talking about a tsunami and how several buildings along their coast had flooded. Knowing that her home was also right along the sea, she immediately feared, "It's drowned my family!" She was upset at the almost inevitable thought and the fact that she couldn't find out any information about them. She was beside herself until finally Uncle Demetrios and Aunt Dorothea brought word that they were just fine, with no damage at all. With all that she had heard about destruction and concern with loss of life, she could hardly believe it, but she was so thankful.

Her family was relieved to hear that she and their extended family in Heraklion were all safe as well. Everywhere they all went for a while, the tsunami was the main topic of conversation. Word got around from people in the region and radio reports that there had been a large earthquake in the Aegean Sea north of them. The radio also reported that multiple territories had been affected by significant aftershocks, landslides and deaths.

More and more the Stavrolakis realized the extent of God's protection. Others had estimated that in Heraklion the waves reached a height of two meters, as far as thirty meters inland from the normal shoreline. And the earthquake had been centered closer to their house in Karidia. The areas just to the west and east of their house had taller cliffs, and still the water had flooded those upper fields. But in their own case, not even the basement area was flooded. Arianna thought that an angel must have been protecting them by stopping the water right where it belonged.

As part of the storytelling, Stella, Barbara and Lea told their parents how unmanageable the donkey continued to be. Stella spoke up, "She really makes it harder than if we didn't have her at all." Nikolas had worked with her also and was arriving at the same conclusion. It really wasn't worth maintaining her when all she could do was carry such small loads that they could carry on their own, and only on level or downhill slopes.

Nikolas told the girls to say their goodbyes (or good riddance as the case may be), and he sold her. The donkey was somewhat notorious in the area, so he wasn't able to get much for her, but he wouldn't have wanted to cheat anyone anyway. Nikolas mourned the loss of a small part of his dream but was happy that she would have an easier life and wouldn't hurt as much. Arianna thought it was a good example of not judging something by its looks.

The girls, especially Stella and Barbara, settled into a summer routine. They woke up with the sun, did some chores until about eleven, swam and then came in for lunch. After about forty-five minutes' rest for napping or reading, they did some more jobs and then swam again in the early evening.

Lea tagged along with Stella and Barbara when the tasks weren't too strenuous. There were various jobs, depending on the needs of the family, and the girls either worked together or took turns. The sisters would often help clean the house, prepare meals and do the laundry. A couple of times a day they walked the goats, usually with ropes so that the girls could guide them to the grass or weeds and away from any growing vegetables. The many harvests throughout the summer required their labors. The girls also spent time either crocheting or working the loom, which Georgia was very good at and was teaching Barbara. Arianna would supervise their handiwork, looking over their shoulders to tell them that they must crochet so many centimeters before they could go swimming.

When August came around each year, they had a practice of taking note of the weather during the first ten days. They believed the conditions of each day would represent the weather for each month ahead. With the recent bizarre exhibition of nature, they were particularly alert to possible disruptions. This general forecast could help them to know the best times to plant the different crops.

It became time again to harvest the tobacco leaves. Over a period of weeks, the girls got up very early, picked the gummy leaves and

208

strung them up to dry. It was tedious, dirty and stinky labor, and they couldn't wait to get it out of their house. They had it all carefully stacked in bundles as Nikolas continued to press the government to sell it. Again the authorities thought the crop was top rate, and again there were delays in negotiations for them to sell it for him. Meanwhile, they had weighed and measured everything and cautioned him against losing a single leaf.

Arianna had not really wanted to promote that crop in the first place. Then they worked incredibly hard only to store two years' worth in their house. But ghastliest of all, suddenly bugs were everywhere. They were drawn to the tobacco leaves. Crawling and flying bugs were all over the storage area. Arianna was incensed and felt so powerless to do anything about it.

Nikolas immediately informed the government of the disaster and insisted they do something. They sent the proper officials from Athens to their house to assess the situation. When they got there, they were apologetic that the leaves were no longer viable for sale. They would have to burn the leaves in a supervised bonfire. Nikolas had a sinking feeling when he realized the futility of all of their efforts, but there was nothing more that could be done. They had to get the stuff out of their house.

The officials weighed everything before burning it outside on their beach. The girls cried when they saw all of their hard work and Stella's plan to be a teacher up in smoke. Plus it smelled terrible. The whole experiment was so disheartening. Nikolas apologized to Arianna. Now that her house was back in order, she was more charitable, "Most of your innovative ideas have put us ahead. Now we know not to try that one again."

In the fall, right after they stomped the grapes for preparing wine, they got ready to make *raki* [concentrated alcohol]. In order to own and operate a distilling apparatus, a permit from the government was needed. Nikolas' father used to have a still, but Nikolas never did. So he approached a local still owner to be put on the list for the next *raki*-making party. After they crushed the grapes and poured the juice in the wooden barrels to make the wine, they collected all of the leftover pulp from the filter and winepress. This residue of either red or white grapes was put it in earthen barrels to ferment for many days.

When it was their allotted time at the still, the Stavrolakis brought the fermented grape remnants, along with plenty of wood to burn and any food they wanted to share. They put the pulp in a copper pot over an open fire. Then they put another copper pot upside down on top of the other and used a water and flour mixture to seal the connection. The top pot had a long tube coming off to the side. The heated alcohol rose as a gas to the top of the pot and through this tube. After it was cooled along the tube, the alcohol was collected from the other side as liquid.

The process took some time, so in the meantime they visited with friends. They could add to the party by cooking some meat or vegetables over the open fire. During each person's turn at the still, many of the components of *raki* preparation had to be carefully measured and recorded for the government. The *raki* was used as a drink in small amounts or as an external rubbing alcohol. *Ouzo* was similar but had more of an anise or black licorice flavor. If they wanted that, they bought it since only certain large manufacturers were allowed to make it.

***

Back in Heraklion, Ioanna wasn't having a very successful attempt at learning to sew. She had been patient for several months but really wasn't learning anything. She figured out that the girls who had come from the other villages had already interned under seamstresses for a while. They were there to learn the arithmetic of the measuring and cutting. So without the same baseline knowledge, Ioanna wasn't able to pick up what they were talking about. Besides, it seemed to her that really all they discussed were their boyfriends and parties. They sent Ioanna to go buy the thread or buttons that they needed, which at first she had no idea where to find. Mrs. Delouraki continued to treat her like a daughter, so at least her living arrangements were a comfort.

One day, Ioanna finally broached the subject with Aunt Dorothea. "I know *Baba* is paying good money and is counting on me to learn, but I am really not learning anything there. I have tried to be patient,

but it has been a long time. Is there somewhere else that I can go?"
Aunt Dorothea did some investigating and set her up with one of the
best seamstresses in the city. She explained the new situation to
Ioanna, who was grateful for the new opportunity.

***

The months passed and the holiday season began. As per the usual
Greek Orthodox tradition, the Stavrolakis fasted from meats, dairy,
eggs and sweets the forty days before Christmas. In all of the four
townships, they could only find one area that had a couple of
evergreen trees. Nikolas and the younger girls walked over to the
ravine a little west of their house where they used to walk the
turkeys. In order to preserve the trees for the future, they only cut a
limb from one of the trees. Arianna put it in a bucket of water in the
house. The girls decorated it with various homemade creations.

Arianna and Georgia made *melomakarouna* [citrus-flavored finger
cookie dipped in syrup and topped with nuts and cinnamon] and
kourabiethes [flaky butter cookies topped with powdered sugar] that
they would enjoy on Christmas day, after the fast. Before every
holiday, Georgia thoroughly cleaned the house, including the
bottoms of the chair legs. After the Christmas Eve and Christmas
services, they feasted and celebrated as a family.

For New Year's, after services they enjoyed *vasilopita* [pound cake].
Following the fun tradition, Arianna had baked inside it a special
treat like a coin. Whoever found the prize in their portion got to keep
it.

***

Ioanna spent the holidays with Mrs. Delouraki and Uncle Demetrios
and Aunt Dorothea. Her aunt was kind to loan her a coat for the
evening Christmas Eve service since it was so cold. She missed her
family at home but was glad that she could be with some relatives.
Several months had gone by at her latest arrangement with a
seamstress, but she still wasn't learning anything. The lady did a fine
job but wasn't really a teacher. Ioanna found herself doing odd jobs
and the lady's housecleaning more than learning to sew. The closest
she came to sewing was picking up the pins that had fallen on the
floor.

211

Ioanna had been looking forward to Epiphany, which commemorated Jesus' baptism on January sixth. Her church back home had an annual service, but in the large coastal city of Heraklion, they had a bigger festival. The priest would bless a cross and then throw it into the sea. Men who wanted to brave the cold water could dive in to search for it. Whoever found it was thought to be blessed for the year. There would be a parade, dancing, food and celebration, and Ioanna was excited to see the Heraklion celebration for the first time.

The seamstress, however, wanted Ioanna to do her laundry instead. Ioanna thought that this was the last straw. Not only was her father paying this lady good money and she wasn't learning, but she definitely wasn't there to do her housework on a religious holiday. Ioanna quit then and there. She enjoyed the festival and then later discussed with Mrs. Delouraki what she should do. Mrs. Delouraki told her, "I know someone who used to be a seamstress but has retired. Let me see if she would be able to teach you."

The retired seamstress was willing to show Ioanna a few things. But since she no longer had a business, they were only able to practice with patterns and paper and no fabric. The lady's eyesight was not too good, but she was at least able to show her how to measure and the basic principles of sewing.

After a little while, Arianna brought Georgia to visit Ioanna. Arianna had bought some shiny pink fabric and wanted her to make a dress for Georgia. Ioanna was nervous about the project but did the best that she could. When the dress had been completed and Georgia tried it on, Ioanna knew something wasn't quite right. It fit well but it didn't hang exactly like it should have. No one had told her about fabric bias. Since she had only used paper as practice "fabric," she wasn't aware that thread line alignment affected the stretch of real cloth.

Georgia wore the dress anyway; she was proud of Ioanna's accomplishment. But Ioanna was conscious of her mistake and learned to line up the fabric correctly before cutting it. The retired seamstress encouraged her that she did a really good job for her first attempt with real fabric. After a rocky start from her various learning experiences, Ioanna finally thought that at least she had taken a step in the right direction, though she still felt far from a sewing career.

Chapter 22

When sixteen-year old Ioanna returned from Heraklion to Karidia in April, she didn't feel very proficient but was willing to try to sew for her family. Before long, she was inundated with sewing requests from members of their community. They brought her all kinds of projects, and most of the clothes or fabrics were in tatters.

One lady brought her an old man's wool coat and a picture of a boy's coat that she wanted made out of it. When Ioanna lifted it to look at it, dust flew everywhere. "How am I supposed to make anything out of this?" Ioanna asked herself. She washed it in the sea and ironed it with a coal-heated iron.

After putting a lot of thought and days of labor into it, the coat turned out lovely. When she was asked how much payment she required, Ioanna didn't know what to say. Her only frame of reference was the ten drachmas that she earned in a whole day of braiding onions. Ioanna asked for ten drachmas (about thirty cents). The lady was indignant, acting as if she were asking for the sun and the moon. Ioanna didn't mean to insult her, and she knew the lady was not able to pay her. "Ma'am, I don't need the money. You just take it for your boy," she told her.

Another time, a lady wanted her to make a robe with velvet, lace and other fancy accents. She brought Ioanna the basic material but none of the accessories. So Ioanna purchased those herself. When the time came for the lady to pay, the same thing happened. In essence, Ioanna was losing money. Glad for the ability to help some people, she continued to accept requests. She often sat under the tree in their front yard and occasionally had a line of people approaching her.

Since their house was on the road between the American base and Heraklion, military vehicles passed by often. A captain noticed Ioanna sitting out front and observed that she was sewing. One day he was driving by with an interpreter, and they saw Nikolas also in front of the house, so he pulled over. Nikolas was dirty from the field and he was leading the horse. "Excuse me, sir," the captain said through the interpreter. Nikolas stopped and greeted him, "*Ya sas* [Hello]!" The captain admired their house and surroundings.

Then the American said, "I am a captain at the base down the road. I have driven by and noticed a young lady sewing and wondered if she might be interested in doing some small sewing projects for us. We would pay her to sew additional stripes on uniforms or other minor alterations." Nikolas wasn't too sure about the idea but thought that he would start by seeing how Ioanna felt. He responded, "We can ask her."

When Ioanna heard the request, she was confident in her ability to help with what he needed and replied, "Sure I can." Nikolas told the men that Ioanna was agreeable but that they would discuss the idea further. The captain thanked him as he and the interpreter left.

When Arianna heard about the American's request for Ioanna to sew for them, she objected, "I know the Americans have been kind, but they are still regarded by most people as outsiders. If these young men come to our house often, it may not be good for the girls." Nikolas agreed, "I am very concerned about our reputation. But if they don't stay long and the sewing is done out front… It could be good money for easy work."

After some deliberation by the family and persuasion by the American captain, they cautiously agreed to try a few projects. The interpreter conveyed their desire to limit the number of visits by bringing several things in one batch.

Ioanna thought the jobs that the captain brought to her were very easy. They even brought her the thread to use. When she had finished, he asked her what she charged for each uniform. She thought for a minute. All she knew was the Greek price, which really she never got. She had tried to charge ten drachmas (thirty cents) for a whole coat, but the captain just asked to add a little piece of material to each side of a shirt. She answered, "Three drachmas (ten cents) per shirt?" The captain thought that was insulting, so he gave

215

her more. Ioanna thought to herself, "Wow, this is the business to be in!"

Ioanna later remarked to her family how polite and gentle the American seemed to be. Georgia teased her, "I think he likes you." Ioanna didn't think so and brushed it off saying, "He just needed assistance with a task, and anyway I am sure that they have strict rules about that."

After a few weeks of Ioanna's sewing for them, the captain again approached Nikolas, "We are expecting many families of the servicemen to come and live on the base soon. If we made a place for her and provided a sewing machine for her to use, could your daughter come to work on the base with us? She can continue to sew the insignias, but we think the families will bring more sewing needs." Nikolas told him that they would have to think about that.

As much as the Americans had done for the community, and especially the children, the Greek people were still distrustful of the outsiders. That, coupled with strict rules of propriety with regards to his sixteen-year old daughter, could cause this interaction to tarnish their family's reputation, even if everything was above reproach.

Nikolas and Arianna knew in their hearts that the Americans were kind and honorable people. But if everyone else on the island considered the girls "ruined," what would their long-term prospects be? On the other hand, the money for relatively easy work could be God's provision for them. And Barbara was finishing the last weeks of her schooling, so she could help in assuming some of Ioanna's responsibilities in the fields and at home. It was a difficult decision.

Nikolas proposed a possible compromise. In addition to hiring Ioanna, could they find a position for Nikolas as well, so that he could effectively be her escort? The captain thought that maybe they could find a place for him as a gardener. He asked them both to go to the base to fill out applications and have pictures taken.

When Nikolas and Ioanna got to the American base, the translator helped them fill out the forms. Ioanna couldn't believe all of the questions they asked on the application. They wanted to know not just their age and address but about all of their beliefs— were they Nazi sympathizers, did they have Communist leanings... They filled out everything and waited to hear from the Americans.

In a nearby area, a family raised pigs and also, not so coincidentally, started a trash-collecting business at the base. Their son came up to Ioanna one day and asked, "Have you lost anything?" Ioanna didn't know what he was talking about and said, "No, I'm not missing anything." He persisted, "I found something that belongs to you, but you have to pay me a good price to get it back." Ioanna wouldn't budge, "I didn't lose anything so I am not going to pay you anything." Finally he gave her the pictures that they had taken at the base. He had found them in the trash. Ioanna thanked him but didn't know what that meant. Maybe the Americans didn't need the pictures anymore, or maybe their applications were denied.

The captain came by again and told Nikolas, "I don't know what happened, but we can't find your applications. Do you mind coming back to the base to fill them out again?" After they kept returning and the applications kept getting lost a few times, Nikolas guessed that the Greeks who worked in the base office were throwing them away. They all knew that the captain was scheduled to be transferred. Maybe the Greek workers figured that he would become too occupied before he left to follow up on their applications, and no one else would know the difference. Nikolas wasn't sure if they were trying to protect Ioanna and her reputation or if they had other motives, but they were glad when Ioanna was finally accepted to work at the base. Nothing had yet opened up for Nikolas.

Before he left, the captain asked Ioanna through the interpreter, "They are still building the area that we can use for your sewing. In the meantime, could you work in the dining hall?" Ioanna agreed, and her hours were set from six in the morning until two o'clock in the afternoon. The work was much lighter than she was used to— refilling the salt and pepper, cleaning the drips from the coffee pot, sweeping the floors or cleaning the tables. They had other Greek workers employed to cook the meals and wash the dishes, but Ioanna was the only person in the dining area.

The Americans noticed how willingly and thoroughly Ioanna worked and asked her if she knew anyone else like her in the area whom they could hire to work with her. Ioanna answered, "I have a sister who is a year older than I am. I can ask my parents if she can come to work here." They agreed and Georgia was hired immediately. She applied one day and started her job the next day.

Ioanna couldn't believe the amount of her first monthly paycheck. Nine-hundred drachmas (thirty dollars) was more than she had ever seen. "And the work was a breeze," she told their parents. Georgia added, "And they are very nice people. They treat us with care and respect."

Stella was glad for her sisters but had other things on her mind. Ever since she made the vow to God that she would go to the distant monastery if He saved her father from the well accident, she reminded her mother of her obligation. She couldn't feel at peace until she fulfilled her promise. Arianna asked around to get directions, and one summer day when they were already at their furthest field in Topos, the two of them followed the river even more south to walk to the church. Stella thought to herself that she had no idea how far it would be when she made the vow. But she felt so much better when she was finally able to say her prayer of thanks at the altar.

A little over a month after Georgia started at the base, the Americans again asked the girls if they knew someone else who could come work with them. When they told Nikolas, he went to Asprada to ask a relative of his if he wanted one of his daughters to work at the base. He started to explain the generous salary and great working conditions when his cousin cut him off, "No way! You bring dishonor to our family name. I will not let my daughter be so disgraced." Nikolas left, thinking that he could identify with his reluctance. But he was a little surprised that even after his girls had tried it out, he didn't trust his own family to vouch for the Americans.

Georgia and Ioanna were a little embarrassed to tell their boss that they couldn't find anyone who wanted to work there. Ioanna tentatively offered, "We have a younger sister, but she is only

218

fourteen. She doesn't even have her legal identification yet." They answered, "We don't care how old she is, as long as she works as hard as you do."

After Nikolas and Arianna gave their permission, arrangements were made for Stella to start at the base the day after the Fourth of July. Georgia and Ioanna knew that the Americans were going to shoot fireworks from the base beach on the fourth, so the family went outside on the balcony to watch them from a distance. Spectacular colors and shapes filled the sky as the girls stood gazing, transfixed.

The next day when Georgia, Ioanna and Stella reported to the base, they were shocked to hear that the base colonel had passed away the day before. The Americans had many things to deal with so they asked Stella to report back on the seventh for her orientation. Georgia and Ioanna continued to serve the very solemn military unit.

When Stella returned, she was shown around the base, and she recognized the temporary buildings that she had seen there as a visiting schoolgirl. Maybe because she was the youngest, the American servicemen and the Greek workers were extra nice and protective of Stella. She and her sisters gained respect by anticipating needs and quickly taking care of them. They maintained a proper balance between staying quietly out of the way and being friendly when others spoke to them.

The girls found themselves learning more English. On her breaks, Stella enjoyed hearing about America, like the Statue of Liberty, the Grand Canyon and Yosemite. Sometimes they showed her maps or pictures. There was also another group who stayed at the table after lunch for a Bible study. They were always so nice and called each of the girls "Sister."

Best of all, Stella liked her paycheck and some of the fun things she could do with it. Since they got off work at two, Georgia and Ioanna were often still needed to help in the fields and do housework. But Stella was younger and Arianna worried that she was so skinny, so she didn't push her to work as hard after putting in her day at the base. Stella sometimes went into Heraklion and liked to buy books or magazines to read. It was also nice to be able to shop for some clothes or shoes if she wanted. With three of the girls earning money at the base, they decided that the next year they wouldn't need to grow cotton to make their own clothes.

One day Arianna asked Stella, "Do you want to save some of your earnings to go to school to become a teacher?" Stella considered it a moment and answered, "I thought I wanted to be a teacher, but now I am not so sure. I am enjoying working at the base." Though she couldn't put it into words, Stella felt there was a sense of excitement and importance at the American base. She thought it was interesting to watch the comings and goings and learn about another culture. While Stella was working there, she started to eat meat again, which Arianna hoped would give her more strength.

In August, Georgia had a couple of days off and decided to stay at her grandmother's storage home in Prasinos Kampos in order to better be available to supervise making the raisins from the field in that area. In the morning, there was a knock at the door. Georgia was surprised, since no one usually lived there, but someone must have seen her. She opened the door to a lady that she recognized from the village. She was dressed in all black.

Georgia welcomed her, "Come in." The lady replied, "No, I just wanted to stop and talk to you here. I wanted to come in the quiet of the morning to catch you. You know I lost my son over a month ago?" Georgia nodded. She knew that he had been tragically killed by a hidden landmine. "I am so sorry," Georgia said sincerely. The woman continued, "Before he died, he told me that he was in love with you. He wanted me to approach your family to ask if you could be his bride."

Georgia froze, not knowing what to say. She had recently turned eighteen, but she wasn't ready for these conversations yet. The woman promised, "You will always be my daughter-in-law." Georgia knew that she was hurting so she didn't argue but lingered sympathetically. As she started to leave, the woman pleaded, "Don't tell anyone. I just had to tell you." The woman wiped her eyes and hurried down the road. Georgia was stunned. She barely knew the young man and had no idea of his intentions. She was sad about the tragedy but she didn't have romantic feelings for him. She felt a little touched and a little awkward about the visit but honored the mother's wishes and didn't talk about it.

Nikolas brought the young chestnut horse to Prasinos Kampos to check on Georgia and the raisins. The faithful mother horse was aging, so for the past several months he had been using the younger horse more. The raisins had not quite dried, so he loaded up the horse with baskets of some of the remaining grapes and headed across to Lithos to check on things there.

As Nikolas came to the hill leading down to the large well that the whole village used to draw water, he pulled firmly on the reins. He knew that the horse already remembered where the water was, and it was a hot day, so he held tightly. But the horse was thirsty and with a burst of energy galloped down the hill.

Nikolas saw his aunt drawing water at the well and shouted to warn her of the oncoming horse, but it was too late. The loaded-down horse accidentally knocked her into the well. Nikolas yelled for help and ran to the edge of the well. "Are you okay?" his voice echoed down the ten-meter reservoir. He heard splashing and shouting, "Help! Get me out of here!" Nikolas was relieved. The well was wide, deep and full of water, which helped her situation.

Other men came running and they rigged some rope to lower Nikolas down and pull them both up. When Nikolas was lowered down the well, his aunt was scared and screaming but appeared to be okay otherwise. As he reached for her, he told her to grab onto him. Her long, thick, wet dress hindered her movements, but she managed to reach for Nikolas. He was able to get her to hold onto the rope then call to the men above, "Okay, pull!"

The men pulled her and then Nikolas out of the well. The aunt was shaken but miraculously unhurt. Nikolas thanked the men and escorted his aunt home, sincerely apologizing about the accident. "I am just glad to be on dry land. Thank you for your help," she sputtered with relief.

When Nikolas got back to the barn at the end of the day, he gave the chestnut horse some water and oats and rubbed her down. Then he patted her mother saying, "I really miss you out there. You have been and always will be the best." He noticed that the black horse had been getting whiter and whiter as it got older and cringed at his next thoughts.

Later he told Arianna about the accident at the well. Then he commented, "I know that can happen with any horse, but I couldn't help but think it might not have happened with its mother. But I can't really use her much— I don't want to hurt her by pushing her to do what I need her to do." Arianna nodded, and he continued, "She's really your horse, so I wanted to ask you about what we should do with her. I don't want to see her die, but I would think that might be even harder on the girls." Arianna agreed, "Yes, she's been with us all of their lives. You think we should sell her?" Nikolas answered, "I don't want to, but we should think about it. We might get a little better price, and I might feel a little less guilty about selling an older horse if she could still do some light work, maybe on more level terrain."

Arianna released Nikolas to do what he thought was best with the older horse, but it took Nikolas a couple of months before he could bring himself to consider any arrangements. He knew that because of their attachment, he would need to sell her to someone out of the area. They tried to prepare the girls as best as they could.

One day a man and his two boys came from the other end of the island to see the horse. Nikolas was away, and Ioanna answered the door and took them to see the horse. The man seemed interested and asked her, "Does she kick or bite?" Ioanna wanted to terminate the deal so she fibbed, "Yes." She was successful at thwarting the arrangement and the men left without her. When Nikolas found out what happened, he was stern with Ioanna, "I know that you care about the horse, but it was wrong for you to lie and interfere with my plans. I am your father and the one who decides what's best. It's not easy to find an easy life for her away from here— you are not to meddle!"

Later when a man came from Heraklion to see the horse, Ioanna did not stand in his way. Arianna and the girls cried when he took off with their beloved friend. She had been a faithful member of the family and it was heartbreaking to see her go.

Nikolas himself struggled to hold back tears and found an excuse to walk off by himself. He couldn't help but think of all that she had helped bring them through— transporting them and their things different places during the war, working the olive press, plowing the fields, taking the sick to the doctor, laboring during impossible destitution after the war, carrying a heavy buffet on her back from one town to another, parading a war bride during her wedding and mothering several foals. She survived after transporting equipment for the Germans and after being hit by a vehicle on a dangerous road. And the countless memories associated with his wife and daughters— how protective she was, the many trips up and down a steep and rocky mountain, the exhilarating ocean swims with her and the years of loyal friendship… There could never be a horse more special to him.

Chapter 23

When school started that fall, Lea was the only girl in the Stavrolaki family to have classes. After being accustomed to following her older sisters around, she was apprehensive about walking to Asprada by herself. Arianna was also nervous about her nine-year old embarking on the long journey on her own, but she knew that Lea would soon meet up with other students along the way. Over the next several months, Lea adjusted to her routine, while the other family members continued their various jobs and responsibilities.

The next spring, Arianna and her mother planned to go to a cousin's engagement party in another village. Her mother came to their house as they had arranged, but something came up and Arianna couldn't go with her. It was Georgia's day off, so Arianna suggested to her, "You go in my place."

Georgia was surprised. Usually she didn't attend many functions. Sometimes Arianna took Ioanna to those things but mostly the girls were kept out of sight, with Georgia usually in the kitchen. Georgia knew that the family needed to be represented and it was her duty to go where she was sent, so she joined her grandmother in waiting for the bus.

When they reached the girl's village, almost everyone had already gathered. There was music and dancing, and they were roasting meats over an open fire. Georgia knew only some of the family members. Although she was a little uncomfortable at first, Georgia was always sweet and friendly and was well received by everyone. She politely conversed with those she was introduced to and offered to help with anything that was needed.

Many other girls were helping to transport the gifts, so a relative handed her a tray with expensive perfume to take from the groom to the bride. After Georgia greeted a few more people, she spent the rest of the evening in the house sitting next to her grandmother, as was proper for a single young lady.

A few days later, Arianna approached Georgia, "Did you have a good time at the engagement party?" Georgia answered, "Yes, they had a great celebration." Arianna gently probed, "What all did you do? Did you meet any interesting people?" Georgia told her about all of the food, music, dancing and fancy gifts. She added, "There were several people I didn't know, but I mostly stayed with *Yiayia* [Grandmother]."

Arianna tried a more direct question, "Do you remember the young man from another town who played with the musicians? He is a friend of your cousin." Georgia thought that her mother was acting strangely, "I don't know who or what you are talking about."

Finally Arianna explained, "We had someone ask us about you through Aunt Dorothea. The young man had been engaged to another girl a while back, but she passed away. He had built a large home and her family had helped furnish it. Her family encouraged him to find another wife and said that they would accept her. He hadn't been interested in anyone until he saw you. He wants to buy you a wedding ring."

Georgia had recently turned nineteen but was mostly more guarded around boys than interested in them. As the oldest, she was always afraid that someone with self-seeking motives would too aggressively pursue her. She felt the burden of setting an example in choosing someone honorable and good. This man might be, but she didn't know him. Even if she had the opportunity to get to know him, she knew that she wasn't ready.

Georgia was grateful that her mother wasn't pressuring her to accept as she replied, "I am not ready to be married to him or to anybody else." Arianna nodded and gave her a minute in order not to coerce her. She then asked, "Do you know when you might be ready? The young man apparently said that if he is going to marry anyone, you are the one. We have to give them an answer because you remember they have been hurt, and we don't want to hurt them again."

Georgia understood that but didn't want to talk about it anymore. Arianna asked, "Do you need a month or two to get used to the idea?" Georgia was starting to get vexed, "I can't give you a date." Arianna clarified, "Not a date, just an approximate time so I can tell them." Georgia said with finality, "I don't want to hear about it anymore. I will tell you how I feel a year from now."

Georgia's spirits lifted when she walked outside and saw their old horse drinking at their small trough at the side of the house. She walked up to hug her as her owner apologized, "We were just passing through and she came straight here." Georgia assured him, "That's okay. I am glad to see her." The man urged the horse back towards the road. Georgia said goodbye, "Go on, girl." She couldn't help but wonder at how things change. She had vivid memories of the war and hard times right after the war, so she was glad that some things had changed. But other changes were sad or scary.

Barbara, on the other hand, wanted a change. She had been out of school for a year since she had finished the sixth grade the previous spring. With her older sisters working at the base the past many months, much of the burden of both the house and fields had fallen on her. She had many recollections of trying to learn things by herself, like the first time she tried to fry something. The oil got too hot, and it splattered and burned her foot— she still had the scar. She was the only one who could walk the goats twice a day. She brought the field workers their meals and worked in the fields herself.

"It's not fair," Barbara told her parents at the dinner table one night. "My older sisters get to earn money at the base. I have to do harder work, including their share, without getting paid and without learning or training for anything." While Arianna praised her and thanked her for helping them keep everything together, Nikolas looked thoughtful and then asked, "Is there any skill you want to learn?" Arianna suggested, "You have learned some fine embroidery and sewing from Ioanna and loom work from Georgia." Barbara answered, "Yes, but I enjoy talking to people more. I think I would like to fix people's hair."

Nikolas and Arianna looked at each other in surprise. In many ways, given the life they had been used to, getting one's hair done seemed like such a luxury. But they knew times were changing, and the profession was respectable. When Arianna didn't say anything, Nikolas said, "I don't know how you train for that, but I can ask around the next time I am in Heraklion if you are serious." Barbara got excited, "Yes, please!"

Nikolas arranged for Barbara to stay with her Aunt Dorothea and assist a beautician in Heraklion. "It's not really formal training, but maybe you can have a break from here for a little while and see if you even like the occupation," Nikolas told her. Arianna worried about her going to the big city and taking this on, as she was only thirteen, but Nikolas reassured her that Dorothea would look after her.

Barbara enjoyed seeing people coming and going and visiting at the beauty parlor. She watched the hairdresser very carefully but didn't do much herself. She handed the lady the rollers or pins and swept the cut hair from the floor. Her aunt didn't want her to be idle, so she also assigned a certain number of centimeters to crochet each day.

After several weeks, the beautician asked Barbara to run an errand to get a beauty supply. She gave her the money and told her exactly where to go. Barbara was eager to be helpful, so she went to the store for her. However because of that, she didn't have time to complete her designated crocheting.

When she explained to her aunt, Dorothea was troubled and told the woman, "She is a young girl from a small town. Anything could have happened, and I am responsible for her. She is going home!" Barbara was a little disappointed but thought that it was probably time to go back and help at home anyway. She thanked the lady for the time that she was able to watch and learn.

When Barbara returned from Heraklion and they gathered together again, Nikolas asked her how she liked living in the city. "I liked it," she replied. Nikolas mused, "Hmm, and I know Ioanna enjoyed city life…" Arianna recognized the look that Nikolas had when he was considering a new venture and wondered what he was up to now.

Ever since Barbara had expressed her frustration with the field work, Nikolas started thinking more about the girls' future. He realized that they really shouldn't have to be working like field hands. Most of them had several years' education, and more jobs might be available in the city. The positions at the base were working out great for now but may not always be available.

Finally, Nikolas came out with it, "What would you all think about saving your earnings to buy a little property in Heraklion and build a house? You could build different stories so that each of you could have a level. That way, if you ever wanted to work or live in the city, you would have a place." The girls were surprised and delighted. They all started talking at once, but Arianna interrupted, "How are they going to pay for this multi-story mansion?" Nikolas ignored her sarcasm and said, "They can build it little by little. And if they aren't ready to move in, it can be rented out in the meantime."

When the girls seemed to be in agreement, Nikolas said that he would keep his eyes open for a good deal on some land. The girls were too enthusiastic for Arianna to object, but all of a sudden it seemed like her babies were all grown up and could be moving too far away.

One fall day when Arianna was in Lithos, Zoe, Nikolas' sister, found her and pulled her aside. Zoe told Arianna, "I had someone ask me about Georgia." Arianna asked, "What about Georgia?" Zoe was impatient at what she thought was obvious, "About wanting to marry her." Arianna exclaimed, "Oh! Who is it?" Zoe told her the name of one of her husband's relatives and stressed, "He would be a very good catch." Arianna told her, "I don't think Georgia is ready, but I will mention it to her and let you know."

Arianna waited for the right moment to ask Georgia. The last time they had discussed such things, she had seemed tense. When Georgia seemed relaxed and was alone, Arianna asked her if she knew the man. Georgia said, "I think I met him once. Why?" Arianna told her, "Your Aunt Zoe said that he was interested in you. I know you said that you didn't think you would marry this year, but I thought I would ask you, just in case…" Georgia replied, "No,

228

nothing's changed. I don't want to marry or commit to anyone anytime soon."

Arianna said no more on the subject but carried the message to Zoe. Arianna was starting to wonder if she could handle this for five girls. Part of her wanted to see her older girls happily settled, but most of her preferred to keep them at home with her forever.

She wasn't the only one feeling nostalgic. One night soon afterwards, they heard a noise outside the house. When Nikolas investigated, he was surprised to see Arianna's old horse. He gave her an affectionate pat, "Hi, girl. What are you doing here?" The horse whinnied, as if in response. Nikolas looked around and shouted out, "Is anybody there?" he rubbed her down a little and gave her a few oats and water but kept her at the front of the house so that the owner could find her.

Arianna and the girls came out to give her a quick greeting, but they didn't stay out too long. It was a little cool outside, and they also didn't want to confuse the horse too much. Nikolas kept an eye out until she was safely returned to her grateful owner. Apparently the horse had traveled a long way to steal a visit with her former workmate and enduring friend.

The next day, Georgia ran over to the *Sterna* field to pick some broccoli and cabbage. Emilios, a young man from their area, was working in a nearby field and came over to say hello to Georgia. He remarked, "Don't you love these cooler days?" Georgia replied, "Yes, it's a beautiful day, sunny but cool."

Emilios asked her, "Did I see your old horse roaming around yesterday?" Georgia said, "Yes, I'm not sure if she ran away or got lost and came to our house last night." He commented, "It's interesting that they can find their way back to the place they were used to. But you had her a long time. Do you miss her?" Georgia sighed, "Yes. She and I were born on the same day. *Baba* got her as a present for *Mama*, but really we all loved her." He gave her a sympathetic nod and then waved as he walked back to his field.

The next spring, Nikolas found a suitable piece of property in Heraklion to buy. Georgia, Ioanna and Stella combined the money that they had been saving and purchased it. They would have to continue to save for a while before they would have enough money to start building, but they were excited to have their own piece of land in the city.

At the base, the girls' boss, who was also a good friend, overheard them talking excitedly about the land purchase and asked them, "Are you still thinking you will work at the base or will you be looking for a job in the city?" They hastily reassured him that they were very happy at the base and had no intention of leaving.

After he was relieved on that point, their boss changed the subject to ask them what they knew about landmines along the beach. Ioanna told him, "There were many after the war but eventually the government sent a large group of men with metal detectors to find and remove them." Georgia added, "But I don't think they got all of them. We have heard about some tragedies that happened even after they came." The man nodded, "Yes, we have too. We are planning on sending our own teams to look for them, so if you see anyone along your beach, don't be alarmed."

When Georgia was picking some artichokes in the *Sterna* field not long after that, Emilios happened by again. He gave her a friendly wave and smile, "How are you doing, Georgia?" She looked up and said, "I am well, thank you!" He asked, "I thought I saw a group of Americans down by your beach. Do you know what they are doing?" She answered, "They are probably trying to remove more of the landmines. They told us that they were going to try to do that since there had been some more accidents." He nodded, "Oh, good. I am glad that you and all of us will be safer." Georgia agreed.

Emilios then asked, "Are you still enjoying working at the American base?" Georgia said wholeheartedly, "Oh, yes! They pay us well, the work is easy and they treat us almost like family. The base is really growing, too, so there is a lot more excitement." Emilios told her that he was glad and then left.

As time had passed, gradually there became more activity at the base. More personnel and families came, and more buildings, like a gymnasium, movie theater and bowling alley popped up. Also, permanent buildings began to replace the temporary structures they had started off with. There was never a pressing need to have Ioanna sew for the families like originally intended, but all three girls were more than content with their jobs in the dining hall. The stigma from the Greek community had lessened somewhat, and more and more Greek people had been hired to work at the American base.

One day in the summer, Stella, Ioanna and Georgia walked out of the mess hall towards the front gate to catch the bus home. Georgia had just learned a new English phrase and was practicing it in her head so she wouldn't forget, "I'll see you." As they walked, they passed a tanned young man with dark hair and eyebrows. He was working on a motor scooter outside. She was a little surprised when the man yelled out some of the words that she had been practicing, "See you Monday, Georgia!" Not even thinking about which language it was, she automatically replied, "*Endaxi* [Okay]!"

As soon as they were out of earshot, Ioanna cautioned, "You know you aren't supposed to speak to the Americans without chaperones around!" Georgia was surprised, "He was American? I thought he looked Greek." Ioanna continued, "It isn't proper." Georgia countered, "That was the first time I heard the phrase that I had been practicing, and I thought I was expected to say something when someone is being nice."

The girls arrived home and greeted their Aunt Anastasia (Natassa), who was wearing a robe and slippers, having just walked up from swimming. The girls weren't sure if she was distantly related or a family friend, but they called her "aunt" out of respect. She was staying at their house for several weeks. "Did I miss the bus?" she asked the girls. Stella answered, "Yes, sorry, it just left." Aunt Natassa was disappointed, "I need to get some medicine from town." Nikolas had recently returned from the fields and offered to go, but Natassa could see that the horse was too tired for a long trip into the city.

They heard the sound of a motor scooter coming their way. Natassa flagged him down. The girls recognized the driver as the American who had been working on the motor scooter at the base, but Natassa thought he was Greek and started asking him where he was going. When he looked confused, she realized he wasn't Greek and in English said, "Sorry!" Natassa had lived in Heraklion and had more English classes in her higher education, but she hadn't practiced the words in a while.

She started to walk away but the man had been looking for an opportunity to get to know the family and said, "Wait, you need something. Can I help you?" She pointed to Nikolas, "This man needs to go to Heraklion." The American replied, "I am going there. My name is Mark Anderson. I can take him." Natassa explained Mark's offer to Nikolas, who nodded to him and hopped on the back of the motor scooter.

When the men returned, the family asked Mark into the house and offered him some water and fruit. He was happy to accept. And he was delighted to capitalize on the opening to continue to drop by every day. Most of the conversations were between Aunt Natassa and him. Arianna acknowledged that he had earned their kindness by doing them a favor but insisted the girls resume their usual duties.

Emilios queried Georgia one day in the field, "The American seems to be over at your house a lot. Is he interested in one of you girls?" Georgia was taken aback, "Oh no. How could it be? I am sure it is not allowed and we don't even speak the same language." Emilios wasn't so sure, but he changed the subject to a more light and fun conversation. He realized that field work was much more enjoyable with a friendly, pretty girl there.

After conversations with Mark, aided by pointing at objects like a cross, Aunt Natassa figured out that he was going to be a minister. He was an only child but had parents and a close aunt who was a doctor back in Texas.

After a couple of weeks, Nikolas became uncomfortable with Mark's repeated visits. He knew that he was nice and that Aunt Natassa enjoyed practicing her English. But he told Arianna and

Aunt Natassa, "We have five girls here. I'm already uneasy that some of them work at the base. I don't want soldiers here all the time." After they discussed it and agreed, Nikolas asked Aunt Natassa to tell him as politely as she could to not come back.

When Aunt Natassa was finally able to broach the subject with Mark, he decided to divulge his true intentions. "The reason that I come is that I like Georgia. I want to marry her." Everyone was shocked.

At that moment, Georgia walked in from outside. She saw everyone staring at her, not saying a word. She looked from Mark's beaming face to everyone else's mortified faces and still no one said anything. She began to feel like she had done something wrong and braved, "What is it?" Aunt Natassa said, "This man likes you." Georgia was stunned. After giving Georgia a minute to grasp that, Arianna added, "He says that he wants to marry you." Georgia had to sit down.

Aunt Natassa told her what they had learned about him, that he knew Jesus, read his Bible and wanted to be a minister. When she told her that he was an only child, Georgia grasped at a polite way out. In all that she had witnessed, mothers were very protective of their sons. Feuds even started over their potential wives. How much more would be the outrage with an only child marrying a stranger from another country.

Georgia saw Mark staring at her and impulsively quipped, "Oh sure, he's the only child. I will marry him only if he brings me a letter of approval from his parents." After Aunt Natassa interpreted, Mark smiled and said, "Okay." He shook their hands goodbye and jumped on his motor scooter, leaving the rest feeling dazed at what just happened.

Chapter 24

After Arianna recovered from her astonishment, the inquisition began, "How well do you know him? Have you talked at the base—how can the Americans allow this? What have you been hiding?" Georgia jumped in, "Nothing! There was only one time when he was working on his motor scooter outside when he said 'See you Monday, Georgia.' And I said '*Endaxi.*' That was it. I was as surprised as you were."

Arianna calmed down a little, "But why did you answer like that?" Georgia was a little troubled at how confident Mark seemed when he left, but she was still convinced, "It will never happen. He is an only child. His family will not let him marry somebody strange and bring her to them. They would want a wedding in America that they could be there for. I have it made— they will reject me immediately. The letter will obviously say no." Arianna wished that she were as sure as Georgia seemed. She didn't want to even begin to think of never seeing her first-born daughter again.

After the shock of the drama wore off, they all eventually went about their usual routines. Tourists from all over came to their area and loved to swim near their house. Stella was interested in hearing visitors talk about the various parts of Crete. Seeing her enthusiasm, different ones asked her if she wanted to join them on her days off. Stella couldn't believe her good fortune when Arianna gave her permission.

Over time Stella was able to see many places across the island. The western coastal cities and rock fortresses with lighthouses in Chania and Rethymno were unique and beautiful. In Heraklion, she toured the old, large church, *Agios Titos* [Saint Titus]. A little south of Heraklion among the green rolling hills was the large archeological site and one-time center of Minoan culture, Knossos. That site took almost a whole day to tour, but history had always interested her.

Further south were more palace ruins, Phaistos, and to the east, the Malia Minoan Palace. She also enjoyed the eastern coastal city of Agios Nikolaos, which had a lake encircled by cliffs with numerous modern houses cascading along them. Further east in Lasithi stood many striking, traditional-style, white windmills.

Stella appreciated each town's beauty, history, churches, monasteries and people. She told Arianna, "Our area is beautiful and peaceful. We are lucky to be able to live right on the beach, pretty much to ourselves. But the other areas each have their own charming personalities." She told her sisters, "I wish you could see..." as she told them details about each place she visited.

Just when they thought that they had seen the last of Mark Anderson, one evening he drove his motor scooter up to the house. Most of the family was outside. Mark walked over, grinning from ear to ear and holding a letter in his hand. Arianna's heart sank.

Aunt Natassa greeted him. He returned the greeting and handed her the letter. "What is this?" she asked. Mark answered, "My parents have given us their blessing." Natassa swallowed hard, wondering how she was going to tell Nikolas and Arianna. As she looked at their faces, she knew that they had already guessed. "Let's go inside," Nikolas suggested.

Arianna called to Georgia and they all went inside and sat in the living room. Arianna offered Mark something to eat or drink, but he politely declined, anxious for things to be settled. Natassa started to peruse the letter. She looked up and told them, "His parents are happy for him and are ready to welcome her into the family." Mark pulled a box out of his pocket and opened it, showing a diamond ring.

Arianna panicked and pulled Georgia into the kitchen, while Natassa continued to make sense of the letter. Arianna pleaded, "Tell me that you are not thinking of accepting this man." Georgia looked bewildered, "You know that *Baba* always taught us that if you give your word, you should never take it back— your worth is tied to fulfilling your word. He said that we've got to be honest even if it hurts."

Arianna was flustered, "Do you know what you are doing? You barely went to school to learn to write your name. Where would you be going?" Heraklion, which at first seemed too far away, was suddenly very close compared to America. Arianna pleaded, "You girls bought the land in Heraklion to build a house. Don't destroy that plan without thinking it through. I don't want you to accept that ring."

Nikolas came in and added his objections, "None of us really knows this man, and you can hardly communicate with him. You would be totally dependent on him in a foreign country." Georgia knew that what her parents were saying made sense but was still conflicted. Her father continued, "We don't want to see you do this, but it is your decision. Just please think through what would really make you happy." Nikolas guided Arianna back into the living room to give Georgia a minute to pray and think. "Lord, give me a sign. I want to do Your will," she prayed.

Georgia rejoined the others in the living room. Her parents were telling her aunt to make sure to make it clear to Mark how little education she had and how they were concerned for her safety. Natassa told him, "She doesn't have a lot of education. She cannot write very much. You would be cutting off communication with her family. And we are worried about her safety. She hasn't seen, but I have seen in your movies that your roads are different than ours. You have lights; she cannot cross the street with those lights. How in the world do you expect a person who has little education to cross the street? She is going to be lost."

Mark said sincerely, "I promise her and I promise to her parents right now that she will never have to cross the street alone. I will always be there to protect her and take care of her."

When Natassa relayed those words, a tremendous peace settled over Georgia. It would be difficult to leave her home, but he loved her to the point of his own sacrifice. He loved God, was handsome, had a supportive family and was to be a minister.

236

America was so far away, but it was a dream land that many aspired to. The Americans had always been so kind to their family, conducting themselves with an integrity that was notable. At his strong words of commitment, Georgia foresaw a glimpse into the incredible destiny ahead of her. She thanked God for her sign. She would keep her word.

Georgia smiled at him and nodded. Mark handed her the ring and she accepted it. A tear slipped down Arianna's cheek. Nikolas hung his head down sadly. After an awkward silence, Mark rose to leave. Georgia sat still, but Aunt Natassa conceded, "Well, at least you can walk outside with him."

It was getting dark as Georgia walked him to his motor scooter. He started professing his love to her and his excitement about their future, but Georgia didn't understand much of it. Finally he kissed his own hand and looked inquiringly at her. She gasped, understanding that he was asking to kiss her. She pushed him away and walked inside. Mark chuckled as he turned on his motor scooter to leave. She was worth waiting for.

When she got back inside, her aunt and parents were still sitting there. They looked at her like, "What are you doing? Are you losing it?" Georgia knew that this was difficult for them and tried to think of the best way to explain her feelings. As she sat in the same chair that she had before, it was quiet enough to hear a pin drop.

All of a sudden, blood started pouring from Georgia's nose. Arianna ran to get a cloth to press against her nose. It continued to bleed as they tried everything to make the bleeding stop. Finally it stopped. Alarmed that the stress was affecting her health, they said no more about the situation and sent her to bed.

Eventually, Nikolas and Arianna became reconciled to the path that Georgia wanted to take. They trusted that the Lord would take care of her when they couldn't. Arianna tried to save her tears for when she was alone.

Mark started the paperwork process that had to be done before they could get married. He thought it best to not put Georgia's parents in the position to have to sign a United States consent form to allow the marriage, so he suggested they get married in March when Georgia would turn twenty-one. Arianna and the girls started preparing the household items and clothing that Georgia would need.

One afternoon, Georgia stopped into the little café between Karidia and Asprada. Some people were exclaiming over the new telephone they had just installed. Georgia was also impressed with the technology and wondered if she could ever call her family here from America. She completed her transaction and started to walk home.

Along the way, she ran into Emilios' sister. "I hear that congratulations are in order," she said. Georgia nodded and responded, "Thank you!" The sister said hesitantly, "You know Emilios really liked you. He even bought you a ring. He was so disappointed when he heard of your engagement." Georgia was surprised, "I had no idea. I am sorry if he was let down. I thought we were just friends." His sister mused wistfully, "You are lucky to be going to America. You must be so excited." Georgia agreed, "Yes, I am!" They smiled at each other as they went their separate ways. Georgia hoped that Emilios wasn't hurt, but she knew that with his personality he would be sure to find another nice girl.

At the end of the summer, Mark was heading out of the base early one evening. He ran into his friend, Ole Svenson, and told him, "I am going to Heraklion. Do you want to come along?" Ole said, "Sure," so they rode the motor scooter towards the city.

When they got close to the Stavrolaki house, Mark changed his mind, "Would you mind if we stop here?" It was common knowledge to the servicemen that down the road at the house with the big trees out front lived some girls who worked at the base. Ole agreed to the change in plan. Mark explained, "You know I am going to marry Georgia, the oldest sister, in March." Ole smiled and nodded but thought to himself, "Now why would he want to do that? No one in his right mind would come over here and marry a Greek girl."

Nikolas and Ioanna were away, but most of the rest of the family was home. They welcomed the men inside and offered them some

238

orange peel preserves and water. Aunt Natassa was still there, so the introductions and most of the conversations were conveyed through her. The men enjoyed themselves for some time and then left.

As they got on the motor scooter, Ole remarked, "Very nice family!" Mark agreed and said, "I knew from the first moment I saw Georgia that I would marry her." Ole was starting to understand the attraction a little bit more but still thought he was crazy.

In the fall, Lea began her last year at the school in Asprada. She felt grown up to be in the sixth grade among the oldest children. For a moment she wondered what her future would be like, but she supposed that she would just work in the fields like most of her family.

Shortly after that, Mark took a fall trip to Israel and Italy, along with Ole. When the Greek people who worked in the kitchen at the base heard that he had left, they protested to Georgia, "I bet he didn't even discuss it with you." "Maybe you wanted to go with him after you are married." "You don't need to marry an American. You should marry one of the cooks." "How about Ethymios? He is very nice and he likes you." "We can help you escape and marry him!" Georgia assured them that she wasn't interested in any such plan.

The early part of the next year was very busy with wedding plans. The girls helped Georgia send out the invitations to family and friends. Mark found an apartment in Heraklion, and Georgia contributed to the rent. When Ioanna protested to her that she shouldn't have to pay, Georgia quipped, "I feel very modern and American." The apartment was partially furnished with some wicker furniture and an ornate bed. Nikolas brought over a table and buffet. Mark was able to get a small refrigerator, which was a new and delightful thing to Georgia.

A couple of weeks before the wedding, Mark came over covered in black soot. "What happened?" Georgia asked. Eventually by piecing together hand motions and limited understood words, he communicated that the furnace had caught fire and soot exploded all over the apartment.

Nikolas, Arianna and Georgia brought some cleaning supplies over and began to tackle the mess. But the more they cleaned, the harder it became since the soot became sticky. It took a lot of effort, but finally they got everything cleaned up. Georgia was touched that her parents not only allowed her to make a decision that tore them apart, but they pitched in to help overcome messy obstacles so that she could have her dream.

Mark was starting to get anxious about the paperwork that had not arrived from the regional U.S. military headquarters. As they got closer to the wedding date, Mark warned them that they may want to keep plans loose in case the permit did not come in time. Sure enough, they had to delay the wedding for a week. As they spread the word among their friends and family, many, thinking of the soot and the delay, said among themselves, "Wow, she must really love him to proceed despite such a challenging start to their relationship."

Partly because of the delay, the wedding wasn't very fancy. The girls baked and pulled together what they could at the last minute. The couple got married at the large Saint Titus Church in Heraklion. Georgia was a beautifully radiant bride. Everyone gathered together and celebrated, many with mixed emotions, knowing that before long she would be leaving them. But for Georgia's sake, they tried to keep the occasion a happy one. Afterwards, Georgia was excited and nervous to go on her first airplane flight. She and Mark went to Athens for their honeymoon.

Although Georgia's family knew that she would be back to live in Heraklion for a little while, they were sad to see her off. Even though Georgia was already twenty-one and Arianna had four other daughters, it was emotionally difficult for Arianna to see her firstborn daughter married. She didn't even want to think about the next step of losing her. Her sisters tried to keep the conversation light. Stella said, "It'll be Ioanna next." Barbara teased, "No, she's too picky. It'll probably be you." Ioanna said, "I may become a nun."

Once the wedding celebration was over, Nikolas was ready to try another experiment in one of his fields. Arianna heard the word "experiment" and remembering the tobacco fiasco became hesitant

240

until he explained that he was talking about a new variety of grapes. That was a little more in their usual realm. Nikolas said that they are called *Kardinali* [Cardinal] grapes. This variety was supposed to be red and very sweet. He said that the government would coordinate with some big international company and they would provide the instructions and the small cuttings to plant.

Since Ioanna and Stella worked most of their days at the base and Lea was still in school, Barbara was Nikolas' helper in preparing the *Kardinali* grape cuttings and the soil. They planted the tiny stick-like plants at specific depths and distances and watered them each day until they were established. Once they started growing, they would steady the plants with poles and wire. Barbara hoped these grapes would be worth the trouble. They probably wouldn't see many mature grapes for two or three years.

One night each year in April or May when the conditions were right and the ocean started to get warmer, the people from surrounding villages liked to gather at the beach for a fishing party. If the moon was out and the sea was calm, they would bring lanterns and their fishing gear since fish would come right to the edge of the shallow warmer water.

The girls thought that most people were there for fun, and sometimes it was hard to stay quiet for the serious fishermen who would shush them to not scare off the fish. The search party used spears or nets to catch whatever they could find— clams, squid, calamari, octopus or other common varieties. Together they would walk along the shore for a kilometer or two, from around the Stavrolaki house to the west towards Heraklion.

The girls carried buckets to keep whatever fish Nikolas caught. Nikolas knew how to choose the right size octopus, since if it was too big it would be too tough. Nikolas caught two of them about a half meter each. He sent Barbara home with them and told her to run back with another bucket. He warned her, "Make sure to cover them so they don't get out." When the group got to the large rock breakwater, the men sprang into action since there were fish everywhere.

Nikolas, Arianna and the girls enjoyed the outing. When they got home, they checked on the octopuses but couldn't find them in the bucket. "I covered them!" protested Barbara. Arianna said, "Well, the sneaky things got out." Everyone started searching all over the house for them. It took a little while, but they finally found them under one of the beds.

In the summer, relatives continued to come to their house to enjoy the beach. Sometimes they stayed the night, especially on weekends. Aunt Dorothea's son from Heraklion was around Stella's age. He enjoyed hanging out with his cousins at the beach. In return, he was happy to escort Stella and Barbara to events in Heraklion, since it wasn't appropriate for young girls to go out on their own. Occasionally they went to parties or church festivals. Stella especially loved to take the bus into the city, meet her cousin and go to the movie theater.

Ioanna didn't care much for these events, although she occasionally went to some local church or family functions with Arianna. Stella reflected at how different her and her younger sisters' lives were from the two oldest sisters. The older girls remembered a lot more of the war and the tough times and were given much more responsibility. She respected them for that but was grateful for her own freedoms and fun. Lea had just finished her last year of school in Asprada. She was allowed to attend some activities, but was still too young to go out too much.

As often as they could, the family tried to get together with Georgia. She had resigned from her job at the American base after she married. At one of their visits, Georgia announced that she would be having a baby near Christmastime. They were very happy for her and congratulated her and Mark.

As the summer was ending, Mark came to visit his in-laws in Karidia. He brought an interpreter with him. After greetings were made and refreshments were served, Mark got straight to the point, "I got my orders. I will be transferred to America in December." Arianna choked up. Nikolas nodded and looked down. Mark continued, "I know that this is hard on you all and Georgia. She may not be able to call or write much, and I don't want to completely cut her off from her family. If you thought that it would be a good thing for any of her sisters and for Georgia, I would be willing to try to take one of her sisters to America with us."

Arianna felt like she had been struck. She was having a hard enough time trying to come to terms with losing one of her daughters. She couldn't imagine losing two. Nikolas asked, "Would you even be able to do that?" Mark answered, "I am pretty sure that we can get the paperwork through somehow, but it may take time."

Arianna changed the subject, "How can Georgia travel so close to her due date?" Mark replied, "I was thinking that she should fly home to my parents in October so that it is still a couple of months before she is due. I know that it is not ideal for her to travel by herself, but I can make all the arrangements and have people to escort her at each connection."

Arianna was worried and overwhelmed. Nikolas told him, "We will need time to think about all of this. Thank you for letting us know and for your offer."

After Mark left, Nikolas looked at Arianna. She walked away, warding him off with her outstretched hand as if saying, "No way!" Nikolas did not particularly want to send another daughter to America, yet thought it was worth discussing. But he knew that pressing her now would be too upsetting.

They didn't bring up the subject for more than a week. At first Arianna felt completely justified in thinking that Georgia had made her choice, but there was no reason to turn the world topsy-turvy any more than that. But over time, Arianna felt twinges that maybe she was looking at it selfishly. She pictured Georgia by herself in a foreign land. And then she wondered if she were depriving one of her other girls of an opportunity that she could never have in Karidia or Heraklion.

Nikolas gradually saw Arianna's demeanor turn from resolve to sadness. He sat and gazed at her, saying nothing. Arianna finally broke down, "How can I do this? How can I send two daughters away and never see them again?" He rose and embraced her, "God will give us grace if it is His will." At last Arianna tearfully admitted, "I think it might be."

After dinner one night, Arianna and Nikolas gathered the girls in the living room. Nikolas told them, "Mark was here a while back and told us that he would be returning to America at the end of the year. He is sending Georgia in October so that it is not so close to her due date." The girls were subdued in sadness, realizing that October was only two months away.

After letting that information sink in, Nikolas added, "He has offered to try to arrange for one of you to go with them if you would like. You could keep Georgia company and see what opportunity you might have there." While the girls looked at each other in amazement and disbelief, Nikolas continued, "We don't want to see any of you go, but we don't want to hold you back from anything that you want to do, especially if it might benefit you."

No one said anything for a while. Arianna clung to a desperate hope that none of them wanted to go. Nikolas prompted, "Lea is the only one who has just been in school. She could continue studying in Heraklion until the paperwork is approved and then expand her education in America." Arianna felt stabbed in the heart. Connecting a name to what had been a general concept made the separation more absolute and painful. And of all of her precious daughters, she had never considered that it would be her baby. After an initial sorrowful reluctance to release their youngest sister, there was general assent among the older girls. Ioanna spoke up, "We are happy with our jobs at the base. It might make the most sense to send Lea or Barbara, and since Barbara has been out of school a few years and Lea just finished in Asprada..."

Lea felt as if the whole world might be opening up to her. It was an exciting but incredibly intimidating thought. Throughout most of her life, she felt almost like a fifth wheel. Her parents and older sisters had been protective of her, but no one had much time for coddling. She understood that the others were ahead of her, so she mostly tried to stay out of the way or help where she could. She often felt like she was in the background or out of focus, too little to be noticed. She

244

didn't feel rejected or unloved but just followed behind everyone else.

Now all eyes were on her, as well as their dreams for her future. Lea looked at her mother and sensed her heart breaking. She knew that Arianna loved all of her daughters equally but that there was a special attachment to her as the youngest. The choices were very hard for them to weigh— a life of struggle but strong familial support and familiar surroundings versus a land of opportunity and love for Georgia.

It was almost too much to grasp in one sitting. They adjourned with the thought that Nikolas would look into arrangements for Lea to begin school in Heraklion. No harm in that, either way. When the time was right, they might ask Mark more questions.

Aunt Dorothea graciously offered for Lea to live with them for as long as she needed. Lea reflected on how God had been preparing her path. Her own mother sacrificed her position in Heraklion to switch places with Aunt Dorothea when her skin suffered in the fields. That open door allowed Aunt Dorothea to now bless Lea with a place to stay in the city. School in Heraklion was more challenging than in Asprada but could be good preparation for classes in America.

Although Aunt Dorothea was always caring and very generous to share meals, Lea knew that her father and sisters were paying for her room and board. She was conscious not to eat too much so that the price wouldn't be raised. Her other aunt, Aunt Nektaria, also lived in the city and often visited and brought food over. So with family around, Lea felt loved and cared for.

Lea noticed that many times when her cousin had a test at school, her aunt made sure that she ate lamb brains to make her smart. She wondered if that worked but wasn't too sure she wanted to try it. Lea walked back and forth to school every day. On most weekends, she took the bus home to see her family and help in the fields. Over time, Stella thought to herself that Lea looked very skinny and encouraged her to eat more. Lea replied, "I eat, I just don't overdo it and I get a lot of exercise."

Mark, with an interpreter, answered more of Nikolas and Arianna's questions about taking another daughter to America. They told him that they were thinking that Lea might be the best one to go with them in order to get the most out of her education. Mark said, "Since she is a minor, she may have to be legally adopted either by someone in my family or by Georgia and me. Would you be okay with that?" Nikolas and Arianna had already come so far in their thinking that they wouldn't allow that to be a stumbling block. So Mark left to confer with his family on the idea and also with the base concerning the regulations.

Ioanna and Stella counted the money that they had been saving to start building their house in Heraklion. Although they knew that it would set them back, they felt that it was only fair to offer to purchase Georgia's share that she had put in for the land. When they discussed it with her and knew that it would be very unlikely that she would ever return or need the property, they bought her out. That day, they felt a little of their dream fade away. There would be a big hole in their lives without Georgia around. Whenever they could schedule it in around their work schedules, the sisters tried to visit Georgia. Since the plans for Lea were still indefinite, they didn't talk much about that idea with Georgia.

Mark discussed adopting Lea with his parents and his single aunt in Texas. At first they thought that either of them should be the ones to adopt her to give the newlyweds some space, but then they questioned their ages and also the regulations. Anticipating Lea's paperwork, they thought that Georgia, as the closer relative, might have an advantage.

The day that Georgia was to leave her homeland was quickly approaching. All of the women were emotionally spent as they tried to help her pack. They tried to be happy and positive for her sake and the baby's, but they also wanted to express how much she meant to them in their last days together. Her mother-in-law sent her two maternity dresses so that she could wear one and they would recognize her at the airport.

246

It was a clear, sunny day in October when the entire family rode into Heraklion to see Georgia off. They gathered on the tarmac and gave her hugs and well wishes. Arianna couldn't help the tears. She was trembling, trying to keep it together. Georgia's sisters were also devastated. Their family was so close, having been through so much heartache and destitution and rebuilding together.

Georgia had almost been their second mother, sweetly and patiently serving and caring for them. She was their model of a hard worker who pleasantly pitched in with no signs of resentment or stress. They admired her for who she was and for her courage in choosing an adventurous new life. Standing there in that moment, they were certain that they would never see her again or ever meet her baby, their niece or nephew. The pain of separation was almost too much to bear. They broke down as they clung to her.

Georgia's eyes were red and puffy as she walked towards the steps to the airplane. Mark walked her as far as he was allowed to go. Trying to comfort her, Mark leaned over and told her, "Don't cry. I will be there in a couple of months, and Lea may be able to come America someday." At first Georgia thought that all of the planning with regards to Lea was wishful thinking or a way to ease the idea of separation from her homeland. It was too inconceivable.

But he continued, "I will keep trying to work on the process to bring Lea to live with us." Georgia realized that Mark was serious and sounding optimistic that it could really happen. The whole idea struck her as impossible. She wondered what all of the ramifications would be.

The flight attendants urged Georgia to board the plane. Mark kissed her goodbye and told her that he would see her soon. Georgia turned and waved one last time to her family and then walked up the steps and into the plane. Her family watched and waited until the plane took off. They stood, waving and crying until the plane became a tiny dot in the sky.

Chapter 25

On the airplane, Georgia hardly thought about her journey from Heraklion to Athens to New York to Texas. Actually, with two stops in Texas and not understanding the geography, she thought that she was flying from New York to Dallas and then to Texas. But the main thing on her mind was her family— what would happen to it? Would Lea actually leave Greece and move to America also?

Although she would love for Lea to live with her, she felt that it would be especially hard on her mother to see her youngest daughter go. Georgia was quite concerned, not wanting to be the source of any more disruption in her family. But she prayed that the Heavenly Father would keep Lea and her whole family in His perfect plan. Before long, she made her connection in Athens without any problem and tried to sleep on her trip to New York.

When Georgia arrived at the New York airport, she slowly found her way through the very confusing customs procedures. Afterwards, she was to be met at the airport by someone who spoke Greek and was to escort her to her hotel. She waited on the curb with her suitcase in the cold, windy, dark night.

Finally, someone came asking, "Crete?" Georgia nodded and started to talk to her but realized that she did not speak Greek after all. The woman ushered her inside and made a call to Georgia's mother-in-law. "I got her," she said.

Then the woman took Georgia to the hotel. While weaving through the dizzying traffic, Georgia was astounded by the large American city, with its bridges and many tall buildings all lit up. She had heard of New York but could never have pictured it. She couldn't believe that she was there, essentially by herself. When they arrived at the hotel, the lady gave the staff instructions to wake Georgia in the morning and put her on the bus to the airport. Georgia was glad to rest but was nervous about finding her flight the next day.

In the morning, the hotel staff pointed Georgia to her bus, but when she boarded, she wasn't sure what to do. There was a bucket in front of her, but she didn't know how to make change. She showed the bus driver the money in her hand, but he was cross with her and she couldn't understand him. She was so grateful when a man jumped up from his seat, helped her make change, gave her his seat and told her where to disembark after looking at her ticket. She thanked him sincerely and hurried through the airport.

Overhead, she heard her name being called, "Paging passenger Georgia Anderson…Georgia Anderson, please report to your gate for final boarding!" Georgia heard the announcement but didn't know where to go. Finally, someone helped her, and she boarded the plane. After she was seated, she realized that she hadn't felt the baby move in a while and started to worry. She tried to rest, but the plane went through a lot of turbulence, and she was very nauseated.

When she landed in Dallas, she was greeted by her mother-in-law, who recognized the dress that Georgia was wearing as one that she had sent to her. They could not communicate very well, but they were happy to see one another. Since the last short flight from Dallas to their smaller city wasn't to take off until late in the evening, they went by limousine to the airport hotel. When Georgia stepped into the limo, there were many businessmen, all dressed up in suits, and she threw up all over them. Georgia was so apologetic and her mother-in-law was embarrassed, but Georgia had no way to warn them and had no warning herself.

When they got to the hotel, a doctor was summoned. Georgia was so fearful that she had lost the baby since she had not felt it move in a long time. But the doctor heard the heartbeat and told her to rest until her next flight. Her mother-in-law was shaken when she heard that the same airplane that had brought Georgia from New York to Dallas had a safety incident on its way to its next destination. She had no way to communicate this, but she didn't want to make Georgia anxious with the news anyway.

Finally, they made it home and Georgia was welcomed and cared for. They sent word to Mark back in Greece, who reassured her family that she and the baby had made it safely to Texas.

Mark's family was very nurturing and supportive of Georgia as she acclimated to her new environment. Georgia had a lot to figure out in her day-to-day life. She marveled at many of the conveniences like a washing machine, electric stove and vacuum cleaner. Soon she got so accustomed to ready-made foods like soup, that when she opened a box of cake mix, she fully expected to see a cake in there. But compared to what she had been used to with the luscious produce of Crete, like grapes and lemons, she was disappointed, and for a long time couldn't bring herself to buy them. Her in-laws went out of their way to make her first traditional American Thanksgiving a special one, with unique and delicious foods and a very cozy gathering of thankful family.

In early December, Mark flew to the United States. Georgia was glad that he made it before the baby was born. A couple of weeks later, they welcomed a baby boy. Georgia's family back home was ecstatic with the news of a healthy baby, the first grandchild and nephew. After having so many girls in the family, they were especially proud to finally have a boy.

Christmas in Karidia that year brought mixed emotions. They were happy that Georgia was living her dream in America with her husband and newborn baby. But it was hard to come to terms with the knowledge that their family would never again be complete for the holidays.

So many times over the past couple of months, there were things that the girls wanted to tell Georgia. When they were in Heraklion, they instinctively wanted to turn down her street, and then they remembered that she didn't live there anymore. It was very difficult to adjust to her not being in Greece, or in much communication. Their only comfort was that the God who was taking care of them in Crete was also taking care of Georgia and her family in Texas.

The next spring, Barbara helped Nikolas trim the *Kardinali* grape plants and weed the area around them. They were coming along

250

nicely. Barbara couldn't wait to taste the grapes, but it would probably be another year or two before the vines would really produce.

Although she didn't know how it originated, Ioanna started to complain of a sore throat. Arianna helped her prepare a treatment of onion warmed with olive oil and lemon for her to press against her throat. When the sore throat persisted, Ioanna saw a doctor who recommended a tonsillectomy. She scheduled an appointment at a clinic in Heraklion for the following week.

A few days later, Barbara was swimming in the ocean and felt an excruciating pain in her abdomen. She could hardly move. Nikolas had to carry her inside. He put her down on the bed and rode to the small café towards Asprada to call the doctor. Arianna noticed that she had some fever, so she crushed some mint in a little oil and tied some of this around Barbara's wrists. When the doctor came, he examined her and had Arianna put something cold on her right side. He said, "It's a good thing that she was in the cool water when the pain came or her appendix might have burst. You need to take her to Heraklion immediately so they can take it out."

Nikolas took Barbara to the hospital, but the doctors there wanted to wait a little while to operate until the swelling went down. It turned out that both Ioanna and Barbara had their surgeries on the same day, but one at the clinic and one at the hospital. With Ioanna's tonsillectomy, she did not have a general anesthetic, so she heard the tissues being cut, saw the blood and started shaking. The trauma of that was almost as bad as the pain afterwards.

Arianna was not too sure how to manage the convalescence of two of her girls at the same time. Barbara, not working at the base, had borne the brunt of the household and field work. But she was not to do anything strenuous for the next six months. Stella teased her, "Ah! You did that on purpose to get out of work!" They all did their best to compensate to allow the girls to recover. Before long, Lea would be back from Heraklion for the summer.

In the middle of the summer once Ioanna had recovered and Lea was back home from school, Stella was able to spend some time with

Nikolas' mother. She was getting advanced in years and had the desire to go back to her hometown for her former church's name day festival. Stella met her in Lithos and took her by donkey to Topos. Her grandmother decorated her donkey with blankets and fancy linens and rode regally, almost like a queen. She had prepared breads and many kinds of foods and brought them along.

Stella couldn't believe how happy her grandmother was. Nikolas' mother loved the town where she had lived as a young girl, and she was able to reunite with some of her distant family members. They stayed a couple of days before returning home. For both Stella and her grandmother, it was a special memory.

The fall crept up again and Lea resumed her schooling. They had not heard much about the adoption or other paperwork, so she continued her studies in Heraklion just in case. She still tried to come home when she could, especially in the fall when there was so much harvesting to be done.

Often Lea would return and no one was home. If they hadn't left a note telling her which field they were in, she would try to piece together from clues around the house where they might have gone. But if she guessed wrong, it could add up to an hour to her walk to try to find them. Arianna felt bad that Lea had to work so hard after studying all week. She was still thin and had never really been strong, but she always worked her fair share.

One day Lea came home for the weekend and found the house all locked up. She knew where the hidden key was down near the lower level of the house, so she took off her shoes and walked barefoot through some weeds. Suddenly she felt an excruciating pain. She didn't know what she stepped on, but it stung her and pain shot up her leg. She dropped to the ground, crying in pain. She thought to herself, "I am going to die right here, and no one will even know." She prayed to God and every saint she could think of, "Please help me! Heal my foot. Don't let me die right here in the weeds."

Gradually the pain lessened and Lea was able to hobble inside the house and tend to her foot. Arianna was worried when Lea didn't show up in the field, so she headed back a little bit early. She found

252

Lea at home with her foot elevated. It was red and swollen. "What happened?" Arianna asked her. Lea answered, "I stepped on something near the beach and it stung me." Arianna questioned, "What do you think it was?" Lea reflected, "I think maybe it was a scorpion. It was an awful pain, but I prayed and it is starting to feel better now."

Arianna wished that they didn't have to work in so many spread out properties. There were so many things that could happen. It was really too dangerous for each person to be off on their own. Arianna hugged her and said, "Thank you, Jesus, for taking care of my baby."

The next summer when they checked on their field in Karidia, Nikolas and Barbara were happy to find several good clusters of *Kardinali* grapes. The government-negotiated companies weren't expecting them for another year, so Nikolas was free to do what he wanted with this crop. They did turn out very sweet, so the family was pleased with this experiment. Nikolas wanted to sell as many as he could. He was proud to be the first in the area to have this variety, so he wanted to present them well to show them off and get a nice price. He supervised Barbara as she laid them in the basket. He insisted that she arrange them just so and not casually throw them in.

Barbara smiled as she remembered many teasing conversations she had with her sisters about the differences in personalities of their parents. Nikolas was easy-going and meticulously patient, while Arianna was always rush, rush. Arianna sometimes lost her patience watching Nikolas cut his toenails. While he was taking his time, Arianna complained, "I have toenails too, but I could cut my nails and they would grow back before you finish cutting your nails the first time." She also gave him a hard time when it took a while to catch some fish, as if he could make the fish bite faster. While he was trying to catch some cuttlefish or an octopus, she would yell from the balcony, "Haven't you caught anything yet? The sun is going down!"

Another contrast was that Arianna was up every morning around five and tried to get as much work done before the sun went down, while Nikolas was not a morning person and liked to stay up late visiting. Since Nikolas was rarely up early, Arianna would sometimes coax anyone walking by in the morning to come have coffee with her. She also had coffee in the afternoon after allowing herself about a ten minute nap, and boy, was she up and going again after that!

There had been other times similar to arranging the *Kardinali* grapes when Nikolas arranged produce nicely to sell it fresh and Arianna rushed him saying, "Hurry up!" But Nikolas told the girls, "Don't listen to your mother. When people see it all laid out nicely, they won't ask you how long it took but will admire how perfect it looks." Arianna retorted, "Who cares?" And yet she cared when the girls did the laundry that everything was scrubbed pure white. The girls were sometimes amused at the differences between their parents and even the contradictions within each of their personalities.

Nevertheless, Arianna was very pleased with the price that they got from selling the *Kardinali* grapes after they had been displayed perfectly. Nikolas had constructed a simple covered wooden stand near Asprada to sell some produce to both Greeks and Americans.

The American base required anyone working in food areas to submit to medical testing every six months. When Ioanna and some other girls at the base were thought to have worms, they held their jobs for them but insisted that they receive treatment. Ioanna could only see a doctor who was approved within the socialized medical plan that she had, so she went to Heraklion. The doctor told her, "Worms are good for digestion. We don't have a cure." Ioanna explained, "But I have to have a cure to work." The doctor laughed at the Americans and recommended an older physician that he knew. When she found that doctor, Ioanna had to stand in a long line of people. The doctor also laughed at treating her for this but gave her something for it.

A little while later, Ioanna was re-tested. She had not been cured, so she repeated the formulation that she had been given. On the third course, she started feeling sick. She had a high fever, pain all over and horrible vomiting. She felt awful, and Arianna tried everything she could think of to try to help her. On her way back to the doctor, even though it was still the end of summer, Ioanna felt so cold that she had to wear a coat. She looked so terrible that as she walked down the sidewalk, people quickly sidestepped her to avoid catching something. The doctor advised her not to take any more pills until she felt better.

Although she stopped taking the substance, her skin began to break out. She went to a few other doctors. One was fearful that it could be the Ebola virus and sent her to a hospital for those who needed to be in isolation. When the doctor there obtained her medical history, he was puzzled until Ioanna feebly pointed to her purse and he examined what she had been taking.

He immediately sprang into action and told Arianna, "Woman, you are about to lose your daughter. This is poison! There is only one place that has the antidote, and we don't have time for you two to get there on your own. Come with me, I will drive you!"

Arianna was in a panic as they hurried to get the remedy. She wondered how this happened. She knew that there seemed to be limited doctors who wanted to try to cure her original condition, so maybe the formulation was risky. Or maybe since she had to have so many repeated treatments… Regardless, as they rode in the car, she kept whispering under her breath, "*Christe mou*," praying that God would heal Ioanna.

They got the antidote and admitted Ioanna to the hospital. After they got her settled, Arianna found out that she had been taking arsenic. Arianna knelt at her bed and prayed to the Lord, "Please save my daughter, please don't let me lose her." Several other family members came to see Ioanna and pray for her.

A little while later, a lady came into her room and told Ioanna about a special church in Athens that was known for miracles and how God had healed her ulcer. When she left, Ioanna prayed, "Jesus, I pledged my life to you years ago. I want to reaffirm my faith and trust in You. Please heal me, as I know You can, without any more promises from me. But as a sign of my gratitude, if You heal me so I can go back to work, I will give You thanks and give the church in Athens my next paycheck."

Gradually, Ioanna's health began to improve. She remained in the hospital for a while and then finally went home. The family was glad to see her home and doing so much better. When she felt strong enough to be on her feet most of the day, she re-took her medical exam and received approval to return to her job at the base. She was able to joke about the experience, "At least after all of that, I was cured!"

In the fall, the family was notified that Lea needed to go to the American Embassy in Athens. Ioanna had been wanting to go visit the church in Athens to fulfill her vow after the arsenic poisoning. So Nikolas, Ioanna and Lea left by ship from Heraklion. It had been two years since they started paperwork so that Lea could live with Mark and Georgia in America. Over the years, various family members had made a few visits to Athens to fill out more paperwork and answer questions. As the three walked into the embassy, they were hopeful that they would finally receive her approval. For hours they waited and were taken from one office to another, talking with different officials and answering more questions.

At the end of the process, their hopes were dashed when an official told them that Lea's authorization was denied. They were so dazed that they barely caught the explanation— something about the child had to have lived with the adoptive parents in her original country for a certain length of time. Mark and Georgia had already gone to America, and Lea had never lived with them in Heraklion. Lea was stunned. The world that she had thought was opening up for her and that she had been preparing for had suddenly crumbled around her. Nikolas thanked the man, and, in a stupor, they slowly walked out of the embassy.

None of them knew what to say. In a way, they were happy that they wouldn't have to be separated. But they had been fairly sure that America was to be Lea's destiny. Nikolas and Ioanna consoled her the best that they could, and then all of their thoughts turned to Georgia. They hoped that she wouldn't be too disappointed.

They took a bus to the church that Ioanna had promised to visit. Ioanna gave her offering and took some time to thank God for healing her from the arsenic poisoning and the original ailment.

They all took a moment to acknowledge God's sovereignty over their lives and the news they had just heard.

Afterwards, they went to the harbor to take the overnight ship back to Crete. The ship was very large, with accommodations for various economic levels, from nice rooms to places on the deck for people traveling with their chickens and goats. They checked in to their modest rooms and then proceeded to one of the upper decks to have a nice dinner together. The sea was calm and the ship was so big that they could hardly tell that they were moving.

They each selected the spaghetti and settled in at their table to enjoy the view of the ocean. By this time, Lea was still bewildered as to what her new future would be, but she was becoming reconciled to not going to America. As she continued to visit with her father and sister, she thought to herself, "Maybe it's okay. My family and my friends are here." They took their time eating and relaxing as they watched the sun set from the upper deck.

Suddenly, without warning, the plates began to slide across the table. Unoccupied chairs skidded across the deck, as the Stavrolakis started to feel the waves rocking the ship. Deafening alarms blared ominously. The staff called for everyone to immediately return to their cabins.

Nikolas carefully helped Ioanna and Lea to their shared room and then staggered to his room. The girls managed to land on their bunkbeds. The ship lurched so much that their packed suitcase glided swiftly from one wall to the other. As they tossed and turned, Lea watched her coat on a hook sway almost horizontally towards her. They started to hear the walls of the ship creak and moan, as if the wind and waves were trying to tear it apart. From outside their room, Ioanna and Lea could hear people screaming, "We're perishing!"

Lea couldn't keep it together any longer; she threw up right where she was. From her lower bunk, she prayed earnestly that their lives would be saved. At that moment it didn't seem very important what or where her future would be, but only that she and her family would have one. Lea had always had a special love for God and the church, but she was not quite ready to go to heaven. She thought of her mother and all of the losses that she had faced in her lifetime— her beloved brother, father, two baby sons and in essence her oldest daughter. Lea didn't think her mother could take it if she lost her husband and two of her daughters this way.

While Lea was crying out to God on the bottom bunk, Ioanna on the top bunk saw a vision. She could still hear the chaos around her, but in her mind's eye, she could see three arches in the sky. She heard a voice say, "*Min fovase* [Don't be afraid], you will not perish in the storm. Fear not about the news that you got today, for it is My will that Lea go to America. And not only Lea, but *all* of you will go to America and testify of Me." Ioanna was so certain of the awe-inspiring and reassuring voice of God that she told Lea, "We are going to be okay" and calmly fell asleep.

At some point in the night, the storm passed and the sea became calm again. In the morning, Ioanna couldn't wait to tell Lea and her father what God had told her. She thought that maybe the three arches she saw symbolized the three amazing promises that He had given to their family. When Nikolas heard everything, it was almost too incomprehensible for him to grasp. He had no doubt that God could speak and that His hand was on their surrendered lives. Beyond that, he didn't want to try to figure it out. But he marveled at the Lord's presence and trusted that He would bring about His will in His time.

From the moment Lea heard the account, she felt peace and was convinced that the words were from God. She knew that there were many times in the Bible where Jesus' first words were "Fear not." And the order in addressing their immediate concern of not perishing in the storm first and then progressing step-by-step to each part of His plan for their lives was significant. She didn't know how it all would come to pass, but she was sure that it would. In the meantime, she couldn't wait to hug her mother and sisters but had no desire to eat spaghetti for a really long time.

Chapter 26

Lea, partially in faith and somewhat out of routine, continued her studies in Heraklion. Arianna, Stella and Barbara had the unique advantage of hearing the bad news of the traumatic voyage and the embassy denial in light of the good news of God's protection and promises. But the idea of all of them going to America was staggering. Instead of dwelling on that, they progressed through their tasks, one day at a time. It was for the Lord to confirm the word and bring about whatever He had in mind, whether it was for them to live there or just visit (a big enough miracle) and *when*... Maybe it was to be more of a symbolic family tie to America. So they continued life as they knew it, trusting God to lead them each day.

The next spring, Ioanna and Stella were finally able to afford to have builders begin their house in Heraklion. The house design was very simple, so there was not much for them to supervise. Stella remarked, "This is really happening! We are going to have our own place." Ioanna agreed, "It's nice to have something of worth to show for all our work." Nikolas chimed in, "A house in the city should be a good investment, whether or not you ever use it. You have worked hard and should be proud."

Shortly afterwards, a letter came from Mark. When they got it translated, they discovered that he was working on another way to get approval for Lea to go to America. "A congressman...?" Stella questioned when she heard, "he brought *her case* directly to the government?" To them it sounded like a long shot. Ioanna shrugged but reminded them, "You never know what means God could use." Nikolas agreed and also admitted, "I have to admire Mark's perseverance." Arianna nodded but still had mixed feelings about whether she wanted this plan to happen.

In the summer, Nikolas hired a team of workers to help harvest the wheat at their distant field in Topos. Arianna sent Barbara loaded with food for lunch for all of the hired hands. After a couple of days of walking almost three hours in each direction, Barbara thought to herself, "This is crazy. Get me out of here." She had heard an old custom that if you throw a rock over your shoulder, you don't have to return to that place. She waited until she got near a church and then emphatically threw a rock over her shoulder. She prayed, more out of frustration than what she really believed, "If there is a God, I don't want to come back here!" She kind of laughed at herself afterwards, but it felt good to vent her feelings.

That year, the *Kardinali* grapes produced in massive quantities. The contracted company sent workers to harvest the crops that they wanted as a part of the original agreement. But they left many of the large grapes for the Stavrolakis. Barbara and Arianna helped Nikolas harvest many large basketfuls to sell. They were so sweet that it was difficult to stop themselves from eating too many.

Barbara told her parents, "I can't believe how tall these vines have grown!" They had formed tall canopies, climbing higher than their other grape varieties. Arianna smiled at Nikolas and said, "I think that we can call this one a successful experiment— but most of your endeavors are!" Nikolas acknowledged, "You all are out here right beside me. I couldn't do it without you."

In September Nikolas, Arianna and Barbara continued to gather the grapes and figs and started to plant the winter broccoli, cabbage and cauliflower. Ioanna and Stella continued their work at the base, and Lea started classes again in Heraklion. It had been almost a year since the United States embassy rejected her application.

One day, they got a letter from Mark. Their anticipation intensified until they were able to bring a translator to the house. He started to read, and they soon realized how important it was. When he got to the part that said that Mark was able to get permission for Lea to come to America, the girls let out exclamations of surprise and joy. "I can't believe it!" Barbara said. "Wow, they did it!" Stella was amazed. Ioanna, knowing how hard Lea was working in Heraklion, guessed, "She will be so happy to hear this." Tears welled up in Arianna's eyes as she admonished, "Let him finish the letter."

260

The translator told them that Mark had convinced a congressman to initiate a private-law bill with the federal government to allow Lea's eligibility, based on the special circumstances that the adoptive mother is her sister. Although she didn't live with both of them for the designated amount of time, she had known her adoptive mother her whole life. Mark was able to get the bill passed, and they were instructed to go to the embassy for more processing.

Nikolas thanked the translator and offered him some payment, which he declined. "Then we insist that you stay for dinner," Nikolas offered. The translator replied, "Thank you, but you all have so much to discuss. Another time." Arianna handed him a basket of fresh fruit and said, "Come by any time."

The girls started talking all at once about plans. How were they going to wait until the weekend to tell Lea? How should they tell her? Who should go to the embassy and when? Arianna couldn't take it anymore and excused herself. Nikolas found her on the balcony. She was staring out at the ocean with tears in her eyes. "The baby I almost lost, I am losing her now," she sobbed as she buried her head on Nikolas' shoulder. He tried to console her, "You'll never really lose her. Love will always connect you, and there are letters and telegrams, maybe even a visit or two."

Arianna struggled, "But she is so little to venture into such a strange, big world. Are we doing the right thing?" Nikolas reassured her, "She is very bright. We owe it to her to give her this chance. God will be with her, and she and Georgia will have each other."

After a while, Nikolas left Arianna to her thoughts. He knew that the ocean, as well as time, could be soothing. But he prayed that God would comfort her and assure her that He would never leave or forsake any of them, no matter where they went. He told the girls to start dinner and let Arianna have some time to herself. The girls' enthusiasm had also waned as the reality of maybe never seeing their youngest sister again started to set in.

When Lea came back home the next weekend, the excitement mounted again. Even though it was a busy fall harvest time, Nikolas and Arianna consented to their quitting early to be home when Lea arrived. Lea was surprised to find everyone home when she got there. "Is everything okay?" she asked. Nikolas spoke, "Yes, but we have some big news. You are going to America!" Fifteen-year old Lea looked from face to face— at first surprised and thrilled as if she had been handed a momentous gift— then realizing how much she was going to miss each of those faces. She hugged everyone, saving the longest for last as she saw how much Arianna was struggling to be happy for her.

All of a sudden Lea felt like there was so much to arrange. There would need to be more trips to the embassy for paperwork. Lea would need to pack, make travel arrangements and say goodbye to all of her extended family and friends. She kept going to school though, since they didn't know how long the finalization would take and didn't want her to fall behind in her studies. Arianna agreed to that reluctantly, preferring to spend every last moment she could with her before she left.

Soon afterwards they received word that more processing was needed in Athens. Nikolas and Stella decided to go together to the American Embassy, and on the way they stopped in Heraklion to check on the house construction. When they got to the embassy, the officials confirmed that Lea was now eligible to go to America. There was a little more paperwork to be done, which Nikolas and Stella were able to initiate.

About a month later after another trip to Athens, they found out that things had progressed, and that it should only take one last visit to pick up her papers. They set an appointment for the end of November. The family expected that Lea should be able to fly to America a couple of days later.

The time passed all too quickly. The weekend before her scheduled appointment at the embassy in Athens and her flight to America, Lea was home in Karidia. Word got out that the president of the United States had been killed, and Lea was shocked. Everyone who heard about it was saddened and upset.

The family wasn't sure if Lea's appointment would be cancelled but decided she should go in order to not miss her chance in case it still

262

stood. Lea packed all of her belongings in anticipation of leaving for America from Athens. Ioanna and Stella planned to accompany her to Athens to obtain her papers and then see her off from the airport there.

It was an emotional time of saying goodbye to family and friends. At only fifteen, it was hard for her to leave everything that she had ever known. As she hugged her parents and Barbara in Heraklion, she held on to God's promise that she would see them again someday.

Arianna sobbed all the way home. It was unbearable for her to forever send away her oldest and youngest daughters. Lea was still so young and from Athens would be traveling all by herself. She asked herself why she allowed this to happen. Nikolas hugged and tried to reassure her, "It was God's plan. He has bigger plans for her than we do."

When Ioanna, Stella and Lea arrived at the United States embassy in Athens on Monday, it was closed because of the American national day of mourning for the late president. Many people were lined up along the streets and officials were stopping traffic and holding people back.

The girls saw two open-top limousines come by and realized that it was the king of Greece and his daughters. They waved to the crowd, and the girls thought that the princesses were so beautiful. Someone said that they were on the way to a cathedral for a memorial service for the American president. The queen had gone to the United States to express the sympathy of the Greek people.

The girls decided to stay at a nearby hotel to try be at the embassy first thing when it opened the next day. They noticed the newspaper headline, "They Killed the Killer." As the girls settled down to rest, they could hardly describe their feelings about all of the happenings. The world events were significant and for a while distracted them from the upcoming separation of their family.

When the embassy opened the next day, Lea and her sisters were near the first in line. She was able to get her final documents and could leave at any time for America. The girls wrestled with jumbled emotions as they headed back to the hotel. Ioanna and Stella had been trying to help her go to America all along, but now that the time came, they were very sad. Lea was glad to finalize the direction of her life. She had been working towards this goal— all of her extended family knew it— and it was considered a great thing to go to America. But at the same time, she was heartbroken to leave so much behind.

The next day, Ioanna and Stella accompanied Lea to the airport in Athens. All three girls were crying as they said their goodbyes. Ioanna told Lea, "Give Georgia and the baby a hug and a kiss for us." Stella said through her tears, "We are going to miss you so much!" Lea replied, "I am going to miss you too. Thank you for your help with everything. Take care of *Mama* and *Baba* for me!" She cried fresh tears at the thought of her being powerless to help if they needed anything. They hugged goodbye one last time, and Lea walked to the airplane.

Lea was more scared than she had let on. She didn't feel that her English was good and was very unfamiliar with large cities and traveling, especially internationally. When she got to Amsterdam, she knew that she was supposed to stay at a hotel, but wasn't sure how to find it. Someone pointed her to the hotel shuttles. She finally got to the hotel and checked in, but didn't know how to operate the elevator. Someone eventually came along and she was able to find her room.

Even after the hotel door closed behind her, Lea was petrified. She had made it this far, but it would be more important to make it back to the airport and board her plane on time. She almost wished that she stayed all night at the airport gate. How was she going to wake up? She didn't know how to set an alarm clock or tell anyone to wake her up. Her family spent so much money to fly her across the world. She was so afraid that she was going to miss her flight and be stuck in Amsterdam. She didn't have a way to reach either her parents or Georgia. She just *had* to wake up on time. Before falling asleep, she thanked the Lord for helping her so far and prayed that He would help her get safely to Texas.

Lea was so nervous that she hardly slept. Somehow she was able to get up early and find the shuttle back to the airport. She had her ticket, and someone had written some information on a piece of paper to show people to help her. With some assistance, she found her gate and boarded the plane. When she finally sat in her seat, she was so relieved that she soon fell asleep. It seemed surreal when she arrived in America. She was so focused on making her connection that she didn't take much time to look around.

At long last, Lea landed in San Antonio. She was met at the gate by Mark and a very bewildered Georgia. Mark wanted to surprise her and hadn't told her where they were going or even that Lea was coming. When she realized what was happening, they hugged and started talking a mile a minute in Greek. Georgia, already acclimated to American fashion, pointed at Lea's hat, "Why are you wearing that thing? Take it off!" Lea had been fixed up in a white dress and hat by caring family members who thought that they were dressing her stylishly. Lea took off her hat and stooped to greet her nephew. She was so proud and happy to meet the little guy— that was one of her happiest moments.

Lea found her bag and they headed to the car. Since Mark and Georgia had driven several hours to get there from their smaller hometown, and it was very late, they decided to stay in a hotel and drive home the next day. Lea couldn't believe how cold it was, "I thought it was supposed to be hot in Texas!"

Eventually they made it home and Lea got settled. Mark and Georgia and Mark's family made her feel really welcome. Before long, she started high school classes in the middle of the school year.

Lea soon realized how little she was prepared, both for understanding the lectures and for the reading and writing assignments. Although she had taken some English classes, fast conversations with a Texas accent were mostly still foreign. Every time the teacher said a word that even remotely sounded like her name, such as leap, leaning or leader, she jumped in her seat, scared that she was being called upon for an answer.

To do her French homework, she used a French to English dictionary and then had to use her English to Greek dictionary to figure out the meaning of the words. Her schooling was very difficult but she tried very hard to do well. Her family never put pressure on her, but she put some pressure on herself. She had been given an opportunity, and she wanted to make the most of it. So she stayed up many late nights studying.

***

Back in Karidia, the family was having a hard time adjusting to having Lea and Georgia gone. They re-read each letter from America four or five times. Their sisters hadn't left much behind, but there were a few old dresses that remained in their wardrobe. The girls were so forlorn that they would hug their sisters' clothes and cry. For Barbara, who was too young to remember the war tragedies and loss of her two brothers as babies, this was the first real heartbreak of her life. Their family just wasn't the same. That Christmas seemed like it was the saddest one they had ever had. They tried to comfort one another by thinking that at least Georgia and Lea had each other now.

Shortly after Christmas, a famous actor-comedian from the United States came to the base in Crete to do a show for the men. This was very exciting for the military personnel and their families. They had set up an outdoor stage for the event. Some other performers came, including a beauty pageant winner. Ioanna and Stella weren't familiar with any of the celebrities, but they were glad to see the Americans' spirits lifted.

Barbara was glad to have a lighter workload in the fields at the beginning of the year, since planting wheat and barley was not considered women's work. She still needed to bring the men food twice a day, and she spent the rest of her time cooking or sewing for her and her sisters' dowries. Meanwhile, Ioanna was concerned at their dwindling combined funds after buying Georgia's share of the property and starting to build the house. She complained to her parents, "It's not fair that Barbara has to stay home to take care of everything. Stella and I are able to earn some money to contribute to the family needs and to our house. Barbara should get a job or go to school to train for something."

266

Arianna, still freshly upset with two daughters leaving the country, said, "This is unbelievable what is happening here. Barbara is not going anywhere. She has to stay here and take care of things. Who is going to take care of all of the businesses?"

Ioanna replied, "There are many farm workers available these days. Even though we only make a little more than minimum wage, it is about three times what some field workers earn, and some of them may take produce for some of their pay." Nikolas, wanting to be fair to each of his daughters, spoke up, "If we can find a good job for her and she wants it, we can release her from her duties."

Ioanna asked if there were any openings at the base, but there weren't. By that time many of the Greeks had realized that the base offered good opportunities. But their boss told them, "There's an officer who lives with his family in Heraklion. They are looking for a nanny for their three children during the week. I can vouch that they are very nice and honorable if she is interested in that position."

After everyone met one another and discussed the arrangements, Barbara accepted the job as a nanny. The family had a big house near the famous ruins at Knossos. Barbara enjoyed getting to know the children, but she also missed being at home.

One night in her room before going to bed she sincerely and desperately prayed, "I am so confused as to what I am doing. I am supposed to be home helping my mother. Why am I here? I am making a little money, but I am away from my family." This family was very nice, but she was so afraid that she might be doing the wrong thing that she was shaking as she prayed.

All at once, she saw a light in her room. She heard words in her mind that she knew were not from herself, saying, "Don't worry, because I am with you always." After that amazing Presence, she felt God's comfort and reassurance in her new path.

Barbara got to know the area and found a park that she liked walking to with the children. The gardens and ducks were picturesque and charming. The lady of the house loved to entertain, and Barbara liked to help her prepare for her parties. Barbara had always enjoyed acting as hostess when anyone came to their house for beach parties. But now she was learning how to do things the proper way according to the Americans.

After several months, Barbara overheard a conversation that her employer was having with a guest. "I can't believe how blessed we've been having Barbara here. She is so kind and hard working. She is a good girl, very proper, and doesn't have a party lifestyle like so many young people do these days. And the kids love her," she praised. Barbara felt gratified that she was appreciated.

***

On her days off in the summer, Stella helped in the fields or took the bus into Heraklion. In the city, she checked on the construction of their house or shopped in the *agora* [public area]. On her way back towards Karidia, she would often get off the bus before the usual stop at their house so she could take some groceries to the field in Lithos or Prasinos Kampos. Her parents were usually out there long days, so she would bring them some things for dinner. On one of her trips to the city, she stopped by to see Barbara. Stella was happy to see where she worked and that she was doing very well.

In September, they heard on the radio that their recently-crowned king, the son of the king that Ioanna and Stella had seen in Athens, got married. Sometime after that, Stella was running some errands in Heraklion. She was about to cross the street when someone told her to stop. She looked up and saw the young royal couple, walking hand in hand. They had crowds and police on each side of them. When she got home, Stella couldn't help but gush, "They were so beautiful and poised. I can't believe I saw them!"

***

Barbara came home on the weekends and for the Christmas and Easter holidays and occasional other days off. So although she was away, with an hour bus ride, she was really never too far. She was happy with her job, but Ioanna and Stella kept their ears open for any openings at the base.

268

Barbara came home for May Day on May first, which was their Labor Day holiday. Most of the businesses closed to allow people to take a break from their busy lives and enjoy nature and the beauty of spring. The girls collected flowers and made wreaths for their hair and larger ones for the front door. The Stavrolakis went to Prasinos Kampos to celebrate in the village. People brought many kinds of foods to enjoy outside in the fresh air while visiting together.

While Barbara was standing by herself, a young man whom she hadn't seen for a while walked up to her. "Hi, Stergios! What have you been up to?" Stergios answered, "I was away on my military training, but I am back now." Barbara thought that was one relief they had as women; they may have to work hard in the fields, but they weren't required to do military service.

He asked her, "What are you doing these days?" She replied, "For almost a year and a half I have been taking care of three children in Heraklion during the week." Stergios thought a minute, "So you're home on the weekends?" Barbara confirmed, "Usually." As he walked away, he told her, "Maybe I'll see you." She nodded and waved.

Stella walked up as he left, "Was that Stergios?" Barbara said, "Yes, he's back from the military." Stella teased, "He's gotten really good looking." Barbara smiled and shyly admitted, "Mmm-hmm."

Other guys visited with Stella and Barbara. The girls were very friendly with everyone. Ioanna attracted attention also, but many were intimidated by her since she wasn't particularly encouraging to them. Ioanna didn't see too many men who seemed to share her interests, mostly in regards to modern ideas regarding life and work and pious devotion to God and the church. In the past, Nikolas used to respond to teasing about having five girls, "They will bring the boys," but he was hoping that they wouldn't come along too soon. Arianna was still having a hard time with two of her daughters gone.

Stergios kept coming up with excuses to ride his horse past the Stavrolaki house on the weekends. Every now and then he would catch Barbara crocheting out on the porch. He struck up a conversation, and she politely offered him some water and whatever else they had as refreshment.

That summer, Nikolas decided to buy a tractor. In addition to using it for plowing the fields, they could use it like an automobile since it could pull a wagon. The whole family decided to take it on a test run to Prasinos Kampos. Off they went, with Nikolas proudly at the wheel and Arianna and the three excited girls in the wagon.

When they rolled into the village, one of Arianna's nephews was enthralled with the tractor and begged Nikolas to let him drive it. Nikolas let him drive them around the square. The young man wanted to show off to those watching from the town square but also didn't know how much gas to give it, so he accidentally lost control of the tractor and turned the wagon over. Nikolas, Arianna and the girls had a few scratches but all got up and said, "We're okay!" Arianna's nephew felt bad that he could have hurt someone, but they only teased him about it (for years).

Finally, a position opened at the base. Barbara gave notice and thanks to the family that she had been working for and accepted the dining hall job. When she saw Stergios next, he asked her, "Why did you take a job at the American base? Are you all so hungry that you have to demean yourself? I had such dreams and plans for you and us and now they can never come true."

Barbara was too stunned to say much in reply, but he was walking away anyway. At first she was embarrassed and disappointed. But then she realized that she didn't want to be with someone who jumped to conclusions too hastily without knowing the real situation or giving her much chance to explain her thoughts or feelings. "Guess he won't be coming around anymore," Barbara chuckled to herself. Nonetheless, she thanked God for the open position at the base and looked forward to her new beginning.

270

Chapter 27

Wheat harvesting time came around again, and Nikolas hired workers for his multiple fields. By that time Barbara had begun her new job at the American base. She enjoyed being around lots of people while earning an income close to home. After Barbara, Ioanna and Stella got off work around two in the afternoon, they joined the others in the fields. Some used a sickle to cut the wheat while others followed behind, gathering it into bundles.

They were in the middle of reaping when a telegram came from the United States. Georgia had a healthy baby girl! Arianna expressed her praises to God, and Ioanna exclaimed, "I am so happy to hear that!" Barbara said wistfully, "I wish we could see her." Stella agreed but marveled at the new technology, "At least we can feel a little connected to them by telegram."

When they finished winnowing the wheat, the family gathered the good kernels into a large mound. With their hands, they made the sign of the cross over the grain, giving thanks to God for His provision. Before taking it home to sort for sale or storage, they waited for representatives from the government to come by and take their portion for tax.

Near the end of the year, the first level of the house in Heraklion was completed. Since none of the family needed to live there yet, they rented it out. With that arranged and the harvesting completed for the season, Nikolas wondered how he might bolster Arianna's spirits.

Nikolas was not able to dismiss his memories of earlier in the year when Arianna got the news that her oldest brother Petros had died. Even though they knew that he had a chronic illness, his passing was difficult for her. It was difficult for Nikolas to see her wail at the funeral for Petros and for her father, whose bones they removed from the family plot to make room for the body. Family was precious to Arianna.

So when Mark sent an invitation to visit them in America, Nikolas encouraged Arianna to go. Arianna's reaction was, "Impossible!" To her the idea seemed as strange as her growing wings. Nikolas pressed, "We can manage things without you, and we can afford it." Arianna conceded that they could probably get along without her for a little while but wondered if she could navigate the baffling travel. Could she really cross half the world to visit the daughters she thought she would never see again?

It had been two years since Lea left and five years since Georgia moved to the States. Barbara prompted her mother, "You can meet your grandchildren!" Ioanna nodded and assured, "We can take care of things here." Stella urged, "Go have a good time and tell us all about it!" Over time, Arianna was convinced to go. Nikolas wished that he could send one or all of the girls as well, but they were all happy for their mother to go and send their love.

Arianna left for the United States in December. She wondered how Georgia and Lea managed with the confusing airports. At least she was fortunate to fly as far as New York on an airline whose attendants spoke Greek. She was amazed that she could put a glass on a tray on an airplane and the liquid wouldn't spill.

When she got to New York, Arianna didn't know what to do. Instead of catching her correct flight, she somehow ended up in Chicago. Someone finally helped her get to Texas.

When she was met by her family, the first thing Arianna said was, "Good to see you! Where's the bathroom?" Lea, who had not been told of her mother's visit, couldn't believe it when she saw her and suddenly fainted. Everyone was alarmed, but Arianna said that she must get to the bathroom quickly, so Georgia showed her the way while Mark tried to revive Lea.

By the time Arianna and Georgia returned, Lea was conscious and the color was returning to her face. Mark was telling her, "I am so sorry, I wanted to surprise you but not shock you with her arrival."

Arianna hugged her and asked, "How are you, my precious girl?"
Lea smiled, "I am fine— very surprised, but happy to see you!"

Once she got settled and rested, Arianna really enjoyed visiting with
Lea and Georgia and her family. It was a joyous reunion that
Arianna treasured. She spent a lot of her time playing with her
grandchildren. She also helped Georgia with the cooking and
cleaning. In addition to catching her up on all her family life,
Georgia told her of how active she had become in their local Greek
Orthodox Church.

When Arianna visited with Lea, she couldn't believe how much she
had matured. She was in the middle of her senior year and was
driving an old yellow car that Mark had loaned her. In addition to
her studies, she worked at a department store. Lea admitted, "The
manual cash register and calculating change was challenging for me
at first since I was unfamiliar with the coins and wasn't great at
math, but I am managing better now."

Arianna asked her, "Have you thought about what you want to do?"
Lea answered, "I had been thinking about becoming an international
airline stewardess since I am doing pretty well with languages and
might be able to fly to Greece occasionally. But I found out that
there are only a few international airlines and they have strict rules.
You have to be young, female and single. So since that couldn't be a
long-term job, now I am thinking of becoming a language teacher."

Having always valued education, Arianna was thrilled, "I am so
happy that one of my daughters may become a teacher. It doesn't
look like Stella will be one after all." She thought that America must
be very special to have teachers who could specialize in just one
area. She continued, "No matter what profession you choose, I am so
proud of you and how hard you have worked."

While she was there, Georgia and Mark baptized their baby girl.
Arianna was so happy to be there for the special occasion. She was
asked to be her godparent, along with Mark's friend Ole Svenson,
who had visited their house in Karidia while he was stationed on
Crete. Now he was living in the same town as Mark in Texas.

When they all went to eat at a Mexican food restaurant, Ole joined them. Arianna was fascinated by a new kind of pepper that she had never seen and asked, "What is this?" Before anyone else could warn her about jalapeños, Ole said with a straight face, "It's a pickle. Try it, it's good!" When the others laughed, Arianna realized that he was trying to play a joke on her. She smelled it, smiled and put it back on her plate.

Later when Arianna asked Lea about any special friendships, Lea told her that with her studies and work she didn't have much time for socializing. But Arianna saw that she was popular with some groups of kids who came to pick her up for occasional outings. Lea explained, "I think they just like that I am different."

At first she went to outings with the brother of a friend. Then there was a clean-cut, business-minded young man named Dan who hung around. But the most serious seemed to be a guy named Stephen. He wasn't very academically minded, but he seemed to be really fond of Lea. Although she enjoyed hanging out casually with large groups on the weekends, Lea was focused on her goal of getting an education. Arianna was happy to see how well both of her girls were doing.

The month passed more quickly than Arianna liked. She was taken to see some different sights that were fairly close by, but it was priceless to her to meet her grandchildren, see her girls flourishing and picture where they were in America.

When she got back home, she had so much to describe to the family, beginning with updates on the girls, descriptions of the grandchildren, their house and then America. Everyone asked her what it was like. Arianna thought about it and said, "It seems like the richest people here are like the poorest people in America. There were so many open highways and a lot of space there— so different than the narrow, winding roads in Crete."

Early in the new year, some of Arianna's relatives were visiting on the Stavrolakis' balcony. Someone had brought over some persimmons, a new fruit for them to try. Nikolas picked one up and looked at it, "It looks like a tomato." He took a bite to prove that it wasn't that different but was surprised how sweet it was. He laughed about it and then suddenly became unresponsive. He seemed to be awake, but he wasn't able to move or communicate. Although it was a part of their culture to make and have some wine occasionally, none of their family would ever think of becoming drunk. Nikolas was not quite sixty years old, but they wondered if he had a ministroke or had just over exerted himself.

Arianna and her brother helped him to the bed, and the next day he was fine. It scared Arianna though, and she pleaded for Nikolas to take it easier, "Let the hired hands take care of everything and you just supervise them." He agreed to cut back on his physical labor.

***

In America one night, Lea had a vivid dream. In the morning, she couldn't shake it so she asked Georgia, "Is Mark adopted?" Georgia was surprised, "Not that I know of. Why, do you think that he is?" Lea said, "I never had any reason to think so before, but I had a dream that he was adopted and that he had siblings who were living in a bus-like thing." When Georgia asked about it, she found out that he really had been adopted. The revelation was surprising at first but eventually helped Georgia to feel closer to Mark and his family and opened up more communication. Later, Georgia told Lea, "I can't believe you found out about the adoption in a dream. That was pretty amazing." Lea and her whole family were coming to realize that God could reveal things in a variety of ways.

Before Lea's high school graduation, Stephen came to see her one night. They sat in Georgia's sitting room and Stephen pulled out a box from his pocket. When he opened the box revealing a diamond ring, all of a sudden Lea felt suffocated. She apologized, "I'm sorry, I can't. I had no idea you felt so strongly. You have been a great friend. I'm so sorry!" Stephen looked crushed when he left, and he didn't come around again.

Lea cried on Georgia's shoulder, "I guess I have been a little naïve. Maybe I led him on when I didn't mean to. I just didn't feel that way about him." Georgia comforted her, "It will be okay. He will be okay. It's better that he know now, and you shouldn't marry anyone that you don't love."

Lea had applied herself so diligently to her studies that she earned a scholarship to their local university. Georgia and Mark were very proud of her accomplishment, especially after coming in at such a disadvantage. In addition, she was granted a Work-Study position as a secretary in the modern language department on campus. Lea was looking forward to the new chapter in her life.

***

At the military base near Asprada, Stella asked for a day off for the middle of May. She had heard that they were bringing the skull of Saint Titus from Venice to the *Agios Titos* Church in Heraklion. She always enjoyed historical things and was excited when her boss gave her time off to go to the special occasion.

The day soon arrived, and Stella took the morning bus into the city. People were already starting to gather in the streets as she made her way to Aunt Dorothea's house, which was near the church. Aunt Dorothea and Aunt Nektaria, who had also decided to meet the family there, quickly greeted Stella then yelled to their grown children, "Let's go! We don't want to miss anything!"

As they started down the street, Stella told her cousin, "This is so exciting! I can't believe that of all places, they decided to relocate the skull here— at *your* church!" Her family could hardly hear her over the many church bells that were ringing and the excitement of the crowd.

Everyone made their way toward the harbor to watch for the ship bringing the relic. Some people held candles or other symbols from their respective churches. Her cousin motioned to Stella, "Look! There is the Archbishop!" Stella looked where she was pointing and saw the Archbishop in his elegant ceremonial robes and headdress. There was a roar from the crowd, so Stella strained to look around the people to see what was happening. A ship was slowly sailing towards them. It seemed like a long time before the ship arrived and was secured in port.

When the officials emerged with the relic, some from the crowds cheered. The Archbishop stepped up to greet the visitors and make

276

the sign of the cross over the honored artifact. Then they carried it through the city toward the church. Stella and her family followed in the procession of people, many of them singing hymns as they strolled.

When they arrived at Saint Titus Church, the officials positioned the relic in a carved wooden canopy adorned with a beautiful tablecloth and flowers. The Archbishop pronounced a blessing and then allowed the others to view it. Only the top of the skull could be seen through the rounded decorative case made of intricately-etched silver and gold plating. A curved protective layer of glass surrounded the metal casing. With the throngs of people, it took a while for them to see the display up close, but the family members waited in line to see it. Later that evening Stella told her family all about it and summarized, "I feel like I witnessed a little bit of history!"

A couple of months later in July, the church in Karidia celebrated the festival of its patron saint. In times past, normally the family went to the church further away in Asprada since the closer church in Karidia was smaller and rarely had a priest. But these days, a priest came more regularly, and everyone was excited to plan the name day festival.

Arianna and the girls worked hard to help prepare several foods for the event. They were excited when the day came, and they walked together over to the church. After setting up some tables outside, they all went inside the church for a service, including a remembrance of all those who were no longer with them.

Afterwards the music started up, and people enjoyed many kinds of food and dancing as they visited with one another. The celebration lasted all day. Several young men tried to use the opportunity to get to know the Stavrolaki girls better. The sisters were polite but kept the conversations casual. They all thought it was nice to visit with their neighbors in a fun community setting close to their home.

***

In Texas, Lea was preparing to start college. She changed jobs from working at the department store to a cafeteria restaurant since it would work better with her classes and Work-Study schedule. She sometimes stood behind the counter and served the people their food, but usually she took a cart around to those seated and asked if they needed refills or anything else. She liked that since she could visit with people.

On registration day in August, Lea was nervous. The university campus was large and she had not learned her way around. Even though she had made good enough grades to earn almost a full scholarship, she did that through hard work and didn't feel like she was yet fluent enough in English, especially for professional writing. She was very nervous about her classes and her Work-Study responsibilities as a secretary. She wasn't just worried about how fast she could type but also her spelling and how to put sentences together.

These preoccupations were on Lea's mind as she made her way through the registration tables to find where she was supposed to sign up. When she found the modern language section and told the man her name, he said, "Oh, yes, Evangelea! I have seen your name. I am the head of the department, so you will be working for me. Let's get you registered and then I can give you a tour of our building."

As the head of the department later guided Lea down the sidewalk, a young man was walking in their direction. The professor stopped him when he came closer, "Jim, this is Lea. She will be working for me in the department. Lea, this is Jim Duncan. He has been an honor student studying languages here for a couple of years. He is president of the modern language club and is very active in the program and on campus, so you will probably see him around a lot."

Lea murmured, "Nice to meet you," but was still distracted with whether or not she will be competent at her job. She didn't want to let anyone down. Jim thought Lea was beautiful with a unique international appearance. He welcomed her, and then they continued in their opposite directions.

After Lea got the tour of her main building, she went to the bookstore to buy her books. As she was comparing the book titles to

278

the list that she received in registration, she heard a voice behind her saying, "I know you!" She turned around to see Jim Duncan, whom she had just met. He grabbed her hand and started enthusiastically shaking it without letting go and declared, "You must be from Bolivia!" Bewildered at this kind of exuberance, Lea tried to get her hand back as she thought to herself, "What kind of knucklehead is this?" She corrected him, "No, I am from Greece." Lea finally managed to get her hand free. They talked for a little bit and then Lea was able to escape.

As the months went by, Lea often saw Jim Duncan around campus. To her, it seemed like when they ran into each other that he was trying to charm her, but she wanted to get her bearings at her new school and job. Rumors of his popularity on the basketball team and in many clubs (and once having five girls riding in his car) reached her and didn't interest her. She eventually found out that he was hanging around a girl named Cecilia Duncan. She concluded that he must be married, so surely he could not be interested in her.

When Jim asked Lea out, she said, "Aren't you married?" He told her that he wasn't. She retorted, "But who is Cecilia Duncan?" He answered, "Duncan is her maiden name. We just happen to have the same last name. We have gone out but are seeing other people."

For a long time Lea didn't believe him, but eventually after inviting Cecilia to lunch, she found out that he had told her the truth. Lea told her that she didn't want to interfere in their relationship and was really there to study. Cecilia appreciated that but confided in her that she had met a nice guy named Dan. Lea was surprised when she put together that she was seeing the same Dan that Lea had gone out with a few times in high school. After that, Lea agreed to go out with Jim. She wasn't sure if it would lead to anything, but they seemed to have some common interests.

***

Meanwhile, Stella had been receiving several advances by both Americans and Greeks. She liked to have fun and didn't want to think about settling down with anyone. When the right person came along, she would think about it, but for now she wanted to keep the relationships casual.

In the summer, a friend from the base told Stella that there was going to be a special music group coming to the base. He asked if she would like to go with him to see the rock band at the broadcasting station. She agreed, but had no idea who they were. When the day came, she met her friend at the station. They had instruments already set up and some chairs along the back for the few visitors who were allowed to go in. When the four young men came in, the others around her whispered and clasped their hands together excitedly. Stella had no idea where the station was broadcasting to, but they played a few lively songs and gave a short interview in English. She thought their unique style sounded really good, and the young artists seemed very polite.

After the program, Stella just sat on her chair quietly while the others gushed over them and thanked them for coming. Some of the band members looked her way, a little puzzled. They had been used to girls screaming and grabbing at them. Afterwards, Stella's escort borrowed a car to drive her home.

Later when she told some people in the base dining hall that she heard the band that came, they were amazed and jealous, "How lucky you are! Do you realize how famous they are all over the world?" Stella had gotten some idea from seeing the excitement of the few others around her, but really she had no clue and started to feel a little embarrassed. She was glad to have had the privilege of seeing them, but she wished that she had paid more attention.

Around that time, a letter came from America. There was a Greek family in Texas who had become friends with Georgia. They had an unmarried son who was a little older. They really respected Georgia and Lea and thought if any of their sisters were like them, maybe she would get along well with their son. They would be willing to pay all of her expenses, just to see if it worked out. Mark had also purchased a trailer and wanted to go on a vacation to see many other states. Would Ioanna want to come to America for a visit?

Ioanna thought about it. She had the vacation time and could scrape together the money. She didn't want to feel obligated to the family and would rather pay her own way. It had been a year and a half

280

since Arianna visited America, and she would love to have a turn to see her sisters and niece and nephew. Nikolas and Arianna were a little nervous about the possibility that she could end up staying there, but they gave their blessing for her to visit.

When it was time for her trip, Ioanna faced similar traveling challenges as her sisters and her mother had experienced. But on the plane to Texas, Ioanna got more and more excited about seeing her family. Georgia was the closest to her in age, and they went through some challenging but memorable times together. She remembered like it was yesterday when Lea was born and she had thought of her as her own baby, she was so protective. And the babies must be getting bigger— would they look like Georgia or Mark? She could hardly hug them all enough when she got there. The first night, even though she was exhausted, they stayed up much of the night talking.

On the day the assumption of Virgin Mary was observed, they planned to go to the local Greek Orthodox church. Lea helped Ioanna with her hair and helped her choose a white dress that had blue on the shoulders. As she walked down the hallway from the bedroom to the living room, she heard Mark laughing. He was letting someone in the door. When the man crossed the threshold, it was as if the hand of God pointed him out to Ioanna and said, "That is your husband." Ioanna blinked back the tears that started to form at the surprising revelation.

Mark introduced Ioanna to his friend Ole Svenson, "He actually has been to your house in Crete, but I don't think you were there that day." Ioanna replied, "No I don't think we have ever met. Nice to meet you." They all got to talking over breakfast for so long that the church had closed by the time they got there. Ioanna was disappointed, but Georgia knew someone who had a key, so they borrowed the key to go in and say a prayer and light a candle.

Ioanna was glad that they fulfilled their religious mission, but all along she was very distracted. Lea noticed and asked, "What do you think about Ole?" Ioanna wasn't sure what to say, "He seems nice. He has a very outgoing personality." Lea prompted, "And good looking?" Ioanna smiled but then said, "I don't know anything about him. He could be married." Lea said, "He is a good friend of Mark's and isn't married. He is a Christian and sells insurance."

Not long afterwards, Ole sent a dozen red roses to Ioanna to welcome her. Ioanna wasn't sure what it meant, but Lea told her that it was a good sign. Ioanna got to know Ole better as he kept showing up at almost all their meals. One night, Mark and Georgia and Ole and Ioanna went out to a steakhouse. By that time, after all of Ole's attentions, Ioanna's feelings were becoming a little more obvious.

As she was talking to Georgia later, Ioanna said, "But I haven't met the Greek family that wanted to meet me yet." Georgia said, "Well you have a choice. If you marry the Greek man, you will never want for anything. If you marry Ole, you will never have enough. He had to borrow money from Mark to pay for your dinner." Ioanna chuckled at her blunt analysis. They all knew that there were things much more valuable than money. But Ioanna felt that she should at least meet the Greek family.

A date was set, and the Greek man was to pick up Ioanna at Georgia's house. As she walked into the living room after getting ready, Ole was on the couch. "What are you doing tonight?" he asked, although he had already been told the whole story. Ioanna answered, "I am going to dinner with a friend of Georgia's." Ole enthusiastically said, "Oh good, go enjoy yourself. Just go out there and have a good time!" He liked her and kind of had a feeling that she liked him, but he was self-confident and thought things would play out.

Ioanna had a good time meeting the gentleman. They ordered steaks and visited. He was very courteous and attentive. He himself had never been to Greece, so he asked her all about their life in Crete. He was a very nice man, but there wasn't a strong connection. When she got back, Ole immediately asked her, "How was it?" Ioanna smiled and told him some of the fun details of the night without saying anything personal.

During her visit, Ioanna also met Jim Duncan, Lea's boyfriend. They got to know each other a little after a few visits. Ole also continued to hang around until Mark, Georgia and Ioanna took their trip north.

282

The Andersons and Ioanna took the camper to explore Yellowstone National Park, the Black Hills and Colorado for a couple of weeks.

When they returned, Ioanna spent more time with Ole, and by the time she left, they were engaged. Ole chuckled to himself, remembering how back in Crete he had thought that Mark was crazy to marry a Greek girl. It was even more ironic that Ole hadn't met Ioanna when he was in Crete, but they happened to meet in a small town in Texas.

When Ioanna returned to Karidia, she told her family all about her trip. She saved the part about Ole for last, not knowing how they would take the news. Tears slipped out of Arianna's eyes when she heard about the engagement, but when she heard of how God had spoken to Ioanna, she felt reassured. Arianna also felt better because she had gotten to know Ole while she was in America. She knew he was a Christian, and she liked him. The couple had discussed getting married in Texas a year from then, so Ioanna still had some time with her family.

As Arianna went to bed that night, she thought back to when she was engaged. After her disagreement with her parents about her arranged marriage, she had vowed that she would never make any of her daughters marry someone that they didn't love. She wondered to herself if there was a loophole in the current situation, since technically she never said that she would actually allow them to marry whomever they loved. She had to smile, though, appreciating that along the way she had come to love her arranged groom. She knew that love sure helped in life's unpredictable journey, and that God's presence and guidance through it were incomparable. With a tear in her eye and half a smile, she fell asleep.

Chapter 28

A very shy American serviceman wanted so badly to speak to Stella but could hardly get up his courage. Stella saw him looking at her so many times that she began to suspect his feelings. He rarely spoke to her himself, but he stood around the other guys who would talk to her. He tended the flower gardens at the base. Stella could see him gardening many times outside the dining hall window. She liked flowers and over time watched their growth, from his planting the bulbs until the gladiolas were about a meter high. One day as she walked towards the gate at the end of her shift, she complimented him on the flowers that he had been working on. He smiled and looked down, embarrassed.

Shortly after that, Stella and Barbara were sitting outside their house after swimming one evening when the bus stopped in front of them. Stella's shy admirer emerged from the bus carrying one of the largest bouquets of flowers that she had ever seen. He walked towards her, while the Greek people and American servicemen waited on the bus. He presented to Stella some of the gladiolas that she had complimented him on; and without a word, he turned and walked back to the bus. Stella managed to yell a "thank you" to his retreating form. She smelled them and smiled while Barbara teased her.

Some time later, he did the same thing, only with red roses. But this time he managed to say, "Here are the roses" before he walked off and got back on the bus. Barbara teased her even more, "Oh now he is getting serious! He spoke to you!" Stella thought that he was very sweet, but thought that she should be careful to not encourage him too much. She didn't want to hurt him. Stella was waiting for lightning bolts, followed by the *perfect* guy— she had the interview questions all ready.

Not long after that, Stella's shy friend was transferred from the base, but more officers were transferred in. One morning, Stella and Ioanna were standing against the wall of the dining hall. Stella noticed a very handsome man take his tray to a table with six other servicemen. She watched him as he sat at the end of the table and stared at her (lightning bolts on both sides). He kept looking at her and seemed to want to talk to her. It didn't take him long to introduce himself, and she noticed that he spoke Greek well, "Hi, my name is Sam Smith." They struck up a conversation and he wanted to see her more.

Over time, Stella and Sam got to know each other after many short visits. He told her that he probably wouldn't be on the island for many months. After the smiles and butterflies, Stella questioned him about his family, religion and disclosed to him that she had no interest in cooking. He smiled and said that was okay. He shared with her his family's concerns that she was only interested in him in order to go to the United States. Stella assured him that was not the case, "Actually I am not really sure that it would be a better life in America. I am very happy here."

After Sam proposed, Stella faced the heart-rending task of telling her parents. She told them while they were in a field one afternoon. Arianna reached her breaking point and snapped, "Absolutely not! We are not sending any more daughters to America!" Stella acknowledged how difficult this was but pleaded her case. They could see that she loved him.

Nikolas was thoughtful and finally said, "We can't stop her. We let the other three go. We have to let her pursue her dreams." As he said the words, his own heart was torn. Little by little his own dreams were changing. After all of their impossibly hard work, he no longer needed a thousand grapevines for each daughter or a multi-story house in Heraklion. Would he ever get the chance to meet his grandchildren or ever see his daughters again? This time when Arianna sobbed in the quiet of the night, he did too.

After Sam and Stella were engaged, they could see each other more often. Stella enjoyed when they had a chaperone or there were enough people around for them to go out to some local places. They had fun getting to know one another more while planning their wedding, which they scheduled for New Year's Eve.

***

In Texas, Jim introduced Lea to his family over the Thanksgiving holiday. It was a little awkward at first since his family thought that things had been more serious with Cecilia, whom they had met and approved. Granted, Lea and Jim had a rocky start. In addition to the other girls in the picture and the name confusion, they shared an awkward first kiss. Lea, wishing to hold him off, gave him the most pointed, sharp kiss, like a rooster peck. He thought, "That's it? Did I miss it?"

For a short time Lea had a car that at almost every stop, the gears stuck. It had been challenging enough for her to learn a stick shift, but in addition, at a stop light, she had to get out of the car, open the hood and unlock the gears with pliers. Often nice gentlemen would offer to help, but she waved and yelled, "No, thanks, I've got it!" But despite these challenges plus full course loads and jobs over the past year, their relationship had gotten serious. Jim's family was gracious and welcoming and his mother even shared her turkey stuffing recipe, which Lea really liked. "We didn't have stuffing in Greece, or this kind of fruit salad," Lea explained admiringly.

When he brought her back to his parent's house in December, the day after Christmas he took her to a beautiful park. By the river, Jim got down on one knee and beginning with, "There comes a time in every man's life...," he asked her to marry him. Lea gasped, "Oh, Jim!" and smothered him with a huge hug and a kiss. He noticed that she never really answered him, but he got the message.

***

The days in Karidia leading up to Stella's wedding brought some feelings of uncertainty. There had been an uprising in the government, and to avoid any bloodshed, the king and his family left the country. No one was sure if Greece would continue to have a monarchy. Additionally, the health of Nikolas' mother was failing. They took her to the doctor who discovered a lack of sensation in her extremities and signs of previous brain damage. When she had been dropped as a child, it must have injured her more than they had

286

thought. The family realized that much of her irascibility throughout her life could have been medically based. But also prominent in Stella's mind was that in the couple of days before the wedding, she didn't have much contact with Sam. The morning of the wedding, she felt a little insecure until she saw his smile at the end of the aisle of the church.

Sam and Stella got married in a church in the suburbs of Heraklion. Everyone thought that they made a beautiful couple. Stella looked stunning in her elegant, rented wedding dress. They didn't have a formal reception but handed out a *boubouniera* [white candy-coated almond wrapped in tulle tied with ribbon] to each guest. Other than the sting that they were about to go to America, the family was very happy for them. Stella felt like she was in a fairy tale and it showed on her face.

Afterwards, they went to the island of Rhodes for their honeymoon. Since Ioanna and Stella's house in Heraklion had already been rented, Sam and Stella rented an apartment for the few months before they were to move to America. They were both interested in travel, so when they could, they visited many areas of the island. They went to some places that Stella had seen in her travels with various tourists, as well as many new places. Sometimes they got on a tour bus so that they could hear what the tour guide had to say. With so much to do and see, the time passed quickly until Stella's paperwork was finalized.

In the year after Stella got married, Stella and Ioanna moved to America, and Lea and Ioanna got married in Texas. Nikolas had felt honored when both of his American sons-in-law managed to write to him in Greek, asking for his permission to marry his daughters. Ole had enlisted Georgia's help, and Jim copied how Lea had written out in Greek what he wanted to say.

The partings were very difficult. The fact that international flights were not so prohibitive helped a little bit. Back when Georgia had left for America, the family almost felt it would be like flying to the moon to ever be able to see her again. But now it seemed like the costs and logistics could be managed on occasion. Even so, their family unit had always been so tight. They lived in close quarters, worked side by side in the fields and at the base and went through the difficult and happy times together. The girls were also very close with their very large extended family. It seemed surreal to Nikolas and Arianna when they were left with only Barbara.

Christmas was very sad for Nikolas, Arianna and Barbara. They were glad to receive letters that everyone was happy and healthy in America, but the house that was usually filled with so much activity and excitement at that time of year was practically empty. Arianna tried to picture her grandkids laughing and playing around a Christmas tree.

The following year after some of the sorrow of separation had abated and they were adjusting to their new life, Nikolas and Arianna began to put many of their hopes on twenty-five year old Barbara. In their loneliness, they clung to her but also wanted the best for her. Barbara started to hear whispers among the different communities at what a catch she would be with all of the property that she would inherit. "And she's beautiful, nice and hardworking, not a party girl," they said. Others added, "Think of all the presents she can get from America, and she can go back and forth to the States." And, "We'd better hurry to arrange something before an American snatches her up."

Barbara didn't really have an interest in going to America; she was happy in Crete. In fact she had not been much interested in getting married. She was happy with her work and her life. Matchmaking opportunities started to pour in, but she declined them. As she continued to hear people talk about her appeal, Barbara became more fearful that whoever seemed interested in her was only interested in her money and property. She felt a lot of pressure to make the right decision since likely her parents' future would be affected by the type of man that she married. She could not judge his character wrongly for all of their sakes. So for now it was easiest to turn them all down. She wasn't ready anyway.

In the spring, her Aunts Dorothea and Nektaria came to the house. They visited for a while, asking if they had heard anything from the sisters in America. Then they mentioned a young man who was a distant relative. "I know that everyone is talking about how much you are worth and you can't trust everyone. But this guy is distantly associated with the family and he is going to be a priest, so you don't have to worry about that," Aunt Dorothea said. The idea of one of her daughters marrying a priest pleased Arianna. And anyone studying to be a priest was probably pretty serious about marriage, since they were required to be married before accepting a position.

Aunt Nektaria encouraged Barbara, "You really should make a decision on someone to marry pretty soon. It would be better to get everything settled. People are starting to get worked up over you." Barbara knew that they were all looking out for her, but all she felt was pressure and fear. She told them, "Thank you. I will think about it." As they left, Aunt Dorothea said, "We can arrange for you to get to know him better if you want to."

Barbara was confused. She knew that they had made some good points. But somehow she didn't feel ready or right about it. She earnestly prayed on her knees, "Jesus, please don't let me make any mistakes. If this man is the right one for me, please give me peace about it. Please guide me in the way that I should go." After many days of prayer, Barbara told her aunts that she didn't feel right about pursuing anything with the man that they had suggested.

A few months later, Nikolas and Arianna were working in the grapevines in Lithos. With most of the girls gone and Arianna urging him to take it easier, Nikolas had leased out some of their property. They had laborers who helped them with their remaining land, but there were new laws limiting how many hours employees could work in a day. The government also initiated laws requiring children to regularly attend school. So much had changed over the years. Nikolas and Arianna had so much to do to finish the work that the laborers couldn't get to that they decided to camp overnight for a while. Barbara had to work at the base each day, so she stayed home.

One of those nights around eight o'clock, her parents stormed in the door. "What's wrong?" Barbara asked. Arianna gasped, out of breath, "Pack as much as you can of your things. You can't stay here by yourself anymore." Barbara started to pack, asking, "Why, what happened?" Arianna answered, "We heard that someone found out that we were away and planned to kidnap you. He was going to get some other guys to help him. But our friends warned us." Barbara questioned, "Where can I go? I have to work early in the morning." Nikolas explained, "We thought you could stay with one of your aunts in Heraklion. Since your boss lives there, maybe he can give you rides from there and back." Barbara packed many of her things in case she needed to be gone for a while.

With more automobiles around, it was getting too dangerous at night on the curvy road to ride in the horse-drawn wagon, and the tractor had narrow tires which were always going flat over long distances, so they arranged for a taxi to take them to Heraklion. Aunt Nektaria was able to take her in. She lived with her husband and son, so she looked forward to having another woman in the house. She was very loving to Barbara in her situation.

Barbara was able to arrange rides with her boss without any trouble. Since Nikolas and Arianna had many crops in numerous fields that would keep them occupied most of the summer and fall, they planned to keep this arrangement for several months. Realizing how serious this had become, Barbara continued to kneel daily in prayer for His guidance.

The cousin she was staying with worked at the outdoor movie theater, so Barbara got a free ticket whenever she wanted to go. Between that, being spoiled by her aunt and finding many things to do in the city, Barbara had a good time. But after a while, she thought that she should make use of her time and see if she could train to become a hairdresser. When she got off work, it was early afternoon and the shops in the city closed for afternoon break, but they opened again in the late afternoon. Although there was no formal training, she interned at a local shop in the evenings.

In the fall at a dinner party, Aunt Nektaria introduced Barbara to a young lawyer she knew. She tried to subtly praise each young person's attributes during the conversation. The gentleman seemed interested in getting to know Barbara. She was polite to him but didn't encourage him too much. That only made him more interested. He spoke to Aunt Nektaria, expressing his serious intentions.

290

Later, Aunt Nektaria asked Barbara about the lawyer. "He's sincere, if you would like to get to know him better. I have known him for a while and he is a nice man," she said. Barbara didn't know what to do. In a way, maybe there was no harm in getting to know someone better. But their society seemed to push things along so fast, she didn't want to get trapped. Barbara prayed about it and again didn't feel right about it, so she turned him down.

For the next several weeks, Barbara prayed so desperately and often that her knees started developing calluses. Although she had a happy life, she felt unsettled. She was away from home and there were men pursuing her that she didn't know if she could trust.

One night as she was praying anxiously, she fell asleep. She had a very vivid dream that she was in the small church in Karidia by herself. She walked up the center aisle of the church to the front where there was an intricately carved picture of Jesus. She stood there and began to cry as she prayed. All of a sudden, Jesus came out of that picture and stood before her. He was tall, bright white and beautiful. She could see through Him as He walked towards her and then walked around and stood behind her. He put His hands on both of her shoulders, looked around towards her face and said, "Why are you crying so much? Don't you know that you are My sister, and I am the One who is going to take care of you? I don't want you to worry anymore because I will be with you all of the time. And you are going to America— this is the answer to your major decision. You haven't known what to do and it hasn't been easy, but you are going to be by your sisters. I am always with you." Then He disappeared.

When Barbara woke up, she knew that the experience was very real. She felt His hands on her shoulders and knew those powerful words were from Him. She was in awe that she had been in the very presence of Jesus. Such peace and happiness flooded her! He loved and protected her more than any person could. She never had to worry. He told her so clearly that He would take care of her. That experience changed her life, and she would remember it forever. No matter what she went through, He was with her.

Chapter 29

Several weeks later, Barbara was working in the dining hall of the American base when she noticed a young man that she had never seen before. He was checking the identification of the men who were entering. After a while, he motioned for her to come over. She knew that she really wasn't supposed to speak to the GIs, but since he was working, she thought that he might need something.

When she got to the table where he sat, he asked her, "What is your name?" She said, "Barbara." When she pronounced it, she used the Greek pronunciation, having a soft "v" instead of a hard "b." When he didn't say anything more, Barbara walked off to resume her duties. Later, he stopped her again, "How do you spell your name, with a 'b' or a 'v'?" She answered, "I spell it with Greek letters, the *Greek* way." He replied, "I think you should spell it with a 'b'!" She wasn't too sure if it mattered to her how the Americans spelled her name. She started to walk off again, but he introduced himself, "I am Allen Davis." Barbara smiled and nodded and went back to work.

When the fall harvests were over and the Christmas holiday was approaching, the family decided that it was safe for Barbara to move from Heraklion back home to Karidia. Barbara told her mother, "Aunt Nektaria loved me to pieces and I learned quite a bit from the hairdresser, but I am very glad to be home!" The hairdresser had let her copy some written instructions on how to do several things to keep for her reference.

Barbara's return was noticed by the community and interest in her was renewed. Arianna was approached on behalf of two other men studying to be priests. Barbara chuckled, wondering if that was to become her destiny. But she knew that there was more to a man than his profession. Not feeling particularly drawn to either of them, she tried to avoid giving a direct answer for now.

Allen Davis walked up to Barbara one day and asked, "Would you like to go out with me sometime?" Barbara had never really been out with anyone and didn't think it was proper, so she replied, "No, thank you. I don't really go out." So Allen tried to get to know her in other ways. He realized that Barbara's boss was her friend, so he became friends with him. Her boss told her one day, "He's a nice kid. He isn't going to have hair for long, but he really likes you." He did not tell her that he had overheard Allen telling a friend that when he first saw her, he knew that she would become his wife.

Allen persisted in getting to know her in small ways. Over time, Barbara was drawn to him because he was gentle, quiet and honest. He seemed young and innocent and very sweet, which matched Barbara's sweet innocence. Their friendship grew without any feeling of pressure. In addition, she knew that he wasn't after her for her property— he knew nothing about it. That awareness took a huge weight off her shoulders.

As the relationship grew more serious, Barbara sensed that a difficult decision was on the horizon. She knew that there were still many choices in local men who were interested in her. And she loved her parents. When her sisters left, she hated to see what it did to them. How could she consider doing the same thing? Since she was the last daughter in Greece, she felt the responsibility for them, as well as the domain that they had built up and still needed to maintain. She loved her homeland and really didn't want to leave, but her feelings for this man were growing and she also missed her sisters.

Just before Easter, Allen came to the house with an interpreter to ask for Barbara's hand in marriage. Nikolas and Arianna were shocked. Since Allen and Barbara had never formally dated, her parents had no idea how serious the relationship had become. Even Barbara was a little surprised at how soon he wanted to take this step. For a moment Nikolas and Arianna hoped there was some sort of mistake; maybe Allen had deeper feelings than Barbara did— until they looked at Barbara's face…

To Arianna, it felt like the room was spinning and the floor was falling out from under her. No! Not again. It couldn't be. Surely Nikolas would put his foot down this time. She was his special charming, affectionate Barbara. Nikolas looked like the wind had been knocked out of him. When he was able to pull himself together, he tried to appear supportive of Barbara as he started to ask some questions. Allen was a Christian, seemed to really care for Barbara and would be moving back to the States soon. Nikolas could not give Allen an immediate answer but invited him back to dinner in a week.

When the extended family found out, everyone was upset. No one really knew Allen and they couldn't understand why Barbara would want to leave. Aunt Dorothea yelled and Aunt Nektaria cried. Barbara listened to all of them, knowing that it was hard for everyone. At length, Barbara explained, "We got to know each other slowly at the base. He is so kind and gentle. I feel safe with him and I can trust him." Then she told them of her encounter with Jesus in her dream and reminded them of Ioanna's vision on the ship. Arianna and her sisters started crying. God's hand was on their lives, and although it wasn't the way they would have chosen, they had to accept His plan.

The next week, Nikolas gave Allen his blessing. It was the hardest thing that Nikolas and Arianna ever had to do. They felt like everything important in their life was disappearing. But it wasn't right of them to put all of the responsibility on Barbara. Each daughter had made her own choice. At least there could be a little more contact— not only were some of the other sisters able to write, but they also sent pictures. And maybe some of them could fly overseas to visit every now and then. Most of all, they knew that Barbara was happy, and God would be with them all.

Nikolas urged Barbara and Arianna to plan a big wedding, "I have been saving for five dowries, but I don't need to give any. Let's celebrate and be happy with all of our family and friends before you have to leave." Barbara was happy to plan for a big wedding in July. Allen spent more time at the house so that her parents could get to know him a little better. They came to really like him.

In May, a letter came from Ioanna that she had a son. Nikolas and Arianna were so proud to have a second grandson. They really wished they could see him, but they treasured the picture that Ioanna sent.

The day of Barbara's wedding was beautiful and clear. They had the ceremony at Saint Titus Church in Heraklion and had two *koumbaros* [best men]. After the ceremony, they had a sit-down dinner for their two-hundred guests at a new restaurant near Karidia. Barbara displayed some of the intricately-designed home accents and embroidered linens that she had made by hand or with the loom. The music and celebration were festive, and Nikolas got up to dance with the others. He made every effort to be cheerful and enjoy the day, no matter what would come later. Arianna preferred to visit with her friends and relatives, many of whom she hadn't seen in a while. They all complimented her on one of the most elaborate weddings they had attended in some time. It was difficult for her to answer all the questions about when Barbara would be leaving. They weren't very sure when all of the paperwork would be ready, and on this happy day, it was painful to remember that she would be moving to America.

After the festivities ended and the cleanup was almost over, Arianna reflected that she was blessed with five sons-in-law who were all Christians. It didn't matter to her if they were of different denominations as long as they all loved Jesus. Her faith was more than a religion to her; it was a relationship. The Lord had brought them through so much, with so many miraculous interventions, that the reality of His presence couldn't be questioned. But she had learned that one key in finding God was earnestly seeking after Him. She wanted that blessing of relationship with Jesus that brings with it love, wisdom, provision and protection to continue in her daughters' families as well.

Allen and Barbara went on an extended tour of Greece for their honeymoon. They started in Athens and went on to the Peloponnese, Delphi, Thessaloniki and Rhodes. At the various sites, they enjoyed the scenery, shops and restaurants of the present as well as the tributes of the past. Barbara was enthralled by the archeological ruins of a Macedonian palace with an all-mosaic tile floor.

When they returned from their honeymoon, Ioanna and Stella's house in Heraklion was vacant, so Allen and Barbara stayed there until the paperwork was approved. As it had been with some of her sisters, it took many months to get all of Barbara's paperwork completed, since she had to petition to change her name, report that she had married an American serviceman and get permission to go to the United States. In the meantime, Barbara spent as much time as she could with her family.

In September, she told her parents that she got her passport— the final step of the process. The realization hit Nikolas and Arianna that she was really leaving, and they were shattered. The next day, Nikolas had an errand to do and went into Heraklion by bus. That hot afternoon, Barbara was visiting with Arianna inside the house when they heard the bus stop and then continue on towards Asprada. They looked out the window but didn't see Nikolas. When they walked out the door, they saw him on the ground, across the road. Arianna gasped, "Nikolas!" Both of them ran over to him. He couldn't talk or move. Arianna and Barbara panicked and started praying as they tried to help him. They struggled to ease him into the house. His right side was paralyzed and his mouth was twisted. Barbara ran to summon a taxi. By that time, they realized that he probably had a stroke. They took him to the largest hospital in Heraklion.

Barbara was devastated. "My leaving put too much strain on him," she cried to Arianna. To God she pleaded, "Please don't let him die." Arianna echoed her prayers but reassured Barbara, "It's not your fault. He is going to be okay." They were both immensely relieved when Nikolas passed the point of danger. But he needed a lot more time and care to regain his mobility and speech. He was in the hospital for two weeks, and his health progressed significantly during that time. When he was discharged, he needed to walk with a cane since he was still weak on his right side. Arianna and Barbara thanked God for sparing his life and helping him to recover.

The ladies forced Nikolas to take it easy at home. They assisted him with some mild exercises but otherwise served him and didn't allow him to walk around much. Nikolas had been active his whole life, and it was difficult at only sixty-three years old to adjust to his limitations. But he was glad to have more time to sit with Barbara. They kept the conversation light to keep his stress low. And Barbara was just the one to do it— she was full of amusing anecdotes and daily observations. At times Arianna wondered if it wasn't good for him to laugh so much, but she could see that their time together was special.

Gradually, Nikolas was able to get around more. He still couldn't run or grip things tightly with his right hand. His right index finger had never been the same since he had been hit in the wagon. His speech was quite good, with only a very slight slurring of his words. He was able to do some light work, still relying on his cane for balance, but he mainly just supervised the workers.

In November, the time came for Barbara and Allen to move to the United States. Saying goodbye this time, Nikolas and Arianna couldn't even pretend to be optimistic. They were all weeping. Barbara felt even worse leaving her mother with the extra needs of her father. When she turned to him and saw the tears in his eyes, she broke down, "I am so sorry, *Baba!*" Nikolas corrected her, "Don't feel bad. We will miss you, but I release you. You have to follow your husband and your own life." All Arianna could manage was, "God be with you." They clung to one another a little longer before Barbara boarded the airplane.

When the plane took off, through blurry tears Barbara looked out of the window at her beautiful beloved land, fading before her eyes. Crete was so much a part of her that she felt like she was leaving part of herself behind. "Please take care of my parents," she whispered to God, "I know this is Your plan, but it is so hard leaving my loved ones behind."

Allen left on an earlier flight, so Barbara had to travel alone. She was nervous about finding her way. After overnighting in Athens, she caught her flight to New York. When she arrived, she was scared and confused but followed the others to customs. The agent did some things with her papers and directed her to a sitting area. She wasn't sure if she had been processed or if they needed more information from her.

After a long time sitting there, she looked up and saw Allen coming towards her in his military uniform. He greeted her lovingly and then said, "Let's get your things; I have the car ready." Earlier, Allen, with Barbara's help, had bought a new car from Germany and had it delivered to New York. They drove to New Jersey to process Allen's discharge from the military. Then they took their time driving home, stopping in various states to visit Allen's friends or extended family.

When they arrived in Texas in the fall, the sisters were so happy to be reunited. Georgia's children had grown more than Barbara realized. "Has it already been ten years that you have been here?" she asked Georgia. Shortly after they got there, Stella hosted Thanksgiving dinner at her home. There was so much lively conversation as they all caught up on each other's news and on the news from back home. How they wished that their parents could be there. They were concerned about Nikolas' health and Arianna's ability to take care of everything. The sisters knew that the bond of the extended family was strong and they were in good hands, but they wished their homeland were closer.

When Barbara met Allen's parents, they welcomed her warmly. They had been so curious what she would be like. It didn't take long for her to enchant them with her pleasing personality. They had recently lost their son-in-law in the Vietnam war, so they knew how precious life was and were so grateful their son and his wife were home. Over time Barbara acclimated to her new life. Allen's parents liked to entertain. Barbara was easily able to step in and help since she had experience from her job as nanny and personal assistant in Heraklion. She thanked God for even that little step in preparing her.

The next January, Lea took steps to get her American citizenship. It was her first good opportunity after waiting the required five years of residence in the States. Right after they were married, Jim had enlisted in the military during the Vietnam War. After his training and brief service in medical administration, he was discharged because of a problem with his back. Now he was pursuing his master's degree, and Lea was finishing her bachelor's degree, both in foreign languages. Lea took her citizenship exam and passed. She was happy when the paperwork was processed and she was an official United States citizen.

With all of the girls living in America, people often remarked how much they looked alike. Stella and Lea, in particular, could almost be mistaken for twins. One day a friend of Stella's told her, "I saw you at the grocery store earlier." Stella replied, "I haven't been to the store recently." The friend insisted, "I saw you, but you were with another man. He was tall and had glasses." Stella laughed, "Oh, you must have seen my sister Lea. She looks a lot like me and is married to a tall man with glasses." Her friend laughed too, almost in relief.

The next year three more granddaughters were born. One was born on Saint Patrick's Day and her mother wondered at the green ribbon on the door. "I thought you said that I had a girl. Why is there a green ribbon?" The nurse had to explain what the celebration was all about, since that holiday wasn't observed in Greece. Another one of the girls seemed as if she could end up growing into some kind of amateur writer someday. The other mother knew that her sister had been in labor for thirty-three hours, so she decided to clean the house and take her time getting to the hospital. But her daughter was born in about eight hours. "What happened to my thirty-three hours?" she wondered, but was not sorry.

Georgia's children were almost twelve and seven and begged her to take them to the air show that was going to be in their town. They were going to have many kinds of airplanes flying and on display. Georgia consented, but when they got there, she froze. At the sights and sounds of the World War II planes, she flew into a full panic. All of the traumatic memories came flooding back. Vivid scenes of bullets piercing the ground at her father's feet while they were running to the shelter and bombs falling while they were hiding in the cave flashed in front of her eyes. She couldn't distinguish what was real right then versus what was in the past; so she grabbed her kids' hands and, in a frenzy, hurried them home. The children did not understand what had been so seared into Georgia's instincts. Later, she apologized to her kids and sought God for the healing of past wounds. Wartime had such an impact on her life, but God's grace and healing was even greater. She thanked Him again for His protection through the many ups and downs in life.

Chapter 30

The next spring, Stella and Sam decided to visit Crete before their second child was born. Stella was almost six months pregnant when they left. Nikolas and Arianna met them at the Heraklion airport. They ran to hug each other exuberantly. "It is so good to see you!" Arianna exclaimed. Stella agreed, "It is so good to see you too, and to be here again." She asked her father, "How are you feeling?" Nikolas responded, "I am just fine. Your mother makes me take it easy." Stella smiled, picturing that scenario, "Good for her!"

Both grandparents were thrilled to see Stella's one-year old girl, calling her *koukla* [doll] and loving her up. They all realized that this was the first time that Nikolas was able to meet any of his grandchildren. They then turned their attention to Stella and insisted that she rest after the long journey.

In the two and a half years between Barbara's leaving and Stella's coming to visit, Nikolas and Arianna moved to the house that Ioanna and Stella had built in Heraklion. They leased out their home in Karidia except for one annexed section that they had built on the side of the house for themselves. They had never built more than one story of the house in Heraklion, but it was perfect for them to stay in town. Arianna had some family there, and it was closer to the doctors for Nikolas' checkups. So Stella and her family stayed with them at the house in the city. They had a nice back yard for her young daughter to toddle around.

They had so much to catch up on. Nikolas and Arianna wanted to hear everything about their children and grandchildren. Stella told them that their last grandchild was born at a hospital that had a tornado come through that same day. There was some damage to the hospital and it was scary, but everyone was okay. Each day, more family members came by to visit with Stella and hear all of the news from America.

During their two-week stay, Stella and the family went by their house in Karidia a few times. They all loved to swim in the ocean. Stella decided to baptize their daughter at the church in Karidia. Violetta, Stella's childhood friend, served as her godmother.

Before Stella left, they had many conversations about Nikolas and Arianna going to America. Nikolas really wanted to see his daughters, all of their children and where they lived but wasn't sure if he wanted to live there or just visit. Arianna wasn't sure how they would manage it but also wanted to go, at least for a time. Stella promised that the sisters would get together to help them with any paperwork if they wanted to come on an extended visa or move there.

After Stella and her family left, Nikolas and Arianna felt an enormous void all over again. Their hearts were sick that they were so far away from their beloved daughters. They almost felt like they were grandparents in name only, they were missing so much. Two more grandchildren were to be born that year. They began to seriously consider— could they really move to America?

Their area of the island was the only life they had ever known. Nikolas had chosen one of the most beautiful, isolated spots on the north shore to build his home and business. They built and rebuilt their house after an earthquake and a war. They toiled so hard on multiple pieces of property spread out over a large area, which could make them difficult to sell. But did they really want to sell it all since they put every last bit of themselves into making the land profitable?

So many memories met them at every turn within their community. Their two baby boys, their fathers and their brothers were buried there. How many close calls God had delivered them from— frostbite, boils, the firing squad, shelling, bombs, mines, well accidents, poisonings, pneumonia, operations, motor vehicle accidents, near drownings, attempted kidnappings, a tsunami…

So many things they would almost rather not remember, and yet it all testified to the protection of God and how as a family they pulled together. They even considered how Nikolas and his countrymen defended their beautiful land against foreign occupation. Many fought hard so that they would have the freedom to live there and preserve their Greek culture.

They had invested so much of themselves in their native country. With God's help, Nikolas pioneered so many innovative ideas to try to get his family ahead in life. And he was successful, even envied among his peers. Similarly, Arianna had so many skills that might not match everyday life in America. When they really got down to the issue, they were fearful to leave their supportive extended family, their land, their culture and their way of life. They would be fish out of water in a foreign place.

On the other hand, they felt like they must somehow see their children again and meet their grandchildren. Nikolas had never been to America; Arianna had visited once but many more grandchildren were born since then. Maybe they should travel back and forth occasionally. But without knowing the language, travel was confusing— Arianna ended up in the wrong city the last time she traveled. They were getting older and with Nikolas not too strong after the stroke, it would be physically exhausting and maybe too strenuous for his health. Not to mention the emotional toll of having to say goodbye each time.

Arianna knew how much Nikolas loved beauty. He particularly loved the ocean. She described the area that she had seen in Texas so that he was able to consider the difference. "Instead of palm trees, they have cactus. Rather than a vast ocean, they have some rivers and lakes but mostly wide-open dusty land. They have some trees, but very few fruit trees," she warned him. They were sure that there were beautiful areas in America, but really no matter where it was, they couldn't imagine any place that felt more like home than their special Crete.

They counted the costs and did consider the sacrifice. But no matter how they weighed it, they realized that their home was where their heart was, and their heart was their kids. It tore at his heart to consider selling all that he had worked for, but Nikolas was ready to leave it all for his daughters and their children. "Let's go," he told her pleadingly. With tears in her eyes, Arianna nodded, not quite ready to verbalize her assent. She was more connected to her extended family and needed a little more time to embrace a major life change.

Before saying anything to their daughters, Arianna wanted to discuss the long trip and physical strain with Nikolas' doctor. The doctor encouraged him to take as many breaks as he could to rest, but didn't see any compelling reason why he couldn't travel. To the doctor, Nikolas appeared almost brokenhearted without his family. So even if he were to balance a possibly healthier state with an empty existence against a short physical strain with a joyous reunion, he concluded, "What do you have to lose?"

Nikolas and Arianna continued to pray a little longer. Arianna, in her private prayer time, sought God, "Lord, we know that You are Love, and You put the love in our hearts that we have for our children. We put You first, but they are second above everything else in our lives. But if the stress of selling everything and then taking this long journey is too much for Nikolas, let us be grateful for the lives that You are giving our kids in America and for the lives You are giving us here. Please give us peace about what we should do."

One day, Nikolas and Arianna decided to take a trip to their house in Karidia. They sat quietly on the balcony watching the calm ocean, clasping hand in hand. Almost as a panorama in front of her, glimpses of the past visions they had been given from God streamed before Arianna. Ioanna as a small child saw the land of another country come close to touch their country. When the amphibious vehicles came, she saw a canopy over their ships and knew that their lives would be affected by the Americans. Barbara had a dream of Jesus and heard Him tell her that she would go to America with her sisters and that He would be with her. Nikolas had the dramatic dream that he was cutting Barbara, which saved Lea's life. Lea's dream of the entire Easter service and Ioanna's vision on the ship showed that Lea had a special, anointed relationship with God and was destined to go to America. And the amazing last part of Ioanna's vision on the ship was that not only Lea would go but *all* of them would go to America and testify of Jesus. Even the night that Nikolas had been detained by the Germans when Jesus appeared and assured Ioanna that her father was safe indicated God's hand of protection on his life. Arianna turned to Nikolas and said, "God has reminded me of all of His promises to us. I am ready to move if you are."

Nikolas and Arianna sent word to America that they wanted to leave everything behind and move to Texas. The girls were thrilled, and yet they knew that the decision had been a difficult one. They had no doubt that the strong family bond back in Crete would allow any of them to return to open arms and hospitality if they wanted, so that helped in thinking about a transition. Accordingly, the girls coordinated among themselves to work with the United States government to begin the process.

While the girls initiated the paperwork, Nikolas and Arianna began to make preparations to leave. Telling their families their decision was very difficult for them. Many of their family members were surprised that they wanted to take such a drastic step, but they understood their wanting to be with their children and grandchildren.

When Christmas came around, it felt a little strange to Nikolas and Arianna. It was surreal to think that it would probably be the last time that they would spend that holiday in Crete. But they looked forward to spending Christmas and all of the other holidays with their daughters in America.

As Nikolas and Arianna thought about leaving the region, they discussed a lifelong dream that had always been in the back of their minds. They had always wanted to go to Israel. Since they were geographically so close, they began to discuss taking a trip in the early spring. Even though they had a lot to do to prepare for a huge move, if they were ever going to go to the Holy Land, this would be the time. After checking with the travel agency to make sure that Nikolas could manage with his cane, they decided to sign up for a tour.

When spring came and it was time for their trip to Israel, Nikolas and Arianna were both happy that they had decided to go. They packed as light as they could, flew to the Holy Land and met the rest of their tour group. They spent several days traveling by bus to many

304

of the biblical sites. Arianna loved seeing the historic churches, with their unique architecture and symbolic ornamentation. Both of them were impacted by walking where Jesus walked. The Bible seemed to come alive as they could picture the accounts of what happened in the various places. They were tired when they got back, but they were grateful that they were able to have that experience.

Nikolas asked Arianna if she wanted to see any of the other islands, mainland or nearby countries. She thought a moment and replied, "No, I think I want to spend as much time as possible with my family on our island. I am sure there are some great places to see, and it was wonderful to see Israel, but this place is so special to me." Nikolas wholeheartedly agreed.

Nikolas and Arianna made several trips to the American embassy in Athens to try to get their paperwork approved. It had been many months since they started the process, and they were starting to feel like they were getting close. It didn't actually seem real to them until they got the approval. When they did, they got busy packing and finalizing arrangements. In all of the times they said goodbye to each daughter, one at a time, they never thought that *they* would be the ones to be saying goodbye and leaving the island. They said goodbye to each of their family members and invited them to visit them in America anytime.

It was almost like a dream to them as their airplane took off. Were they really leaving behind everything that was familiar to them? Their beautiful land and fruit of their labor… they had to let it all go to embrace the most precious part of life— love.

They departed on an airline whose attendants spoke Greek, and Sam met them at the airport in New York to help them connect and fly with them to their final destination. When they arrived, they were greeted by their loved ones. Tears of joy flowed at the long-awaited reunion. Nikolas' heart was full to finally see his grandchildren. At that moment, there was no doubt in their minds about their sacrifice. They were home.

***

Chicago area church, spring 2000

Lea stood in front of a group of women, encouraging them to persevere in their daily lives, relying on the love and the power of God. She shared from the Word of God and her personal testimony about how God can intervene *suddenly*. "Wait on the Lord and trust Him for the fulfillment of His promises. Some of you have felt like a horse ready to run, but you feel that the reins are holding you back. You are saying, 'Will I ever experience the breakthrough?' Know that when the sudden season of God comes, you will see the fulfillment of your miracle. Stay in an attitude of expectancy. Don't let the enemy put doubt and fear in your mind, but speak words of faith and remember to seek *God* more than the promise."

Lea went on to share examples from the Bible about individuals who experienced God's sudden timing: "Suddenly the blind man was healed by Jesus. Suddenly Saul had a dramatic conversion experience. Suddenly Joseph was taken from the prison to the palace, and suddenly Esther went from obscurity to the throne. Ruth came out of a place of mourning and famine into divine connection and provision. Your answer may not come when or how you expect it, so don't limit God. The man at the pool of Bethesda had been crippled for thirty-eight years, and he was waiting for someone to put him into the healing waters. But in God's sovereign way and timing, Jesus stood before him and healed him with a single command."

"If you are still waiting for your miracle, don't lose heart. Keep trusting the Lord. In my own life, I was the youngest of five daughters on the island of Crete. Things didn't look good for me. There had been a major war, and there were many, including our family, who had tremendous needs. Had I stayed there, I probably would have never attended high school or achieved much in life. But I know about God's faithfulness and divine intervention."

Lea proceeded to tell her testimony of Georgia's marriage, and her family's struggle to let first the oldest and then the youngest leave the island. She shared about the government initially denying her permission to immigrate to the United States, and about the terrible

306

storm that assailed the ship they were on. "Yes, there were hardships, delays and disappointments along the way, but what Jesus promised in the midst of the storm came to pass. The 'no' became a 'yes' and the impossible became possible. It may take time, but God is not a man that He would lie— what He promises, He fulfills."

Then Lea told about God's greatest promise— the promise of salvation. "The God of the universe, wanting a personal relationship with us, created us with a free will to choose to love and follow Him or sin and go our own way. God is holy, pure and perfect, so when we sin, our imperfection separates us from Him. He loved us so extravagantly that He sent His Son Jesus to earth as a man. Jesus lived the perfect life we should have lived and suffered the agonizing death that we deserved. Jesus demonstrated His power over death, the consequence of sin, by rising from the grave. Personifying both God's justice and His mercy, Jesus paid the penalty for our wrongs and provided the Way to make right our relationship with God the Father."

Lea continued, "The Bible says that all have sinned. No matter how good we are or how hard we try to do the right thing, we could never earn salvation or eternal life by the standards of the holy God. Jesus' sacrifice was the only payment that could ever be good enough. By God's grace, if we believe in Jesus, accept His sacrifice for our sin and surrender our lives to Him, we can be assured of His presence in our hearts and eternity with Him."

"That doesn't mean that life will always be easy. My family and I had our share of difficulties, but God consistently provided protection, guidance and provision along our journey. God has a destiny and plan for your life— your life will have new meaning in Jesus. His Holy Spirit living in you will help you to love God and love people in fulfilling your purpose. If you are ready to receive Jesus as your Lord and Savior, please pray after me:

Dear Jesus, thank You for dying on the cross to take the punishment for my sin. I believe that You are God's Son, and You died and rose from the dead for me! I ask You to forgive me of my sin, come into my life, and give me the power by Your Holy Spirit to live for You.

I surrender my life to You and confess you now as my Savior and my Lord. Amen."

Lea reassured those praying that prayer that according to Romans 10:9 they can know that they are saved. She encouraged them to find support in a good local church and to read the Bible, beginning in the New Testament. Then she prayed individually for those wanting prayer for other needs.

At the end of the meeting, a lady came up to her and said, "Thank you so much! You don't know what a powerful impact the message and personal ministry time just had on my life." She proceeded to tell Lea how the Lord touched her and then asked, "Do you happen to know where the German graves are on Crete?" Lea answered, "No, I'm sorry, I don't. Why?" The lady replied, "My father, a German officer during World War II, was stationed in a small town near Heraklion. He didn't want to be there and always looked for ways to help anyone that he could on *either* side of the war."

Lea told her that she just got goosebumps, "That's about where our house was, and our uncle ran into a kind German officer who after their conversation spared our house from the bombings. Most of the other houses in the area were destroyed. And there were other Germans who had a hand in sparing our lives. The idea that in God's providential plan, all these many years later I may have helped someone from the family that helped mine— or even someone of German heritage— is an incredible blessing from the Lord."

Over the next several months, Lea couldn't get that conversation with the German lady out of her mind. It would be just like God's goodness to interweave destiny's tapestry with different individuals demonstrating His love in action on different continents, decades apart, coming around full circle. In awe of this divine appointment and His entire plan through her whole family's past and future, she marveled, "What an amazing God we serve!"

EPILOGUE

Nikolas and Arianna had eleven grandchildren, whom they loved, prayed for and watched grow up. For a time, they helped a couple of their daughters manage a Greek restaurant that they owned. All five sisters completed the requirements to become United States citizens. After their many years of sacrificial labors and prayers, Nikolas and Arianna were able to witness some of the material and spiritual blessings from the Lord that were realized by their children and grandchildren. Their legacy, shaped by their own fathers and others in their family heritage, was a testament to the multi-generational impact of prayer and spoken blessing.

The whole family continued to grow in their faith in God and served Him in various ways. They valued their Greek Orthodox upbringing but expanded the depth of their personal relationships with Jesus Christ. With a greater understanding of His grace, their prayers changed from desperate bargaining with God to communicating with a loving Father. They also came to know the power of the Holy Spirit and began to recognize that He had been at work throughout their lives. Evangelea's name and remarkable baptism foreshadowed her call to full-time ministry as an evangelist. She has considered it a privilege to bring the Good News to many nations, including some that were involved in her native country's past, exemplifying the love and forgiveness of Christ.

All of the family is exceedingly grateful to God that throughout their unique history, during both the good and the turbulent times, He was there.

The End

Made in the USA
Middletown, DE
12 January 2020